D1556099

The Stargazers

[illegible]

[illegible]

[illegible]

[illegible]

[illegible]

[illegible] *Sunday Mirror*

[illegible]

[illegible]

[illegible]

[illegible]

Praise for the novels of Harriet Evans

'This sweeping, absorbing story is a treat' **Adele Parks**

'Her characters are finely drawn . . . The reader becomes deeply immersed in this charismatic family's fortunes. The result is that rare and lovely thing, an all-engaging and all-consuming drama' ***Daily Mail***

'This epic, absorbing novel is full of intrigue, emotion and characters who'll really stay with you' ***Fabulous Magazine***

'Utterly gorgeous and filled with flowers and paintings, secrets and heartbreak . . . and always hope' **Veronica Henry**

'I was blissfully carried away by this intelligent (she's as good as the great Rosamunde Pilcher), classy and superbly executed family saga' ***Saga***

'A really superior modern saga, with utterly true to life characters' ***Sunday Mirror***

'Fabulously gripping' ***Prima***

'I love it on so many levels, the immense feeling of place, the slow, irresistible sense of being drawn deep into the family and its story, and the strange hovering of menace somewhere in the idyll. Wonderful' **Penny Vincenzi**

'Spellbinding' ***Independent***

'Evans is the reigning queen of the big house family saga . . . The sort of book that has you ignoring family and friends long into the night' ***i newspaper***

'Gripping' ***Irish Times***

'Gorgeous' ***Stylist***

Harriet Evans has sold over a million copies of her books. She is the author of thirteen bestselling novels, most recently *The Beloved Girls*, a Richard and Judy Book Club Selection and the *Sunday Times* Top Ten bestseller *The Garden of Lost and Found*, which won *Good Housekeeping* Book of the Year. She used to work in publishing and now writes full time, when not distracted by her children, other books, gardening, her jumpsuit collection and now stargazing, having acquired a telescope whilst researching *The Stargazers*. She volunteers with Inspiring the Future, is an ambassador for the London Library and last year was elected to the Management Committee of the Society of Authors. She lives in the greatest city in the world (Bath) with her family.

By Harriet Evans

Going Home
A Hopeless Romantic
The Love of Her Life
I Remember You
Love Always
Happily Ever After
Not Without You
A Place for Us
The Butterfly Summer
The Wildflowers
The Garden of Lost and Found
The Beloved Girls
The Stargazers

A Winterfold Christmas (e-short)
Rules for Dating a Romantic Hero (Quick Read)

The Stargazers

HARRIET EVANS

First published in Great Britain in 2023 by
HEADLINE REVIEW
An imprint of HEADLINE PUBLISHING GROUP

1

Cataloguing in Publication Data is available from the British Library

ISBN 978 1 4722 7142 6 (Hardback)
ISBN 978 1 4722 5109 1 (Trade Paperback)

Typeset in 12.5/14.5pt Garamond MT Std by Jouve (UK), Milton Keynes

Printed and bound in Great Britain by Clays Ltd, Elcograf S.p.A.

Headline's policy is to use papers that are natural, renewable and recyclable products and made from wood grown in well-managed forests and other controlled sources. The logging and manufacturing processes are expected to conform to the environmental regulations of the country of origin.

HEADLINE PUBLISHING GROUP
An Hachette UK Company
Carmelite House
50 Victoria Embankment
London EC4Y 0DZ

www.headline.co.uk
www.hachette.co.uk

For my darling dad Philip Evans 1943–2021,
whose memory is a blessing

'Remember to look up at the stars and not down at your feet. Try to make sense of what you see and wonder about what makes the universe exist. Be curious. And however difficult life may seem, there is always something you can do and succeed at'

Stephen Hawking

Author's Note

This book is set in the past and at various points reflects, in language and attitudes towards misogyny, anti-Semitism, racism and homophobia, opinions and words that would not be acceptable today.

Iris

During those last days, before she becomes too weak, she finds she remembers it all once more, piercingly clearly. As if to die, she has to live through it again. So much of it is pain, the pain that has burnt within her since she was very little.

So she writes it down, though her hands are slow and stupid, the letters childlike, and the doltish nurse looking after her keeps interrupting to ask if she wants a drink or her hand held. *Leave me alone, you fool*, she wants to shout, but her voice has stopped working so she smiles instead and they think she is wonderful.

'Isn't she wonderful,' Carole says, sobbing over her. They all think she's wonderful.

She writes it down – why? So they will understand? So they will know the truth? She does not know why she writes it down. But she remembers. Everything.

1922

Her mother's hands stroking her pale hair, how soft it always felt, a caress every time.

'It's my house; I don't see why I should give it up.'

'Fane is not your house, darling. It belongs to your Uncle Clive and he will live here when he returns. If he returns.'

She likes the idea of an uncle. She has read a book where a little girl has an uncle who brings her sweets and a bird's nest and they are jolly together.

'When will Uncle Clive come back?'

'I don't know, darling. No one knows.'

She remembers, too, the kiss her mother drops onto her forehead, the words she uses.

'We must be very kind to your uncle. He has suffered a great deal. It will be a terrible shock for him, to return after so long, to have to take up the reins, learn how to run everything.'

She remembers the milky panes of glass in the little room that was hers above the monumental portico, which always felt to her like the entrance to a vast temple. She had been to the British Museum last year. She was only eight years old and had stood still and stared for what seemed like hours at the statues, pillars and gateways of civilisations buried in the sand for centuries, uncovered and carried across the sea to London. The mystical carved griffins, five times her height, that once stood guard at the gates of the fabled city of Nimrud. The crumbling panels showing the king hunting lions, the arrow piercing the flesh, their huge paws like kittens, the dying fall. I live in a palace too, she wanted to say to the tweedy little man next to her, staring in awe at the ancient marble. Only it is not thousands of miles away. I came up by train, this morning. It is a terrifying, wonderful place. It is my home. It is called Fane Hall.

She considers what she should give this uncle of hers who will come from Canada, the other side of the world. She was only five when her father died, in the last days of the war, 1918. She remembers his last visit home quite well: his large bristling moustache, the feel of his hands as he hugged her tightly when she sat on his knee. He smelt of pipe tobacco and spicy aftershave. He liked to drop kisses on her hair, and whisper in her ear. 'My brother had eyelashes like yours as a child, dearest. Sandy white. Just the same.' She remembers the sound of the horn of the car that came to take him back to war. How he got up, cupping her head in his large hand that last time. She will always remember that. She hates car horns.

It is often lonely growing up at Fane. She is the only child, apart from the boots boy who is three years older than her. But when she says she is lonely Mrs Dennis, the cook, tells Iris she must not be so difficult, for she is a lucky girl. She, Mrs Dennis, is very busy and does not have time for her whining. She hears Mrs Dennis talking about her to one of the maids. 'Nasty white eyelashes. Sneaks around pretending to play, but she's a sly little thing.'

She is happiest outside, where she can see the stars, the birds, mark the seasons, hear the wind in the trees of the woods beyond the park. In summer, the sound of the breeze ruffling the leaves is like whispering, and in winter it bends the bare branches and makes them howl. She loves the blancmange-pink dog roses in the hedgerows that in autumn become jewel-coloured rosehips of ruby and garnet. She watches the swifts as they swoop over the long, waving grasses of the parkland, squealing and curling. She has a dormouse as a pet, and one winter a quite tame robin who flies to her windowsill every morning looking for the crumbs she sweeps into her pinafore to save for him. Nanny Pargeter frowns at her when she discovers her doing this in the kitchen garden one afternoon. 'Nasty, dirty habit. You must try harder, Lady Iris. Remember you are your father's daughter.'

She tries not to be naughty. Often, she doesn't understand things. Often, without meaning to be, she is naughty, and is scolded, and Nanny Pargeter will take a slipper to her. She understands she is very lucky, to have the honour of looking after the house for her father until Uncle Clive gets here, lucky to live here when millions are poor and starving and had no clothing and heating in the long winter just past. When soldiers who fought for their country are begging on the streets, their ragged uniforms where their legs or arms once were tucked into their jackets. When the map of Europe that Miss Gulling, her governess, shows her most mornings up in the Star Study has scribbles all over it from where she has crossed out countries, written new ones in – 'Yougoslavia' – in a careful hand. When so much lies in ruins.

Miss Gulling travelled extensively before the war, in Germany, Austria, Switzerland and France, and she tells her stories of schlosses and ancient countesses and mountains so high you cannot see the tops because they are in the clouds. Miss Gulling evidently had a Life before she came to Fane Hall to teach little Lady Iris Fane. She believes Germany has been humiliated by the terms of the peace agreement and must rise again. She says Germany should have been invited to participate in the Olympics, that their boys would have beaten Abrahams hands down, that Abrahams isn't a true Englishman. She says: 'Germany will be strong again – you wait and see.'

Iris's mother was most careful to appoint the right person. She is careful about everything to do with appearance: her daughter's clothes are ordered from Harrods, her night things from the Army & Navy arriving swathed in tissue paper, then carefully altered by Nanny; her deportment is regularly corrected, hours spent sitting on a chair, walking the corridor with her small shoulders flung back lest she should be round-shouldered; as for her friends, there are none, as she might not be mixing with the right people, and the new Earl Ashley might not approve of sending her to school to mix with common girls. 'We do not know what your uncle will think is best for you when he returns.'

When he returns. This is what they always say.

One day she says: 'What does he have to do with it?'

Nanny Pargeter, folding clothes in the corner of the nursery on the top floor, along the corridor from the Star Study: 'Naughty child, how impertinent you are. He is the head of the family, and he will say what happens to you.'

'That's enough, Nanny. Oh, Iris darling, you do look dreadful, so bedraggled. Have you brushed your hair?'

Iris is drooping with tiredness, but she says: 'Yes, Mama. One hundred and fifty times.'

Everything must be properly done. Yes, she is fortunate.

Nanny Pargeter, Mrs Dennis the cook, Miss Gulling the governess and her mother – her life is ordered by these four women, and the grounds of Fane, which is her own world. She knows every inch of it, and she is clever, so she remembers what she is told. The black marble statues, one of Hermes, the other of Cassandra, greeting visitors as they cross into the vast hall. She loves Greek myths, like her father, her mother tells her, and his father and all the way back to the first Earl Ashley. Her favourite, of course, is the Odyssey, with men turned into pigs, and magic, and witches, and one-eyed men. And Penelope and Telemachus, waiting for Odysseus to come home.

She knows she is a disappointment, twice over. She should have been a boy, and she is not a boy. Then, she should have been a pretty girl and she is not; she is plain, like a monkey, if a monkey had pale eyelashes, pale hair, pale skin, and asked too many questions. She knows adults don't like her. She sees their assessment in their eyes when she is wheeled out if visitors come to call, trussed up in her petticoats and pinafores, hair twisted into curls that never sit quite right.

Fane Hall is a long, flat-fronted mansion built in the late eighteenth century, with an East and West Wing which curl out from the frontage towards a kitchen garden and a stable block. At the centre of the house is the portico, protruding, a vast stone canopy with six Corinthian pillars, as tall as the British Museum's, upon which rests a pediment flaking with age and a frieze of carved objects – a vase, an oak, a sun – running the length of the portico, which casts the central hall into darkness.

Once, it was the finest house in Sussex, perhaps in southern England. Now it is slowly, gently, falling apart. She knows her dear mother cannot manage it all. She is not the sort who ever could, not like the stiff-backed great ladies who come to call on her mother and patronise her, who should have lived at Fane, who would know what to do.

Her parents met because her father saw her mother playing at the Wigmore – in those days still known as Bechstein – Hall. He carried her cello back that night for her, through the streets of Marylebone. Her mother didn't know for several weeks that the gentle, kind man she called first Mr Fane, then Arthur, who alternately waited outside for her after every performance or left bouquets at the stage door of violets, then roses and notes in looping handwriting on thick, creamy paper, was an earl, Lord Ashley, of storied, glittering Fane Hall. Her mother, the daughter of unworldly middle-class artisans, simply had not understood what marrying a man like that would entail. She says this once to her daughter, with a little laugh, and Iris knows what this means, and she never says it again.

Lady Ashley cannot do accounts, or 'deal' with Mrs Boyes, the new housekeeper, or discuss poaching with the gamekeeper, or organise committees for the purpose of Good Works. She knows what an elegy is, and how to reach fourth position, how to master a Beethoven sonata. But she tries so hard: Iris sees her weeping as she attempts to knit socks for the poor, and cannot get her hands to work, her slender, clever hands that can play anything, but, God bless her, absolutely cannot knit.

Increasingly, her mother is only happy when she is practising, up on the top floor. The deep, melancholy sound of the cello reverberates through the house. It echoes across the empty rooms, bouncing off dusty chandeliers and the wooden shutters, most of which are fastened tight shut these days. Iris knows there is no money, that her father has gambled much of it away, and she knows the house is dying, and yet she loves it passionately, to her bones, this connection to her darling, kind father, who lies now in Belgium, his grave untended, unseen by anyone who knew him. There are many little things that will pain her throughout her life, words and sounds that stab behind the eyes and hurt her head in the course of the day: Belgium. Car horns. Cellos. Hand-knitted socks. Fathers. Fathers.

But she doesn't see any of that – not yet. She knows only that Uncle Clive will return, and then the house will come alive again.

So they pass, the days and nights, engulfing her like snowdrifts in winter, clouds of dust and seed in summer. Two women, waiting for someone else to come and live in their house.

August 2020

'How extraordinary,' said Sarah Forster, coming into the large, cluttered kitchen. 'You'll never guess what's happened.'

Gently she moved the mess on the kitchen table – a packet of seeds, two coffee mugs, a pile of junk mail, an old bowl filled with dead biros, unsharpened pencils, rusty paperclips and coins – out of the way, and dropped a package onto the table.

'Barnard Castle's banned day-trippers,' said her daughter, Friday.

'Not yet.' Sarah unhooked a mug from the dresser, touching the warped old wood, as she did every morning, saying the words she said only to herself each day. *Good morning, all souls in this house.*

She poured herself a coffee, wrapping her aching fingers round the warming china, and winced: her hands were bad today.

Her heart was racing. She tried to ignore it, to breathe.

'I heard the doorbell go,' said her granddaughter Esmé, leaning forward and tapping the package. 'So it must be something from the postman. That facemask I ordered for you from Etsy's arrived.'

'No, it was for me. And I'm not wearing a facemask that says "Gotta Blame It on My Juice" even if it means I get fined,' said Sarah. She smiled at Esmé, but Friday saw the puckered line on her forehead.

'What is it, Mum?'

Sarah sank down onto the ancient kitchen chair, which creaked alarmingly; everything in the house was, like her, ancient. She gave a small laugh, and pulled the package towards her. 'It's the strangest thing. This has arrived from Vic.'

'Who?'

'My sister,' she said to her granddaughter. 'You've never met her.'

'You have a sister?' Esmé put her phone down; she even managed to look vaguely interested.

Sarah knew her daughter was watching her. 'Yes.' She moved the fruit bowl, then the keys, ineffectually. 'But we – Well, I haven't seen her for years.'

'Did you fall out?'

Sarah looked down at her coffee, as if surprised she was still holding it. She was silent for a long time. 'Not really,' she said eventually. 'It's – sometimes it's easier not to see people any more.'

She traced Vic's address on the back of the jiffy bag with one stiff finger, the diamonds and sapphires on her engagement ring glinting in the late summer light. Then, briskly, she ripped open the package, gingerly removing a thick, battered pamphlet, its staples brown with ancient rust. '*Stargazing: A Guide for Beginners*' it said across the front in a crisp 1950s sans serif font.

Oh, where was Daniel?

'Stargazing,' said Esmé. 'Grandad would like that.'

'I was given it,' Sarah said. 'A long time ago, by –' and her voice faltered.

A sheaf of papers, folded inside the pamphlet, slid out. The first sheet, a letter.

'Dear Sarah,' she read out loud.

'I trust you are well and have survived these last few months relatively unscathed. All is well here in Ingotsham, though quiet without Robert, who died last year.

'She never told me,' she said, looking up. 'Oh, poor Vic.'

Her fingers were trembling. She pressed them to her lips, eyes scanning the page as she read to herself, rapidly.

How are you? How is life in The Row? I am pleased to see that you are still there (how wonderful that you, like me, are still in the phone book). Are you still playing? Is Daniel still alive? I hope he, and the girls are well too.

I am writing after all this time as the trustees of Fane have been in touch. They are reopening the house to visitors, and would like to invite us to attend a ceremony there in August.

It seems that during the lockdown the warden undertook an inventory, and found some boxes in the attic. They have been there for decades, ever since Iris died, I suppose. There was also this pamphlet, under the bed she died in. It must have been there for decades. I thought you would want it.

She also found these papers, an account of Uncle Clive's arrival at Fane and Iris's early years. Her health was failing but it is very clear to me it is our mother's handwriting.

I didn't know what to do, and then I realised after what has happened with the pandemic over the past six months it is ridiculous to have this silence between us. I didn't telephone or write to you about Robert. I wanted to tell you. But I couldn't bear your sympathy. I knew you would understand my pain. No one else does. I think we've come to believe we've always worked best at arm's length. But . . . oh well, life is too short, Sarah. If the last few months have taught me anything it's that. I don't want to end up like her. I can't.

Don't worry: I'm not asking to be best friends.

But we were *best friends though*, Sarah found herself thinking, and her breathing grew laboured, her eyes pricking with unbearably painful tears. *You were my world, Vic, and I loved you so much.*

She read the rest, her voice soft.

Read what she has written. I wonder what you make of it? It changes everything, if it is true. (And I think it is true.)

I said to you once that I think of the past now, that is to say our childhood, as rather like living with wolves. Everything was so chaotic, so terrifying, so confusing. The wolves were at the door and we ended up eating ourselves instead of making them disappear.

Anyway – read it.

With my love.
Your sister,
Victoria
x

Sarah stood up, and pushed her chair out of the way. 'Excuse me,' she said, nodding. 'I'll – I'll just –'

'Is she revealing all the family secrets, Gran? Is she going to have you cancelled?' Esmé offered, but Sarah simply smiled and left the room.

Friday, who had said nothing all this time, frowned at her daughter.

'Leave Granny alone for a bit,' she said. 'She doesn't like to talk about what it was like, growing up.'

'Why?'

Friday stared at the kitchen door, which was banging in the wake of her mother's exit. 'You learn how to be a parent based on what happened to you. Granny – Well, given what she's told me, I'm amazed she made it out alive. I'm amazed I did too. You have no idea what she went through. I don't think she fully understands it, either. Oh dear –' She gazed around the kitchen, the absence of both parents keenly felt. 'What's happened, I wonder?'

The sound of her mother's cello echoing through the house drifted down the stairs. 'We should both leave her for a while,' said Friday, tidying up the breakfast things. 'Let's go back to the flat today, Es. We were only meant to stay here for a month or so. And it's been nearly six months.'

'It's been great, though,' said Esmé awkwardly. 'I didn't want to come here . . . I thought it'd be awful. Now I don't want to leave.'

'Well, me neither.' Friday gazed out of the window into the little garden at the dark quince tree where the fruits hung high up, still small, tight, pale green. 'I love being back here. We were lucky, you know. But it's not our house, Es.'

'No, it's much nicer.' Friday laughed. 'Oh, Mum, let's stay a bit longer. Just till we go on holiday. If we get to go, that is.'

'All right. I'll see what happens. See what's in the package Vic sent her today. It might change things.' Friday was silent, listening to the cello, the plaintive, sweet notes that hung in the still summer air. She glanced down at the letter, still on the table.

'The wolves were at the door,' she said after a while, quietly, almost to herself. 'Poor Mum. Poor Vic.'

Esmé shrugged. She was fifteen and the past – Well, it was simply that, wasn't it? Dead, and buried. She bit into her toast, looked back down at her phone.

Part One
1969

Chapter One

September 1969

'Hold on tight, Sarah! Hold on! Are you ready?'

Are you ready?

'Yes, Daniel darling,' she said, unable to believe it was really happening. 'Yes, I'm ready.'

'This turning is bloody awkward. OK? Here we go, my bird. Here we go!'

The sun shone with the full force of late September, bathing the cobbles of The Row with the last of summer's silky light. As instructed, Sarah Forster held on tight to the door, while her husband reversed and swore at the same time, the noise from each activity growing proportionally louder the less success he had. A Hampstead matron scuttling past, with neat coils of silver hair and gloved hands gripping a rigid handbag, glanced at them in covert horror as Daniel, swearing and rocking the gear stick back and forth, inexpertly tried to negotiate the van they'd borrowed between the wooden gateposts denoting the entrance to The Row.

Later, Sarah would appreciate her husband's loudness in public, his obliviousness to others' judgements. Then, she was still not quite used to it, and though she smiled, patting his arm encouragingly, she wanted to sink down into the footwell of the seat, cover herself with the road atlas and remain there till it was all over. She felt like this quite often.

'Bloody *hell,* Sarah!' Daniel muttered furiously as the car lurched violently and the Hampstead matron, terrified, ran for cover up a side street. 'The British hate cars – that's their trouble. We hate progress, and anything that's unusual. Look at the state of British industry! Why have this bloody gatepost here! Why!

Why make our lives harder? It's our street, after all! I'm going to write a letter.'

'Who to?'

'To whom, my adorable Philistine. Is there a mayor of Hampstead?'

'There's the GLC.' The van was bunny-hopping down the last few yards towards the oval-shaped private garden and Daniel steered it left, braking gently. Sarah drew a long, silent breath. They were here. This was The Row: the dense trees, heavy with summer's last flourish, the cooing pigeons, the shouts of children playing in the central garden, surrounded by two crescents of redbrick houses, some hung with silver tiles, some with gables, or balconies, or turrets. It was like a film set, a child's toy town. Her eye flickered from one to the other. *Which one is it again?* She looked round. She had the feeling she was being watched.

This is our house, she said quietly to herself. *And so it begins.*

'We're here, darling,' Daniel was saying. 'Finally. Now, who's this fool blocking the way? Oh, damn, I think it's a neighbour. Good afternoon!'

'That's me,' came a woman's dry voice. 'You must be the new bods.'

Daniel climbed out of the car. 'We most certainly are.' As Sarah got out and shut the door, Daniel was shaking hands with a tall woman standing in front of the gate next to their house. She held a cigarette in one hand and a trowel in the other. She sported a silver crop and wore a black polo neck and slacks; completing the look was a huge pair of round white sunglasses.

She gave them a brisk but warm smile. 'I'm Diana, Diana Catesby. Glad to meet you.'

'Ah!' said Daniel, still pumping her hand up and down enthusiastically. 'As in Catesby, Ratcliffe and Lovell.'

'He was my great-something grandfather,' Diana said carelessly. 'Catesbys of Ashby Manor, don't you know.'

'Well, well. I'm Daniel Forster,' said Daniel. Diana nodded and gave him another quick smile. 'Of the Ashkenazi Jewish Forsters of Ukraine and Germany via Petticoat Lane and Sussex, you know.' Sarah wanted to disappear again, but Diana laughed. 'And this is my wife, Sarah.'

'We can't have that. Where are *you* from, Sarah?'

There was a pause. 'Oh,' said Sarah, 'I'm like the Nowhere Man. From Nowhere Land.' She put her hands on her hips, and inexplicably did a little dance, before stopping, blushing furiously.

'Sarah's my wife?' said Daniel somewhat uncertainly, as if he wasn't sure she'd agreed to it.

'So, you've bought Thorpe's place,' Diana said, moving on without comment. She raised her eyebrows, with a slight smile. 'Well, well – welcome.' She laughed. 'It's in rather a state. Rather strange, thinking of anyone other than Adrian Thorpe there. They were a lovely family. I suppose that's a rather tactless thing to say.'

'Not at all,' said Daniel. 'I'm glad they were lovely. And I'm glad they left it in a state. We wouldn't have been able to buy it otherwise.'

Sarah was scanning the brickwork, the window frames, the front path, the cracked stones where weeds flung themselves up towards the sunlight. Silvery tiles covered the top half of the house, rising to a fringed white wood gable, and at the corner, in front of chimneys as tall as cathedral spires, was a turret, a curved princess's tower. The leaded windows glinted in the afternoon sun. Several were cracked, or broken entirely.

Well, Sarah said to herself, *it's going to keep us busy, I suppose.*

She gave a smile at the memory of the previous night, their last in the little flat in Islington, their first home together. They'd eaten pasta around the tiny table in their tiny kitchen, sharing a bottle of wine and making each other laugh till they were weak with stories of their respective days – how she'd got lost in Peter Jones, looking at curtains, and had to back away towards the underwear department when she thought she saw Susan Cowper, the most dreadful girl from school, replete with headscarf, pearls and gloves (she was a year older than Sarah, so twenty-seven).

Susan had glanced over, and bared her remarkably large, horsey teeth, as if recognising, or scenting, Sarah, and Sarah had stumbled backwards against a mannequin and, thinking she was being assaulted, had caught the mannequin's arm and wrenched it off, before dropping to the ground, like soldiers on manoeuvres. Later, she had made a joke of it to Daniel, but her blood was pumping, her cheeks flushed and she was astonished at the rage she felt, seeing Susan again, after all those years, after everything.

Daniel had laughed until tears ran down his cheeks at the way she told it, and Sarah had laughed too, at the image of herself, staggering backwards, assaulting a mannequin. Daniel had told her about how that very day he'd tried to help an old lady across the road by gently taking her arm, whereupon she had angrily shaken herself free and shouted, 'Unhand me, sir!' before striding rapidly in the other direction towards Judd Street.

'Oh dear,' Sarah had said, gripping the sides of the table, their joint laughter ringing around the small flat. 'We're not going to become sedate and boring and talk about property prices and the EEC at dinner after we move to Hampstead, are we?'

'Never,' Daniel had said, and raised his glass. 'Not us. To never being sedate! Long may sedateness be discontinued!' And they had both found this, for some reason, funnier still.

Perhaps it was unspoken nerves. Sarah thought of the evening now, looking up at the house. She felt eyes on her, again, and shivered, wrapping her arms round her thin frame, encasing herself in her own warmth.

'Well,' said Diana, 'I don't want to hold you up. We'll have a drink soon, yes?' She removed her sunglasses with a flourish, waved her hand and hummed, her eyes rolling slightly back in her head. Sarah stared at her, fascinated. 'Great to meet. Listen, I'll leave you cats to it, but do, do shout if you need anything.'

'Why do I know the name Adrian Thorpe?' Sarah said, after Diana had turned and, swaying back down the path, vanished inside.

'She was stoned,' said Daniel, staring after her.

'No!'

'Well I never,' said Daniel. 'What a gal. Stoned, at midday.'

Sarah sniffed curiously. 'Are you . . . *sure*?'

'Oh, I'm sure. Did you see her pupils? Wide as her eyeballs. And she had bare feet. This is a good neighbour, Sarah,' he said happily. 'I like this house.'

'Daniel – it isn't too much for us, is it? We're not flashy Hampstead up-and-coming types – we just want somewhere simple, don't we?'

'Don't you remember?' He took her wrists in his, holding her hands inside his. 'I promised you I'd give you a home, a proper home. I did.'

'You did.'

'I did,' he repeated, as if it was worth saying twice.

'I know, darling. I know. But – Adrian Thorpe!' Sarah clicked her fingers. 'I've got it. The newspaper editor. He edited *The Times*. Didn't he used to visit Churchill during the Battle of Britain? Didn't he basically dictate public morale?' She turned towards the house, chewing her lip. This is . . . *his* house? Yikes.'

'It's not his house, Sarah, it's ours,' said Daniel. He took out a key then picked her up, swinging her into his arms, and kissed her, one hand holding the back of her head, his lips searching her, pulling her towards him. She could feel him inhaling, feel the shuddering breath inside him, and then he broke away, and looked down at her. 'I love you. Sarah, I love you so much,' he said, kissing her lightly again as he pushed open the front gate with his hip and she hummed the opening bars of Elgar's Symphony No. 1, which always reminded her of ceremonial marching. Daniel nodded. 'Oh, that's very good,' he said, setting off down the path as if she were light as a bird, whilst she sang.

Inside, it was so quiet that Sarah's ears rang with the noise of the van on the cobbles and the sensation, which she'd had since she'd woken in their Islington bedsit that morning, of falling, constantly, through space and time. She stared back through the curved redbrick porchway of her new home, at the patterned glass where entwined red and green shapes twisted into a knot, then again into the large, echoing hallway, where the Victorian tiles, patterned with stars, spread away from her, like a sea of galaxies, a path out towards the back of the house. It was chilly inside, dark and still.

'Stars,' she said, nudging Daniel. 'Look, on the tiles.'

'See? Didn't I say? The hall was piled high with rubbish the old guy's grandchildren were storing here while they argued about what to do with it. So I didn't see the floor; I only noticed it today,' Daniel said. He hitched his jacket around his shoulders, as if he too found it cold. 'It's a good sign.' He pulled her against him.

'I don't understand how we got this house.'

She had been on a tour of Austria with the Pembroke Quartet when it came back on the market, and had had several agonised phone conversations with Daniel about it. 'It's perfect,' he'd said. 'It's our house. I'm telling you it's our house!'

When she'd returned to London – she'd thought the decision had been left open – she was slightly surprised to find they'd bought it, that it was a done deal. Their little flat was increasingly uninhabitable: fungus, mould, mice, a leaking roof and an invisible landlord. It was time to move. But from that to – this?

As if reading her mind, Daniel bent down and kissed the tip of her nose. 'Everything OK, Mrs Forster?'

'Absolutely,' she said. 'Just feeling rather strange, that's all. Where's my cello?'

'It's in the car. I'll go and get it. Don't worry. First thing in.'

She was fiddling with the open wires coming out of the light switches when he returned with a box of books, staggering over the threshold.

'Open the first door will you, Sarah? There's the study.'

Sarah looked around at the large, well-lit room with its curved windows, and the ecclesiastical-looking stained glass, the baronial fireplace, the empty shelves. 'Here's where the old man ran his empire, I guess. It's the study. This is where I'll write, and you can practise.' He took her hand and pulled her along the corridor. She was smiling. 'And in the evening we'll move through into the kitchen. We'll have dinner parties, all-day parties, brunch. Sarah, I'll bring brunch to the English.'

'You lived in New York for six months, Daniel. Stop pretending you're Damon Runyon.'

'It's in my Jewish soul. I felt more at home there than anywhere. Apart from when I'm with you, I mean.' Sarah rolled her eyes. 'Now, look at this –'

He opened the kitchen door and she gazed in alarm at the large, echoing kitchen, the vast pine dresser that stood on the long wall to the right of the door, the cold stone floor, and more and more empty shelves, empty cupboards, all needing to be filled with – their *things,* their lives. At the back were dirty French windows giving out onto a tangled mass of brambles and bindweed that was the garden. He glanced towards her, and saw her face. She put her arm round his shoulders.

'I love it.' She ran her free hand through her hair till it stood on end, like a duck's tail. 'It's a wonderful house, Daniel, but can we afford – all this? It's a mansion!'

'It's not a mansion. It's a semi-detached house.'

She could hear the disappointment in his voice: they had already had this conversation, and here she was, raking over it again, on this special day.

'I know. I know the wiring needs doing and the floorboards are rotten, and the glass needs replacing, and we'll have to clear the garden, sort out the damp, buy furniture, oh, everything. I know but – listen. Don't be the Sarah who sees problems. Be my bird, the one who sees horizons, wants adventures, who has to have her cello, to play. Who says "why not?" instead of "why?". Isn't that what we promised each other? Come.' His fingers tightened round hers, and she looked down at his large hand swallowing hers, the fine, long, graceful fingers, the strength in them, the gentleness and grace.

She didn't say what she wanted to, which was *I've lived in chaos before – you know I have.* Instead, she said: 'We did. And it's going to be wonderful. I just need to get used to it. Only I don't understand how you have the money.'

'You don't need to worry about that.' He saw her jaw tighten. 'OK. It's more than we could afford. But not much more. They wanted cash, and I have cash, from Aunt Miriam's will, peace be upon her.'

'You used up all Aunt Miriam's money?'

'On a house!' Daniel said, his voice raised. 'I didn't bloody blow it all on the nags, or at the Coach and Horses, Sarah! I bought us a house! Listen, I'm not saying it won't be tough. We'll be poor for years, my angel – you have to go out on tour immediately and I have to write a huge airport bestseller – but it's all going to be worth it. We'd have been crazy not to go for it. It's where we build ourselves. Think about what you've managed to accomplish, by yourself, since you got away. What *she'd* do if she knew.' His face was lit up now. He was waving his arms around, his wicked enthusiasm almost infectious. He led her upstairs into the vast drawing room. 'Here's where we'll sit in the evenings, and read, and listen to the radio, and watch TV. Look.'

'There's a balcony,' said Sarah. 'I've always wanted a little balcony.' She smiled, and it was OK, and not so daunting. She closed her eyes, and suddenly she was there. She could see herself in summer, windows open to the street, the trees moving outside, someone or something padding around at her feet, and in winter a chair beside the window, a fire burning in the grate, wood smoke curling towards her, rain drizzling outside.

More and more rooms: box rooms with square dents in the carpet where the bed had been, tiny lavatories, huge bathrooms with clanging lavatory chains and claw-footed baths on more cold, bare tiles – Sarah wished she could simply put down cork matting right now. To have it all sorted out, this unwieldy, terrifyingly grand house where other people wanted to live and where ghosts seemed to be about to pop out at any moment. The Thorpes, all of them, coming back to claim the house. And all the time the feeling she was being watched, by whom she couldn't say, wouldn't go away.

On the top two floors were two bedrooms each. The second floor had a vast room overlooking the back garden and the garden of the house beyond, where a little girl sat, reading a book against a tree. Above, behind the houses, was the green expanse of the Heath.

'This is our room,' Sarah said, turning round, holding up a finger, as a bird sang in a tree outside. 'Look at the sky. Look at the view. We can look at the stars, Daniel.'

He was staring down at the carpets, not at the view, but he said: 'I know. There's a tiny balcony there. With binoculars, it's dark enough here we might even be able to see the Milky Way – I don't know –'

'Daniel! Stargazing.' And suddenly the joy of it flooded her – they would live here, and sleep in this beautiful room, and it was affordable, thanks to Aunt Miriam. She felt a pang of guilt that she'd met Aunt Miriam once and secretly thought she was kind of mean, an old nosy parker who frowned at Sarah and at one point pinched her hip, as if disappointed with Sarah's form – too much of it or too little, Sarah never knew, just that she was wrong in some way.

She breathed in, a ragged, happy breath. 'Oh, Aunt Miriam. I love you.' She looked down at Daniel, who was pulling energetically at a floorboard under the carpet. 'I love you too, Daniel Forster. I can't believe it. I can't bloody believe this is where we live.'

He turned. 'Yes?' he said. 'Oh,' he said, following her outstretched finger, pointing at the view. 'Oh yes.'

She gave him a small smile, but her face was serious. 'I do love you,' she said, the words thick in her throat. She held his face between her hands, kissing his temples, his eyelids, his wide cheekbones, his nose. 'I love you more than anything, anyone, ever.' She kissed his lips, and pressed herself against him. 'Don't ever leave me. Don't ever let's move.' She kissed him again, almost feverishly. 'Here. We're here.'

'We are,' he said, not smiling now, his gaze intent. 'Come down here.' His hand slid up her leg, slowly, slipping into her knickers, sudden, quick, and she gasped. He pulled her down, onto the floor, and they made love, slowly, exquisitely, joyfully, feeling like children, playing at grown-ups, camping out for a night in someone else's life.

Afterwards, Daniel slept, his face twitching as it always did when he was deeply asleep, and she lay there, happiness flooding her, listening to the sounds of the house and the trees outside, the noises of her new home, her new life, until her eyes closed.

A noise thudded through Sarah's head; something seemed to be shaking. She could hear a dog barking, and for a moment didn't know where she was. She sat up with a start, mouth dry. She was naked, her nipples tightening in the breeze from the open window. Next to her, her husband lay prone, creamy, ropy muscles tight across his shoulders and back. She gazed at him for a second, thinking how pleasing he was, how much she enjoyed simply looking at him.

The noise came again and she realised it was someone banging on the door. Her front door.

'Daniel.' Everything came flooding back. She yanked her long floral dress over her head. 'Daniel, darling. Someone's at the door. Did you park the van in the wrong –'

Daniel didn't move. Sarah pulled on her plimsolls as the knocking grew louder. 'Coming!' she shouted. Her left hand skimmed the smooth bannister rail, worn and soft from years of hands resting on it. It was warm.

The front door was heavy, and true; it sat exactly in the frame. Sarah paused for a moment, her hand on the lock. Her first visitor. It was all wrong. She pushed her hair out of the way, smoothing down her dress, as if she were twelve again and standing outside Miss Parker's office, waiting for the hammer to fall. Her hands were sticky with Daniel on her, on her fingers, her stomach, between her thighs. She was very aware she was naked under the dress.

Suddenly she smiled. She wasn't twelve any more and this was her house. She opened the door.

'Good afternoon!' A bright, round face smiled at her. 'You must be Mrs Forster, I heard from the Thorpes that was the name. I wanted to introduce myself.' She held out a small, doughy hand.

Sarah looked down at it, blinking. Gold rings, studded with diamonds, turquoises, garnets, cut into the swollen fingers, each nail a gleaming, pearlescent almond shape. Sarah shook her hand. 'I'm Sarah Foster.'

'Oh yes. I'm Georgina Montgomery and we're in the Cottage, just at the other end there.' She peered over Sarah's shoulder. 'You've just moved in? Sorry to be so nosy. I'm – well, we all are – *desperately* curious to know who swept in and carried off this lovely house! And I said to Monty, I'm just going to pop over, just *pop over*, to say a little hello, and he said "Jolly good idea, darling," and here I am! He's resting. Bit of a farewell do last night for Lara and Henry . . .' She passed a hand over her forehead. 'Diana knows how to pour the drinks – that's all I'll say about *that.*' She gave a loud laugh, like a honking duck. 'Ha! Ha! Ha!'

'My husband is upstairs,' said Sarah, not wanting to explain further. 'We'd love to have you over for –' She frowned, watching Georgina's eager face to see if this was the right thing to say. 'For soon . . . would be lovely,' she finished, wishing Daniel would wake up.

Was this what you did with neighbours? How did you live, in a house, in a street like this? How did you do any of it? Houses, marriage, families, careers, futures. She didn't know the rules. Every new thing tripped her up.

The first evening after they'd got back from their honeymoon, spent in Portofino, flushed with sex and sun and wine, Sarah had set to making her new husband a meal, and hadn't realised that you cooked onions gently in butter or oil on a low flame. She had turned the heat up to the highest setting, burnt them to a cinder, and the neighbours in the tall, packed five-storey house had all, every one of them, complained. Sarah had gone into her bedroom and cried at the failure of it, the crushing reality of life compared to her in a headscarf, thong sandals and a red dress, sitting by the sea eating *spaghetti alle vongole.* Daniel had cooked instead.

The first time he'd asked her out to dinner he'd taken her to a little restaurant off the King's Road and halfway through she had disclosed she'd never eaten out before. 'Monica's mother took us to tea when I stayed with them in the holidays,' she'd had to explain, flushing with shame. 'But not for meals.'

She could not explain what she was remembering was restaurants with her mother, leaning across the table groaning with all the food she could order: lobsters, veal escalopes, gratin dauphinoise, grabbing their skinny little arms, hissing: '*When the waiter takes that couple's plates into the kitchen, we leave. We get up and walk, then we run, you understand? It's a joke, Victoria, don't snivel for God's sake! It's all a bit of fun.*'

She and Vic never ate the meals, their small stomachs curdling with fear about what was to come. Their mother, of course, merrily guzzling everything down until she was ill the day after, unable to move. 'A bilious attack – leave me alone, you cretins,' she'd hiss, and the curtains would be drawn, and there was no one to take them to school or make them food.

She hadn't known what to order that first time with him and sat staring in misery at the menu. And then, because he was Daniel, he'd understood. He'd known what to do. 'That's first, that's second – you know how it works really, Sarah,' he'd said. 'Pick something you like the look of. That's all that matters.'

'It's exciting, you see, a new family, on The Row,' Georgina Montgomery was saying. 'Might as well tell you now, I wanted Monts to buy the house, but he wouldn't. Said it wasn't worth it. And then they knocked down the price and you nipped in there! I'm furious about it, but he wouldn't be moved. And here you are!'

Floorboards creaked above Sarah, and she started. She wasn't sure if Daniel had heard this. He had a habit of wandering around with no clothes on. Her fingers tightened on the door. She wished fervently, right then, that it was just another ordinary day in Islington, and she was fighting her way through the crowds out of the Tube station after rehearsal, cello strapped to her back, clutching her string bag on her way to Chapel Market, plucking Daniel out of a pub where he'd be discussing art or literature with some old Islington roué, staggering back up the four flights of stairs, putting two eggs to boil on the tiny gas hob, collapsing on the bed together, entwined, pulling each other's clothes off, noises rising, the heat, the feeling of him inside her, pushing, holding back, then deeper . . . deeper . . .

She shook herself as a breeze ruffled the overgrown jasmine climbing up beside the front door, plucking at her long flowery dress. Behind her, she heard Daniel's feet, thundering down the top flight of stairs. *Play a part, Sarah*, she told herself. *Play it as if your life depends on it.*

So she smiled. 'I'm glad to hear you wanted the house too. Makes us feel we've got good taste. Might we invite you and your husband over for a drink soon?'

'Do, do. Pop a note through the door. And we'll explain who

everyone is, what you need to know.' Georgina's eyes glittered. 'You've met Diana. I happened to see you arrive, you see. Diana's a lovely lady. Now, we're the corner cottage, there. One of the small houses. Not really The Row. But we're right on the Heath.' She pointed behind them at a little redbrick gatehouse, one of two flanking the wooden gate at the other end of the oval. Beyond it rose the trees of Hampstead Heath. 'I told Monty, I'd only live on The Row, you see. My aunt lived here and it was my life's ambition to own a house here one day. She was Number 4. Professor Gupta lives there now.' She leaned forward. 'He's Indian, you know. Keeps himself to himself.' She looked as if she was about to say something else, then added, 'Poor Lara and Henry. I do feel for them, but of course, *you know*.'

Daniel's voice boomed out behind Sarah. 'Good afternoon.' He put his arm round her shoulders, extending the other to Georgina. 'I'm Daniel Forster.'

Georgina actually lowered her lashes, and looked up at Daniel through them. 'Good afternoon,' she said. 'Georgina Montgomery. Very nice to meet you.' She tapped the glass on the porch, and Sarah saw then the curling entwined shapes that she'd noticed on the way in were letters. A. E. T. Georgina followed her gaze. 'Ah, yes. You know, Sir Adrian bought the house for Eveline. *She* was Russian,' she said, nodding at Daniel. Years with Daniel enabled Sarah to understand what people like Georgina meant. She meant Eveline was Jewish. 'And you know what happened . . .' Georgina trailed off, and looked down.

'No?' said Sarah politely – what else could she say?

'Well, she killed herself. Here in the house. Weeks after she gave birth to their daughter. Oh dear . . . I hate being the one to tell you . . .'

'Oh no,' Daniel said softly. 'That's terrible.' His arm tightened round his wife.

'He'd had the whole house remodelled.' She pointed behind them, a regretful small smile playing about her lips, as though she was sad about being the one to tell them. 'Their initials are everywhere. Even on the tiles. A.E.T. It's short for Aeternum. Eternity in Latin.'

Sarah turned. She saw, stretching away from her, the star

pattern she had admired on the way up. How it was not a pattern at all, but the letters again. A.E.T. Eternity.

Georgina was gabbling now, the muscles in her shiny face working fast, eyes darting from Sarah to Daniel. 'I know Lara loves the house. But she's awfully glad it's over, poor lamb. I don't know her well, but I hear that's what they say, though I'm no gossip, Sarah – that's not me. The swing in the garden is where her husband Tony proposed to Lara. She stayed here the night before she was married. Lovely girl. Very – reserved, no surprise with all she's been through. Ever so clever, she's a photographer you know. Takes lots of photos of round here. So that's nice! Yes, we're all very close here.'

'We'll be glad to know them,' Daniel said in his warm, make-all-things-better voice. 'Now, Mrs Montgomery, I really ought to get on with hauling my wife's possessions inside.'

'Time and tide!' said Georgina with a tinkling laugh. She bared her teeth at them, eyes widening again. 'Well, well! We'll have that drink, then!' She looked expectantly at Sarah. 'Soon! Welcome once again.'

Then she turned, and trotted down the path, letting the gate swing shut with what seemed like some relish to Sarah, who stood watching her go.

Daniel blew on her neck. 'She's crazy.'

'Did you think so?'

'Oh, absolutely. Maybe there's something in the water this high up out of town. I told you we should have stayed in Islington.'

Sarah felt a bit sick. It was being ruined. 'Did you know any of that? About the owners, and the house, and all of it?'

'No. But I wouldn't listen to her. I don't think any of it's true, and even if it is . . . Think about where you grew up. Where I grew up. Who cares what happened here in the past? Listen to me. I promised I'd return the van to Eddie today. So I'm going to go now, but I'll be right back.' He stopped. 'Sarah, darling. Of course this feels scary to you. I understand why.'

'You do?'

He held her wrists and looked at her fiercely, his dark eyes burning into her. She could not look at him. It was too frightening, the enormity of it. She felt his beard, bristling against her cheek, his arms round her, as she rested her head on his shoulder. 'Sarah, listen to me. *Listen.* We're going to have kids, and pets, and a life. And we'll live here, and I'll write books and you'll make music and babies.' His hand slid over her flat, warm stomach, and she rolled against him, against his hard, solid frame, the softness of the worn plaid shirts he always wore, his comforting scent, spicy, sweaty, Daniel. 'We'll die here. After a long, long life together. We're here. No one else. Their problems are their problems. Not ours. This is a clean slate. I promise you, Sarah.'

'Yes,' she said, pressing herself against him, wishing they could simply stay like that, like they had been on the floor wrapped in the eiderdown, with the owls hooting behind the house, for ever. 'Clean slate.'

'Good,' he said. 'Now, come here, Mrs Forster. Jeez, I love you.'

Chapter Two

April 1970

Seven months later

'I've had a letter from Vic,' Sarah called from the kitchen. She swallowed some tea, rather gingerly.

There was a grunt, then a muffled curse, then silence from the study next door.

'She wonders whether we are enjoying Hampstead.' Sarah considered, then tossed aside her burnt, dry toast, as a loud banging came from the study. 'She thinks it's – Oh, where is it. "Has the exoticism of North London worn off yet?"'

'She means the Jews. She's fixated on us,' Daniel called back over the sound of the banging. 'Tell her you're screwing one. Tell her you like his—'

'I won't, thanks very much. Anyway, she wants to come and visit.'

'AHH.' Daniel emitted a bellow of pain, and something made a popping sound. 'God dammit!'

'With Robert.'

'Wowee. Two for the price of one. A bargain.'

'She did write at Christmas to ask if she could visit. I can't keep putting her off – Daniel, what is that noise? What are you *doing*?'

'Birdie,' Daniel called faintly, as though he were trapped under something and unable to breathe, 'can I finish this? I'm at a pretty crucial stage.'

There was silence. Sarah sipped some more tea, looking round the freezing, dirty kitchen, and drummed her fingers against the sheet of music she'd been looking over. Daniel liked hearing her practise while he worked. He said it helped him concentrate.

She, however, found it difficult to keep her focus, and preferred to practise upstairs where her precious cello was out of the way of upturned nails, flying forks, spitting fat or any of the other chaos that came with life with Daniel.

'OK,' he shouted after a few minutes. 'Come and see.'

Cautiously – the other day he had balanced a ladder against the bedroom door and Sarah, coming in after a practise, her mind still entirely on Schubert and fingering problems, had opened the door and sent him flying – she entered the study.

'Oh, Chri—Oh, wow,' she said, concealing her horror. 'Daniel – what have you done?'

'It's original,' he said, avoiding her eyes. 'What do you think? Be totally honest.'

'Totally honest? Really?'

'Yup.'

'It looks like an explosion in a custard factory. It's terrible. I mean – sorry. I didn't mean that. Goodness.' She pressed her fingers against her mouth, laughing. 'You look – gosh.'

Daniel put one hand on his hip and pouted, pointing one leg. 'Like it, do you? Hm?'

He was dressed in one of the old shirt dresses she'd worn to rags at music college. His hairy legs and toes were splattered with paint. He had a tea towel wrapped round his head as a scarf, but his beard, too, was flecked with yellow.

Yellow seemed to have flecked itself everywhere, in fact, gilding every surface, smearing where he walked. He had taken the boarding off the fireplace to reveal the ornate tiling and the curling wrought-iron grate beneath, and had painted them all primrose yellow.

'Shouldn't we,' said Sarah after a moment, 'get the builders to—'

'We don't need builders,' Daniel said, struggling to put the paint lid back on. 'I know lots of guys who can advise me, chaps in the pub, and so forth – we can do this ourselves. Look,' he said, as she opened her mouth, eyes narrowed. 'Have faith, my bird. I'll make it look really professional. It's simple. See? We merely get the chimney swept and take that board thing covering the flue down and hey presto.'

'We merely –' Sarah bit back a sharp retort. 'Do you know how to do that?'

'Well. Not really.' He peered at the tiled fireplace. 'Isn't it ugly? To be honest, I rather regret it now. Too draughty. And now I can't fix it back in place.'

He shivered. After he'd graduated and was working in America, in the early days of their relationship, Daniel had lived in Greenwich Village in an apartment so cold that when Sarah went to visit him, the morning after her arrival, she woke up to a covering of snow on the quilt and a gentle blizzard floating in through the rattling window. It had not bothered Daniel. He'd grown up in a flat in a crowded terrace in East London, then been evacuated to a cramped cottage with a range that was lit first thing and kept the house cosy until night, then fetched up in a set of rooms in college at Cambridge where fires were replenished throughout the day: he had always been relatively warm. The cold didn't get to her, of course: she'd learned to block it out since that first winter at school, as other little girls had shuddered in bed, racked with tears and the pain of stiff, swollen fingers and joints, of hot-water bottles freezing solid in the night. But she hated it. Hated what it did to you, how it ruled everything, being cold. Daniel didn't fear cold the way she did.

This fear made her voice peevish, and she heard it, and hated it. 'Why on earth did you take it off without making sure we could put it back on again? All this winter we've both done nothing but complain about how cold this house is. You must be mad.'

'I thought we could get a fire going again.' He stared at her, paint on his face. 'You know. A cosy fire, burning away in the room, me typing away, a cat, maybe – you know? A cat, lying on a rug – you upstairs, rehearsing – and you love yellow. I thought you'd like it.'

In 1968 she'd been on tour in America and Daniel had flown out to join her. It was April, and beautifully, deliciously warm. They were married in City Hall, Sarah in a primrose yellow Halston jumpsuit, the most expensive item of clothing she'd ever bought. And since then yellow had become her favourite colour. Sarah looked around, at the swathes of patchy yellow and the floorboards flecked with tufts of raspberry wool, like berries, squashed on the ground – Daniel had sworn it would take ten minutes, if that, to peel away the ancient pink carpets and reveal the lush original oak floorboards beneath. She glanced into the hall, where he'd chiselled away half the paint on the delicate spindles of the bannisters. As of two hours ago, she couldn't get into the sitting room, because he'd been sorting out his books, including the huge pile he'd acquired from various of his favourite bookshops on Charing Cross Road. A tower of them had collapsed, somehow wedging themselves between her school trunk and the door, barricading themselves in, an event Sarah took to be symbolic.

She took a deep breath. 'Wellllll . . . I think half the chimneypots have blocks over them to stop the birds nesting in them. Taking them off is quite a job. And the chimneys will need sweeping, and relining – I'm not sure we have the money at the moment to . . .' She trailed off, for she knew the answer.

'OK, OK,' said Daniel, eyes on the floor, and Sarah felt like a criminal. There was an awkward silence, broken when the grandfather clock in the hallway, which she had found at an antiques shop just up the road and which, miraculously, still worked, struck the hour.

'Heavens,' Sarah said. 'It's twelve?'

'Yes,' said Daniel, looking at his wristwatch, which was covered in primrose paint. 'Oh Lord, Sarah—'

'No . . .' said Sarah, smearing the paint off his watchface frantically. 'It can't be twelve. No . . .'

She hadn't wound her watch up that morning, having mislaid it in a pile of books two days ago and had been so glad to find it she hadn't noticed it was running forty-five minutes behind when she put it on. 'Oh God. It is twelve,' she said as the pips sounded on the radio in the kitchen. 'Christ. I'm really late.' She patted ineffectually at her face, her hips, then her thighs. 'I need the cello, darling. I have to be in Marylebone at one. The concert is at one –' She went pale as she remembered. 'Daniel – it's in the sitting room. Have you managed to get into the sitting room yet?'

There was a short silence, and Daniel, in the ratty old dress, stood on one leg then the other.

'Listen,' he said, immediately understanding the gravity of the situation. 'I'll shin up the drainpipe outside and get in through the window.'

'You can't.'

'I can. It'll be fine.'

It was a cold April day. Spring had not arrived yet; there was no warmth in the ground. The Heath, which everyone kept saying was the most magical place, and wasn't she lucky to live so close to it, had been a sea of mud for the last six months. She and Daniel had gone for a romantic walk on New Year's Day, bundled up against the icy frost covering the black, gooey mud and both of them had slipped, sliding almost extravagantly down a hill into a dell, Sarah twisting her ankle.

Daniel dashed out now into the front garden, grabbing the omnipresent ladder from the porch, and was picking his way up it towards the sash window above the window seat. She watched him, from the overgrown front garden, her heart hammering.

'The concert starts at one – I'm an idiot, darling. I'm so sorry – My watch –'

'Don't worry,' he said sharply. 'I'll get in there, I promise. Go and get your things, so you're ready to leave the moment I've got it out again.'

As Sarah reappeared, bag in hand, satchel packed, shoes on, hair brushed, she saw Georgina, passing by, head swivelling in to see what was going on. 'Oh! Good morning, Georgina,' she said.

'Dear me! Locked out again!' said Georgina in a bright voice.

'Not quite – something is blocking our way into the sitting room and –' Sarah's throat was tight. She thought Georgina must watch them through a telescope, choosing only to rush outside when disaster befell them. She smoothed her hair back, took a deep, calming breath and tucked her bag over her shoulder.

'Any luck, darling?' she called.

Daniel was trying to reach in to open the window. 'Jesus – *no*,' he said, in exasperation.

'Daniel, you have to –'

'Hey, kiddos!' A window on the second floor next door opened, and Diana's silver-white head appeared. 'Trouble? You OK, Daniel?'

'I am, Diana,' said Daniel, trying to maintain dignity, whilst perched half in, half out, like a crab atop a spindly wooden spade. 'How are you, dearest?'

'Oh, I'm good. Lakshmi has particularly blessed me with her light at the moment,' said Diana, exhaling and nodding with certainty. Diana's latest obsession was Hinduism and she and Daniel, who were thick as thieves, spent a lot of time discussing religion over a bottle of wine. Sometimes Professor Gupta joined them, sometimes one of the other neighbours.

'I read that pamphlet, by the way,' Daniel called down to her. 'Thank you – lots to think about—'

Sarah moved from one foot to another, wanting to scream. 'I think I might just go, Daniel,' she said eventually when he couldn't reach the catch on the window after a second attempt. 'There'll be a cello I can use at Wigmore Hall. I'm so sorry—'

'Sarah!' Daniel turned round, and the ladder rocked against the wall. 'Darling, I'm sure I can climb in – give me a minute.'

'But,' she said, trying not to sound like a petulant child, trying not to panic, 'I don't *have* a minute.'

Before she knew it, she had grabbed her things and was hurrying down the street, tears blinding her eyes. Everything was wrong. She had to be calm, and organised, before a concert, and it was a mess, all of it. She had scrambled into the Mary Quant black wool belted mini-dress with the pockets and the sharp white collars, her only clean concert outfit, but it was crumpled, with a tiny mark where she'd dropped jam on it the last time she'd worn it. And it smelt a little, under the armpits. Her hair was dull and greasy, not thick and backcombed. It needed washing.

But it was Daniel with whom she was disappointed, with whom she was irritated. She knew the Daniel who dreamed big, who wrapped her in love with his plans for the future. She had not yet come across this Daniel, who made a mess of simple tasks, who made grand plans and never quite went through with them, who sat in his study all day doing – what? *Nothing*, certainly not writing the sketches for his friend Terence's revue *The Ox and the Ass*, which he was actually paid for, or planning out the serious book on Britain in the sixties he'd told everyone he was working on. Whilst she, Sarah, practised for at least an hour, usually two, every day, and had rehearsals and concerts and meetings, walking the pavements of central London with her cello strapped across her back, the soles of her brogues worn paper thin so that, when she pushed them from the bottom, she could feel the contours of her finger, poking up, wanting to burst through.

Perhaps it's different, being a musician, she would tell herself, when she came back to find Daniel asleep at his desk, a copy of the *Evening Standard* fluttering above his head with every guttural breath. (He had time to go out and buy the paper, but not time to tidy the garden, or finish painting the skirting board, or clear away the upturned plug he'd rewired and left by her side of the bed for her to step on.) I have a vocation, she'd remind herself. I was born into a different class, whatever that means. He doesn't have the confidence I have. He lost everything. He had nothing. He has –

He has no bloody clue, was what she couldn't help thinking.

At the top of The Row, by the gate that led out to Oak Avenue, Sarah found she could no longer see properly. She wiped her streaming eyes on the black cuff of her sleeve, then fumbled in her pocket for a handkerchief – that was another thing about Daniel: he never had a handkerchief on him, whereas six years at boarding school had taught her that stepping out without a handkerchief was a crime on a par with arson. She carried on walking, rubbing her face firmly with the hanky. This was a trick she'd picked up as a child, make your face red and get the blood circulating, and the puffy bloodshot eyes will disappear more quickly.

Come on, she told herself. She blew her nose purposefully, picking up the pace and humming to herself, hearing the music swelling and falling away. She wondered if she should stop at the telephone box and call Wigmore Hall to ask them to make sure Joseph's cello was easily accessible – she'd seen it there two days ago, and knew he was touring – it must be.

Oh, the mess of their house!

Briefly, the vision of her best friend Monica's flat flitted across her mind. Monica had got married last summer – the opposite of Sarah's 'hole in corner American affair' as her sister had referred to it in a letter afterwards. A church in Guildford, six bridesmaids (Sarah was one of them) in peach Shantung silk, bouquets of baby's breath and peach carnations, a reception for a hundred and fifty at her parents' house. Monica and her stockbroker husband, Guy, happily installed in a flat given to her by her father in Earl's Court. Now Monica was pregnant, and was giving up her job as a publisher's secretary. They were leaving London next year for Surrey; they had everything planned out. 'I like it that way,' she'd said with a shrug, when Sarah and Daniel had gone there for dinner a few weeks before. 'I expect you think it's awfully bourgeois.'

'Mon! Of course I don't.' Sarah had patted the back of her friend's huge astrakhan waistcoat, then her cheek. She hadn't meant to, but wanted to touch her, to feel the connection to her darling friend, who knew it all, who made her feel safe, who understood her in a way no one else did, and now seemed so vulnerable, biology taking her over: her skin clear, almost translucent, the curious dichotomy of her thin face and arms and her distended stomach, as if the baby was sucking everything from her. She looked younger, almost the age they'd first met; Sarah felt protective of her.

'Well,' said Monica, shrugging, 'I'm rather looking forward to doing nothing all day and just looking after a baby. It seems so easy compared to having a job. And, besides, Guy and I like planning ahead. Knowing what's what.'

'Yes,' said Sarah. 'It sounds marvellous – Won't you need something else to do, though? I mean—'

'Oh God no. Look how happy Mummy was, doing nothing. We're all set. Aren't we, Guy?'

'Absolutely, old girl.' Guy had drained his glass and squeezed her hand, looking Sarah up and down. 'Want to retire by the time I'm fifty. Need to plan for that.'

At the thought of Guy, still only thirty-two, his red face, red wine, red trousers and Daniel's impression of him – 'Golf one day, Dannyarl, old maan?' – on the interminable Tube journey back to North London, Sarah allowed herself a smile.

'Oh, Guy's all right,' she'd said to him. And it was true. They had very little in common but their love of Monica and for that she was immensely fond of him. After all he had, indirectly, led her back to Daniel, many years ago.

'Really?'

'You know he is. I don't agree with him about lots of things. But the thing about Monica is we were always so different.'

She thought of how Monica would laugh at her now, gently, kindly, for being so highly strung. They had always found something to laugh about, even when life seemed awfully serious. When Monica's asthma had been so bad that she'd gasped for every breath and Sarah said nothing, just held her hand and stroked it, for hours at a time. When Sarah cried at night after she'd left home, and Monica had climbed into bed with her, and hugged her, and she always, *always* had warm feet. How Sarah missed her, missed living with her every day, her sweet half-moon eyes, her kind smile, her light-brown ringlets. And suddenly Sarah found she was laughing. It was so silly – it didn't *matter*, being locked out of the very room her cello was in, living in chaos, any of it. She loved Daniel, she adored him, and he loved her, and this was teething stuff. Everything could be wonderful if only she'd loosen up. Sarah blew her nose again, defiantly, and thus barely noticed stumbling into someone, pitching headfirst over their foot and falling, falling onto the ground.

'Oh God. Oh my God. I'm so sorry, so very sorry – your lovely dress is all torn – Oh God, your knee – look at it!'

Sarah looked down. Her knee was bleeding, deep red with little black bubbles of gravel scattered across it, and yet it didn't seem to hurt. She kept smiling, even as the woman she had tripped over gazed in horror at her, hands pressed to her mouth.

'I'm so sorry. It's almost as if I stuck my foot out on purpose. You went over quite heavily. Are you all right? Nothing broken?'

'I don't think so.'

'Oh! It looks bad, though. Are you sure you don't want to wash it, at the very least?'

It was extremely discombobulating, tripping when you were grown up. The ground was much further away than when you were little, and you fell more heavily. Her knee was agony, but Sarah said: 'No, no, I'll just press –' She looked down at her handkerchief, drenched with snot and tears, and gave a small gulp. 'Oh.'

The woman reached into the pocket of her dress and handed Sarah a perfectly pressed handkerchief. 'Have this. Keep it. I've got loads.'

It had the day of the week embroidered on it, with a delicate yellow flower below. 'It's Thursday?' said Sarah to break the silence, after she'd pressed it to her knee, down which blood was oozing slowly.

'Yes,' said the stranger. 'I know it's rather childish. It's a quirk of mine. One of many.'

She was more of a girl, really, tall and slight and dressed in the most gorgeously beautiful floral maxidress trimmed with cream lace that made Sarah, scruffy, hot, depressed and bleeding, quite dizzy with envy. Her slender neck and collarbone rose out of the coral red, yellow and green floral pattern of the dress and her fine blond hair fell about her face, shimmering in the light, as she bent down to look at Sarah's knee. 'It's quite deep, but I don't think you need stitches.'

'Gosh no,' said Sarah, who had once played on in a lacrosse match with a dislocated shoulder. 'I'll be fine. Listen, it's so kind of you. Let me wash it and get it back to you – where do you live? Are you on The Row as well? I've been there seven months, but I'm still not really sure who's who.'

The woman smiled. 'I'm not on The Row, no.' Without warning, she hauled Sarah to her feet. 'You're right – you'll live,' she said with a gentle smile. 'But rest up, won't you? Sweet tea, read a book for a bit, you know.'

'I will – this evening.' Sarah blinked, telling herself it wasn't so painful. That she shouldn't worry. 'I'm awfully sorry to be rude, but I really have to rush off now. I'm late for a concert.'

'Oh.' The woman looked rather taken aback. 'Listen, it is rather nasty. Clean it and take care it doesn't get infected.'

Sarah nodded, and looked at her watch, and her eyes widened. 'I will, I will. Thank you so much. I must go. I'll be late.'

In the quietness of The Row behind her, she could hear someone laughing, another voice raised, which she knew was Daniel's, but she didn't have time to run back and see if he'd got into the drawing room, rescued her cello. If she hobbled all the way, she might just make it.

Waving, she set off as fast as she could. She had reached the brow of the hill before she remembered the bloody rag tied round her knee. 'I'm Sarah Forster,' she called. 'I don't know your name but – we're Number 7 – The Row – do knock next time you're passing.'

The young woman watched her, shaking her head, her slim, delicate frame impassive. 'Be careful,' she called after her, her gentle voice carrying on the April breeze. 'Honestly. Be careful, Sarah.'

Later, travelling back on the Tube, Sarah found she could barely stay awake: her head kept falling forward, and she would jerk up, terrified of missing her stop. The sensation of Joseph's unfamiliar, half-a-size-too-large cello between her legs, and the drawing of the black synthetic material of the black tights she'd borrowed from the cloakroom attendant over the spongy, raw wound, which throbbed with pain every time she bowed, was a peculiar, cumulative kind of agony. Afterwards, she limped to John Bell on Wigmore Street and had her knee washed and dressed by a kindly pharmacist, who tsked in a pleasing manner.

'That's a nasty cut. You might have to have stitches if it doesn't heal tomorrow.'

Sitting obediently on a chair, swinging her other leg, she thought over the progress of the day, from amusement to irritation to utter despair and rage to pain and kindness and then to losing herself, for short, sharp seconds only, in the beauty of the Schumann String Quartet No. 3.

'Bloody great concert,' Oscar Gould, their manager, had told them. 'The EMI chaps were most impressed. Sarah, they said they loved your expression, in particular.' Jolyon, the ancient first violin, scowled – he had been against hiring Sarah out of music college originally, and went out of his way to make life as difficult for her as possible. 'They want you front and centre on the album cover.'

'God no,' said Sarah with a shudder, ignoring Jolyon's snort of disapproval.

The Northern Line was empty, the scratchy peach and brown seats comforting, the flickering lights soporific, the faint scent of a Turkish cigarette at the other end of the carriage almost soothing. Sarah blinked heavily again, looking down at the grooves on the floor, cigarette stubs, betting slips, Tube tickets. This was her career and even if Daniel might not remember what she'd sacrificed for the cello, what collateral damage there had been, she knew.

When she opened the front door half an hour later, she could hear laughter coming from the back of the house. Sarah sniffed. Thick smoke – cigarette smoke, marijuana smoke and smoke from something burning – filled the hall. Wearily, she limped down the corridor, narrowly avoiding a pot of paint, and pushed open the kitchen door.

Daniel was sitting at the kitchen table, surrounded by women, wreathed in smoke. Two empty bottles of wine stood in front of him, Joan Baez wailing loudly on the record player. As Sarah came in, he leapt to his feet.

'Birdie! Hey!'

'Something's burning,' she said, unable to look at him, because she hated being cross.

'It's fine. We put it out. Just a newspaper. Made a bit of a mess.' He gestured to the sink, filled with the charred remains of the *Guardian*, loose pages crumpled up into the sink like petals of a black-and-white flower. 'Now, listen – I eventually broke into the sitting room, I tidied it all up, and I've put your cello in the study. How was the concert?'

'Fine.' Sarah unhooked herself from her handbag and looked around. Her back ached, her leg ached, her eyes ached with the smoke and the effort of not crying like a silly little girl.

Next to her, Diana stubbed a joint out on a side plate.

'Hello, doll. How are you? Been in the wars, I hear.'

'Oh.' Sarah blinked at her, peering through the fug. How did she know? 'Nothing serious.'

'Want some wine?' Diana waved the bottle at her.

Sarah shook her head. 'A cup of tea.'

Daniel used to make her cups of tea when she got back late from rehearsals, her back aching. He knew to make it sweet, just one and a bit teaspoonfuls of sugar. Sarah put the kettle on the hob. She folded her arms and leaned against the cupboards. All of her ached, she realised, her jaw, her shoulders, her knee.

At the table, someone said something, and the others laughed. It was like being in school again, staring down the long, brightly lit refectory at a crowd of girls around a dark polished wooden table, knowing they were whispering about her.

'Sarah!' Daniel called to her. 'Diana's asking you what you played today, honey.'

Sarah shook herself. 'Oh,' she said. 'Sorry. Some Schumann. A bit of Mozart. Always a crowd pleaser, Mozart, but the Schumann's my favourite.'

'I love Mozart.' Diana stretched out her long, long legs, encased in gold lamé palazzo pants, and leaned back in the chair. '"*Lacrimosa dies illa*" and all that,' she warbled, in an uncertain soprano.

'Brava!' Daniel clapped. Diana nodded modestly.

'Leading light in the Highgate Choral Society, in my day. Adrian used to say he loved hearing me through the wall, singing in the bath, you know.'

I wish you'd all go home. Go home and leave us alone.

'That was a very long time ago,' said a voice from the other end of the table. 'Sarah doesn't care about the old days, Diana.' Sarah turned and saw, with a start, the woman who had helped her off the pavement earlier that day, sitting next to Georgina. 'Hello, Sarah,' she said with a small smile. 'Nice to see you again. How's the knee?'

'You –' said Sarah. 'Hello!' She stared at her. 'Goodness, I'm sorry I didn't spot you there. Daniel, this lovely woman helped me today.'

'Oh, Birdie. What happened?' Daniel looked on in concern, but didn't move.

'I was rushing and I tripped on the way to the station.' She smiled at him. 'I went to the chemist. She told me—'

Daniel interrupted eagerly. 'Birdie, I'm so sorry about earlier. You know after you left I felt so guilty I decided I'd try some gardening and I hit myself in the face with a – What's it called, Diana?'

'A hoe,' Diana said loudly, with her eyes still closed. 'You're an idiot, Daniel. After the disaster in the sitting room he was most worried about you. Kept saying he'd let you down, you deserved better – Oh, my dear. What a state. I took him to the allotment to distract him, Sarah. Showed him my veg patch. He tries to help and hits himself in the face.'

And indeed when Sarah looked again at her husband she saw he was sporting the beginnings of a black eye – red, swollen, fading to purple at the edges. 'Oh dear,' she said. 'Are you all right?'

'Fine, fine.' Daniel waved his arms happily. 'All's well that ends well. I was walking back feeling very glum, I tell you – well, who do I bump into but Georgina, and she tells me that this young lady is waiting outside the house.' He gestured with approval at Sarah's stranger. 'And I invite them in, to see what we've done with the place, and we get to talking, and then Diana comes to apologise—'

At this Diana opened her eyes, and said, furiously, 'Never explain, never apologise. I did no such thing, you fool.'

Unperturbed, Daniel continued. 'So we've spent the afternoon hacking away at the garden, with Lara's approval.'

Lara. Sarah looked again at the stranger, her mind flipping through the bewildering amount of information she had acquired since moving to The Row. *Lara.*

'You're Lara Thorpe? You lived here.'

'I am,' Lara said, nodding. 'Lara Cull, these days. Sorry I didn't introduce myself properly this morning.'

Sarah couldn't explain why she felt cross. 'Oh, no, of course not.'

'I could see you were rather flustered. I didn't think it was the right time to explain I'd grown up in your house and my grandfather was Adrian Thorpe. I'm very glad to know you both. I hope you're happy here.'

'Lara's a photographer,' Daniel said, stumbling slightly over the words. 'She's offered to take your photo if you need it for the – for work.'

'Oh! Thank you,' said Sarah, smiling at Lara, but Lara didn't smile back, just nodded, looking at her intently.

'God, I'm absolutely wiped out,' said Diana, rubbing her forehead and eye with one flattened hand. 'One more drink, then I'm off.'

'One more drink!' Daniel slapped Diana on the back. 'She's game for one more, my friends! Look!'

His eyes were shining, his smile broad. Sarah saw how much this meant to him, these ladies round the table. The company, the mess, the free exchange of ideas, of stories. She wished, oh how she wished she could throw off this cloak, the one that dragged her down and made her worry all the time, about everything, about the gathering cloud above them, about daring to hope for contentment. Her head swam – she steadied herself, as Lara, who had been watching her, leaned across and said in a low voice: 'I'm sure the state of the house when you moved in must have horrified you. I'm so sorry.'

'No,' Sarah found herself saying. 'When I was younger I had a . . . Where I lived was much worse.'

'I can't see how!' Lara laughed, almost wildly.

'Sarah,' Daniel said, a note of warning in his voice.

Sarah felt a jolt of irritation, which she should have recognised as extreme fatigue. She heard herself saying: 'One day I went into the bathroom closest to our bedroom, and I pulled back a dust sheet and there was a dead cat in it. Mummified.' Lara's face froze. 'I have seen worse. Really. Someone scrawled swear words with a scalpel into every wooden panel in the dining room. I didn't know what most of them meant. Still don't. There were so many glass cases of stuffed birds that had been smashed or damaged – you'd find their legs, snapped off, lying on the floor, and the rats would climb up and eat them. Really. You don't need to apologise.'

Lara leaned back in her chair. Sarah knew she'd said too much. Everything was melting before her eyes. 'I'm not feeling that great, and I don't want to be a –' Blackness was falling in front of her eyes, like dark rain. 'I'm going to go and drink my cup of tea and lie down for a while. You carry on. Please,' she said.

Lara stood up. 'You're very pale.' She glanced at Daniel, but the others had turned back to their discussion about some old boyfriend of Diana's. 'I'll see you upstairs, shall I?'

'Thank you,' Sarah said weakly. Lara took the tea cup from her.

Upstairs, she put it down on the side table, and produced a rug from somewhere. 'Lie down on the sofa,' she said. 'Here. Gosh, you don't look great.'

'Everything is in chaos,' said Sarah softly. Somehow, she knew Lara understood. 'I don't do well with chaos. I like to have things calm. And I can't see a way –' Lara said nothing, but simply draped the rug over Sarah, then tucked it around her. Sarah stared down at it. It was soft Scottish woollen tartan, in navy and green. 'I've never seen this before. I'm not sure it's ours.'

'Well, it was left behind,' said Lara. 'I thought it must have been as I've missed it. We kept it in here.' She patted the window seat by the French windows. Sarah stared. 'I had no idea that lifted up,' she said, pointing at the seat.

'Well, now you do.'

'You must take the rug back.' Lara shook her head.

'Of course not. It's yours. It was in the house when you took possession.'

'That's not the point. Take it.' Sarah held it out to her, but Lara simply stared at her and Sarah lowered her arms, embarrassed.

There was something comforting about the act of hugging the soft brushed wool, feeling its springy warmth. Lara nodded. 'I'll go now and let you rest.' Sarah started to protest, but Lara said brusquely, 'It's lovely to meet you properly. I'm glad you like it here. See you around another time.'

She pressed her shoulder lightly, and disappeared. Sarah sat still for a moment after she'd gone, then pulled at the rug where Lara had tucked it in just slightly too tightly. She closed her eyes.

At some point in the night, she must have clambered into bed, for she woke the next day with a start from a deep sleep at the sound of something banging. Her head ached, and shards of memory from the previous day started to jab her waking brain. The banging stopped, then started again. Sarah pulled on her dressing gown and went slowly downstairs.

Daniel was in the kitchen, hitting something with a hammer. The dregs from the previous evening's gathering were scattered around the kitchen: cigarette butts, remains of food, dirty glasses stained with the ruby-red wash of wine.

He looked up as she came in. 'Hey. How are you?'

'I'm OK.' Sarah tried to shield her eyes from the ashtray, which had a peach stone in it, covered in ash.

'I slept downstairs. I didn't want to wake you. I couldn't get rid of Diana, or Georgina.' He screwed up his eyes. 'God. I feel rotten.'

Sarah was silent. She picked up a bunch of flowers.

'They're from Lara. She dropped them off this morning. She wants me to meet her husband. He's a producer. She thinks we'd get on. She's saying thanks.'

I think you belong here, the note said in small, curling writing, like a child's. Sarah took the note, folding it in her fingers.

'He seemed nice. He was with her. Tony. Tony Cull.'

Sarah nodded.

'Look, I'm sorry about yesterday.' Daniel rummaged around and handed her a piece of toast. 'I was about to bring you up breakfast. On a tray.' He waved the tray in the air with the other hand.

'You don't need to. Daniel –' She cleared her throat. She wasn't sure what was going to come out. But she had to tell him.

'Don't say anything. I'm terrified of what you're going to say. I've been in a real funk, Sarah. I didn't know how to tell you.' He rubbed his face. 'I can't work. I'm stymied by what we've taken on. I don't expect you to understand.'

'Oh,' said Sarah, and a weak sweat seemed to flood her. 'Oh, Daniel. I do.'

'I was stupid. This house – I love it. It's the dream.' He came towards her, dropping the tray onto the counter with a loud clatter. 'It's everything I wanted for us. Our family. Our – I don't know! Our story. But – oh Jesus, what *have* we done.'

He smiled his huge smile, and ran his hands through his hair, so it stuck up. He was grinning, but his eyes had tears in them. 'I was up late last night talking to the others about it,' he said. 'You know what? I think we should just admit defeat,' he said. 'Acknowledge we're in over our heads and sell.'

'I don't want to.'

'You're safe with me. You know that, don't you? She can't get you.'

She can, though. She does every day.

'We're staying,' she said. 'Daniel, it's our house now. I don't want to move.'

He caught her in his arms, smoothing her hair away from her face.

'You're so beautiful at the moment,' he said, kissing her. 'Your face, your skin – there's something about you. You're so beautiful, and I love you – Sarah Forster, I love you so much. I want to live in you. I want you.' He pulled her towards him, his hands pushing between them, stroking the side of her breasts, her hips, his lips on hers, tongue pushing between her lips, and the smell of him, clean and fresh but slightly wood-smoky, was unbearably arousing. She forced herself to look at him, really hold his gaze. She was terrified, but she realised she had to see the whites of his eyes. To make him understand she was on the verge of folding in two, like the cardboard cut-out dolls she'd been given as a birthday present by a classmate. She had bent them over to hide them from her mother inside a book, and they never stood up again.

Sarah caught his wrists. 'I love you,' she said. 'But you have to work. You have to make money. You have to do more comedy sketches. You have to go and see your agent and stop gadding about with Diana to matinees and asking people over for afternoon drinking sessions. Do you understand me? And I have to play. I can't have my cello locked in rooms. I can't be late for concerts. I have to be able to practise. I'll die if I don't. You know that.'

'Of course I do,' he said, almost impatiently. They gazed at each other, breathing slowly, deeply. Neither moved. Daniel reached up, and stroked her collarbone. 'Sarah – darling. Let's make a baby. I want to make a baby with you. Now. Don't you?'

She stopped, and pulled away, and he saw she was smiling.

'What's wrong?' he said.

'Yes,' she said, kissing him. 'Only it's too late for that.'

'What do you mean?' Daniel was still, his jaw clenched. 'Honey—'

'You did it already. There's a baby in there already, Daniel.' She put his large, wide hands over her stomach. 'It's a baby. I was trying to tell you all of yesterday, and – oh, yesterday was just a disaster. It's our baby. So that's why we're staying. And that's why you have to work and I have to work and – oh, everything's great.'

They were quiet in the hall, holding each other, and then – only this time, Daniel firmly drew the bolt on the front door, and the curtain over it, and they came together, suddenly, more abruptly than ever before, but it was a new start. She knew it. Now there was no going back.

Chapter Three

June 1971

Fourteen months later

A soft tap on the door woke Sarah with a start. Was it daytime? She glanced at the clock by her bed: she'd only been asleep for twenty minutes, but so deeply it was like being plunged from hot water into cold. The muscles in her face didn't seem to want to move.

Another knock.

Mustn't wake a sleeping baby.

Should she whisper 'Come in'? Should she do nothing, and risk this person knocking even louder? Her back was always painful now: because she didn't sleep, didn't sit properly, spent most of her time in bed feeding this child who didn't show any gratitude, just screamed and drank, screamed and drank, and then glared at her with a round, solemn face and dark eyes, just like Vic's.

Mustn't wake a sleeping baby. Tears leaked from Sarah's eyes.

Daily life was now terrifying, fraught with the possibility of disaster at any point: the house of cards collapsing, each card fluttering, wayward onto the ground. Each card an extra hour's sleep, remembering to pack a nappy pin, the nappy cream, remembering to 'strap baby in!' as the midwife had put it. Remembering to put on knickers, and not to cry on the bus, remembering to grin otherwise men in vans would lean out and would say 'Sun's shining, love! How about a smile, then!'

Her world was so small: reduced to nipples and tiny toes and holes and milk. And the person was still knocking.

Very quietly, she said, 'Come in.'

In her cot, Friday moved slightly, fists clenched. Daniel's head appeared round the door.

'Hi, honey. Do you want a cup of tea?' He advanced into the room slowly, holding out a steaming mug. Sarah nodded.

'Thank you,' she mouthed.

He held out the mug to her with its handle so she had to take the hot side. She hated him.

'Listen,' said Daniel, sitting down on the bed. 'Ah. Birdie – Georgina's downstairs. She wondered if you wanted to—'

'Nope,' said Sarah, taking a tiny sip of tea. 'This has sugar in it.'

'I thought you'd like some sugar. Sweetness, you know.'

'I don't.'

'Sorry.' He nodded, castigated. 'Sorry. She was saying it's a lovely day, and do you want to take Friday and go for a walk on the Heath?'

Sometimes Sarah found there were lost moments, long seconds where she couldn't remember who she was. She wasn't a musician, wasn't the girl who married Daniel in New York in a yellow silk jumpsuit. She wasn't the one who saved Stella, who helped her fly, who gazed at stars with the Bird Boy on summer nights. She was Friday's mother. That was all she remembered.

'No thank you.'

'Sarah,' said Daniel, biting his lip. 'It might do you good to—'

'I know. But I'm – I'm so bloody tired, you –' She took a deep breath. She hated using this angry, thin, contemptuous voice and yet she heard it more and more. 'It's easier to stay here.' She reached out a hand towards Friday, stirring in her sleep.

Daniel picked up her hand, and moved it away from the cot. He kissed it. 'What about if you don't have to go out. Listen, honey, why don't we have some people over on Sunday?'

'Us?'

He laughed at her. 'Yes us, who else?'

She felt despair that he thought this could be fixed by her sitting in the kitchen talking about Gore Vidal, or what Kenneth Tynan made of some new play. She just wanted to be in bed, asleep, or, because sometimes, in a great smacking punch of irony, because she couldn't sleep all of a sudden, in bed, with a cup of tea and a Georgette Heyer novel.

'*Hellooo?*' She could hear Georgina calling up the stairs.
'She cares about you, Sarah. We all do.'
'Thank you, darling, but can you tell her—'
'Daniel! I'm lonely down here!' Georgina called coquettishly.
'She's lonely down there, Daniel,' Sarah said.
'Yes, yes,' said Daniel crossly, and, despite herself, Sarah had to hide a smile behind the corner of the eiderdown. She looked down at Friday, who had started crying, then at Daniel. She wondered – does it occur to him, to pick her up? He slept through her screams at night. He said he was able to. 'Rather embarrassing, actually, but I do,' she'd heard him telling Misses Pam and Barbara Forbes, the sisters opposite, who had given shy little giggles. 'I sleep like the dead. No conscience, you see!'
'I openly despise that woman,' Diana had told Sarah, the previous day, when she'd brought round a packet of brandy snap biscuits and they'd sat in the wilderness of the garden, Diana gently rocking Friday in her pram with a silver-slipper clad foot. 'She's getting worse too. She reminds me of a cow, munch munch, and her laugh. It's like when the Canada geese fly south every summer. She's unhinged.'
There was something about Diana's fury that was so funny Sarah had found she was properly laughing, throwing her head back with amusement. And at times, like being in the garden with Diana, Sarah felt as though a wonderful life was within touching distance. But then the cloud would come down again, the one that obfuscated all her attempts to be good. The one that told her she couldn't, wouldn't be able to do this.
She couldn't understand why *her* baby didn't sleep yet. Ever. Why she, Sarah, kept crying herself, all the time. Why her stitches still hurt and why breastfeeding was still agony, eight months on. Why Friday still didn't smile at her, why you became invisible when you pushed a buggy, why other mothers in the playground spoke to their babies as if they were morons. 'Let's change your liddle biddle nappy wappy, Charles,' a woman had said the other week at the park and Sarah had stared at her, completely bemused. Was that how you were supposed to talk to them?

As Daniel retreated downstairs, Sarah fumbled with the ribbons on her nightdress, and freed one aching, solid breast, to attach Friday to it – but Friday wriggled, squirming in anger as milk squirted into her eyes, making her almost rigid with fury. One little hand, the tiny fingers splayed, batted at her in outrage.

'Oh well!' she could hear Georgina saying, her voice echoing through the house. 'What a *shame*. Poor *Sarah*. I heard . . .' and her voice became indistinct as she lowered it. Sarah tried to listen, but Friday was clamping down on her nipple now. It was like someone was slicing it off, slowly, with a blunt knife. Sarah tried not to think of the pain, tried to pretend she was somewhere else. Where? On a warm Tube carriage, rocking to and fro, on her way to a rehearsal, cello clamped between her legs, reading a Margaret Drabble, the faint fug of someone's cigarette nearby. Yes. Her fingers dug into her palm. The nails were long now. The pain was good, it was a good pain when she did that.

Why was Georgina bothering? Why didn't they leave her alone? And suddenly, for some reason, Sarah remembered how, on her birthday, Vic had stolen a lollipop from the newsagent's round the corner from Pelham Mansions, and run back all the way home. 'For you!' she'd shouted, wild with exhilaration. 'Happy birthday, Sarah!'

They'd always tried to get each other something, no matter how hard it was, so that there was one present. And this had been the sweetest present, in all ways.

To her horror, the door opened and Georgina's head, all set curls and pearlescent eyeshadow, peeked round.

'Come on, dear. I told Daniel I wouldn't take no for an—' she began, but stopped, unable to hear herself over the sheer volume of Friday's screams. 'We'll go for a walk when you're finished,' she bellowed, eyes glancing down at Sarah's half-naked form in disgust.

'Really. Not today, Georgina,' yelled Sarah, struggling to hold one breast and one baby in each hand, and gasping as a stabbing pain shot through her breast. Georgina tried to speak, but Friday's mouth was wide open, the tonsils, tongue, roof of her mouth purple and blood red. And she screamed, and screamed, so loudly that eventually Georgina, eyes wide in horror, held up one hand.

'I'll come back,' she bellowed over Friday's howls, accepting defeat. She narrowed her eyes, and Sarah saw how the eyelids crinkled, how the pearlescent eyeshadow flaked as she did so. The rest of her speech was drowned out by Friday's screaming, and eventually, miraculously, she had no choice but to back out of the room.

'Well, thank you for getting rid of her,' said Sarah to her daughter, once they were alone. Without realising it, she carried on rubbing Friday's tummy, and Friday stopped screaming. Her huge eyes opened and closed, and she looked up at her mother, almost curiously.

Who are you? she seemed to be saying. *I know you! You're the person who's always here.*

'Yes, thank you,' Sarah said to her again. 'Well done, baby girl.'

Friday waved her clenched fists at her as Sarah stroked her soft, fine hair. It was long at the front now. It stuck up, like a quiff. She was eight months old, and really quite delicious, despite everything.

The quiff reminded her of Vic's old boyfriend, Graham, or Quiff Graham, she and Mon had christened him. Vic had gone out with him in her final year, the year where Sarah had followed her around for months at a time, trying to speak to her without success, until her final day when she'd come to find Sarah and, without warning, flung her arms round her sister from behind, clutching her so tightly that Sarah couldn't breathe. 'I'm sorry,' she'd said, her voice croaky. 'So sorry.'

It occurred to Sarah that being this tired had its upsides. It shook life up, made her remember things that had drifted out of sight, settled in dark corners in her mind. She found she kept thinking about Vic. Vic had been the first-born. Was it like this for her?

'You,' she said to her daughter, gently corkscrewing her finger towards her rounded tummy. 'Are a lot of trouble.'

Friday's eyes widened, and she waved her legs and arms in the air, as if she were a surfer. She blew some bubbles, making a rumbling, satisfied sound. Sarah watched her, mesmerised. Something in her chest hurt, as if her heart were squeezing itself, trying to make room, trying to open up. She had been knocked out for most of the birth, had woken up to find a baby in the room and Daniel grinning idiotically at her, and since that moment in autumn she had frequently wondered: how do I know she's my baby? What if I wasn't pregnant? What if it's all a trick? But she didn't say this to anyone, of course not. They'd think she was mad. She *was* mad, but no one must know.

There was a knock on the door, breaking the thread of the little moment and making Friday jump. Her eyes bulged again, and her mouth turned down at the edges, in a comically clownish fashion.

'Sarah, just one thing – I'm so sorry –'

'For Christ's sake, Georgina,' said Sarah firmly, trying not to let the white-hot fury she felt rise into her voice. 'I said go away!'

A head peered round the door. 'It's me,' said Lara, her eyes dancing with amusement. 'Daniel said I shouldn't bother you, but I just wondered if you wanted a walk on the Heath. It's not so hot now, and there's a breeze.' She came into the room, holding a bottle. 'Hello beautiful,' she said, staring at Friday, who blew some more bubbles.

'Yes,' said Sarah, climbing slowly out of bed, and smiling at her daughter. 'I'd love that. Let's go.'

The pram was one Daniel had acquired from a junk shop in Camden. It was huge and unwieldy and slightly unstable, so Sarah had to push it slowly, terrified it might founder on a treacherous rock, jolting Friday out onto the roadside, her small skull crushed on the road. Nowadays, she saw disaster everywhere she looked.

They walked along Lime Avenue. The heat of the day hung in the still air, heavy with the sweet, deliciously fresh fragrance of lime blossom. Sarah heard music, for the first time in months, the gentle, melodious pull of a cello and realised she was humming. She inhaled: the scent was intoxicating. She glanced at Lara.

They'd been near neighbours for eighteen months, but Lara was still an enigma to her.

The previous day the Pembroke Quartet's latest album had arrived through the post. The postman hadn't been able to fit it through the letterbox and had hammered on the door, waking Sarah from a delirious nap. She had stumbled downstairs, foggy with rage, and torn open the brown paper in front of the postman. There was the new LP, featuring her doe-eyed gamine stand-in, a young cellist called Miranda Hawksley. The quartet stood self-consciously around some stone steps, all wearing black polo necks, holding their instruments. Miranda's left leg was draped, rather oddly it seemed to Sarah, over the edge of her cello. One fingernail was pressed against her white cheek and her brow was slightly furrowed.

'Cor. Who's she, then?' the postman had said curiously, jabbing a smeary finger on the cardboard sleeve. Sarah had slammed the door on him, not caring that this was the rudest she had ever been in her whole life – records like this were broken every day by her now – and padded slowly back upstairs to her room. She knew they'd have to let her go; it was clear. She hadn't been able to continue to play with them whilst pregnant and, as Oscar had explained to her, they could hardly pay her for doing nothing now she'd had a baby. But it hurt, that was all. And she kept seeing Miranda's face, calm, certain of herself, wherever she looked.

Her beloved cello stood in the corner of the room. She thought of it like a princess in a tower, one she had rescued from the darkest recesses of Fane. In the afternoon light, it sometimes cast a shadow like another person, waiting for her patiently, arms folded.

She knew she could unzip the case and take the instrument out. Run the sweet-smelling, hard rosin over the bow. She could do so at any time. And yet she didn't. Something stopped her, for the first time since she'd started playing, and it was terrifying, this musical silence. And she didn't know why, but she felt Lara understood.

'We used to walk this way every day,' said Lara suddenly in a quiet, dreamy voice. 'If it was a slow news day, my grandfather would put the newspaper to bed and come back to see us, and he always wanted to walk on the Heath. He'd point out the different trees, and the birds. We'd walk as far as Highgate Ponds, then turn and go back. When Pa was well enough, we went to Kenwood.'

'How wonderful, to have this, growing up,' said Sarah.

Lara spoke in a rush. 'Well, I didn't know any different. And it was rather strange, when I look back on it. No other adults in the house: once there'd been lots of us. I had an older brother who died, you see, and then my parents died . . . From the age of about eleven it was just us and my grandfather.'

Sarah didn't know what to say. 'How did they die?'

'Ah, my brother – he died in an accident on the Tube. He was hit by a train. It was a crowded and – well.' She stopped. 'Six months afterwards, my parents went to a cottage in Wales for a holiday. The boiler leaked. Carbon monoxide poisoning.'

'Oh, Lara,' said Sarah involuntarily. 'How – awful. How –'

She put her hand on Lara's arm, awkwardly, but at her touch Lara flinched and moved her hand away.

'So after Henry went to boarding school it was just my grandfather, and Mrs McClean, whom he brought in to ma-Clean, which was a joke I heard rather too often.' Lara raised her eyes to Sarah's and Sarah felt again that shiver of recognition. 'I don't know if you know this, and sorry to be so gloomy, but my grandmother killed herself not long after she had my mother. In the room you sleep in.'

'Yes,' said Sarah softly. 'I did know.'

'I hope it doesn't upset you.'

'No,' Sarah said frankly. She didn't know how to explain that other people's ghosts did not bother her. 'It doesn't.'

'Good.'

'I'm sorry,' Sarah said, feeling a flush of embarrassment start from her chest. 'That's a terribly insensitive thing to say. I didn't mean it as it came out.'

Lara shrugged. 'Don't worry. I shouldn't have asked you.'

Sarah didn't want to know, and yet she knew she had to so she said, 'If you don't mind awfully talking about it, would you tell me what happened to her?'

'They think she lost her mind. Something about having the

baby – that was my mother, Jane.' She shrugged, almost indifferently, and turned away. 'She was only nineteen.'

'How awful.'

'She started having visions. She couldn't sleep. She thought she was a terrible mother. She went quite mad and my grandfather called in lots of experts. She tried to climb out of a window.'

'Why?'

'Well, they had locked her in, you see. She kept escaping onto the Heath in her nightgown. They were going to send her away to an asylum and the day they came for her they discovered she'd hanged herself.' She stopped, and stared at Sarah. 'When my mother met my dad of course they had to live with Pa – that's what we called him. That huge house, all on his own. So we were all together, Pa, Mummy and Dad, my big brother Sam and us two – Henry and I are twins. Pa worked most of the time, but he came home to a very happy home.' She smiled, her eyes crinkling at the sides. 'Everyone wanted to be us. It was that house on the street, you know, friends of my grandfather, refugees from Austria and Germany, colleagues from the paper, people making music, thumping out tunes, arguing about politics, art, literature. Until – well, you know. I buried both my parents and my brother in the space of nine months. Enough time to grow a baby. It felt like that. I can't explain, but it did. And then everything changed.'

'Oh, Lara.' Sarah tried to steady her breathing, to get a grip on the pram handle, though her hands were sweating so much it kept slipping out of her grasp.

The young woman climbing out of the window, trying to escape. *It's not about you*, she said to herself. *This was another life, another person. Nothing to do with you.*

Lara shrugged. 'After we lost Sam—'

'Sam was your older brother, yes?'

'Yes,' said Lara. A smile played around her mouth. 'He was enormous fun. Very like my mother. Loved music. Loved making noise. Evenings in the kitchen, all of us bashing something, my father on the piano. *You're* a musician,' she said, almost accusatorily. 'You must know what that's like.'

'No,' said Sarah. 'I didn't grow up in a house like that. Lara, what happened to your other brother?'

'Henry went to boarding school as soon as he could, when he was thirteen. He still loves institutions. He joined the army. He's got his clubs. I hardly see him. But I couldn't bear Pa being on his own, so I stayed behind, and I see now it was rather a quiet way to live. He'd work till four then walk with me, but he'd go back to his study after that, five or six till midnight, so I was rather alone in the house. I think that's when I first became interested in photography. Looking through old photos, wanting to make new memories, new images.' Her eyes scanned the horizon, the kites flying in the distance on Parliament Hill. 'There was a family whose garden backed onto ours, on Christchurch Avenue. A family of five, lots of books, always laughing, tramping up and downstairs. They looked so nice. There was a girl, around my age, tall and slender – I'd watch her going up to bed. I'd think, *I wish you could be my friend. That should be me. I wish—*'

She broke off and looked down. Sarah thought of the little girl in the back garden she'd seen on their first day there. She knew what she meant. How alone she felt, sometimes.

'I'm so sorry—' she tried to say, but Lara cut her off.

'Let's not talk about it any more. You went to Haresfield School, didn't you?'

'Yes, I did,' said Sarah, a little surprised. 'How did you know that?'

'I knew someone who was there.'

'Oh.' Sarah didn't ask whom. 'Did you get sent to boarding school?'

'No, a day school round the corner, rather full of bluestockings. Daughters of the important people nearby. I changed my name, so I was a Thorpe. They knew I was his granddaughter, you see. That sort of thing matters to those people. And I – wanted him to know I felt I belonged with him. We were the only two people left, Pa and I.' She gave a twisted smile. 'Most girls my age were so grateful to be going off to university, and I didn't want to go. You see I wanted to go back –' And Lara stopped, her small, pale face frozen. 'What

I wanted was to go back to a house full of sound and music – and I couldn't.'

'Oh, Lara.'

'But it was all right. Especially the dreadfully cold winters in the late fifties, the two of us next to the fire in the drawing room, cosy as anything. He'd read me books, *The Water Babies*, *Oliver Twist*, *Alice in Wonderland*. Mrs McClean made delicious cakes; we were very snug. But then I'd go to the kitchen and see our names on the wall. It's hidden by the dresser now, you see, but we signed our names. The whole family. And I'd stare at it and sometimes – I couldn't really bear it.' She stopped abruptly. 'That's enough. Where are your people, then?'

'Well,' said Sarah. 'Our father died on D-Day. We lost touch with his parents, my grandparents. They were in Yorkshire.'

'And your mother?'

'Yes, she's still alive. There, there, little one.' She busied herself fussing over Friday's blanket.

'Was boarding school masses of fun?'

'No,' said Sarah flatly.

'Oh, it always sounds fun. Midnight feasts. Very jolly.'

'The reality was the opposite I'm afraid.'

'How so?'

'Oh, I slept in a room with rags blocking up the broken panes of glass. The oats had weevils, you'd spot them in the porridge. There was a girl there called Minnie in my sister's year – she hadn't seen her parents for three years, and there was a rumour they'd simply forgotten where they'd left her. When my best friend Monica left, she couldn't do multiplication. But I learned the cello there.' She stopped, because to talk about it was still painful, then swallowed, and said, 'And I met my best friend, Monica. But it wasn't the sort of place where you sent your daughters if you liked them, let's say. Or else you thought it was the sort of place where you'd meet the right people and you didn't care what the school was like.'

'Why were you sent there? Because they wanted you to meet the right people? Earls' daughters, and all that?'

'Not in my case,' said Sarah.

'Oh, I see. You *are* an earl's daughter,' said Lara teasingly.

'No, I'm not.'

'You lived in a stately home, anyway.'

'No, I didn't,' said Sarah. She pushed the pram and caught up with it.

'I heard you did.'

'How?'

'From the girl. Who was at school with you. I don't remember her name.'

They were both silent. Confused, Sarah peered sideways at Lara. She was hopeless at reading social cues, couldn't do it. She hadn't had the practice. Was this how friends talked to each other? Or had she annoyed Lara, said something she shouldn't have?

'It wasn't stately, or a home,' she said eventually.

'*It wasn't stately or a home!*' Lara imitated her. 'Well, how very la-di-da!'

Sarah wished she was alone with Friday suddenly. She wanted to watch her round little face, staring up with wonder at the sky and the lime trees, her dark eyes following everything, her hands reaching out to clutch at what she saw. *I am here, little one.* She leaned over, to blow on her, and Lara said:

'Thank God you're not one of those besotted mothers, you know. Who only wants to talk about their baby.'

But I do want to talk about her, Sarah thought suddenly, fiercely. *I want to talk about her all the time. How clever she is, reaching for things with her plump little hands. How her laugh sounds so filthy, like a smoker's. How she claps when Daniel and I come into the room, and when she wakes up she is furious, and then she sees you and smiles and it's like sunshine. How terrifying it is, loving her. How different it is to the way I love Daniel, how sometimes it's like warm air, filling up your lungs, and you can't catch breath, you're suffocating, and yet you want to keep filling up on it . . . How I'm not ready for it. I keep thinking about my sister – why do I keep thinking about her? Wondering what it was like, in the dark, dank flat, on her own with our mother?*

But this was one of the things she didn't know: how much you talked about your child, and with whom. So she kept quiet. Lara was silent too as they walked further along the path, and then she stopped and pointed. She said: 'We found a dead body over there, you know.'

'What?'

'Henry and I. We were building a den in the woods. It was a young man, curled up in a ball.'

'What had happened to him?'

'Well, I don't know, do I? He had a thick red mark round his neck – that's all I remember.' She put her hands up to her neck, unconsciously. 'It was swollen in places . . . like a scar – but it wasn't a scar . . . He was naked.'

Sarah put her hand over her mouth. Since having Friday, she felt she was missing a layer of skin. She had no resilience, no depth; she was paper thin.

'Well, the bottom half. He was wearing a shirt. He smelt, and Henry put leaves over him.' She swallowed, as if the memory were there, present with them, and she turned away, looking in the other direction. 'Pa paid for his funeral. They were always finding bodies there. You know, Pa's grandfather remembered them hanging them from trees. Highwaymen, and thieves, you know. Someone on the street, he murdered his girlfriend, bludgeoned her to death, dragged her into the bushes, just over past the ponds, there.' She pointed. 'They didn't find her for months. Barely any of her left by the time they did.'

Sarah looked around, at the mothers in pinafores pushing striped buggies, the decorous ladies with dogs, the businessmen walking home from the City, one with a bowler hat slipping slightly to the side. It didn't seem real. And just then Friday started crying, a thin cry that said, I have had enough. Sarah looked at her watch, and was astonished to see it was almost seven o'clock. 'Gosh. Let's go back,' she said awkwardly. 'I had no idea it was so late. Friday should have had a bath – she should have had a feed. She should be asleep in ten minutes. I'm supposed to be sticking to a routine, you see.'

'Oh goodness, what does it matter? You've had some fresh air and exercise,' said Lara with a shrug. 'I think you both needed it. And she's fine, isn't she?' She pointed at Friday, who was crying more loudly now, an actual wail.

According to the nurse, the world would fall apart if Friday didn't stick to the routine, let it slip by even five minutes, and Sarah tried this every day and every day something went wrong.

She was amazed over two hours had passed without her realising, when her days were so circumscribed.

They turned and started walking back, Sarah pushing the pram as fast as she could. Lara's pace was slow, and Sarah thought she didn't want to leave the Heath.

They parted on the doorstep of No. 7.

'Hope you enjoyed yourself,' said Lara. 'Let's do it again.'

'Next week,' said Sarah firmly. She smiled at her. 'Morning, perhaps. I'm up early.'

'Absolutely.' Lara ran her finger behind her ear, pressing it, trailing it in her hair. As if something in her skull pained her. 'Any time. Maybe I could take a photo of you, of Friday, soon?' She glanced in a disinterested way at Friday. 'Tony's bought me a very expensive camera. He says it keeps me busy.'

'That's – nice of him.'

Lara said: 'He likes me to have something to do. So he can get on with his life.' She shook her hair, so it flowed around her face, silver-water ripples. Friday started to cry more loudly. 'Goodbye, Sarah. I'm glad we had this time together. I'm glad to get to know you a bit better.'

And she turned, and dashed down the path, before Sarah could reply.

Inside, Sarah threw the key down on the table and hung up her cape, whistling softly under her breath. The kitchen door flung open, and Daniel rushed towards them.

'Thank God. Where have you been?' He lifted his daughter out of the pram.

'You told me to go out,' she said.

'Where have you *been*, though?'

'I went to the Heath! For a walk with Lara!' Sarah was suddenly struck with hilarity. 'Daniel, honestly. What a drama you make about everything.'

'Sarah! I couldn't find you. I looked everywhere.'

'How ridiculous you are,' Sarah said, for once feeling as though she had the upper hand. 'You can't have looked very far. We had a lovely walk and it was great to be out, so thank you for the suggestion.'

'She's an interesting girl, isn't she?'

'Very,' said Sarah. She sniffed, and smelt cigarette smoke. 'Hello, Diana,' she called.

'Hey, kiddo,' Diana said. 'Daniel, I told you she hadn't been murdered. Come back – it's your turn.'

Daniel was cradling Friday, who was now so furious Sarah knew that when the storm broke it would be truly awful. But she'd had a walk, and talked to someone who was interested in her, and her legs felt tired for the first time in weeks, tired with activity. As Friday's screams escalated and Diana tut-tutted under her breath and Daniel desperately rocked Friday against him, Sarah paused for one second before removing her from him and taking her upstairs, starting the routine all over again.

'You don't need to yell at me,' she said to Friday, and smiled to herself, as if she'd made a hilarious joke. For once, she felt insulated against it all, for a little while.

Chapter Four

September 1971

One year, Sarah had not returned to school on time, but two days late. She'd been at a cello holiday camp, and got the start-of-term date wrong. A missed train, no telephones and a power cut meant she spent a night on a bench at Victoria station, and another at Monica's house, turning up on the doorstep after Monica had gone back to Haresfield.

'Oh dear, Sarah,' Mrs Powlett had said, wiping her hands on an apron, the only time Sarah ever saw her flustered. 'What have we got here?'

She had spent the night at Frencham Court, then was put on the train the next day, clothes hastily washed and pressed, trunk repacked, and had arrived to find the dorms full, the friendships already alarmingly readjusted and recalibrated, the covering of impermeable tightness wound around not only her schoolmates but the teachers too. Worst of all was that Vic didn't come to see her, didn't seem to have noticed she wasn't there.

She never regained a sure footing that year at school, which was Vic's final year. She was always playing catch-up – the good desks gone, the crushes decided upon. Only Monica was a constant, Monica and the cello.

This experience was one reason Sarah had an obsession with dates and times, though still she frequently got them wrong, was late, misjudged the time, as if time was playing with her, running differently to others. She checked and rechecked the paper tickets for her tours with the Pembroke Quartet ten times a day. She wrote everything down in the pages of her slim, gilt-edged W.H.Smith's pocket diary and checked the diary twice, three times a day. And still events tripped her up. It was mystifying.

This particular golden September day, Sarah was feeling rather chipper: Daniel had gone into town that morning for lunch with friends at the French House and wouldn't be back for ages. He was wearing his floral tie and his silly velvet jacket he was so proud of, and she knew they'd go on to the Coach and Horses, and he'd stagger home at midnight to lie in bed the following day, plaintively asking for toast and sweet tea. He had finished his polemical non-fiction title about the decline of English literature, and was waiting for publication, writing comedy scripts again with the lounging, chain-smoking, casually arrogant gang of chaps he had met during his time at Cambridge.

Daniel's gift for making friends was extraordinary: Miss Minchin the publisher's reader down the road, the station manager at Hampstead Heath who sometimes popped in for tea on his way home, Professor Gupta across the road, the rabbi with whom Daniel went for long walks on the Heath, Diana, of course. But this ability also made her protective towards him, though she never said this out loud. The comedy boys he worked with and with whom he was lunching today were sharp, competitive, insanely insecure. They had all gone to public schools, where they'd honed the finer points of superiority until they could spot a fake, or someone who wasn't quite *quite*, at fifty paces. They dressed up as women, foreigners, anyone who was different to them, and asserted loudly that this was *satire*, my dear. Sarah didn't think it was.

But she didn't say this to Daniel as he hurried off down the garden path in the golden September sunshine, clicking his heels together like Dick Van Dyke in *Mary Poppins*, waving one long hand goodbye.

'Bye, Friday!' he'd shouted joyously. 'Bye-bye, darling! Hope you feel better today, be a good girl for Mama!'

After he'd gone, she had taken Friday to the doctor's, dragging the cumbersome pram up the steep Victorian steps (she'd never noticed before Friday how many places weren't set up for people with prams, or those who couldn't walk: Tubes, buses, shops, libraries). Friday had had croup the previous week, which had been terrifying, and she still had a temperature and didn't seem that well, though of course the moment they reached the doctor's she had thrashed around in her new buggy, pink-cheeked and curly-haired, squawking loudly at everyone, like a crow.

'Aaaaaaarp!'

'When do they walk?' she had asked the doctor, to try and cover the shame at wasting their time with a clearly healthy baby.

'Aaaaaaarp!'

'Now, don't you worry about all that, Mrs Forster,' Doctor Jenkins had said, with an airy wave. 'They'll walk when they're ready.'

'I wasn't worried,' Sarah had wanted to say. I was curious. One of the things she found most bewildering about becoming a mother was that every question or request for information was met with stonewalling, or brushing aside. 'I simply want some facts,' she used to mutter under her breath. 'I don't know about this and I want to know.'

With the cello, you practised. You played and played, until your fingers hurt, and you were better. How did you practise at being a mother? How did you improve, get better?

'Ah. Mrs Forster again,' the nurse had said. 'Well, you're a big girl, aren't you, my goodness!' she'd said sternly to Friday, as if Friday was some kind of freakish circus exhibit.

September sunshine poured through the gaps in the buildings. It leaked through the heavy darkness of the trees. Sarah longed to go back to the Heath, spread a rug on the ground, to lie there and feed Friday little thirds of banana, and then pull her onto her chest and cuddle her, the two of them dozing in the warm shade, Friday's soft, warm weight rooting her to the ground. But the nurse told her again as she weighed her, making Friday cry as she transferred her to the surprising cool of the metal bowl that held her, that Friday was susceptible to illness because she wasn't being kept to a routine.

Sarah had meekly nodded, bumped Friday back down the steep steps again, and started walking home. She'd agreed to meet Lara on the Heath for a walk; Lara was going to photograph Sarah. The buggy kept getting caught on the stones, and Sarah tried not to think of how sick she was of it, how much she hated Daniel for buying it, and the council who hadn't fixed the cracked paving stones, and that nurse, most of all how she hated September, how nervous going back to school made her, every single year. She thought of Daniel, who was probably dawdling in and out of bookshops on the Charing Cross Road waiting for lunchtime, humming happily to himself as he picked up an old green Penguin, or a Rider Haggard. She did not begrudge him this day out, far from it, especially since the previous week he had finally accepted her argument that the Victorian tiles musn't be covered up with thick primrose paint, and had carefully removed it, which made him dizzy with fumes. He'd talked even more than usual, tried to do a handstand and fallen over, then gone into the garden and picked a bunch of flowers and taken them to Diana, who said they were weeds and told him to go and lie down.

Life with Daniel would never be dull – she understood this now. And, two years since they'd moved in, she could see the house starting to shape itself to them, not the Thorpes. The fireplaces had all been uncovered, the chimneys swept. The bannisters were stripped back to bare wood. Sarah had had William Morris Strawberry Thief curtains made. She had found, at a stall on the Portobello Road, a Tiffany lampshade, which stood on an old mahogany sideboard at the edge of the room. Rugs on the floorboards from India covered the parts of the varnishing that hadn't been so successful. Their books were finally arranged in shelves made by Daniel's mysterious friend Dennis O'Malley, a carpenter who appeared without warning, and drank in a pub in Kilburn which he said darkly 'was the kind of place an American's welcome, but not an English person, if you get me, Daniel, if you get me, but you're Jewish, so I'll risk it,' and who took Daniel to the pub where he introduced him to a man he said was descended from Grimaldi the clown, to Daniel's delight.

'Well, doesn't that make him a bigot, as much as Georgina?' Sarah had said to him crossly.

'It's everywhere,' Daniel had told her, letting his hands flop. 'Sarah, I hope you'll understand, but I hope by the time Friday's grown up she won't need to understand. It's everywhere, my darling.' And he would never say more than that.

Pushing the buggy with one hand, Sarah looked at her watch and realised she would be late for Lara. It was hard to pin Lara down. Tony kept her busy, taking her to dinner with showbiz clients, and she was often working out of town. Sarah didn't want to seem needy, but Lara had said she'd pop round several times that last week to photograph Sarah playing the cello and Sarah, stuck at home all weekend with an ill baby and a husband with a deadline, was desperate for someone else to chat to. She had even started talking back to *I'm Sorry, I'll Read That Again* on the radio. The idea, perhaps, that she could open up the cello case, take it out, let her fingers stray over the fingerboard whilst Friday was distracted by Lara. She had not played for months.

'Nice to see you've got visitors, Mrs Forster,' said Professor Gupta as Sarah turned into the road.

'Visitors.'

Sunil Gupta pointed towards her house. 'She must be family! She looks just like you. Wonderful.'

Sarah blushed, rather taken aback at the idea Lara could be seen as family. 'Lara's not family, Professor,' she said. 'She's a friend.'

'Sarah,' someone shouted, from the top of The Row, and she turned. 'Sarah, sorry. I can't make it today. Something's come up.'

It was Lara, leaning out of the first-floor window of her flat, her face pale, in a thin vest that showed her childish figure.

Sarah looked up at her. It was so unlike Lara to yell out of a window, to appear in any way unpolished. But here she was, hair falling over her face, eyes red rimmed, cigarette in hand. She could see Tony behind her, patting her shoulder.

'That's OK,' Sarah called up, trying to hide her disappointment. 'Are you all right? Can I bring you anything?'

'No,' said Lara. 'I just can't. Not today.'

As Sarah was saying, 'I hope I'll see you soon,' the casement window slammed shut, and the curtains were drawn across, and Sarah was left standing in the middle of the road, rocking the buggy, wondering again what she'd done to mess things up and why it mattered. Tears pricked her eyes. When she walked on the Heath, she tried not to mind the other mothers pushing buggies along together, happily sharing confidences and tricks about bath time and dummies and rusks. It was like being at school, trying to work out the rules, and she still wasn't there, and she knew why. She knew why.

Behind her, Professor Gupta cleared his throat and she jumped, having forgotten he was there.

'I didn't mean *her*, dear Mrs Forster,' he said with unusual emphasis. 'I mean that lady on the doorstep of your house. *She* must be family.'

He jammed his pipe back in his mouth and nodded at her as Sarah turned, slowly, in time to hear a voice say:

'Sarah? Is that you, finally? We've been waiting for ages. Almost gave up and went back to Norfolk.'

Sarah's legs felt as though they were turning to water. The buggy jolted, trundling slowly down the road, as if drawn back to the house. She ran after it, catching it with one hand, to find her palms were slippery with sweat. At the gate she stopped, and raised her hand to the figure in front of her.

'Hi, Vic,' she said.

'Hello, sister,' said Victoria. 'You weren't expecting us, then.'

She was the same, utterly the same.

How long had it been? Five years? A quick coffee at a Kardomah before Vic caught her train. Sipping politely, not really looking at each other, not really saying anything.

Her sister's beautiful face, the fine bones, the dark eyes – Friday had the same eyes, liquid and furious. Sarah swallowed. She didn't know what to say. For a moment, they simply stared at each other, tension crackling expectantly between them.

'I—' Sarah began.

'Ah,' said Victoria. 'Well. Daniel said he'd told you, and I did ask him to check. I thought it was fixed but –' She lifted her pendant watch from her waistcoat and glanced at it. 'Robert, have you had your pill?'

'Yes,' said Robert quickly. He patted his tweed jacket, then took a pill from a tiny silver box and popped it into his mouth.

'Perhaps we should go,' Vic said, and Sarah shook her head.

'No, please don't. Don't go, Vic – it's just – Come.' She dragged the buggy onto the doorstep, and patted at her pockets, ineffectually. 'How are you, Vic? How is everything?'

Victoria entirely ignored the question, bending down to look at Friday. 'How are things? This must be Lucinda.'

'Friday.'

'Sorry?'

'Her name's Friday.'

'How unusual.'

'We liked it . . .' Sarah said weakly. 'It was Daniel's idea. He wanted something that wasn't like other names.'

'An excellent choice, then.' Victoria nodded at her niece as if entering a business meeting. 'Well, I have to say it's lovely to see you both.' She leaned forward, giving her sister a very brief, glancing whisper of a kiss. 'Robert?'

'Yes?'

'Sarah.'

'Hello, Sarah,' said Robert, kissing her, his cowlick falling across his face so Sarah felt a sandwich of hair and saliva on her flushed cheek.

There was a short pause as Sarah tried to regain her breath. 'Do you *have* a key?' said Victoria, in a tone close to sympathy, as if she wasn't quite sure Sarah lived here.

Sarah fumbled for a minute in her patched and grubby navy mackintosh. 'Yes!' she said with relief. 'Come in, do.'

'Right,' said Victoria, going in ahead of her. 'And Robert, do you have the bags?'

'That's your aunt,' Sarah whispered to her daughter as she followed behind her brother-in-law, lifting the buggy over the high front step into the chilly hallway. She saw, with dismay, the abandoned sheeting, the chisel, the flakes of remaining paint, the turps and varnish hanging like a cloud in the atmosphere, and the dust that flew up everywhere as she pushed Friday inside. 'I suppose he's your uncle.'

The visitors stood in the hallway, looking around.

'Well here we are!' Sarah cried. 'Just leave your bags here.'

'Right here, in the doorway?'

Vic was here, in the house. She was here, and she would *say* things, and Sarah would have to think about their childhood, and she would ask Sarah things. And neither of them would tell the truth, and there was no way to be honest, and no way they could entirely abandon the other, either. It was how it was: wolves, prowling around the door.

At first, as she fussed around making them a boiled egg for lunch – 'so sorry, the butcher's wasn't open' – she told herself it wouldn't be too bad. That she and Victoria had weathered many storms as children, and could learn to have a new relationship, free of their parents. But as she sat them down, and pulled Friday into her wooden highchair, she looked around in despair and realised it would never be like that.

'I'm so sorry –' she said for the eleventh time, clearing her throat simply to make some noise in the echoing kitchen. She gave her sister, fiddling angrily with some string, an apologetic smile. 'Daniel's out at an important business lunch. He'll be back any minute. I'm sure.'

He wouldn't, obviously. He wouldn't be back for hours. Rage, against all of it, swamped Sarah. She felt slightly out of breath, as if she were late for school again, lugging her metaphorical trunk of possessions up the metaphorical steps.

'I suppose he got the date wrong,' said Victoria, twisting the string into a neat coil. 'Hey ho. We both know how extremely busy you two are.' She opened the drawer of the kitchen table. 'Does this go here? Good grief, Sarah, what on earth is *in* here? It's mouldy.'

'Oh dear God,' said Sarah, as Friday started to yell in outrage at something.

'Aaaaaaarp! Aaaarp!'

'I'm sorry. I think it was an orange. Or maybe some cheese. How disgusting. Put the string there, thanks.' She pulled open the drawer of the dresser, which took up most of the wall and was where most things ended up, at some point or another. It wouldn't budge. 'Oh dear. I think it's swollen shut. It's very old, came with the house . . . We've had so much rain . . .'

'It doesn't matter,' said Victoria, dropping it onto the counter.

'I have to feed Friday,' Sarah said. Robert looked up from the Penguin paperback he'd pulled from a teetering pile of books.

'Go ahead,' he said.

'No,' said Sarah firmly as Friday's wails grew louder and louder. 'I'll do it upstairs.'

'I'm surprised you're still doing that,' said Victoria, spreading her legs slightly wider so she could plant them ever more firmly on the floor.

'Yes, well,' said Sarah faintly. She estimated she had about thirty seconds before Friday went utterly berserk, straining at the straps of her high chair. She had developed this cry of late that honestly sounded like a police siren. It was unbelievably loud – how could she have once thought a new-born baby's cry was the loudest sound there was? When Friday was aggrieved, it sounded like someone being murdered.

The lunch was not ready . . . But she had to make a snap decision. Sarah poured the boiling water out of the pan, scalding herself lightly with a few splashes, then filled the pan with cold water from the tap, waited a few moments then, plucking a plate she'd stacked on the draining board that morning, she briskly put the two eggs on the plate. Her fingers burnt as she did – the eggs hadn't cooled at all. They'd barely be cooked, she knew that. She handed them the plate, noting as she did that it was very badly washed up, streaked with butter and marmalade, and slid the plate across the cluttered kitchen table.

'Here you go,' she said, gaily, over Friday's screams. 'Lunch! And do make yourself at home. I'll be as quick as I can.'

She plucked Friday out of the chair, too briskly, so that she caught her legs on the wooden tray, and Friday screamed even louder. Turning in the doorway, she saw her sister and brother-in-law staring at the small dirty plate on which rested two barely cooked eggs in their shells.

Something bubbled up inside her, and she found she was trying not to smile.

'The trouble is, not that there's anything wrong with Ted Heath *per se*, but that he's just dreadfully common,' Victoria said. She took a sip of tea, one foot rhythmically pushing her niece's bouncy rocker on the floor beside her. 'You knew where you were with Douglas-Home. And Wilson at least didn't try to hide it. But Heath is an *awful* man.'

'Aaaaaaarp!' Friday shouted happily at the assembled room, but only Sarah jumped.

'Ghastly oik,' said Robert, turning the pages of his Penguin.

'More tea?' said Sarah.

'No, thank you.' Vic slid the tea cup away from herself, across the side table, one foot pushing the rocker more vigorously now. 'Rather stewed, I'm afraid.'

There was a short silence. Sarah shoved her hands into her pockets. 'Well, it's great you're here . . . We've finished this room and we're rather pleased with it . . .'

She had persuaded them upstairs, into the drawing room, it being the only room of which she was vaguely proud, but Vic had pointed at the curtains. 'Goodness. What an odd pattern.'

'It's William Morris,' Sarah had said confidently, as though that were all that needed saying.

'I'm aware of that. It's just rather *odd*. I mean, birds don't *behave* like that. Why have you taken up the carpets?'

'Oh, to give it a more natural feeling.' Sarah wanted to show these were deliberate choices. That she was an adult. 'The carpet was raspberry, and very worn.'

'I should have thought if it was good enough for Adrian Thorpe it was good enough for you,' said Vic, shrugging. 'Didn't he know Churchill?'

Churchill never claimed to be an expert on curtains, though, Sarah wanted to say. 'It's our house now, I suppose,' said Sarah with a smile. 'So we can make all the mistakes we want.'

'Yes . . . I see.' And Victoria sat back, gazing around her.

Tension flickered between them: Vic when she was little had delighted sometimes in just being cruel for no reason, because life was hard, because their mother was a bully, because everything was unstable, and because she was a big sister. Sarah told herself she'd weathered it before and she would again. She bit her lip.

'How's life in Ingotsham?' she asked politely. Robert stirred slightly.

'Oh, all very good.' Vic shifted forward. 'Wonderful little

place, really, not much, not glamorous like your rackety life in London, Sarah! We're very happy there. Beautiful countryside, the garden is coming along nicely and of course the walks are jolly good. It's all – yes, jolly good really.'

'Yes,' said Sarah, who had visited her sister in Ingotsham once and been struck by the lack of any walks, let alone jolly good ones, unless you thought walking for hours down a muddy, thin path along the side of a flat, waterlogged field filled with cabbages was a good walk. Vic had appeared totally energised by it, Vic who now pretended to like muddy shoes and hunting animals and 'making do', Vic who before they went to Fane had been a Londoner to her core, a girl of interiors, of longing for new dresses and singing hit parade records, always wanting to walk to Fortnum's, who as a child most enjoyed ballet and reading beyond anything else. At Fane she became the Vic who liked horses and pony stories. At school she became Victoria, aloof, cutting, cool. She was adept at shrugging previous versions of herself onto the ground, sloughing them off like a dead skin. Sarah was the only one who had seen all these different Vics, who struggled to see which one was the true reflection of the sad, pinched-faced young girl with huge eyes and pale skin who cried into her pillow when she thought Sarah was asleep.

'And have you been on holiday anywhere?'

'Us? Holiday!' Vic gave a huge, bellowing laugh. 'Goodness, Sarah, what a world you live in! We can't go on *holiday*. We don't have the need to dash off to the other side of the world on a *whim*. And, really, when you're in the countryside, you don't really need to go anywhere. The garden and the animals can't be left in summer. And we wouldn't want to go, either. No, we're *verrry* happy at home. Dorcas had kittens – that's kept us busy. And one of the sheep has a prolapse.' She smiled with grim pleasure at Sarah. 'Taken up quite a lot of my time. I've had to sit up with the stupid girl. Nasty things, prolapses.'

'I know,' said Sarah. 'I had one.'

Vic looked angrily at her, then chewed the side of her lip. She was silent for a moment, and Sarah felt it coming.

'Any communication with Fane?' Vic said eventually.

'No,' said Sarah.

'You haven't taken Friday down to see her?'

'You must know I haven't.'

'Don't be like that, Sarah. I'm merely asking—'

'I know, but the way you ask it is couched in such a way that I have to respond like that, as you put it.'

'You can't simply pretend she's dead.'

Sarah gripped the edge of the arms of the chair. 'Why not?'

'Her first grandchild,' said Vic. 'That's all.'

Where was Daniel? He was the only one who understood, who could make the past vanish, soothe her fears about the future. Sarah swallowed.

'Vic. I can't go there. You know I can't.'

Vic shrugged, her mouth tugged down at the edges. 'Isn't it all in the past, now?'

'Why are you suddenly defending her?' Sarah stared at her. 'Has she got to you?'

'What are you implying?'

'That she's stuck a little pin in you like those butterflies Uncle Clive used to catch. Just to watch you squirm.'

Robert yawned, ostentatiously loudly.

'Sarah,' Victoria sighed, 'sometimes, don't you think you're a bit . . . *over the top* about our mother? About it all?'

Sarah found herself laughing. 'Oh, she has. She has got to you. I wonder what it is . . . Robert's tax issues. Monica told me you mentioned it to her. Has Iris bailed you out? Or does she know what happened with Mr Williams? What you did? What you're responsible for?'

'Sarah, you're just being difficult,' said Victoria calmly, but Sarah saw the twitch, in the corner of her eye. 'I simply felt I ought to be in contact with her. *One* of us ought to, anyway. Robert, stop yawning, for Christ's sake.'

'Just being difficult. That's funny. Try telling that to Uncle Clive, to Stella, to ten-year-old you,' said Sarah. She looked down, saw her hands shaking. 'Don't you remember what it was like? Don't you remember Peter Pan and Wendy, Vic?'

'Who were Peter Pan and Wendy?' said Robert, looking up.

Victoria shrugged, but she touched her hand to her twitching eye, in annoyance. 'Nothing. They were – nothing. Go back to your book, Robert.'

'Victoria. She should be in prison for what she did.'

'What do you mean?' said Victoria. 'She's been to prison.'

'I outlined it to a friend of ours who's a lawyer last year. No names, of course. But he was definite that if people were willing to testify we could charge her with abuse and neglect.' She could hear her voice, high-pitched and harsh. She sounded unhinged.

'Abuse!' Victoria gave a scoffing noise. 'Listen, Miss Marple—'

Sarah waved her hand. 'I think I know why you're doing this. Saying it was all all right and nothing much, that I'm making a fuss. Is it that it's too uncomfortable to admit what it was like to your posh country friends? Is it that if you tell yourself it wasn't so bad you don't have to face up to it? That we never knew if there'd be food, and we were always hungry? How we slept in the corridor of the flat because she'd locked us out and gone away and we didn't know where else to go? The time she slammed the door on your hand? The bedroom at Fane? The smell? How about the fact no one intervened, that people just pretended she was odd? You want to forget all of that, just so you can boast about growing up in a house like Fane, seem grand and important? Well, fine. We had to survive somehow. But that's very strange.'

Sarah glanced over at Robert, still utterly absorbed in his book. She found it extraordinary that he could concentrate. Friday wriggled, and Sarah looked at her longingly, wishing she could be alone with her, feel her cool, plump cheek against her lips. Her stomach ached.

'She's got to you.' She pointed her finger. 'Begging for food. The slaps. The smell, Vic . . .'

'I went to see her,' Victoria said unexpectedly. She stood up, leaving Friday's rocker to bounce back, which it did, most alarmingly. Victoria hugged herself, then swung her arms out, then plunged them into her dark corduroy flared skirt. She wore a pie-crust white shirt and a quilted Liberty fabric waistcoat, and if her shining dark hair had been longer – it sat just above her shoulders – she could have been someone from the Victorian era. Sometimes she'd move, and Sarah could catch a glimpse of the thin-faced, urgent, passionate girl she had once been, the one who'd hugged Sarah and read her stories, the one who was always in front, who cared for her when no one else did.

'You went *back* there?'

'Well, I was going to tell you. Robert and I both went. Over the summer. It was – quite extraordinary, really. She's—'

'Are you going to tell me she's changed?'

'Changed?' Vic raised one shoulder, leaning her cheek against it, like a child again, considering the question. 'In a way. She's not well, for a start. I think there's something wrong with her.'

'Of course there's something *wrong* with her, Vic.' Sarah wanted to laugh. She was cold, nausea trapped in her throat, her body shaking in the warmth of the room.

'I mean – some kind of illness.'

'She's dying?'

'I don't know.' Vic shrugged, and for a moment she looked uncertain. Uncomfortable. 'It's jolly odd, though. Whatever's the matter with her is something that now one's a grown-up one sees it's more than merely a bad temper. I mean, she doesn't see the world in the right way. I don't know why.'

Her sister's bluff carapace was gone for an instant, her dark eyes swimming with tears.

'Well, I don't either,' said Sarah, and to her horror she found that tears were springing into her eyes too. She brushed them angrily away. 'But we suffered as a result, Vic – how can you forget what it was like?'

'I don't forget,' said Vic in a low voice. 'But I can't let it rule my life. I have to put it aside. Sarah, I have to.'

Sarah shook her head. 'I can't.'

Either side of the fireplace, they sat, unable to breach the divide, as Robert turned another page of his book, and Friday babbled, quietly, to herself.

Perhaps I should ask her to leave, Sarah thought. *Tell her I can't have her in the house, that it's too hard, that I can't forgive her.* And instantly she knew if she did that Vic would leave, and that would be it, the final chance to have her sister in her life gone, the slender threads snapped, and she couldn't quite do it. Eventually she said:

'So what happened? Where did you stay?'

'She's still got a couple of rooms at the top of the tower. They're quite nice. Of course everything else around it is ghastly, really dreadful, such a shame. She doesn't do anything. Just sits in bed and listens to the radio and smokes. That's it, really. I saw Mrs Boyes – the church needs a new roof, someone's stolen the lead. It's really a dreadful problem round our way, you know. I suppose it's all this unrest with young people not having jobs, and the like, but there's a beautiful old church with a Norman font that they got into last week and ripped the lead off . . .'

But Sarah did not hear what her sister was saying. Her voice faded out and she was back there, lying on the platform looking upwards at the ink-dark night almost indiscernible from the oak trees around them, blinking and allowing her eyes to slowly, slowly adjust, before she opened them and the sky above was spread before her: the Milky Way, like a vapour cloud bubbling with silver and gold and red and the stars, dotting the sky, and the more you looked the more you saw until, really, all you saw were stars, and you wondered how you'd never realised it before, that they were above you, all the time, you simply had to notice them . . .

'Sarah! Are you listening to me?'

'I was thinking,' Sarah said, rubbing her eyes, and clearing her throat. 'Sorry.'

'Anyway, I think you should go back,' said Vic suddenly. 'Do you good. Show her Friday.'

'I barely think of it any more. I couldn't go back.'

'Don't lie, Sarah,' Vic said.

'I said I couldn't. Leave it there. Let's both leave it there. Do you understand?'

Vic shrugged to an invisible audience, as if to indicate that she wasn't the problem.

Silence fell again. And then, to Sarah's huge relief, she heard the sound of the front door downstairs violently banging open, and a voice singing loudly.

'I'm half crazy, all for the love of you!' Friday looked up, at the

sound of her father's voice and stared at her aunt, who started pushing the rocker again, furiously.

'It won't be a stylish marriage . . .

I can't afford a carriage . . .

But you'll look – Oh, shit! Shit! Ow!'

There was a loud thump.

'He's fallen over our case,' said Vic solemnly. 'We should have taken it upstairs.'

Daniel appeared in the doorway, still swearing softly under his breath. Even from where Sarah was sitting, she could smell the rich, sweetly fuggy fumes of alcohol, sweat, cigarettes, pot, meat juices, rolling off him like the mist off the fields in the late summer mornings.

'Hello,' he said, holding up one hand to wave as if it were incredibly heavy, looking at it in surprise, then at them, then letting it drop. 'Vittory! Bobert! How *you*!'

'Very well, thank you,' said Victoria. She was almost smiling. 'You had a good lunch, I take it, Daniel?'

Robert glanced up from *The Long Divorce*. 'Ah. Daniel. What?'

Daniel turned to his wife and enunciating very carefully said: 'I got. The wrong day. Didn't I?'

She shook her head. *Not now*. 'Did you have a good time?'

'I did.' He blinked. 'Nice chaps. Jolly lolly. Now . . . ho ho ho,' Daniel said, advancing towards his daughter, but he stumbled slightly, towards the side table, and Sarah saw it unfold in slow motion, his body falling against the chair, arm flailing to stop himself, knocking the table, the stewed cup of tea on it, hitting it hard, so that it flew up in an arc towards Victoria, hitting her in the face, dark tea sluicing her body, her red neck, her shirt with the crisp ruffles, the delicate floral pattern of the waistcoat, the edge of the liquid raining down on Friday, who started to cry. Daniel fell to the floor.

'Yikes,' he said, head in Vic's lap. Tea dripped down her astonished face. He patted her knee. 'Oh, Victoria.'

'I say,' said Robert, looking up again. 'What's going on here?'

Vic stood up, brushing herself off. 'Goodness,' she said, and she reached into her pocket for a handkerchief. She wiped her face first, then her niece's, then picked her up and put her on her hip. 'Shush, there, there,' she said, and patted her back, firmly but Sarah caught the look she gave her, the dark, fierce passion Vic had always felt she had to keep tamped down. 'None of that nonsense. Here,' she said, handing her to Sarah. 'I need to change out of my clothes, and this child needs a bath. It's obvious you had no idea we were coming, Sarah. I don't know why you didn't make that clear from the start. I saw a fish-and-chip shop on our way down the high street; should I send Robert out to get some supper for us all?'

'Oh!' Sarah looked around as Friday squirmed on her hip, staring at her aunt. Suddenly, like stepping through a door, back to it all, she remembered her sister as she had been. Small, determined, unbowed, unafraid. Her face as she answered their mother back that time in the car, opening the door, the whirring wheels, the sound of her fall. Her mouth, grimly set as she drove off with Miss Parker. She had eaten a snail, after losing a bet with awful Bobbie Thomas, the vicar's daughter, at Christmas. She had met Robert at a dance at veterinary college when he had helped the principal, an old friend, out of the door, and decided to marry him, pretty much on the spot, and when Sarah had asked her why she had said: 'It's everything I need. I know it's not for you, but it is for me. So.'

Yes, this was Vic. This was her sister. 'You're right. And that's a wonderful idea about the fish and chips. Yes, please, if he doesn't mind.'

'Course he doesn't.' Victoria nudged Robert, who immediately stood up, sliding the book into his jacket pocket, and saluted. 'Why don't *both* of you have a bath. I can help Daniel tidy the kitchen. And then,' she said, with relish, 'let's have a bloody drink.'

'It's funny how your sister grows on you,' said Daniel. He dipped the wooden spoon into the orange casserole pot on the stove, and licked it, ruminatively, then handed it to his wife, who did the same. 'Hm, that's good.'

Vic and Robert had been there for five days. It was Sunday, and Daniel was cooking lunch.

'More salt,' said Sarah. 'You never put enough in. Under-seasoning is worse than over-seasoning, Daniel.'

'We can argue about this, but you know that's crazy talk. You just need to trust the ingredients.' He shook the merest dusting of salt from the ceramic pig into the pot.

'Put more in now. Not enough salt leads to more salt usage in the end. People end up oversalting their meals and the flavour's ruined.'

'It's ruined, is it?' He was laughing, and Sarah shook her head at him, and folded her arms. They were facing each other in the little alcove shape of the kitchen units where the old range overlooked the mess of the garden. It was a chilly morning, and heavy autumn dew had soaked the long grass in the tiny dark garden, dotting the copious spiders' webs so they shimmered in the gloom. 'It's not ruined, Sarah darling. Not everything ends in disaster – you need to know that.' He threw some more salt in, then leaned forward and kissed her. 'There you go, my bird.' She reached out for more, but he put his hand on hers. 'What do Jews bring to a new home? Bread and salt. Bread, so you never experience hunger. Salt to bring flavour to life. There's the flavour. But it's all here too. I love it here with you. Just us, like this. Don't laugh at me; don't say I'm being earnest.'

'I won't.'

Daniel kissed her. 'Come here. I'm sorry you had such a bad night.'

'It's fine.' Sarah wrapped her arms round him, put her head on his chest. She was dizzy with tiredness. Friday had woken every hour from midnight to six and was now out for a walk with Vic, but Sarah couldn't relax. There was no relief in the absence of her baby, just anxiety about night time, about when it would start up again, about what this night would bring. Why didn't Friday sleep? She was almost a year old. She didn't sleep, she thrashed and yelled and demanded more milk and howled as if her heart was breaking. The doctor said nothing was wrong. She ate like a starving man rescued from the desert. She just didn't like sleep, and it was worse than ever at the moment, and ordinarily it wouldn't matter but now . . .

Sarah tried to articulate this, to tell him what Vic arriving had done, how it upended everything when it was already chaotic and how the last few days she, Sarah, found she couldn't control the depths of the feelings that swamped her. Sleep, or lack of it, was driving her mad and, though Daniel offered to take a shift, for her to sleep upstairs, whenever they tried it, he slept through and she invariably woke on high alert like the meerkats in London Zoo, upright, alert for danger at the slightest sound.

When they were first married, they had stood like this all the time, quietly listening to each other, holding each other, not moving. Now, as Sarah listened to Daniel's heart beating in the scratchy wool jumper, she said softly: 'I wish she'd just . . . go.'

'Listen, kiddo. I know Vic's tricky. But you should give her a chance. She's come because she wants to spend time with you.'

'I know her better than anyone, Daniel. She doesn't want intimacy. She never did.'

'That's not true, Sarah—'

Sarah held up her hand. 'Daniel, love. You don't know.'

Daniel licked his fingers. He grimaced, and carried on stirring and Sarah knew he was on the verge of being irritated. 'OK. But she wants some kind of relationship with you. And she's sweet with Friday.'

Sarah stared down at the gloopy red stew, bubbles slowly bursting and spraying hot juice on the stove. It was true Victoria had taken a shine to her niece. Vic insisted on walking her extremely fast around the Heath, talking briskly about horseflesh and how to avoid sheep becoming flyblown. She gave her baths and scrubbed her chubby face with a rasping flannel, and read her books that were far too old for her, like *The Railway Children*, but Friday didn't seem to mind.

'I'm not sure she'll understand *The Railway Children*,' she'd ventured, and Daniel had clicked his tongue, as if disappointed.

'Babies develop extremely fast,' Victoria had said briskly. 'And anyone can see Friday is obviously very intelligent. Who knows what she understands?'

If she'd been Friday's mother, this would have been a ridiculous thing to say, but somehow, because Victoria was Friday's aunt, everyone nodded, sagely. It *was* obvious.

In addition to everything else it brought up for her, Vic's

presence made Sarah feel even more invisible than usual. Everything she had achieved since leaving home had been hard-won. Only Daniel and Monica understood this. She had got to music college on a scholarship, survived on grants and wearing one of Monica's mother's old coats in winter till it fell apart. No one had paid her rent or her tuition fees or bought her birthday presents. She lived on tinned food and when she couldn't afford food, coffee from the café below her bedsit. Her body was, after all, used to getting by on very little.

'You're underweight, Mrs Forster,' the doctor had told her when she went for a check-up before Friday was born.

'Yes,' she'd said wearily. 'I know.'

She had worked, and worked, practising till her fingertips were red and tender, then calloused. She had scraped a living in orchestras and quartets and funerals and functions, barely surviving, as London burst into life around her when the sixties took hold. For several years she felt, with grim amusement, that Swinging London and the explosion of everything was for people who could afford it. She couldn't go to Mary Quant or visit clubs to hear music she liked: she didn't have enough money for the bus fare most days. She had no safety net. If she hadn't been asked to play at that tedious Royal College of Music alumni sherry party, she wouldn't have met old Mr Mulliken, and if she hadn't met Mr Mulliken he wouldn't have recommended her to his Colony Room pal Oscar Gould, and she'd never have got the Pembroke Quartet.

All these gains, like crawling along a gritty lane, scratching out a path for herself on and on, an inch further each time, and now she had grown something and given birth to it, something that wanted feeding and nurturing all the time, always wanted more than she was able to give, something that was undoing it all. She knew these feelings were evil, unnatural, but she couldn't stop thinking them. And since Vic had turned up they had become amplified, so they were all she could hear now, the anger, the rage, the desire to break things, to wreck it all.

The worst thing of all was Sarah knew there was only one person who would understand how she felt, and that horrified her.

Her gaze drifted, fatigue clouding her eyes. On the wall behind the oak dresser, on the far side of the kitchen there were the names of the Thorpe family: Lara and her siblings, etched into the tallow-coloured paint with a splattered fountain pen, surrounded with swirling patterns. Time had worn away most of the ink, but some of the scratches remained, if you could see into the narrow gap between wall and wood. Most were indistinguishable, or cut off by the dresser itself.

1950!

Sa -
Lara w
Henr
H

Sarah wondered when they had written their names. On Christmas Day, or someone's birthday? After a jolly Sunday lunch, whilst the adults were snoozing upstairs in the sitting room? Or was it whilst someone was banging out tunes on the piano? Sometimes Sarah felt Lara and her family were all there, waiting for her to go, and they would resume. Sometimes at night she was certain she heard a knocking at the door, and wondered if it was Adrian Thorpe and his family, come back to reclaim the house, to live in it properly.

The front door banged open. Victoria and Friday entered the kitchen, back from their walk, fresh-faced and smelling of the outside, of leaves and smoke. Vic lifted Friday up out of the buggy. 'Who's coming for lunch, then?' she said. 'Quite exciting, to be this sociable. Robert and I are living quite the life here, I must say.' She gave an almost girlish giggle.

'No one's coming for lunch,' said Sarah pettishly. She didn't want anyone else to enjoy themselves today, if she couldn't.

'Yes, they are, you remember, Sarah,' said Daniel. He gave a little bow. 'Us, the family.' Vic went slightly pink. 'Then Diana, and Georgina, and Monty. Monica and Guy, and Lara and her husband. All neighbours, apart from Monica and her husband, whom you know, of course.'

'Who's this – What's this for?'

Daniel gestured at the stew. 'Lunch,' he said with a laugh, as if she were the stupid one. 'I told you, didn't I? Honey, I did.'

'You – didn't.'

'Sarah –' He shrugged, rather helplessly, and she knew he'd told her, and she hadn't taken it in, and whose fault was it? His? Hers? And would it make any difference anyway? 'Oh! I'm sorry. Well, today is the first of Daniel Forster's Legendary All Day Sunday Lunches. Daniel and Sarah Forster's, I should say. They'll be here soon.' From the hallway came a forceful knock at the door. The house shook, and Sarah jumped. 'Right now, in fact,' Daniel said.

'It's twelve o'clock,' said Sarah, steadying herself with one hand on the dresser. Everything was dizzy. 'You don't ask people for twelve o'clock.'

'It's All Day Sunday. The whole point is you ask them for whenever they want to come,' Daniel said, and he danced past her, his large, rangy frame sliding past Vic, gripping her elbows. 'What else is there to do on Sundays, my bird? Shops closed, pubs closed, absolutely everything dead. So glad you chaps are here too! The first of many great lunches in this house.' He disappeared down the hall, and she could hear him opening the door. 'Well, Miss Georgina!'

There was chatter, laughter, shoes scraping across the mat. In the silent kitchen, the sisters stared at each other.

'It's fine,' said Vic. 'Just go and get changed and put a smile on your face.'

'It's not fine.' Sarah didn't know how to say: I can't talk to people. Everything in my head is buzzing so loudly I can't think. I can't even sleep when I try to sleep. And Daniel will pass out upstairs this evening and I will clear everything up, and then Friday will wake up every hour again and then tomorrow will be a write-off, and it just goes on, and on.

She reached forward and took Friday from her sister.

'Look, we'll go,' said Vic. 'Avoid lunch. One less thing for you to – Robert and I ought to leave soon anyway . . .' Her eyes were wide, and she looked at her niece treading water in Sarah's arms. A bubble of stew burst, and a tiny drop shot into the air, hitting Sarah's hand with a scalding *pop*.

'No, you mustn't go,' said Sarah weakly, shifting Friday onto her other hip, and she and her sister stood together, hands almost touching, as the sound of laughter swelled in the hallway. 'Oh! Hello, come in, come in to the kitchen! Hi, Monica! Hey, Guy.'

'Well, there she is! Lady Madonna, there with the baby!' Guy, Monica's husband, advanced towards them, arms outstretched, gold buttons on his blazer clinking. 'Marvellous to see you, Sarah.' He glanced at her breasts, then at Friday. 'Ah . . . This must be the little one.'

'Well spotted,' said Sarah, and Vic gave the slightest snort – of shock or amusement, Sarah couldn't say.

'Hello, old boy,' he said, making a funny face. 'You're going to be a rugby player with a face like that, aren't you?'

'She's called Friday.'

'What? Oh Lord, I'm an idiot. Listen, she's marvellous.' Guy slapped his hands together. 'Mon! Mon darling, I've put my foot in it again. Where are my cigs?'

'Oh God, Guy, what have you said now? They're in your pocket.' Monica appeared in the kitchen doorway, immaculate in a sunflower-yellow bouclé pinafore, white pumps, daisy hair clasp nestled in her brown bouffant. She clasped her hands together. 'Look at this lovely house. I wish I hadn't left Toby with the nanny! I could have brought him, Sarah, and they could be friends.' Her kind, but horrified gaze ranged over Sarah, taking in her shift dress, her bare feet, her unkempt hair. 'My darling Sarah, it's glorious to see you. Are you well?'

'She's fine,' said Vic, striding forward. 'Monica, how nice to see *you*.'

Monica's eyes widened even further, just a second, but she had immaculate manners, and at no point did she betray her surprise at seeing Vic. 'Vic, how lovely. Well. A Fox sisters double act! Quite like the old days.' Briefly, her hand closed over Sarah's wrist, wrapped round Friday's body. *She understands.*

'Golly, this is a turn-up for the books,' Mon whispered in her ear as Vic turned to greet another guest. 'How's it been, having Vic here? You coping?'

'Of course,' said Sarah, still not able to enjoy the arrival of this beloved but unexpected guest. 'Thank you for coming.' She knew she sounded mad, but Monica, unfazed, turned back into the hall, where Guy was arguing about the miners with someone.

'No, Guy. Don't be rude. Go and have a cig outside. Darling, I'll just get the wine we brought . . .' And she disappeared back into the hall.

Sarah held Friday tightly, feeling the warm, plump solidity of her little frame against her shivering body. She could not see properly. She could hardly breathe. They were at the edge of the crowd, and no one was listening to them. Almost like the party had started and they were nothing to do with it.

It was just her, and Vic, and Friday in the kitchen. Sarah said desperately: 'I can't do this. I don't like people dropping by, Vic.'

'I know. But you married Daniel, Sarah. You need to learn to cope with it.'

'Tell me how,' Sarah almost shouted. Friday stiffened in her arms and Daniel, half in, half out of the kitchen, turned back to look at her. 'Tell me what I should do, Vic. You've got it all worked out. To get through this, now, carry on for the rest of our lives. What do I *do*?'

Vic glared at her, and hissed: 'Just pretend. Pretend you're normal. Isn't that what we've done all our lives? Isn't that what other people do?'

'How, though?'

Vic shrugged. 'I didn't have children, for starters,' she said, crisply. 'I knew I wouldn't be able to do it. After her.'

The two of them looked at each other, just as Georgina bustled into the kitchen. 'Hello, Sarah, dear. Awful! Monty's being so rude to your husband, Sarah. Says he looks like an evacuee in his khaki shirt!'

'What can I do?' said Monica, reappearing with the bottle of wine.

'Very good question,' said Victoria calmly. 'Daniel is very dear, but he is hopeless and he's made no plans other than this delicious stew. Monica, would you please set the table? Georgina, get the glasses please, they're on the dresser – that's it, there. I think we'll need that wine, there. Sarah, I'll take the baby. You go and get changed.'

In her bedroom, Sarah faced her own reflection in the full-length mirror as she took off her old clothes. A white, doughy body, half skinny, half slack. Her face, a less distinct version of Vic's, the cheekbones less defined, the hair lighter, the eyes hazel – almost a vaguer, fuzzier edition of Victoria, someone vanishing, melting away. She thought for the first time that, of the two of them, she was more like their mother, though this couldn't be true, as the one thing everyone agreed about Iris was that she was very beautiful. Perhaps I'm like her in character. I have all the badness.

The sounds in her head were louder than ever. Downstairs, the noise of arrivals swelled, more and more people, cramming into her filthy, damp kitchen, Daniel loving it all.

She pulled the dress – a navy tunic with cap sleeves and large pockets – over her head. The noises from downstairs grew louder. She stared past, into space. 'All right,' she said.

At the bottom of the stairs, hanging her coat up in the hallway, she found Lara.

She stared at Sarah. 'You look nice. I've never seen that dress before.'

'Daniel bought it for me last week.' She couldn't really remember – her vision was blurring and she rubbed her eyes. Had he? Or had she bought it? She could hear Georgina's voice, rising above the melee. *'All I'm saying is,'* she was saying, *'they're probably harmless but they should get their hair cut.'*

'I'm so glad you're here, Lara,' she said feebly. 'I really can't seem to get a grip on anything lately. I feel I'm – totally losing control.'

'Oh,' Lara said awkwardly. 'I am sorry. What a shame.'

Just pretend you're normal, Victoria had said. *Isn't that what other people do?*

They'd all had too much to drink when the idea was first mooted. A post-Sunday lunch fug had settled on the table. Empty plates from the stew were pushed to the side; the chocolate mousse that Daniel had flung together and which hadn't really set was half eaten in every bowl. The only other sound was Robert, periodically flapping the pages of the *Sunday Times*. When the talk turned to the back garden, the overgrown tree that was blocking light into Diana's kitchen, and how Diana wanted to find a saw to chop it down, Sarah stood up, and gave an 'excuse me' grimace.

No one took any notice. She went wearily upstairs, listening to the babble in the kitchen, separating into strands of conversation.

'I say,' Daniel was calling after Diana. 'Before you start hacking at it, I'd better check with Sarah—'

'Sarah won't mind,' said someone. 'You've been here two years, you know. She'll be glad of the extra light. Chop the thing orf.'

'I think you should check with her first, though,' she heard Monica say.

'Lara – what do you think?' said someone else. 'Do you mind?'

'Oh yes,' Georgina said. 'Lara, dear, do you mind?'

In the doorway of the bedroom she stopped, only partly surprised to find Vic bending over the cot, cooing down at her niece. Sarah stood perfectly still, in the shadows, and watched as her sister lifted Friday against her, so her little round head popped up over her shoulder, and she was staring at her mother, bright eyes wide open, astonished.

'Good girl, good girl,' Vic was murmuring. 'Good little one. My precious one. My precious darling.' She was kissing Friday's cheek. Still, Friday watched Sarah, her face impassive, and still Sarah knew what she was trying to communicate, for the first time. She knew Friday did not understand what was going on, that she knew something wasn't quite right.

Victoria started swaying, with Friday pressed against her. 'Mama's baby,' she whispered, her slender figure turning slowly in the vanishing September light so that for a moment she herself looked like a girl again. Sarah pressed herself against the door, an intruder in her own child's nursery. 'Mama's little, little baby.' And then Vic breathed in, and with a juddering, sobbing expiration, exhaled.

'Somewhere there's another land –
Diffr'ent from the world below –
Far more perfectly planned
Than the cruel place I know . . .'

The hairs on the back of Sarah's neck rose, stiff, trapping cool air, like ice. She was shivering, she was back there, she was there. She went silently into the bathroom, shut the door, then pulled the clanking chain of the lavatory and made a loud show of washing her hands and humming, opening the door again with a bang. She came into the room, making her voice brisk.

'Vic! I was about to get her. I wondered why you were so quiet all of a sudden, little one,' she said briskly, leaning towards her sister and taking Friday from her.

Her sister gripped her niece tightly, her fingers actually clamped round her small, woollen-clad frame. The sisters stared at each other, for no more than a second. Vic's face, the fine chiselled cheekbones, was rigid. Nothing was said. Sarah pulled Friday away, and turned, clutching her tightly to her. Laughter swelled, downstairs, the front door slammed, some activity building to a crescendo. Someone was going to get a chainsaw.

'See you down there,' said Victoria at the doorway, and she took a small, jagged breath. Sarah nodded. It wasn't going to be said now, what she wanted to say.

Vic tucked her hair behind her ear. 'I think we'll be off tomorrow,' she said. 'Robert's keen to get going.'

Someone had come in downstairs, and there was general merriment, and shouts of 'Watch out!'

'All right,' said Sarah. 'Vic – I am glad you came.' She swallowed. The wolves were at the door. Everything, every emotion was flooding her. She could barely see. It was as though black ink were being poured in a fine film down a screen in front of her dry, tired eyes. Vic hesitated for a moment, then turned and left, and Sarah knew she should stop her, ask her to stay again, invite herself up to stay with her. But she didn't. She listened as her sister's light tread landed on the stairs.

The noises were too loud now. She understood that she had to do something, to break the cycle, to take action otherwise she would be lost. Perhaps it was even too late. And she knew what she had to do.

Friday watched her with interest as Sarah laid her back in the cot and flew around the room, gathering this and that. She picked her up, clipped her into the sling, and then, darting into her bedroom, pulled a few items from the vast mahogany wardrobe Daniel had bought from the Kings Road, which they'd had enormous trouble dragging up the old curving stairs into their room. It was in there now; they'd done it. She couldn't look at it, her eyes blinded with tears.

She crept downstairs, but the noise from the kitchen meant no one heard her. They were arguing about the tree now, and the best way to attack it, and whether Diana ought to do it or whether she was too drunk. She left a note for Daniel on the hall table, propped up against the telephone. She nearly abandoned the whole plan as she heard his voice from the kitchen. How this would hurt him. But it was for the best.

Ten minutes later, she was standing on East Heath Street, hailing a cab to the station.

The trains ran until seven on Sunday evenings. Friday had fallen asleep again, but woke up as they boarded the train. 'You're going out of London,' said Sarah, kissing her soft head, and staring out of the window as the train pulled out of the station. 'We're running away.'

Sunday evening was the strangest time, the longing and sadness, especially with these early September evenings, the light sliding from brightness to deep gold, the lengthening shadows on the tracks pulling her out towards Fane, and those memories of not wanting to stay at school, yet desperately not wanting to go back.

She was going back.

Chapter Five

Sarah woke with a start, looking at a bare white wall, and rubbed her eyes, breathing as though she had been running. For a brief moment, she didn't know where she was, couldn't drag it out from her mind, and she panicked, until it started to come back. All Day Sunday. The stew, spitting on the stove. The heat, the noise, Victoria nuzzling Friday's body.

Somewhere there's another land . . .

Next to her, Friday slept on, her arms flung up above her head, her legs spreadeagled like a snow angel. Sarah gazed at her daughter, marvelling at the translucent, waxy pink perfect fingers, curled into a fist. How tiny her ears were, no bigger than a new two pence piece. How neatly she slept, utterly still, apart from her chest, rising and falling. She looked like Daniel.

Suddenly a daddy longlegs juddered overhead, swooping down next to her. Sarah jumped, and batted it away, ineffectually. September was the time for daddy longlegses. She remembered the first weeks at school, how they would zoom into the room, tangling themselves in her hair. She got out of bed, and bashed it against the wall with a shoe. One leg kept twitching, but she couldn't bring herself to hit it again.

She sat back down on the bed and looked round the tiny, empty room, blinking.

Once she'd opened the door to the past, crossed the threshold, it had been remarkably easy to simply keep going. It was almost liberating.

She and Friday had arrived with nowhere to stay, but though the Burnt Oak, on Fane High Street, was apparently closed (it being Sunday evening), she could hear the sound of bells denoting Evensong was over, and something made her stand outside the church.

The pub was at the edge of the village, next to the church, which in turn gave out onto the edge of the estate. She waited, holding Friday's little feet, and within a few minutes Bobbie Thomas emerged from the porch, waving goodbye to the vicar, a tall, etiolated man with pale grey eyes who gaped at Sarah, and Friday.

'Sarah Fox! As I live and breathe! Gosh!' Bobbie called, and Sarah nodded in relief.

Roberta Thomas had been the vicar's daughter, and she was now running the Burnt Oak pub. She had never left Fane. Bobbie, always too eager, said that of course they had room at the inn. Of course Sarah could stay. She stuttered as she showed Sarah up the narrow stairs to the long low room with the small windows through which the last rays of the evening sun poured silken September gold light onto the ancient eiderdown.

'I'll bring up some soup,' she said, wiping her hands on her apron. 'We've another guest over the way, lovely gentleman who stays here Sunday to Thursday. He helps up at the hall with her –' She broke off in confusion. 'Your mother . . .'

Sarah smiled at her gratefully. 'Thank you, Bobbie,' she said, sinking onto the bed, untangling Friday from the sling. 'I'd love some soup.'

'Oh! Right away, of course. Of course!'

She knew Bobbie's enthusiasm was not rooted in any kindness or friendship but a gossipy fascination. *You want to know why I'm here*, she wanted to say. *You want to know what I might do.* When the soup arrived, she fed Friday a bit of it, and gave her some breast milk and a bit of normal milk – she was desperate to stop breast feeding and was gradually weaning Friday, with mixed results, but this time Friday, sitting on the floor of the tiny room, picked up the pieces of soup-soaked bread and chewed them happily, though the mess on the floor was considerable. They sat in silence, smiling at each other, during this strange meal.

'Well, we're here,' Sarah said eventually. The last thing she did as they both began to fall asleep was to wedge a pillow next to her and her daughter. She was terrified of rolling over and squashing her and in fact all night she dreamed that she had, that she was suffocating her child.

That next morning, she walked along the high street slowly, pointing things out to Friday. There was the tiny garage, and there Mr Stevens, now very bald and very bent, scratching his head, wiping down a filthy axle. She hurried along so he didn't see her. There was the post office with the bottles of sweets behind the counter, though no longer with dear Mrs Boundy standing behind, waiting to help you, the Bird Boy, scribbling away in the corner. There was an antiques shop, a new addition to the village, next to the tea shop, both for tourists, she assumed: Fane had always had daytrippers, but it had added notoriety now. And there at the end the vast manse, which was now divided into shabby flats. It had once been the home of the local GP Dr Brooke, a good man who had taken in the Bird Boy and died of a heart attack in the middle of the high street one day. Next to it, the oddity of the tiny village: a taxidermist's, where the dead birds went in and came out in cases, shuttled off to the hall for the lords who had killed them. She and Vic had hated the place. Now, the windows were shuttered, the building dirty and dark, the sign – Leveson's Emporium of Birds – half fallen off, the wood split, the paint peeling and gone.

To her, the village seemed like a film set, not quite real. At the end of the main street stood the gates to the house. Long ago, the first Earl of Ashley, 'Great' George Fane, who had rebuilt Fane and was her great-great-great-grandfather, had realised that he missed the bustle of London and might want to walk into the village if a barmaid attracted his eye, or if Leveson's Emporium was working on a new find of his: an otter, a kingfisher, a peacock. So he had two entrances built – one a luxuriant driveway that curled through the vast parkland a mile away, its entrance on the main road, and which gradually was used by no one, and this one that led into the estate from the village.

Sarah approached the gates, clasping Friday's small wriggling feet in her hands. The gates were tall: three yards high, the railings painted a rusting dark blue, fluted and curling into graceful shapes at the top. The bottom was blocked off by matching dark blue metal panels, preventing a full view into the estate. Sarah knew what was behind it.

She stood there, shifting her weight from one leg to another. Now she was here, she didn't know what to do.

'I should have thought this all out a little bit, Friday,' she murmured into her daughter's head, shrugging her tired shoulders. 'I lived here,' she said softly, pointing towards the barred gate as they approached. 'It was my great-uncle's house. My mother's uncle. He was an earl. It's called Fane, Fane Hall.' She pointed at the peeling, faded sign. 'I thought you might like to see it.' Friday made a small *craw* sound, and babbled a little, legs swinging. Sarah kept on talking to her, trying to ignore the tremor in her voice, how much it upset her to say these words out loud. And just then, as she was hoping the gates would come crashing down, or that maybe she could push it all over and discover it was, in fact, all made of cardboard, there was a rusting, creaking groan and the sound of metal teeth scraping over gravel and, to her horror, Sarah saw the gates were opening.

A slim figure stood in the flood of morning light between the rusting blue panels. She had a pink dress on, the colour of delicate rose petals, and a matching jacket. Her white-blond hair was twisted neatly up on her head. It gleamed in the sunshine. She was close enough that Sarah could see her huge, empty pale eyes. Sarah, still wearing her now-grubby dress from yesterday, faced her.

Lady Iris walked towards her, close enough that Sarah caught a whiff of lily of the valley and was back, suddenly, on the hot stinking day in Pelham Mansions, not sure – always not sure. Knowing this was how it was, sensing it was very, very wrong.

How thin her face was, and her wrists, they were like sticks. She was barely human, when you looked at her. They hadn't really eaten, any of them, for most of Sarah's childhood, so it made sense, but the sight of her curiously large hands, so well known – it was a jolt, when so much of it seemed unreal. It wasn't. She was here; it was real.

Slowly, calmly, Sarah stared her down. She tried to take in

more details, hungry for them. The elegant cut of her mother's beautiful two-piece suit, the soft cloth falling just so, the white enamel floral buttons glinting in the sun. Her fine bone structure, the pale yellowish skin stretched over it, the intense pale blue of her eyes and the white eyelashes, set far apart in the bony head, the silver brush of the fine blond hair, the glint of diamonds in her ears.

Sarah had never understood why people said her mother was beautiful. She thought she was ugly, in the way very, very beautiful, wicked people can be. There was something terrible about the tightness of her skin over her apple cheeks, of the direct glare of the eyes, boring into her.

'Well, well,' she said in her low, beautiful voice, and her expression didn't change. Sarah had forgotten that her mother had a curious way of speaking, where her face didn't move, but her eyes fixed on you, without expression, like a snake, or a lizard. 'I heard you'd come back. Come to see what I've done with the place?'

Sarah couldn't speak. She carried on looking at her, holding on to Friday's little feet.

'It's funny,' her mother said. 'It's *very* funny you're back. But you can't go inside.' Her voice hardened. 'It's my house.'

'Oh, I know that,' Sarah heard herself say. 'We know it's your house. You won in the end. Even if you had to wreck everything else to get there.'

Her mother's eyes widened, so wide the eyeballs bulged, clear out of their sockets and Sarah could see, with horror and yet fascination, how yellow they were, how bloodshot. She smiled slowly, a huge smile that showed her black teeth, her silver filling, her white tongue. 'Oh, this *is* fun! Let's see . . . is that why you're here, after all those years of silence? To be . . . what, some moralising force for good?'

'I wouldn't bother,' Sarah heard herself say. 'I'm here because I can't stop remembering things. What kind of mother you were. What you made us put up with. How awful it was.'

'Listen to me, you little shit. You don't know.' Her voice was soft. 'You don't know how it was at all. It's my house.'

Sarah sighed. 'It wasn't ever your house. It was Uncle Clive's.

And it's gone because of you.' She leaned forward suddenly, unaware until that precise moment she was going to do it. She pushed open the iron gate with one mighty shove. Friday whimpered.

Her mother laughed, a loud, pealing sound, like bells, and walked backwards, still facing Sarah. Sarah followed her. She stepped across the threshold, waving away the clouds of dry September dust kicked up by the gate. She was inside the grounds. She stared past her mother, her legs wobbling, as though they were suddenly filled with liquid.

The great sweep of Capability Brown landscape of English parkland was gone, the oak and elm against the rolling, gracious space, the drive that curled up away from you towards the main house. It was all gone. It was most strange. Blinking, Sarah tried to understand, to look at the rows of streets with small boxy houses, fanning out in front of her. Twenty yards on, a man was standing out on the pavement of the main street, cleaning a car. He had leather patches on the elbows of his jumper. He was whistling.

She realised her mother was watching her, grimly waiting for her response.

'I didn't realise it was all gone . . . Is the Burnt Oak still there?'

'Of course it's still there,' said her mother. 'It will never be taken down. It's what made me see the truth. It is my link to the past, the reminder. I didn't do any of this lightly. I had to do what I had to do when I got out. It was a ruin.'

'Because of you.'

'Not me. Never me.' She was quite calm. 'I saved this house. It's my house, after all. I saved it from him. He tried his best. But I got it in the end. So I had to get the money to stay here somehow.' She gestured towards the new-build houses, where the parkland had been, where the edge of the old house should have begun and was now, Sarah could just see, a cul-de-sac. 'But I'm still here, and it's my house. Who cares who else is here too? I got my way.'

Hearing the old words intoned again for the first time in years Sarah suddenly snapped.

'Always this, over and over – my God,' she hissed. 'After

everything that happened, everything, this is all you can say?' She untied the sling round her neck with trembling fingers, and swivelled Friday round, so she was facing her grandmother. Friday instantly pulled her knees up to her tummy, waved her fists, and started crying. Sarah stood in the gateway, holding her daughter above her head, like a totemic symbol, or a sacrificial victim before the altar.

'This is my daughter,' she called as her mother backed away.

Her voice bounced off the walls of the new buildings surrounding them. 'She's my baby. I never understood it before, and now I do. You're evil. What you did to us was evil. We were children. And I've come to tell you – you don't matter any more. You don't exist, as far as I'm concerned.' Her voice seemed magnified. 'I'm glad I came. I'm glad.'

There, by that low brick wall, she had first heard Stella cry. There she had run across the landscape to church that fateful Easter Sunday. There she had watched the stars come out, one by one, the Bird Boy by her side. She swallowed, as she thought of him, thought of that night. The night we were just stargazers.

Her tired arms ached with the effort of holding Friday up and her body sagged. Why on earth was she here? Vic had told her to pretend, to do what normal people do. But none of this was normal – she was not normal – and for the first time in her life Sarah did not care.

She lowered Friday and hugged her.

'I'm going now,' she said. 'I wanted to show Friday who you were. So she'd seen you.'

Her mother pointed behind her. 'You're so *tedious*, Sarah. Don't you care, what I've done, how I've saved this place? Other people understand. They know the truth. And you don't even ask.'

'I'm not interested,' Sarah said.

'Not interested, she says! God, I'm bored of you,' Lady Iris called after her, her beautiful, bell-like voice ringing out as Sarah turned back towards the pub. 'You don't care what I did for you, and your sister. You don't care what I went through. What happened to me. You're utterly second-rate, and I'm glad you've reminded me of it. I can barely remember your father, but he was so stupid he got himself killed, of course, and I see now how disappointing it is, but you're his child, not mine.' The vein throbbed on her smooth forehead. 'Go away. Take your whining brat and get out. Get out! It's *my* house!'

'I see prison didn't change you, then,' Sarah said, and her mother's face froze, and she swore at Sarah, again and again, her voice rising. She was still screaming at her as Sarah walked back towards the pub.

'It was *my* house! Don't you understand?' She pushed the gates, kicking them shut, her voice reverberating, the rusting metal panels bellowing as the gates clanged shut on Sarah. 'I saved it. You stupid girl . . . You stupid girl. It's mine now . . .'

Daniel arrived two and a half hours later. He must have driven off the moment she called him, crying, from the phone box. She was sitting in the graveyard of the church, Friday squalling lightly. She recognised the sound of the old Morris Minor and stood up, then ran. She strapped Friday into the carrycot they kept on the back seat and climbed into the front.

'Drive,' she said, then kissed him, firmly, on the mouth. 'Just drive very fast. Now.'

He stared at her. His eyes had hollows under them. His jaw was gritty with a day's fine growth of dark blond beard.

'OK, darling. Did you see her?' His hand reached for hers, squeezed her fingers. She nodded.

'Vic was telling the truth. She's not right in the head, Daniel.'

'Well – of course,' he said.

'What does she do all day?' Sarah was gabbling. 'I don't know how much of the house is left. Some of it. I suppose she stays inside looking out of the window. She never did know how to talk to people, have a normal conversation: we never went to the newsagent's, or saw friends. But it's worse now . . . She's – Yes, something has gone. What happened?'

But she told herself she knew the answer, and there was some comfort to it. Her mother wasn't sane, and perhaps there was no point in asking. As they sped down the high street, Sarah put her hand on his leg.

'I'm sorry for leaving.'

'That's all right,' he said. 'I'm sorry too. But you shouldn't have gone like that. I was so worried.'

'I left a note.'

'I didn't find it till this morning. It was on the floor.'

'But I weighted it down, so you wouldn't miss it.'

'Someone moved it, then. We were all looking for you.'

'I had to go,' Sarah said, after a few moments of silence. 'I couldn't cope any more.'

'Darling girl – I'm here –'

'I know. I can't explain it. It's been bad lately. Very bad.' She brushed a tear angrily off her cheek, as if it had no business to be there. 'I had to see if going back helped. See if taking Friday there helped.'

'Did it?'

'I don't know. Probably.' She was clutching and unclutching her fingers. 'Daniel, you don't realise. I need you. Much more than I realised. And it's terrifying.'

'Why is it terrifying, darling bird?' His hand settled on her writhing, anxious fingers. 'It's fine. That's how it should be.'

'You're everything to everyone. And you need to be everything to me. And Friday.'

'I am everything to you. You're everything to me, both of you. You have to understand that.'

She said furiously: 'You try too hard to get everyone else to adore you. You can't; they won't – that's what I've learned.'

'Oh, don't I know it.' His voice was hard; he took his hand away. 'I know how much you hold it against me for loving you.'

She looked out of the window as the roads grew wider, busier, taking them back into town. They had never spoken like this before.

'I don't mean to.'

'Sarah, I know you don't. But you should have told me how you were feeling before.'

'I—' she began, then stopped.

'Don't fall silent. Don't do your party trick.'

'What party trick?'

'Being quiet, making me do all the work, Sarah. It gives you the power. You always have the power, when you hold it all inside.'

In the back of the car, Friday snuffled and Sarah turned round to stare at her. She was lying, looking up at the ceiling, her legs in the air. Sarah said simply:

'I didn't realise how bad it had got. Daniel, you talk about me as if I'm not there. You're surrounded by your coterie, these girls who adore you, and it's like I'm not there.'

He gave a great shout of laughter. 'Come off it. I'm not screwing any of them, if that's what you mean. It's only ever been you.' His voice seemed to shrink, grew quieter. 'You know that. Since – for ever.'

'I assume you wouldn't, Daniel – that's not my point.' She paused. 'Look. I ran away because before Friday we had a plan. It was us against the rest of the world, the two of us . . . We'd do the house, and earn money to pay for it, and then work it out.' Her voice grew quiet. 'But it turns out I can't do it. I don't know how to.'

'How to what, my bird?'

'How to be that person. The wife. The hostess. I can't be her. Most of all, I can't be the mother. I get it wrong, all of it, every day. I don't know how to *be* like that.'

'You can! You are. Sarah, look at you. You're used to performing. You're an amazing mother. You're wonderful, darling. It's all wonderful – you just need to relax.'

She pulled her hand away. 'No. Daniel, listen to me. The house is too huge, and we can't afford it, and . . . I can't see a way back to work, and you're further away from me than ever, and even when we're together you – you plan stuff like All Day Sunday, you exclude me – you don't realise you're doing it, but you are.'

'I'll help you, whatever you want. I know you have to start playing again.'

'Maybe.' She nodded, and rubbed her tired eyes.

Daniel's voice shook. 'We'll work it out. You can start practising when we get back. I'll take Friday some afternoons. Something like that. Just please – don't do that again. Promise me.'

'I won't,' she said. 'I can't.' And she gripped his hand.

'Keep talking to me. Tell me what's going on.'

'I will. Not right now, though. I love you, Daniel.'

'I love you too, Birdie.'

'I kept thinking about him,' she said, quietly. 'About the Bird Boy. About Stella. About all of them.'

'I can't believe you went back.'

'Me neither,' she said with a short laugh.

'I honestly don't know how you survived it all,' he said. His hand was warm, and heavy. They sat in silence, and she clung on to him, the total, steady comfort of him.

'So,' he said when they were on the A40 back into town. 'What was she like?'

She didn't know what to say. 'She was . . . the . . . same? She dresses more smartly. I think she has money from somewhere. Sold some of the remaining good bits, I suppose. You know why I'm glad I went back? Sometimes I wonder if I'm just being unfair. Unreasonable. If I've misremembered.' And she shook her head. 'I'm not, and I didn't. I didn't make any of it up. It's frightening, being near her.'

They were silent as the suburbs grew more urban, less green, and she could see, in the misty autumn morning, the hazy outline of the city ahead.

Their route into town took them across the new Westway A40, a concrete ribbon weaving above the houses of West London. The city was alive. When the car slowed, she could smell cooking aromas from the streets below, see the Post Office Tower shining in the distance, the tallest spire in a city of spires. A plane glided silently overhead, and on the road underneath she could see two children in matching red jumpers, dancing alongside their father, on the way to school. She belonged here. She was going back home.

'I'm sorry again that you missed the note. You must have been so worried.'

'Well, I was, but . . . Listen, Sarah.' Daniel rubbed one eye. 'Before we get back home . . . I have to tell you something. There was a bit of trouble after you'd gone, you see.'

'What kind of trouble?' Sarah looked down and noticed, for

the first time – *how could she not have seen it earlier*, she would wonder afterwards – that his right hand was encased in a huge bandage, like a mummy. Mummies. Part of the end had come away from the safety pin, and was flapping gently in the breeze from the draughty car. 'Oh my goodness. What happened? Did you get into a fight?'

He gave a rich, amused laugh, like a giggle. 'Me? Come on. When did you know me start a fight? Much less wade into a fight someone else has started. No. Georgina attacked me with a saw.'

'*What?*'

In the back, Friday gave a little cry of distress. 'It's OK, my little one.' He turned back to his wife. 'So we noticed you'd gone. But not for a while. You see, Diana came back with the chain saw. She wanted to cut the branches of the apple tree in the garden right back. And Lara got really upset. *Extremely* upset. That was the apple tree she used to sit in, apparently. Henry got a swing for his fifth birthday. They'd play on it all day. Her big brother, the one who died, what was his name? Oh, he used to sit there for hours when he was studying. So she's in tears, and Georgina gets very worked up, starts calling her a sly little minx –' He blinked, at the memory. 'I do think Georgina is pretty mad. Then Diana got involved. She starts shouting at Georgina, actually at Lara. Goes into the garden and starts hacking at the apple tree, says she's had enough of it, of all the brambles and everything getting into her garden and climbing over everything. Ah – I tried to stop her. But Diana's – she's a lot to handle when she's had a drink, you know? Georgina too.'

'Oh, I can imagine,' said Sarah wryly, wondering why it took men twice the time to understand things women saw immediately. 'So what happened?'

'Well, so Diana's sawing away at the damned tree, and Lara is sobbing on the floor – she was really upset, it was awful, Sarah. Heartbroken, that's what I'd call it.' He stopped for a moment. 'Like she was in physical pain. She's so interesting, isn't she? So tightly furled, you know.'

'Yes, that's it exactly.'

'I think she likes being sad,' Daniel said, unexpectedly. 'I think she wears it, like a cloak. It's easier for her than facing up to things.'

'What happened next?'

'Of course. So anyway, Diana puts the saw down and goes over to her, throws her arm round her. She's all, "Oh, Lara, it's in the past now, dear girl." And Lara won't stop crying. She's curled up. Georgina's in the background absolutely fuming, you know? She picks up the chain saw, like Diana stopping cutting the tree down has really offended her, and she starts lopping more bits off. And Lara suddenly starts yelling – screaming, more like it – and saying things like –' Daniel put on a most disconcerting falsetto. '"Oh! Every branch is my past! Stop it, just stop it!"'

'Oh, good grief.' Despite herself, or because of it, Sarah started to laugh.

'Diana's telling her she has to get over it. Georgina is getting more and more worked up. Monty's been really quiet – he's just there drinking with Monica and Guy. Your sister comes back and sees what's happening, and makes Monty intervene with Georgina. So Monty huffs into the garden, jabs me on the arm and says, "M'wife's very upset, Forster," like it's some Regency drama and he's about to challenge me to a duel. And I say, "I think we all need to calm down."'

'Darling, that's so impressive of you.'

Daniel said in a hollow voice, 'It was mad, all of it, Sarah. It's as if everyone went collectively crazy. I didn't know what to say, to be honest. Georgina turns round. She's got the saw. And she shouts: "You men, you just sit there doing nothing! Can't you see what's going on? Right under your nose?" Monty says, "Look here, old girl, why don't you sit down," and she shouts, "Leave me alone," and waves the saw at him and me, like it's a finger. And then suddenly – oh goodness.' Daniel stopped, and wiped his forehead with his shirtsleeve, then blinked at the road ahead. 'Robert appears.'

'*Robert?*'

'Yup. He's been dozing upstairs, listening to the radio. He just barges out through the kitchen into the garden and starts bellowing: "The noise is *unbearable*. Stop this disgraceful display *immediately*. Stop it."'

'Robert?'

'Robert.'

'Well. I'd never have thought it.'

'The shouting woke him up. That's the only reason he got upset,' said Daniel. 'So Georgina is all startled, and he marches towards her, you know: "I am the very model of a modern major-general". Georgina is furious. But Robert doesn't quite realise how furious. She had this vacant look in her eyes and – oh, Sarah, it was crazy! So she slices the saw through the air. Like she's . . . I don't know, Pussy Galore in *Goldfinger.* And I close my eyes and . . . it hits me.'

'The saw?'

'Yes! there's a sort of thudding sound and Robert says quite calmly, "I say, old girl, you've hit the bullseye." I look down, and my shirt is sliced open, my wrist is bleeding and then I glance over and . . . well, Robert's finger is on the floor. He was leaning against the door,' he said by way of explanation. 'His hand was in the way when she waved the saw around.'

There was a small silence. 'Daniel,' said Sarah. 'Are you telling me Georgina . . . *sliced one of Robert's fingers off*?'

Daniel nodded, slowly, eyes ahead. 'He's in hospital. It wouldn't stop bleeding so they had to admit him. I mean he's fine. But he's saying Georgina's a bloody madwoman, and he wants her thrown in jail.'

'I'm not surprised.' Sarah blinked, trying to get her head round it all. 'So she's been arrested?'

'No. But your sister says Robert wants us to go to the police. She says the house isn't a safe place for them to visit any more.'

Sarah rubbed her cheeks, thinking of the sound of Vic singing softly to Friday. 'Do you know something,' she said. 'I don't think it is. Poor Robert. Poor Victoria.'

'Sarah. Can I ask you something?'

'Of course,' she said.

Daniel was suddenly serious. 'How old were you both, when you moved back to Fane? Do you remember it?'

'Of course I do. I was twelve. Vic was fourteen.'

'Of the two of you,' he said, 'I think you got off more lightly.'

Sarah found herself saying, 'Vic's OK. She's more than OK. She finds it hard to be normal. We both do.'

'I wouldn't love you if you were normal.'

'Oh God. Don't lay it on so thick, my darling.' She laughed. 'Where is Georgina, then?'

'Oh, she's in hospital too,' said Daniel, almost gaily. 'She fainted after it was over, hit her head on the floor and blacked out.'

'No.'

'I'm afraid so. We were rather worried. And I would have noticed sooner, but it was all still in chaos, and then we were looking for Lara. She disappeared. Just ran off. I didn't bother looking for her after we found Georgina, I'm afraid to say. Anyway, just as I was leaving to come and get you this morning, Monty came round. He said he was on his way to pick Georgina up from the hospital. She has a large white bandage, apparently. And she's very embarrassed.'

The harvest moon was still in the crisp morning sky. They were climbing through Camden, the roads becoming wider, flanked with trees and grand, dilapidated houses; cracked dirty stucco and peeling paint.

The last twenty-four hours had already taken on the quality of a dream, a film, like the eerily quiet village. Had any of it happened? Was it real? Her hand stole to her husband's again, and he squeezed it, then gently moved it away as he gripped the wheel, steering them up over the canal bridge, towards Kentish Town, the Heath and home.

For better or worse, Sarah knew she'd achieved something yesterday. As they edged down the cobbles of The Row, and she saw the house, shining in the midday sun, she was happy.

'I'll open the door,' she said, jumping out and staring up at the house. 'I'm so glad to be home, darling. I'm so, so –' She stopped. A window on the ground floor was broken. She pointed at it. 'What's that?'

Glass lay splintered on the red diagonal paved bricks, twinkling in the sunlight. A scarf, which had been Daniel's birthday present to her, lay twisted on the ground, a few silver teaspoons splayed inside it.

'Shit,' said Daniel. He climbed out of the car, but Sarah was running down the front path. The door was open.

He found her sunk to the ground on the cold, hard tiles, squatting, head in hands.

'I'm so sorry,' he said.

'You left the French windows open, I suppose.'

'I guess so. I'm a bloody idiot. I'll call the police. Is your cello . . .'

She nodded. 'It's in your study there, look. It's fine. They don't realise that's the most valuable thing in the house, of course. But they took the earrings you gave me. And Friday's teething ring, the silver one from Monica. And, darling – don't go in there!'

Daniel marched into his study. She got up and followed him in, stumbling slightly. She could hear Friday, crying madly in the car.

Showers of paper littered the floor like sanded snow. Typed sheets, ripped into ribbons. The ribbon of the typewriter, pulled out and twisted amongst the paper, black and white. Books had been pulled off the walls, some open, some closed. The room smelt of something, undefined, unpleasant, musky, bitter. In the kitchen, they had smashed everything. The telephone had gone. Upstairs, in the sitting room, the candlesticks from Sarah's godmother had gone, and the paintings on the walls, and all her jewellery, such as it was, but what was worse, of course, was the loss of safety, of privacy, of feeling as if they made it their own place.

They saw how they'd got in – Sarah was right, the French windows had been left open, and they'd simply walked in off the little passageway at the back of the garden. They had left via the front door, dropping the scarf and teaspoons and some other little silver trinkets Daniel had collected from Portobello Market. They were littered now over the front garden, beetles, spiders, scorpions, all made of silver beaten thin and worked into spindly legs and stings, and they had been trampled on. One was red.

'It got him. He must have stepped right on it.'

'Look, there's blood on the front path.'

'That might just be from Robert, yesterday,' Daniel said, picking up a silver spider.

They shot a quick, grim smile at each other. Sarah went to the car and extracted Friday and then they used Diana's phone to call the police – their phone line had been cut.

Later, when it was just them, and the front window was taped up with packing tape and brown paper, and the local bobby had promised to make sure his nightly beat included a look in at The Row to make sure there wasn't anything suspicious going on, after Daniel made them all pasta, and after they had put Friday to bed and pottered round the house, clearing up every last trace of the burglary, they sat on the stairs, exhausted, each holding a whisky.

'I'd miss you if you ran away,' he said. 'You and me. It's pointless otherwise. We don't work on our own.'

'Don't worry,' she said. 'I won't do it again.'

'I meant what I said in the car. You need to start playing again,' he said. 'What was the first thing you did when you got into the house? You made sure the cello was there.'

'Of course I did, Daniel—'

'No, listen to me. It's your life. You can have that life and this life too. We'll get a nanny. Work something out. I just think you've been away from it too long. You'll play professionally again, I promise.'

She leaned over him, kissed his face, his dear sweet face. He kissed her back, pulling her onto him, and she straddled him on the stairs, holding his hands, kissing him, so that he was pinned between her legs, and her weight was on him, and they were both laughing, and she saw he was crying. Tears came to her eyes, different tears. She carried on, though, and stopped, only to say:

'I don't want to be like her.'

'What, my bird,' he muttered as his hands fumbled with the buttons on her shirt.

'Doesn't matter,' she said, and she took him by the hand, and led him upstairs, and undressed him, item by item, and kissed him, head to toe, and told him what to do to her, slowly, intently.

That evening was when their second child was conceived.

Sarah knew it as it was happening, as Daniel released himself inside her with a pulsing shudder of release and a loud, urgent cry, as she pulled him into her, her legs twined round him.

She really believed she had to give something up for something else to survive. She did not hear music any more. Once, it had been in her head, all the time, the low, solemn beauty of the cello, the sound of the echoing wood, the delicious pinch of her thin fingers pressing on the cool hard strings.

But she never said it. Who'd believe her? No one except Vic, and who knows if she would see her again.

No one ever sat Sarah down and explained to her that she was trying to build a family and a home with no knowledge whatsoever of what that entailed. She'd never had a birthday party, or sat on her mother's knee. She'd never been hugged when someone waits for you outside school, crouching at your level, smiling broadly, arms flung wide. So what she came to believe was to succeed at this – that is, her life at No. 7 The Row, being a mother and a wife – she would have to finally forget her old self. After all, her old self was her childhood and she knew, they all knew, she could not live like that. But Sarah failed to understand that if you push memories down they don't go away.

Sometimes Sarah would look at the cello, now relegated to the corner of the sitting room. She would stare at it, unseeing, rocking babies, folding laundry, trying to get to sleep, and only then could she allow herself to think, to remember. About how she had wrested the cello from Fane, in the days when it still stood. Memories, like shards of glass, jagged, incomplete, glittered frequently in her fractured mind. And, because she had now gone back and unlocked something, during the long, long days and years of motherhood, where boredom swirled together with terror, it started to come back. What she desperately wanted to say aloud, to tell. Her childhood, her and Vic, the whole huge terrifying mess of it.

Part Two
1954

Chapter Six

From 1st August 1954 Lady Iris Fane is to be found at:
Fane Hall
Fane
West Sussex
Please address all future correspondence to her there.

'Write faster,' my mother said, appearing in the room where Vic and I were sitting on our metal trunks, leaning on books, laboriously writing the same note over and over on little pieces of card. 'Well done, Victoria. Three more to go, hurry up.'

She started humming:

'Somewhere there's another land –
Different from this world below . . .
Far more mercifully planned
Than the cruel place we know –'

The cloying scent of lily of the valley followed her as she bent over. 'Well, that one's not very good,' she said, snatching one out of my hand, lightly slapping the side of my head and ripping the card in two. 'Nor that. Nor that – oh dear. Victoria *darling*, do those again for that cretin Sarah who can't even write properly. Hurry up, do. How exciting it is! Aren't you excited?'

She crouched down, the dove grey silk of her skirt puffing out like a mushroom cloud as she knelt in front of us. Vic wrinkled her nose to keep from crying, and shifted her cramped hand on the *Girl's Friend 1953* annual that was her constant companion.

'We are,' she said, blinking hard. 'Aren't we, Sarah?'

I nodded. My fingers ached, my back ached and lunchtime had come and gone, but there was no point in saying it.

‘I want you to watch your behaviour.’ Our mother closed one hand over my wrist, holding it just a little too tight, twisting it just so that it started to hurt. ‘You aren’t London children now. You’re my children, Lady Iris’s girls, and we’re going back to Fane. You must watch yourselves. Do you understand?’ She jabbed a finger at the wall where the engraving of Fane Hall in its chipped black frame hung behind us.

I stared up at the picture of the house, at the thick lines of the cheap image, reprinted so many times the ink blurred the delicacy of the original, which – as we knew, for we had been told many times – hung in the library of the house.

‘Lady Iris Fane,’ she said, her voice cracking. ‘Finally. I am coming back.’

‘I’m sorry,’ said Vic, swallowing. ‘M-Mr Thoday was on at us again today. He says he wants to know when payment can be expected. I – I—’

My mother, whirling round in a circle like the fairy on a wind-up jewellery box, stopped suddenly. ‘What do we say when people ask us that?’ she said, that perfect smile bared at Vic.

‘I – I – I don’t know where Mummy is,’ Vic said, stumbling over the words. ‘But he – he said that I’d said that too many times before.’

Our mother glanced out of the window. ‘It’s so unspeakably vulgar, the way these people go *on* at one. Well, no bothering about *that* now. Look at that handwriting. How nasty. Aren’t you ashamed of yourself, writing like that? Write faster, please. We leave in ten minutes. Do try to look excited, won’t you?’ Two lines, like speech marks, carved between her brows. ‘I planned this all for you. I wish you’d remember that.’

Our trunks, the picture, and our pens and the pieces of card were all that remained in the bare sitting room of our flat on the second-floor mansion block in a seedier corner of Kensington. We had always lived there, so I did not find our strange, uncertain life there all that unusual, even though our mother’s shadow loomed large over everything. In later years, knowing what came next, I was to look back on our time there almost fondly. We were near the park, and the Albert Memorial, which was my sister’s great obsession one summer, and we had twice been taken to the Proms with dear old Mr Green, our neighbour and we could walk to the grocer's and the butcher's and to school by ourselves, and the milkman, Dennis, was our friend. We didn't know any different, of course, but we loved London, with its grimy, wet air, the craters left by bombs in which we climbed around, scrabbling over upturned bedroom walls and floor boards, our thin legs permanently grazed, feet crammed into too-small T-bar leather shoes, our faces always dirty.

We went to Minas House, a little school for nice girls round the corner from our flat. It was a fairly sub-par educational establishment in the basement of a vast Georgian mansion run by a kindly woman who would not, nowadays, be allowed to have the pastoral care of any children, but for whom we felt a great affection because she was quiet and utterly predictable. I didn't know that you had to pay for the school and I don't know if our mother ever actually did. There are many things, now, that I don't understand, and I suppose that is why childhood is so fascinating to us all. We will never fully grasp the circumstances into which we are born and grow up.

Our mother did not pay for lots of things. The daily helps who lasted only a few weeks because she never settled up, the fees for management of the block of flats and the man who waited outside to pounce on her, shouting at her. New school shoes, food in shops – Iris was good at knowing when to exit, to escape. We often left grocers or Woolworth's at the right moment and ran, she laughing down the street, shouts of reproach following us as we tried to keep up with her, short legs tumbling over one another, terrified we'd be left behind and captured; our fear of the unknown was greater than our fear of her. Vic would usually be sick afterwards.

We had known for a week that we would be abandoning London to move to Fane and, when we awoke, we were told that today was the day. As we finished the cards – I wonder now to whom they were sent, who would want to know, except people she owed money to? – Iris was watching out of the window for someone to leave Pelham Mansions and when she said the time was right, we had to go, fast.

As we dragged the trunks along the cold tiled floor – mine

leaving a white scratch – and bumped them down two flights of stairs, I did not fully understand we would never come back here again, that one part of our lives was now over. One of the residents, an elderly colonel who lived next to Mr Green, opened his door and when he saw it was us, he said something horrible under his breath about my mother and shut the door again.

'What did he say?' Vic was panting behind me.

'Don't worry,' I said. She was my big sister, but sometimes our roles had to be reversed, so we could stand up for each other, work together or stay safe. We were close, tight, two halves of an oyster, clamped together, hiding ourselves away. 'He's jealous. They're all jealous because they know now Mummy wasn't making it up. We're leaving. I think she was telling the truth about the inheritance, you see.'

On the journey out of London, Vic and I huddled together in the back of the car not saying a word. It was a cold day, despite it being July. We wore our new school uniforms, as we didn't have any other nice clothes. They were stiff, and itchy, and I hated the brown skirt, which was too long and, as it was a kilt, fell open all the time.

My mother was only ever ill at ease in a car. She could not drive, really, and did not care to, but when our father didn't come back from the war she had to learn. I don't remember what colour or make our car was. There are many things about our childhood I don't remember: my mind has simply filtered them out.

I do remember there was a roadside inn, called the Green Man, where our mother pulled over and went inside to make a telephone call. We followed her inside – one thing we had learned, both of us, was to take our chances where we could, as we were never sure when meals would come.

The landlord gave us each a pickled onion, which made us feel sick for the rest of the drive. To mitigate this Vic produced an apple, which she had taken from a tree overhanging the road. Since it was only July it was still green, and not ripe, and made us feel even worse. We sat in silence as Iris bumped over uneven roads. She sang that hateful song again, loudly, happier than I'd seen her for years. 'I've warned him I'm coming now,' she said. 'He can't say I didn't warn him.'

'Shall we ever find that lovely land of might-have-been?
I can never be your king nor you can be my queen'

The final approach to Fane is along the drive. It snakes like a ribbon up and around the estate. It took us five minutes to make the journey from the gate to the front door. The road cut through an ancient oak woodland, then dipped a little and our stomachs lurched. Then we started to rise, up and over a bank and we could see the whole house, the vast, gently rolling parkland, the stables behind. We were high up, almost floating down as we descended towards the buildings.

I had forgotten what it looked like: the length of a London terrace, tall flat windows divided into squares, the stone golden-grey, a crumbling balustrade running along the top and this vast, lowering central portico sticking out at the centre of the frontage, enormous thick pillars, also crumbling, casting the central flank into gloom. Odd panes of glass along the façade of the house gleamed, catching the late afternoon light. The park-land around was completely silent.

Our mother breathed out, slowly. Her eyes drooped, as if so overwhelmed she might lose consciousness. 'Magnificent Fane,' she said.

But to my horror I found myself thinking, *Gosh, what an ugly house*, and was afraid she might read my mind.

I could see the Burnt Oak, standing a hundred yards or so in front of the blank, crumbling façade. It was said that in Eliza-beth I's time just after the original manor house was built (of which there is no pictoral record) Sir Rodderick Fane had con-structed a platform in a vast oak tree to gaze at the stars with his friend, the magician and astronomer John Dee. One night, the tree was struck by lightning. It had stood for hundreds of years, and its destruction was said to be a bad omen. 'Fire begets fire,' the locals said.

My great-grandfather, I think, built the new Burnt Oak, and it's a private joke that people don't understand it's not a tree any more. It's hard to explain it. In summer, it is so hot to the touch that it sizzles in the heat of the day.

As we drew closer to the house, I could see more detail on the vast portico, jutting out like a ship. The pediment and roof were decorated with a stone frieze of the symbols by which the first Lord Ashley wanted to be known: a peace lily, a dead fox, a flag and a telescope, for the stars his ancestor discovered.

Stars were important to the Fanes. They – we – loved them, because we loved *discovering* things. First Sir Rodderick, who discovered a new comet and who prepared drawings for what could have been a forerunner of the telescope, many years before it was invented, all the way down to my mother who knew the Pleiades, the Cygnus, Betelgeuse glaring red on Orion's shoulder: it was her favourite because she said it was an angry star, red and bright. She had spent hours watching them all as a child, perched on the Burnt Oak. 'We are all made of the dust of stars, nothing more,' she had screamed at us once, when we had complained about something – I think the cold: we were always cold, or hungry. When Vic and I went to watch the Coronation procession in the rain, unpicking the front door because she had locked us in, I found a sandwich that had been dropped in Green Park. It was wrapped in silky smooth wax paper, white bread with thick slices of sweet-salty ham, tangy cheddar and some tomato chutney, and we shared it with utter joy, the chutney spicy and sweet on our tongues. I can still taste it now.

'Here we are, then.' My mother was peering out of the window. She stopped the car outside the vast portico and leaned back in her seat, hands gripping the steering wheel tightly. I saw then she was shaking.

The house was the same as I remembered it, but the closer you looked the more decay you saw: weeds growing in cracks, broken window panes, chunks of stone missing from carvings. In front of one window was a pile of wood and glass, as if someone had thrown something out at some point. A crack stretched up the side of the West Wing, and ivy had got into it, dark tendrils curling around the opening. The monumental scale of everything, compared to the small spaces we inhabited everywhere in London, was overwhelming. Vic and I looked around the landscape, not speaking, avoiding one another's glances.

'Stay there,' our mother said, and she got out of the car and bounded up the first two wide, cracked steps to the house. She was muttering something like *they should have been outside to welcome us*. I didn't really see why. But she was itching, and winking, and it was scary when that happened; you knew she'd blow soon.

She pulled the huge, rusting bell pull, a clanking chain behind a pillar. She shouted: 'Oh! Uncle Clive, we're here!'

The last time we'd visited Fane, Aunt Dolly had been alive. This would have been after the war, after the soldiers lived here, when most of the damage was done, but even then it still felt like a grand, stately home, and Aunt Dolly and Uncle Clive very much the centre of it. Uncle Clive relied on Aunt Dolly, whom he had met in Canada when he was out there prospecting for gold after the Great War. Dolly was short and bustling, with small darting black eyes like an animal, and a taste for the finer things, expensive perfumes from Paris, peacock curtains from Italian silk manufacturers, Lalique lampshades, smashed and broken, lying in corridors, and always the half-eaten boxes of chocolates, the foil wrappers of which still relatively littered the house. She was profligate, but shrewd: the house began its true decline when she died and our great-uncle was in sole charge, for Dolly would not have lost the Turkish diamonds brought back by Arthur, the second earl, or given away the Holbein painting, taken in lieu of tax. She would not have let the roof in the West Wing collapse. She would not have had James Lees-Milne writing waspish letters about the decline of Fane Hall to *The Times*, which made my mother screech with rage.

'But can't you make a fuss?' Vic had asked her, jabbing her knife at a stale, hard bread roll. Vic was less afraid of her than I. 'Can't you say he's not fit to live in the place? Doesn't it say in that letter that Fane needs to be saved?'

I remember our mother had looked at Vic, dipping the bread roll in her glass of water to soften it, and I was worried she'd reach out and slap her, which she sometimes did. But she hadn't. She reread the letter again, eyes moving from her paper to Vic. And then she'd said: 'Perhaps.'

So I blamed Vic for us coming back here.

My mother had never liked her uncle, but for a few years they had at least been in touch and we'd occasionally driven down there for lunch; I vaguely remembered odd, always cold meals in a huge dining room that every time we visited seemed more and more crammed with broken or discarded things: lopsided chairs, rotten rugs, packing cases smashed open, boxes of cracked china.

It was about seven years prior to our 'return' that my mother properly fell out with them and after that we only went on Open Days. We would get up very early, and be first in the queue. We would wear disguises, because Iris said Uncle Clive and Aunt Dolly loved being surprised. Sometimes, Iris would dress me and Vic up as boys, especially the year we had ringworm and our hair was short. Sometimes, she would wear a wig. She loved making things into what she said were games. We would surprise Aunt Dolly and Uncle Clive by tapping them on the shoulder. It was during one day like this that Aunt Dolly took us into her pretty little study and gave us toffees, and a cup of milk each, and then, when we disclosed how hungry we were, sent out for a plate of sandwiches, meat paste and cucumber, and let us eat as many as we wanted, asking questions in her cosy voice, the accent slightly Canadian, slightly Cockney. Vic and I were fond of her, even if she did call our mother some rather unladylike names, and even if our mother's wrath afterwards was terrible.

'We've tried so hard with your mother, girlies,' she told us in her soft, agreeable way. 'She's broken your Uncle Clive's heart.'

Another year we came to the Open Day and Iris borrowed a dog from somewhere to enter into the Best Dog competition. When we arrived, she was furious that they'd put down linoleum over some tiles and hung rope around the place, so visitors knew what route to stick to. 'So common, so common.'

I knew how it went with her: something would annoy her then it would just get worse and worse. Iris raised her hat when the dog won and said in her strange, darting, soft-and-loud voice to Uncle Clive, who was giving out the prizes: 'Everything in this house is mine, so I should get first prize!'

Aunt Dolly, I remembered, had buried her face in her fat little hands and sobbed, and the guests had dispersed, and I heard Uncle Clive saying awkwardly to one of them, 'My brother's daughter. I'm so sorry. It's rather –'

Difficult? Awkward? There were no words to quite sum up the extraordinary way my mother simply decided the house was hers, and Uncle Clive should let her have it.

'You have to rid yourself of this obsession, my dear Iris,' Uncle Clive had said, as she walked to the car, jabbing us between the shoulder blades so we hurried. 'Remember why they called you Iris. It is Latin for rainbow. Try and be a rainbow in our lives, dear.'

So we had not been for a couple of years, but, after the letter in *The Times*, sometime that spring, a youngish solicitor from the family's firm had come to the flat at my mother's request to discuss matters with her. We had not been allowed to meet him. He wore squeaky shoes. There had been a lot of shouting and Iris's quietest voice, the really scary one, and then silence, followed by a loud groan, and the solicitor had left hurriedly – we'd seen him go down the steps outside – very dishevelled, as if he'd dressed quickly after swimming, was how Vic put it.

The result of the newspaper article was that she'd discovered her father's executors were duty bound to protect and preserve Fane, which it seemed Uncle Clive was not doing, and in addition that she was allowed to visit whenever she wanted. We were giving up the flat in London and, as my mother was a trustee and also a beneficiary of her father's will, she should be allowed to take possession of 'certain items at Fane', and to live there under the terms of the will. In addition to this, we were to be sent to boarding school.

This is not how she put it to us, though. She was crying, her slim shoulders juddering, her mouth slack, her eyes slightly rolling back, with the strange white lashes fluttering. It was awfully embarrassing. 'Girls, I'm allowed to move back to my house. It's what Daddy wanted, all those years ago. He would never have wanted me to be discarded like this. He would have understood.

Dark forces, keeping me out. Dark, dark forces.' She pronounced certain words in a flat, odd way that no one else did: Gullsss. Nivuh. Ayet.

'You're making all this up,' Vic had said. She puported to be furious about leaving Mr Green and the Albert Hall and our friends, such as they were, at Minas House. But mostly I think she knew it was a bad idea. 'You've just got that man to agree with you that you should live there again because there are stories in the newspaper about it. It's Great-uncle Clive's house – he inherited it when your father died. I don't know what you're doing, but stop pretending that it's some edict on high.'

Our mother had slapped her so hard round the face that Vic's head flew to one side, and she had finger marks on her left cheek for two days. She got to stay off school and read *Famous Five* in bed in case tradesmen saw her, and I was jealous.

Vic nudged me and we climbed out the car, disobeying her instructions for once, but our mother didn't notice. We stood on the top step for a long time, Iris ringing the bell again and again with so much force flakes of rusting black paint fell from the clanking chain onto the steps.

Then silently, swiftly, someone opened the door.

My mother stretched her hands out behind her, pushing us both back. I watched her walk through the vast doorway, strangely diminished now by the scale of the portico.

Peering into the dark black-and-white tiled hall I could just make out the two great statues on either side of the door, one a man in gleaming black marble, wings on his feet and some dead animal dangling by his side, the other a woman, arms raised to heaven. We were left waiting on the steps. There was an unpleasant smell, though at that point I didn't think much of it.

I looked at those long, pockmarked steps up to the house, at the gravel drive, disfigured and patchy, a bit like our heads after the ringworm, at the weeds growing up everywhere, at the windows stuffed with material where the glass was missing. I thought how sad it was that the house was like that, and how nice we were going to make it. Iris kept telling us that. 'One great house a week is being blown up or knocked down, girls. Nothing left of it. Nothing. Not Fane. I'm going to save it.'

I don't know how long we waited outside, but it was getting dark. I only know that suddenly Vic nudged me. 'Time to go in, Sarah.'

'Yes,' I mumbled, following her.

'Hurry up, please.' My mother was standing in the hallway, clicking her fingers at us.

We entered through the huge, glowering portico, walking between the great pillars. We'd never gone in this way before. Inside, it was almost dark. I coughed, my empty stomach churning acid. 'That's horrible,' I said, but Vic nudged me again, sharply.

'Shhh,' she said. 'Just – be quiet, Sarah.'

I looked at her in surprise, for the smell in the hall was disgusting. Like unmentionable things we had been told never to discuss. Sometimes I catch the edge of it on hot days, or once when a dead man was found in the flats down the road from the Heath after three months, or when our drain was blocked. It was all those things. You never stopped noticing it. It was in your nostrils, all the time. I pinched my nose for the first day or so, as if I could make the smell go away, as if I could control it. My mother's slingback heels clattered over the tiles, the two of us creeping behind her. Whoever had let us in had retreated, and we heard laughter, footsteps thudding away.

Cold evening light flooded the hall from top to bottom. I could see the statues in more detail now: the black stone gleamed in the light. The man was holding a dead hare; at the woman's feet was a dead bird. In the recesses around the hall were white marble busts of men with wigs on. High, high above us, so high that for a moment – only a tiny moment – I thought it was real sky, was a powder-blue ceiling, dotted with roundels, each one with a fresco, gracious Venus, noble Mars, and so on. Below it, a chandelier creaked slowly, the dull lead crystal not minded to glitter.

Vic said slowly:

'What's that room there?'

She had turned right and wandered towards the stench. I followed her into a red drawing room that I remembered had once had a vast picture of King George II. Now, there was nothing on the walls. The red wallpaper was torn in places into strips, and flapped gently. Vic gave a little cry, and then I noticed the rest of the room, and flinched.

There were glass cases everywhere, filled with dead animals – foxes, hares, otters and most of all birds – sea birds, goldfinches, iridescent kingfishers perched on branches. They were piled up against the ruined silk red damask of the other two walls, haphazardly stacked one on top of the other. Some of the glass cases were shattered, and the dead birds were simply exposed to the air. One of them – a wader – had fallen from its mount, its leg snapped in two, and it lay on its side, staring up at nothing.

The more one looked, the more details one picked out – a claw, a broken case, matted fur. I turned away after a few moments, unable to bear it.

'I wish we were back in London,' I said, quietly. Vic said nothing, but slipped her hand into mine. The thought of our tiny, warm bedroom there was almost overwhelming. It was small, that room. This place was uncontainable, vast; there seemed no end to it. We stood in the gathering gloom, shivering in our school blazers, hands clasped.

Eventually, our mother reappeared, and said shortly, 'It's late. Come with me, girls. Bedtime.'

Her mouth was a straight, short line, no expression in the huge blue eyes. I said, in a small voice, 'I need to use—'

'Oh, for God's sake. Here.'

She directed us to an ancient water closet and lavatory at the back of the house, where the stench was even worse and, with it, the distinct smell of damp. The smell stung Vic's eyes, and the dust and hair and – whatever else was in that house made her rashes come up particularly badly.

Whilst both of us peed and took the chance to drink some water from the tap, which was a trick we'd learned early on in childhood, Iris waited outside in the corridor, grinding her teeth, obviously irritated. I knew not to ask her for dinner, that the moment had passed, and I prayed Vic would not do the same. The red carpet had obviously not been rolled out for her by Uncle Clive or whoever was here.

'Was that Uncle Clive you were with?' Vic asked our mother.

'Yes,' she said. 'But he's not going to bother us. He'll stay at his end of the house. That's how it will work.'

We could hear him, or someone anyway, shouting from the other end of the house. Distant, haunting cries that swept through the long rooms, softly lapping at us in waves of sound by the time they reached our ears.

'Come on,' our mother said, slender hand gripping the black railing. 'Let's go upstairs and find your room. I asked Mrs Boyes to come back as a favour one time for us and make the beds up. Silly woman – well, we'll see, now I'm back. We'll see who sticks, who swivels.'

Down an unlit narrow corridor on the first floor she flung open a narrow door. 'Here,' she said.

The room was small, long and narrow, barely the width of the window. Two beds ran end to end. At some point it had been a child's bedroom. There were traces of wallpaper on the walls, in a pattern of fairies and small woodland creatures. Someone had written 'My rume' under the windowsill, in small italics.

'You can choose your beds,' Iris said, as if this was luxury of the first order. She flung open the folded shutters, and gave a small scream as hundreds of dead flies and wasps, trapped between the glass and the wood, fell to the floor, crunching under her feet. She crouched down, muttering, and swept them under the bed with her foot. Bile rose in my throat, I climbed onto my high bed and felt a spring dig into my knee through the ragged quilt.

Our mother had told us that we'd have a room each, but we didn't mention that. I wouldn't have slept on my own in this place for all the tea in China. However, Vic did mention the smell, and even Iris, for once, did not get cross. She said that it was something gone bad and that it had been got rid of.

'Tomorrow you can get up early and go out and explore the

grounds,' she said, as she stood in the doorway. 'This is your home now. You will have a wonderful time. I did, when I was little. Exploring.'

'We need food for tomorrow,' Vic said.

My mother kicked at the wainscoting, viciously. 'For heaven's sake, Victoria. Shut up. Just shut up. You never thank me. You never show any excitement. You moan and whine, both of you. Look what I've given you!'

For the first time I realised she reminded me of a small child, one of those little toddlers I'd seen at the Serpentine in London who would scream when it was time to go home, unable to regulate their feelings.

Vic sat up in bed, her hair a dark, toffee-coloured static tangle. She cleared her throat and said boldly: 'We want breakfast before we go out to explore, and a packed lunch to take with us. We are hungry.'

My mother's face clouded over. She rubbed her forehead hard with the flat of her palm, shoved our suitcases into the room with her foot and said: 'Ungrateful wretches. You've no idea what I've done to get us here. If you knew what I'd been through. Good night. Hope spiders don't crawl into your mouths.' But she didn't hit us, or pull our hair, or twist our ears, or say something so cruel it stung, and she might have done.

Vic sat up for a while reading *Well Done, Dilys, Duffer of the Fourth!*, which she had borrowed from Kensington Library. I watched her, my knees drawn up under my chin, hugging myself to stay warm, wanting her to talk to me.

'You know you won't be able to take that back now,' I said officiously, after a while.

She shrugged. 'I know.'

'They'll issue you with a fine, Vic,' I said. Vic was punctilious about her library books. 'Do you remember what happened to Colonel Brigham? He had to go to court.'

But she raised one side of her lip and gave me a scornful look. 'Honestly, Sarah. What are they going to do? Ask Scotland Yard to track me down with a sniffer dog? We're never going back to that library again. Besides, absolutely no one cares what happens to us. Don't you understand that?'

Vic had never spoken to me like that before; it felt worse than a slap from our mother. I shrugged and lay back down in bed in the cold, damp sheets, pretending not to care, but tears pricked my eyes. There were sounds inside the house – near, and far. The *toc-toc-toc* of something in the floorboards, and the faintest hum of an occasional insect. I could hear a wind-up gramophone, or radio, and some dance music being relayed through the walls, tinny and uneven. And what I thought must be Uncle Clive at the other end of the house, still shouting about something. I wondered if he was there at all, or whether it was just a ghost.

None of it felt real. Was it real? I had been told all my life this was where we belonged, but it didn't feel like it. From outside came a shrieking call past our window, answered by another far away in the trees. I shivered, trying to nestle into the eiderdown, but it was too slippery.

We didn't ever tell other people about Iris, what it was like to be her daughter. Once, at school, I was called into the headmistress's office and accused of having passed on lies. I got very upset. I do not ever, ever, ever tell lies. You would understand why if you were me. I do not ever lie.

I can't remember what happened but afterwards Vic said it was a jolly good show; apparently I had lain down on the ground, drumming my feet on the headmistress's carpet and crying so hard I coughed and was slightly unwell in the back of my mouth. Vic was sent for, and the head talked to her, then she came over to me and crouched down and stroked my hair. I was in the corner, curled up. I just kept saying, 'I'm not a liar. I don't have lies.'

'Lice,' she said. 'You have lice. Headlice. We both do.'

We were both sent home for spreading lice and I remembered thinking as we walked home, silently crying, scuffing the paving stones, that we must have caught it somewhere, off someone. But they didn't ask us about that.

I can still feel the depth of our misery, the fluttering anxiety, knowing we had to solve this problem ourselves. We knew our mother would either create a scene at school and make it much worse or simply refuse to help, so on our way home Vic strolled into the chemist's opposite us, next to the Tube station, and whilst I was chatting to the nice man behind the counter she stole some of the American lotion they had next to the hairbrushes and tortoiseshell hair grips. We kept oiling our hair, as we had heard a lady on the bus once say it makes them drown. We were not children others much liked to play with anyway, and this did not endear us to anyone. I wondered whether, at this new school, we'd be welcomed as the lost souls we were by a gang of cheerful pupils. I hoped so.

When I woke the next morning, my neck was stiff. I could feel the muscles pulling, tearing, as I turned my head to see where I was. Then I remembered. The smell was still there, and it seemed worse than before.

I sat up in bed, unable to move my head easily, and hugged myself. Vic was still fast asleep, snoring. Carefully, I knelt and leaned towards the casement of the window, pulling at the rusting metal knob on the cracked wooden shutters. They juddered open, and I gasped.

A pink-orange sun hovered just above the woodland towards the East Wing. In front of me, the parkland lay glinting with summer dew. I could see spider webs, and wild sedge grasses, glittering in the morning light.

Something caught my eye – the movement of two rabbits hopping across the fields to the woods beyond. In the centre of the parkland stood the great Burnt Oak, its shadow falling across the silvery grass.

The birdsong was so loud I wondered it did not wake Vic. A calling, trilling, ribbon of sound, mingling with the mawkish caw of rooks in the woods. There was another noise too. I listened again, trying to make it out, straining myself to hear it. Something was calling me. Perhaps it was the beginning of my turning away from childhood, perhaps it was ancestral voices, beckoning me to involve myself in the house. Something changed within me that moment: when I remember Fane, I have to acknowledge that for all of the sadness and terror and danger, living there enabled me to see the world differently, and perhaps it began when I heard that cry.

I dressed in my old school shorts and Aertex, pulled on my plimsolls and crept out, along to the vast circular balcony and down the stairs. The smell grew worse the further towards the centre of the house I went. I walked past the white marble heads of old men, the vast black marble statues by the entrance. The nostrils of the dead hare dangling at the man's side seemed to quiver in the early morning light. The woman's lips, raised in a ghastly rictus, were unsettling, as if she'd been trapped in lava, forced to spend eternity like this.

There was a rustling sound from quite nearby – I hoped it was mice, not something worse. I had heard mice yesterday, scampering under the floorboards in our room. Hurriedly, I turned the heavy fluted iron doorhandle, as quietly as I could. The chill of the cold flagstones in the hall meant I was shivering as I emerged onto the huge stone portico and stole carefully down the steps.

The fresh dew soaked my canvas shoes. The air was as sweet as honeysuckle nectar. I was outside. I was free.

I stopped, and looked back at the house. I remember that moment so vividly, as that is when I first heard a scream. A long, drawn-out shriek, like pain.

Chapter Seven

When I was eight, I decided I wanted a birthday party. I invited three friends over from school. I wasn't old enough to understand how different our childhood was from others, but I was aware that one must be complicit in our strangeness, and was usually compliant. So I don't know why I broke out of the mould on that one occasion: perhaps my brain was changing, folding in on itself in preparation for growing up. I don't understand it. But I went to the three most popular girls in the year, and I told them they were invited to our flat for tea.

'My mother has said no presents,' I kept saying, winking, as if it were a secret joke. 'My mother has ordered a special cake from Harrods. Your parents may pick you up at six thirty.'

Even the memory of it makes me feel sick, not nauseous, but a swooping, soaring, freefall feeling of utter terror and then sadness. Because they came – *why?* – with me, trotting down the street from school, holding hands. I remember the excitement on their faces as we rounded the corner into the white-stucco crescent where we lived, the confusion as I pressed the bell. 'It's a flat,' I said grandly, then led them up the filthy stairs, stinking of cigarettes and mould, and opened the door.

'I've bought Jenny, Lucinda and Elizabeth home, as agreed,' I said, advancing into the flat, carefully. 'For the birthday tea.'

My mother pushed herself up from the kitchen table, with both hands. A smile spread across her face. One of the girls said 'hello' in response, as if she thought Iris was pleased to see her. What a life that girl must have had. Where signals were clear.

'Oh,' Iris said, that smile plastered across her whole face. 'You did, did you? Well, this is going to be fun.' And she gestured to the bare shelves, the coolbox.

I won't say what happened. I won't say how they were ready on the stairs, waiting to be collected together, their coats buttoned on, tightly holding hands, their knuckles white.

'You have to take us all,' Elizabeth told her mother, turning her tear-stained face, jam in her hair, towards her. At one point, when she'd asked where the tea was, my mother had flicked a spoon filled with jam at her, and told her she was a nasty, common little girl. 'We made a pact. We have to go *now*.'

I don't remember her mother at all. I just remember the softening of Elizabeth's face, as she stared *at* her mother because she was safe now, because her mother would make everything all right.

I never had anyone else back ever again.

I don't cry often, because once I start it's hard to stop. But I feel the weight of tears, somewhere between my eyes, when I think of that me: small me, how bold she was, how stupid. How she just wanted to be normal, for once.

There was one kind girl at the school. Her name was Hannah Rose Wilde, and she used to give me an apple most mornings. She had large green eyes and short brown hair and she never said anything, but smiled at me and every morning would say, 'I thought you might like an apple.' She was my age, my class. After the terrible birthday party when we were ostracised, she was the one girl who carried on talking to me, making gentle jokes, including me in games if she was allowed to, and, when they were in season, bringing me an apple. I don't blame the other girls. I would have done the same. I do not know what happened to her. But I wish I could thank her: some days she was the reason I felt some warmth, some goodness inside me.

I was thinking about Hannah, about whether anyone would notice us now we were marooned here, about one day feeling normal, and wondering if other people felt normal, and if so what it was like, as I crossed into the parkland. In September, my mother had informed us yesterday with glee, someone would mow the long, long grass, going round in a circle, driving the tiny fieldmice and voles further into the centre of the waving grasses until there was no protection left and they had to scarper, like lit squibs across the newly naked land. Looking back at the house, the dilapidated and rusting garden furniture upended around the side, the broken windows, I wondered who had the job of taking care of the garden, for even I could see that this was unlikely to happen, that this was not a house with gardeners, no matter how much they were needed.

A shrieking, unearthly noise caught my attention and I froze. I looked around, making sure no one was watching. There was movement above me and I glanced up: low in the sky was a bright star, still visible in the morning light, fading gently into the day.

Thud.

Suddenly something soft and heavy landed behind me. I turned, heart racing. From only a few feet away came a strange rasping, gagging noise, a rustling as if something were trying to escape.

For a second, I wondered wildly if it were a shooting star, dropping out of the sky, falling to earth here, and I forced myself to look down, into the broken, dewy grass.

It was an owl. She was small – if I'd pictured them at all I thought owls were big, terrifying, but not her. (I didn't know she was a girl, not then.) I crouched down, moving away from her to give her some room. Her feathers were softest white with caramel edges, her front dotted with black spots.

Slowly, she opened her eyes, like black pools of liquid, and gazed at me with no expression whatsoever.

She had a heart-shaped face with darker, short, stubbly feathers in outline, almost as if someone had drawn it on with pastels. Mesmerised, I reached out, very tentatively, to stroke her, but she shrieked, and I saw then that one wing was twisted out, not gathered against the body like the other. She made a strange gurgling sound.

I was both terrified and excited by her, by the huge scaly

talons that looked as if they belonged on a dinosaur from pictures we'd seen at the Natural History Museum, not a bird. Her beak was long in that heart-shaped face, and very sharp. I peered at her, utterly transfixed; I had simply never seen anything like it before, never been close to an animal like this, not unless you counted London dogs and cats, or rats and mice, which I didn't. Birds were not something you saw close up. They were in trees, or the air, above you.

She cried out again, and then made the horrible gagging sound. I was so sure she must be in pain. Somehow it was unbearable. I still can't explain why. It tore at me, the knowledge that she was powerless like this. I knew nothing about owls, but I knew they didn't belong on the ground, like chickens. My heart ached for her. I was a little girl in pain, but I didn't know that. Panic closed around me – what should I do? Then she reached a leg up and, with one scaly talon, scratched at the heart-shaped face, combing the bristling feathers. Then she opened her eyes, and I turned my stiff, aching neck and we stared at each other.

For the rest of my life I will remember the two of us looking at each other in surprise, in that field between the house and the woods, the furzy haze of late summer mist hanging over the landscape, the faintest pink of the sky with the one star steadily burning above us. I felt as if we were on the edge of the world.

I don't claim that she loved me, my Stella. I don't claim that we saw past the bounds of human and bird, or any of that rot you sometimes see gets talked about. I simply know that our connection was one that defines what it is to exist. It said: you are alive. I matter. *You matter.*

The injured wing moved a little, and she made a small, odd sound, then the gagging sound again. A small, brown . . . *thing* came out of her mouth as she coughed, and it fell to the ground. I looked down at it on the grass: a pellet, made up of tiny, needle-sharp femurs, a skull no bigger than my fingernail, shards of bone and gristle.

It was so unexpected – I said, out loud, 'Oh, yuck!' It would have been funny were it not for the fact that I was sure it meant she must be dying. I stepped away and, unsteady on my feet, still half asleep and desperately hungry, I stumbled and fell backwards into the wet, soft grass, and as I did she briskly, violently flapped her wings, and somehow righted herself again. When I scrambled to my feet again, rubbing my eyes, she was gone.

I looked up into the Burnt Oak, but could see no movement. I stood as still as I could, swaying slightly in the long, dewy grass.

Barn Owl. Somewhere, some Ladybird book at school or Encyclopaedia Britannica entry swam into my consciousness. She was a barn owl. I don't know why it had stuck, but it had. The heart-shaped face, perhaps. The white form, like a ghost, flying across the fields. Something Iris had said: Iris had loved birds as a child, she'd told us once. Birds, and stars.

I stayed a few moments more, hoping for another sight of her, then turned back towards the house. I saw it clearly now in the morning light, square on, the thistles on the driveway, the boarded-up windows, what it had become.

Why had we come here? What would she do with us? What was in her mind? I don't think I had ever thought before about my mother's *role* in life: we lived in Pelham Mansions, went to school and tried to avoid her, and at the weekends we played with each other in the communal garden or went about Kensington together, arm in arm, while she went out on business.

The birthday party came back to me again. I wondered who would notice we'd left London, whether school had been told. I wondered what other parents would say. Why hadn't Elizabeth's mother said something to anyone after she collected three small girls in torn clothes and a state of distress from a rundown flat that two of their schoolmates lived in? Besides Hannah, no one at school asked how we were. No teacher enquired as to why our cardigans had holes in them, why our feet bulged out of our shoes, why we lingered in class, walked so slowly home, why Vic was cautioned twice by the tobacconist next to the school for shoplifting. These were kind people, but they never asked. Even after the disastrous birthday party, no one took an interest in our obvious neglect, the fact we were always thin, always tired, with puffy shadows under our eyes because our mother frequently shouted and screamed late at night about something, anything, that had angered her, sometimes waking us up to bellow in our ears that she hated us. Not one person asked.

So when, later on, I started receiving praise and applause, and people were kind to me, I never trusted them. *You didn't notice me when I needed you to*, I would think, smiling at the portly ladies in bouclé suits and pearls, the gentlemen with bald, shiny pates and horn-rimmed spectacles and an air of satisfaction, those who clasped my hands and told me I was a clever, talented young woman. *It suits you to be pleased with me now, but now is too late.*

I think I woke up at that moment, started to realise we were here for good, that it wasn't a weekend away. I went round to the side of the East Wing where the stables flanked a courtyard of cracked flagstones with yet more luxuriant weeds standing up in green and yellow spikes. The stables had been used for target practice by the soldiers. The doors hung off the hinges and every single window had been shattered. It was nine years since the end of the war and the world had changed utterly – last year we had crowned a new queen – and yet in all that time no one had thought to remove the doors, taken out the glass. I went into the East Wing through the back door, making for the kitchen.

Here was even more chaos than the West Wing, everything jumbled up together. Bronze pans, dulled with age and mildew, hundreds of jelly and pastry moulds, wooden spoons and shards of willow-pattern china in bits on the terracotta tiles. A mouse scuttled across the floor and I jumped. But otherwise it was quiet. And – I noted this – it was relatively warm.

I could hear footsteps close by. The smell wasn't so bad here, masked as it was by the scent of pipe tobacco. Then – I jumped again – another mouse dashed past me, in a straight line. I followed it, curiously.

In the third room, furniture was piled up in a haphazard fashion, almost like a game of jacks. Alone on a shelf was an earthenware bread bin. I edged past two broken dining chairs and opened it up, and there was a packet of Fortt's Bath Oliver water biscuits, dry as anything but creamy and not too stale. I gobbled three, palming them into my mouth until I gagged. But, as I turned to go, pocketing the remaining biscuits for Vic, a large, wrinkled hand landed, heavily, on my shoulder.

I screamed, twisting it off, and a voice behind me boomed: 'What are you doing in my kitchen, little girl?'

I was spun round, roughly, and found myself facing a tall, elderly man in a red-and-gold silk dressing gown. His face was long, grey and thin, vertical lines of dirt etched into the skin like marks on a tree. His hair was grey too, and stood up straight on his head. He loomed over me. I could smell tobacco, and his breath, milk-sour.

'S-s-sorry,' I said, staring up at him, realising I had seen him before, years ago. 'Oh! You're—'

A mouse, wriggling frantically, swung between his thin fingers of his other hand. He waggled it at me. 'I'm your great-uncle, and you can damned well get the hell out of here. This is *my* house.'

My vision swam. Everything seemed to dissolve, to be expanding at the same time, and I felt myself sliding gratefully to the floor.

When I woke up, I was sitting outside in the courtyard, leaning on the back doorstep against the door. The breeze was pleasant, the smell not quite so bad. I could hear piano music on a gramophone just inside. Uncle Clive was next to me. He handed me a glass of milk.

'Drink this. Come on.' I glanced down uncertainly at it. 'You silly little girl. There's no mouse in it. Good, good. I wouldn't waste a nice juicy mouse on you. Drink it. You've had a shock. Hm?'

I took it, gingerly, and drank. It had something sweet, and fiery in it. I screwed my face up, and he said, 'It's brandy. Used it to pep up the miners if they'd been in the cold for too long.' He ran his fingers through his thick, dirty-looking hair. 'Here, have some of this.'

It was honeycomb. He sliced some with a knife, and gave it to me, balanced on top of a piece of salty, creamy cheese. It was the most delicious thing I had ever tasted; I can still taste it. I still think about it. I snatched a glance at him, and he smiled at me.

'Nice, isn't it? The bees have plenty to spare, that's what I tell them anyway. Now, which one are you?'

'I'm Sarah. Victoria's the eldest.'

'You're – eight?'

'Twelve.'

'Twelve.' He looked surprised. 'Good grief. I forget things, you see, since Dolly died. Suppose you think I should have been sending you birthday presents all this time.'

I didn't know what to say to this, so I shrugged.

'Why are you here?'

'Oh . . . Iris says we've come to live here.'

'Does she.' He gave a rich laugh that turned into a cough, and banged his chest with his fist so violently that the door shook, and the needle on the record jumped, with a small scratch. 'Well, she might think that, but you're wrong. What else has she told you?'

He had a rumbling, scratchy voice, curiously terrifying though it wasn't loud, with the edge of what I thought was an American burr but which must have been Canadian, from his time prospecting in the mines. I didn't know what to say to him, and fear – for him, and for me and Vic, at her anger – gnawed away at me. I looked down, and a tear fell onto the ground.

'Listen, Sarah.'

'Yes, Uncle Clive?'

He shook his head. 'I'm not your uncle. I'm your great-uncle.'

'She told us that was what we should c-call you.'

'Of course she did.' He flicked one finger on my cheek. His eyes, close up, were grey, like the rest of him. He was very thin. And dirty – there were folds of dark grime not just in his face but on his nails and neck and around the edges of his clothes. 'Oh dear. I'm sorry to say, my dear, that you and your sister, you are collateral damage. That's what we used to call it in the army.'

'What's that?'

'We had a saying, out in Lakeshore Mine. When the wolves

are at the door, you have to find a way to get rid of 'em. Otherwise you'll just end up eating each other. You'll tear yourselves apart trying to work out how to escape 'em. Does that make any sense?'

'Yes.' I nodded, and a sad smile worked its way across his face.

'Thought it might.'

There was a scrabbling sound behind us, and he turned, and almost leisurely picked up a mouse that had been creeping behind us, spreadeagled, beady eyes darting from Clive to the door. He held it, squeezed it tightly so that its eyes bulged, and it seemed to pop. It stopped squeaking. Then, taking it by the tail, he swung it against the back door, hard, so that something snapped.

'Another piece for the pie,' he said.

I felt sick, and bent my head, swallowing. Uncle Clive took no notice. From the other side of the courtyard, towards the centre of the house, I heard our mother calling, and heard Vic's answering voice.

'Did she shout like that in London?' he said, disdain written on his face. 'God, when will she give me some rest? Has she said how long you'll be here?'

'Yes,' I said seriously. 'I suppose we thought she was staying here. For ever.'

'You're a taking little thing, when you smile,' he said, flicking me under the chin, 'and you look like all the Fanes gone by. Those eyes, that dark fair hair, that quizzical expression. Listen to me, Sally. Your mother destroys things. She always has done. I came back to take up my inheritance when she was five, and the first time I saw her, I knew . . .' He twitched, involuntarily.

'What?'

'I knew there was something different about her. Something . . . wrong.'

There was silence. 'Oh,' I said.

His voice was hoarse, and he rubbed his throat, as if unused to speaking.

'She was so quiet. Watching, waiting. You never knew what

she'd do next. She hated me from the start.' He rubbed his nose. 'Perhaps – I don't know, I could have done better. She was just a kid; she'd lost her father; her mother was a fool. But nothing seemed to bother her. I watched her as a child, dropping birds' eggs out of her bedroom window, sticking her head out to see them on the terrace below.' He clapped his hands together, violently, and I jumped again. 'Splat!' He shook his head. 'She'd play tricks – small things at first – you'd think it was nothing. Hiding enamel boxes, then accusing a servant of stealing so they were dismissed. Accusing decent people of hurting her. She was vile to poor Dolly. Absolutely vile. Called her names. Used to hum, constantly, around her, then ask what the problem was when she lashed out in irritation. My darling Dolly was a sweet girl from a nice family; they'd emigrated to Canada, worked hard. I plucked her out of her home and took her back here and into this Bedlam, and she . . . she made her life hell.'

I felt I had to defend her. 'She says she has been cheated out of her inheritance.'

'That's rubbish. She lies every time she opens her mouth, that one. She inherited a great deal. She's spent it all.' He peered round at me to see how I took this. 'Hah. Didn't know that, did you?'

'Really?'

I wasn't sure this could be true. The mystery of what our mother did all day had long ceased to interest us. She spent a lot of time being measured for suits, Christian Dior, Hardy Amies, and so on, but there was never money for food, or furniture, or clothes for us, as I have said. She went to lunchtime concerts whilst we were at school; she took us once or twice to a cello recital, and embarrassingly made us sit in the front row, leaning forward and watching far too intently. She cried, and clapped too loudly. Other people moved away. Once, we saw her walking very fast towards us in Hyde Park, when we'd walked to the Albert Memorial after a half day at school. We hid behind a tree. After a few minutes, she came back the other way and we realised she was walking up and down Rotten Row, just marking time. Sometimes, she wasn't back till very late. We knew she drove to Fane sometimes, and just stood outside, or walked in the grounds until she was ejected or until it was time to drive home – she didn't like driving in the dark.

'Yes, really. Your father left her some money. Old Murbles told me so. Not much, but enough. And she gets an allowance from me, not that she ever acknowledges it. Does she ever mention that? No.'

'Oh. Well, th-thank you.' My cheeks burnt with embarrassment.

'I'm sorry for you.' Uncle Clive stretched out his legs on the back step, and put his hands behind his head. He sighed. 'Your mother has had one aim in life since she met me, which is to do away with me. She likes to imagine her father left her the house. We're in the final act, you know, rather like Wagner, if that's the right chap. She wants you out of the way to get on with destroying me, and then we'll see, we'll see what happens. But, as I say, Sally, I won't let her. She doesn't understand she'll destroy Fane if she carries on like this. Finish the work the soldiers started.'

'She's always talking about the soldiers. But I don't know what she means.'

'Eight different battalions from three different regiments were stationed here in the war. Then Polish special forces. The Poles weren't too bad. It was our people. Some of the things . . . Dolly and I had to move out to the gatehouse. We'd hear the shots, the sounds of wood cracking as they smashed up the staircases for firewood. When we came back – dear God.' His face was twisted. 'I can't complain, of course, but we're still not right, ten years later. Nothing's right, Sally. Our age is over, you see. My lot, we're done for. And sometimes I wonder if it was all worth it.'

'What was? The war? Surely you can't say that, Uncle Clive.'

'Not the war.'

'Then what?' But he didn't answer. His milky eyes were focused on the distance now, and I wasn't even sure if he knew I was there. I clambered to my feet, my legs still rather wobbly, and he handed me another piece of cheese and honeycomb.

'It's very nice to see you again,' I said.

'Hmm. You poor mite. Look here, come and see me again, would you? But let's pretend we're not friends,' he said, helping himself to another slice of honeycomb. 'It's easier for you that way. I've dealt with your mother before. I don't need to tell you what she's like. She's come here to get rid of me and she'll get her way.' His mood seemed to change suddenly, like clouds scudding across the sky. 'Be on your way, now. Off you go.'

I didn't know how to say that I didn't want to be his friend either, but his wing of the house was warm and he'd given me some food. I wasn't particular. I took the food and left him sitting on the doorstep, long, skinny pyjama-clad limbs sprawled out, looking up to the sun.

Chapter Eight

The sound of a car coming up the drive was rare enough to be an event. Still, though, visitors came, disturbing our strange isolation, as July went by. Sometimes it was bailiffs, sometimes historians concerned with the fabric of the house, coming to beg Uncle Clive to catalogue what remained. The Georgian Society turned up about two weeks into our stay, asking to see the Robert Adam panels, and when he eventually came to the door – my mother never did – Clive slammed it in their face. Sometimes it was sightseers – 'Gannets,' Clive used to shout after them – people come to gawp at the slow, pillowing collapse of yet another English country house. It was said two houses a day were vanishing that summer of 1954, whether because of demolition, fire or neglect: our history erasing itself in front of our eyes. We had done this, my great-uncle said one afternoon, gloomily surveying the disintegrating rear of the house from the stable block. As a nation, we had brought this on ourselves.

'I think Hitler mostly did, to be strictly accurate,' Vic said in the Thin Room, as we called our bedroom, one night. 'Seems a bit harsh to blame it on soldiers who didn't want to be here in the first place.'

But I agreed with Clive. The smell came from human waste, uncleared and fossilised in several of the lavatories, untouched since the soldiers abandoned the house in 1947. The stench then must have been even worse. Now, it just clung to everything, a rotting miasma. The majority of the damage done to the house was because of the soldiers. But there were other smells too – decaying smells, like flowers left too long in a vase, breaking down into slime. And odours of wood and tobacco smoke, too, draped over everything.

When you opened the window of the Thin Room on those

long hot summer nights, you caught the scent of grass, and hay. One of Uncle Clive's last acts before my mother moved back, whilst he still cared enough about the house, was to paper over cracks in the walls of the house with wallpaper paste and newspapers from the last year or so, which we found in a box in the room next to ours, torn into strips. We would lie on the damp eiderdowns those summer nights and pick out two strips at a time, eliding news stories to make each other laugh.

THE VARSITY RUGBY MATCH, OXFORD:
A NUCLEAR CRISIS IN RUSSIA.
MRS CASTLE OBJECTS: STOP THAT COLD MEAL FROM
BECOMING UNAPPETISING BY ADDING A DAB OF
RAYNER'S MANGO CHUTNEY
RAVENSHALL DEMOLISHED BY ARMY UNIT AS VILLAGERS
WATCH – ASK THE MAN FROM THE PRUDENTIAL.
QUEEN ELIZABETH THE QUEEN MOTHER WAS PRESENT
THIS EVENING AT A CONCERT AT ST JAMES'S
PALACE IN AID OF EISENHOWER, UNDER
ATTACK FROM SENATOR MCCARTHY.

Scraps of news from the real world, so far away from us now. What else did we do, that summer? We lay on our beds, shivering – it was never warm in the house – and read old books. We crept from room to room, opening doors, picking up odd things like chair legs and smashed pieces of plaster, dead birds in cases, mouldy bolts of material, eaten away by a fungus.

Our mother spent most of her time in a set of rooms on the floor above us in the West Wing: we could hear her stamping across rotten floorboards, the sound of objects being moved around. She talked loudly, her voice echoing into the emptiness, and played records, and the wireless. Occasionally, we would hear her descend the staircase and tramp along the corridor towards the East Wing to see Uncle Clive. We knew this because there would be the sound of things thrown, of voices raised – shouting terrible, rude, disgusting words. Uncle Clive knew some language, so did my mother. She would tell him to leave. Tell him the house was falling down around his ears. That he was forfeiting her future, the future of a great house. That he was endangering his nieces. That she would report him for any manner of transgressions: black market activity during the war. Harbouring a Nazi air pilot who had crash landed in the field. Burning precious books to keep warm.

'I'll huff and I'll puff and I'll blow your house down,' she said to him a week or so after we arrived, her eyes glittering at him over the long dining table. But he just laughed.

It was one of the few times we tried eating together, all of us. Vic and I had cooked watery cauliflower cheese with curdled milk and the barest suggestion of cheese. There was a lot of cauliflower cheese around then, and boiled cabbage. After I left school, I never ate either again.

We sat in what had been a library and was latterly a billiards room before becoming the officers' mess, which is why it had been saved from the worst of the soldiers' degradations. It was a long, thin room, with the Adam panelling the Georgian Society was so concerned about and a series of Chippendale bookcases, lined with brown and gold books shut up behind glass, which no one ever looked at. It was remarkable that they had survived at all, in fact. In this room only, you could still imagine you were in a gracious, if slightly worn, stately home.

Uncle Clive looked up at my mother, his eyes raking over her. She was so beautiful that night, a film star in a photograph come to life at the end of the table, and I could not help staring at her, marvelling at how in repose, her lovely face was calm, the bones of her neck and collar and skull like finest sculpture, her hair swept into a twist, fastened with pins. She wore the one piece of jewellery she had from her father, a silver star pin she'd stuck into her hair.

My mother repeated herself, her eyes bulging.

'I'll huff and I'll puff, Clive . . .' She sat back in her chair, blinking.

Clive carried on eating, his voice muffled with food. 'You can make all the threats you want, but not at dinner, Iris, please—'

But she ignored him. 'It's *my* house—'

'Excuse me,' Clive said, thumping his fist on the table in frustration. Cauliflower and watery sauce splattered everywhere. 'You know as well as I do, because we've had this conversation innumerable times, that no one will believe you. Stop embarrassing your children, yourself, your family name, you pathetic woman.'

My mother said, 'It was my father's. It should come to me. To me.' She wasn't bothered, or upset. I noticed for the first time the almost robotic, neutral intonation of hers, totally at odds with her film-star appearance. Not just that she pronounced words in a cut-glass accent, but more than that: How her voice never had any expression. She sounded like a doll with a string on its back, parroting lines: 'I've come back now. How many times do I have to explain it.'

Uncle Clive wiped his mouth with his napkin. He put down his fork, darting a glance at me and Vic, who were watching, heads bowed, trying to pretend we were somewhere else entirely. 'Your father may have wanted you to inherit and not his brother, but the house wasn't his to leave. It's entailed. Your mother was utterly misguided in letting you carry on with this delusion.'

She stared at him. 'It's—'

But Clive cut across her, his voice quieter than ever. 'You're not stupid, Iris. Dolly used to say you were, stupid I mean, harping on the same damn business all the time, but you're not. You're mad, like your mother was. The will leaves the contents of the house to you, under the advisement of the trustees of the Estate. I, and one other person, am a trustee. Now, I don't know what that solicitor told you, but we do not allow you to dispose of anything. We do not allow you to sell anything.' He swallowed, but something caught in his throat so he gurgled as he spoke. When he recovered, he said: 'You are a mother, with an allowance, and a perfectly decent life. Instead of looking after your children, you choose to debase yourself like this . . . Look at them. You never talk to them. You never think about them. Women like you should be locked up.'

Our mother's mouth opened and shut like a fish. 'I'll blow your house down,' she said eventually, throwing her cutlery down on the table. She stood up.

'Just wait and see,' she said, holding up a finger. 'One day the truth will out. I'll get rid of you. And I'll blow it all down.' She kicked the door hard, with her pointed silk shoes.

'Temper, temper,' said Uncle Clive. I looked at him. He was smiling for the first time in a long time.

'Sorry,' Vic said, as if we were the cause of it all. *Sorry.*

'I blame her father, for not explaining the situation to her mother better. She was beautiful, but an idiot. Iris is the same.'

I wanted to say that he was wrong: she was awful, but she wasn't an idiot. I sometimes thought she was too clever, but I knew that didn't make sense.

'Listen,' he said, wiping his mouth, and standing up too. 'I'll get rid of her somehow. But you can stay here whenever you like. That's all right. I'm warning you, though, don't play favourites and don't take sides. Find something else to do.'

The fact he thought this was a normal thing to say to two girls and that we thought it was normal to hear is maybe the strangest part of it all.

My sister carried on eating, left arm curled round her food, reading her ballet book, which she'd surreptitiously balanced on her lap under the table.

'She doesn't care, does she, that one?' Clive said, jerking his head at Vic. 'She'll be all right.'

He stood up and left, so it was just Vic and me, sitting in silence. I knew Vic was listening, but she carried on reading.

'Find something else to do.' In fact, we did have interests, Vic and I, and that is what helped us survive, I think. A year ago, our mother had said we could learn ballet and the cello respectively. She said she had come into some money from a godmother and this is why she could now afford it. That, before, it had not been possible, and that is why she'd said no. We knew this wasn't true, but did not contradict her. Why? Why had she changed her mind? I will never know. So, back in London, Vic went to Miss Philippa Hyde's Studio near Gloucester Road once a week and learned to plié and fouetté, and I learned the cello with Mrs Julia Marshall-Wessendorf, in a flat next to our school. She was a friend of the headmistress, an evacuee who had managed to flee Berlin with her son. She only wore black, and sometimes when I played she cried, which was off-putting. But I had use of a tiny cello, and Vic and I were not back at the flat until seven o'clock on Tuesdays, and our mother liked that. Once, we came back early, and a man was leaving, stuffing his shirt into his waistband. 'Wotcher,' he'd called to me as I lugged my cello up the stairs. He'd run a finger round his collar. 'I say, you must be one of Iris's chits. Awfully sorry to dash orf.'

As with everything in our lives, we experienced this without much judgement, only relief that she was busy.

I can't remember why it was the cello I learned, but then I don't remember lots of things. The curious thing is I think my mother suggested it herself, and, if she did, I have one thing for which to be grateful to her. It makes me uncomfortable to think about it, that she might have cared, or thought about what I needed. (It's easier to think of her as a villain. Yes, that's funny when I think about it.)

A week after we arrived in Fane, Vic announced she was going riding.

'What?' I'd said, assuming she was joking. We were alone in the breakfast room, off the Rose-Red Drawing Room.

'I thought I'd take up riding,' said Vic. She shrugged. 'I can go riding at the stables near the village. Iris has arranged it.'

'She has?'

'Yes, some man in the village asked her if one of her daughters wanted to learn to ride.' Vic didn't meet my eyes.

'What man in the village?'

'I don't know, Sarah! Gosh! Someone. He has a stables. The vicar's children learn with him.'

'What about the ballet? I thought Miss Hyde said you couldn't ride and do ballet – it's bad for your thighs.'

Vic ate some more toast. 'I don't know if I'll go on with the ballet. Ballet's for London. I need to find something to do here, and at school. Something other girls do. So I'll be gone most days. I want to get as good as I can.'

'Oh,' I said, trying to hide my surprise. Vic had been obsessed with the ballet.

'You might,' she said, pushing her chair back, and leaving her bowl on the table for Mrs Boyes to take away, 'find something to do yourself, Sarah. I can't babysit you all day.'

Since we'd arrived at Fane, we had increasingly, silently left each other alone. We didn't question what the other was doing. So I simply said, 'I hope you have a fantastic time, Vic. Sounds terrific.'

We had some help in the house now and it was a relief someone was there, someone who would put food on the table, hold some of the chaos at bay. Mrs Boyes had been with Uncle Clive since the beginning, but she had left several years ago now because she hadn't been paid for over a year. She lived in the village, and was the one whom my mother had persuaded to wash and iron the bedlinen and make up the beds before our arrival, and at my mother's behest – I have no idea how my mother got her to agree to it – she now started coming in again every morning.

She cleared away the breakfast things, cleaned what she could – not very much, given that three-quarters of the house was either rubble, inaccessible or beyond hope – did the laundry, prepared a hot lunch, which she served at one and a cold supper, which was left out in the breakfast room for us to help ourselves to. Even though he had treated her badly, she was loyal to Uncle Clive. She had come to Fane as a war widow and he had given her the job of housekeeper. She had a curious, sideways way of staring at us, sort of assessment and distrust combined.

Fane was like a remote island, and the park was the sea, separating us from the rest of the world. I had not properly met anyone else from the village that nestled behind the boundary wall just beyond the house. Vic and I had walked to the village once or twice, and bought ices from the post office where kind Mrs Boundy the postmistress would try to engage us unsuccessfully in small talk. We had no small talk. We had posted cards to those girls whom we liked to kid ourselves might be regarded as school friends – *It's awfully jolly here Pam, I hope to have you to stay one day* – Vic had written, optimistically, in her rounded, tiny handwriting. Pam, of course, did not reply.

The village was small: one street with an ancient church, an old, gabled pub and the post office. Just beyond was the hated taxidermist Leveson, source of the curlews, peacocks, birds of paradise, parakeets, ravens, robins – hundreds of little robins, jammed into case upon case – owls too, of course – stacked in cracking towers of glass around the house.

Behind the high street were two ill-defined tracks with tumbledown houses on each side, tiny workers' cottages so small that I, now twelve, was the height of the front door. Most of them were half derelict, like Fane itself.

'He doesn't have the funds to repair them,' I heard someone saying in the shop, the first time we went in.

'He had the funds to live it up in London and coat that wife of his in furs, didn't he?' This was the landlord of the Burnt Oak, who'd been injured in the First World War and lost a son in the Second. 'Spent all his money on gambling, hasn't he? Ruined this place, ever since he came back from wherever it was, if you ask me,' and he would have said more, but he was shushed by Mrs Boundy. I'd looked up in confusion, not wanting to have heard the conversation at all, but the only person to meet my eye was the Bird Boy, who we had been told lived above the post office, where Mrs Boundy treated him like her own son and fussed over him. He had smiled at me and nodded, then gone back to his book.

Mrs Boundy's own son, a printer, had been killed in a raid on Paternoster Row. As for the Bird Boy, Vic had learned from the vicar's children with whom she had started riding that he was an evacuee from London. He'd been evacuated quite late, towards the end of the war. One day he had got the train with Mrs Boundy to see his mother and sister, back to Cable Street, and when they arrived not a brick of the terrace was still standing: the whole street had been flattened the night before. They had dug for survivors, but it was hopeless. They never found anyone. I wondered afterwards countless times about where they ended up, if they were still beneath the new houses built up over them. Mrs Boundy and the Bird Boy had walked back to the station, caught a train back to Fane and on arriving he had simply said to her: 'I don't suppose I have anyone left now, Mrs Boundy. Can I live with you?'

I don't suppose I have anyone left now.

Having a home with people you loved in it. Walking back to it, finding it in ruins. There was something about this that hurt me so much I could feel it in my chest, even though it was nothing I had experienced so far. Perhaps that was why it hurt.

The Bird Boy was long, and thin, and hollow-chested, with round shoulders and light brown hair. He hung around the graveyard, especially at night-time, always with a pocket book and pen in hand. He did not associate with the vicar's children or any of the other young people in the village. They called him the Bird Boy, because he sat alone up on the Burnt Oak, they said, perched there like a bird.

'He's odd.'

'He's different.'

'He's not from here.'

He did not speak. Which is to say, I had been into the post office several times since my arrival on some flimsy pretext, and he never spoke. But when the landlord, Bill Done, said that about the estate cottages and Uncle Clive, the Bird Boy had looked up at me, his eyes burning into mine. As if he *wanted* to speak, to say something, but couldn't.

I asked Vic about the cottages that evening.

'They belong to the estate, but no one lives in them any more. It's for the best they fall down really,' said Vic in her most officious manner.

'Where did the people who lived there go, then?'

She shrugged. 'How should I know? They just left. But it's not fair to expect the estate to house them for ever, is it?'

'Why not?' All these people, displaced by war, moving to new estates, popping up everywhere. We'd seen pictures in the strips of paper torn up in our room, and on the drive down. People moving out of old bombed-out neighbourhoods in London into brand-new houses. I thought again about Stella, for that is what I'd named the owl I'd found, not knowing if it was a boy or a girl, because of the stars overhead dappling the sky from dusk until early dawn. If I woke in the night – a nightmare or Vic crying out in her sleep – I would go to the window, stare out, amazed at the light in the darkness, the millions of tiny lights pricking the sky. I wondered where she'd gone. How she had flown away, out of sight, vanishing in an instant. I thought to myself that one day I would be brave, go out at night by myself to the Burnt Oak, sit out and look for her, and look at the stars.

In those late summer days, I took to wandering through the empty rooms, sorting through things, to try to return some order to a corner or two. One book at a time, placed back on a chipped shelf half eaten away with wormwood, was still progress, of sorts.

One day – who knows how long after we came to Fane – I stood back to admire what I had done in one room, known as the Star Study. The desk had been upended, home to mice, and piles of papers – letters, photographs, newspapers – stuffed in drawers and cupboards and holes in the floorboards. Someone had slept in a corner of the room, there were quilts and sheets and stained, heavy-looking blankets. I'd righted the desk and cleaned the mahogany (which as well as being dirty had some kind of fungus growing on it) with the beeswax polish I'd found in Uncle Clive's kitchens. I'd put the books back on the shelves, and carefully spread what papers and photographs and maps I could salvage out on the floor, flattening them with books, then rolling them back up into tubes. They stood in the corner, each carefully labelled by me: 'Old map of Oxford', 'Photos of men from village?', 'Map of the stars'.

There was one drawer in the desk that always stuck halfway when I tried to open it. There were papers and photos in it. That morning, when I pulled it, it miraculously opened. Perhaps the hot, dry weather had caused it to shrink back to the right size. I lifted out the remaining papers, and spread them on the ground.

I knew that Uncle Clive had already been discharged and left for Canada when his brother was killed. He wrote from the small mining town where he was living, prospecting for gold. He had thought he would be the second son, free to do what he wanted. I had already found letters from him to his parents, most eaten away, or so damp that they were illegible. I would peel letters away from each other with intriguing phrases like 'bear attack' 'lost in the vast deep' and 'poor fellow: frozen to death standing up in the snow' in his sloping, grey-blue copperplate.

'Dearest Mother, I am thinking of you all the time. The loss of darling Arthur is a terrible blow. What a dear brother he was. What a remarkable man. I shall return as soon as I can. Communication is very difficult. I send you all love, your grieving son.'

I liked these letters. I liked finding evidence of love in this house, in this family. Arthur was my grandfather, Iris's father and Clive's brother. He had died in the Somme. Uncle Clive had been at Gallipoli. He had won several medals. There were letters about that in this bundle, too.

'Jolly proud, but there are others who deserved it too – can't help feeling the title got me pushed to the front of the queue – I was with men so brave you'd cry your eyes out if I told you some of the scrapes we were in – Mother, I kiss your photograph every day, please say you do the same. I miss you and Father very much. All love, your son Clive.'

The modesty of the man! It made me see Uncle Clive in a different light, not the grim, shuffling ghost with whom we shared the house now, but a young man. Smiling, capable, kind.

One of the photos was of a group of men, I thought in Canada, as they were standing in front of a shed, holding pick-axes. One man had a veined lump of stone in his hand – the others were pointing to it. Uncle Clive was holding up the man's sleeve, which when you looked closely was just material, as the other man had no right arm. They were all smiling broadly, Uncle Clive's smile the most manic of all. There was something unsettling about it. There was a dog sitting at the feet of the man holding the stone, looking up at him. I liked the other man. He was smiling, though his eyes were tired, and full of pain you felt even down the years.

I turned the photograph over.

Clive Fane, Donald Chalk & Tugie. Lakeshore Mine, 1921

Donald Chalk, I thought, suppressing a giggle – *what a strange name.* I looked at the dog, a dear little Jack Russell. Uncle Clive wouldn't talk about the war; he didn't talk about prospecting for gold, either. What things he must have seen, what things he never spoke of. I wanted to feel sorry for him, but I couldn't. I wanted to be able to side with him against my mother, to say that she was trying to steal the house from him, persecute an old man. And I couldn't.

There was a pair of binoculars squashed away next to the desk; though the lenses were scratched, they still worked. There were many more maps of stars, but some of them were best thrown away; some had noughts-and-crosses games on them, crude drawings, bits torn off, and some had been scrunched up and shoved in the windows with missing panes of glass. Others had even been burnt in the grate. Carefully, I wound the binocular strap round and put it on the desk. I leafed through the photographs, putting them carefully back in the drawer. The sense of order, of peace it gave me to have quiet, and control, was extraordinary. I thought about Uncle Clive's friend a lot. His kind, sad face. What had happened to him? Was he alive? The thought of these men, lost in history, no children to remember them or mourn them, gradually fading from memory, haunted me.

Time seemed to stretch and crease in those long, light, echoing days at Fane. Sometimes I felt as though we had always been there; other times I could not believe how quickly it was going, how August was already here and soon we would be leaving for school.

It had been raining for three days, solid, unhappy summer rain, and there was a chill in the air. I set off along the worn path through the fields towards the woods, which was my usual walk. This time I took the turning left towards the church on the edge of the parkland, because I had seen rabbits there yesterday, and was enough of a city child still that the sight of a bunny was thrilling.

Halfway, I stopped in the middle of the track at a shrieking, unearthly sound above me. I looked up and saw a creature hovering in the air and, with a flash of white, turning towards me, then diving to the ground.

I ran towards it. Sure enough, there it was, nestled amongst the heavy, wet grasses, the owl again. She lay still, with her eyes closed. I noticed her beak again, so sharp, like another talon. Her feathers were damp. She shivered.

Without thinking, I picked her up, nestling her amongst the folds of my skirt, my heart thumping. She was warm, and very light.

Instinctively, I did not turn back towards Fane. I walked towards the church, towards the sound of someone calling and whistling.

As I drew closer to the church boundary, I looked up and with a dart of surprise saw the Bird Boy sitting on the wall. He cupped one hand round his mouth and gave a screeching, hissing whistle, so eerily accurate that I looked around for the bird nearby.

'I thought it was you,' he said in an unexpectedly deep voice. 'Have you got her?'

I was so surprised at the sight of him that my own voice came out as a squeak. 'Yes.'

He jumped off the wall. 'Good. May I look at her, see how she is? They hate the rain. I've noticed her around, flying in and out of the nesting box outside the church. She's hungry, you see. I don't think she's learned how to feed, or maybe she's fighting with her siblings. I'm afraid she's probably half dead.' I unrolled my cotton skirt. 'Next time, remember body warmth, not material. Keep her warm by keeping her next to you.'

I nodded. 'Right.'

'Take her in your hands. She's young.'

'How do you know it's a she?' I said.

'The spots on her chest. Males don't have them.' He gave a soft whistle. I stared at her. *I called you Stella.* I wanted to say it out loud. 'Ah. Look at her. She's hungry. I think she's given herself a shock. She's dived for a vole and missed her target and she's not practised enough at hunting and the ground's too wet.' His low voice was kind, and soft. 'Yes, old girl. I say, rather a rough landing, eh? Let's get her some food, shall we?'

'What can we give her, though?' I said, thinking of the burnt wholegrain toast Mrs Boyes served up each morning. 'I'm not sure—'

In answer, he pulled a dead mouse out of his pocket. 'Here. She'll eat this. She has to learn how to, otherwise she won't survive.'

I thought of Uncle Clive, killing mice just for the sake of it, not doing anything with them, when Stella was dying for food. The sky was a pearly white, flecked with grey, and flickers of brightness. It was still quite cold. No one else was around. Behind us, a shadow flashed over the church tower.

'The mother abandons them after a few weeks,' he said seriously. 'They're left to their own devices. Around now's the time they're truly off hunting, trying to survive on their own. It's very – it's very tough for them. I have a penknife.' He said this with some pride. 'Dr Brooke gave it to me.'

He leapt up off the wall, and turned round, taking the knife from his pocket and, putting the mouse on the stones, began cutting it up. I tried to watch, but I couldn't. I closed my eyes, like the owl, and I felt her in my hands, her soft, gentle warmth, feeling the faint, faint fluttering of what I thought was her heart. She was so light, really just air.

'Will she eat it like that?' I pointed to the raw, bloody, dark meat with the brown skin still attached in his hand. He gave a short laugh.

'She only eats it like that.'

The owl opened her beak, and to my surprise she let the Bird Boy put some in her mouth. Then more, and more.

'Shall I get her some water?'

'I don't think they need water. They need little animals, their bones, their fur, their gristle. Helps them no end, but when they're this weak we have to help them.'

I nodded. We sat down against the church wall, the great open expanse of white sky above us, the silence around us, damp ground underneath.

'Isn't she beautiful,' he said, and one hand gently stroked the caramel and gold-brown feathers.

I stole a glance at the Bird Boy. In the fresh, damp air, away from the house, I could see him properly. I liked his low, amused voice, gruff with misuse. How awkward he looked, his thin shoulders hunched around his ears, his thin face not quite formed yet, half boy, half adult, his dark eyes that flashed with amusement and feeling. I didn't know any boys, and he was older than me, I was certain, but I didn't feel shy. We sat quietly, as Stella tore the dead mouse to bits, pecking away at it, gobbling limbs and hunks of flesh, and it was strangely restful, rather like bringing order to one of the rooms in the house.

'Where do you catch mice, then?'

'All over. Mrs Boundy's cat died, so it's been easier since they've come back into the post office. And there's always mice in the churchyard. Barn owls go for churches, you see. They like all that death. They're like ghosts – they make no sound; they move at night – then a flash of white and bam, they land on you and you're toast. If you're a vole, that is. I say, she likes you, doesn't she. She's very still.'

I had wanted a pet all my life, something to take care of, nourish, hold. I thought of the time I brought back the kittens, and Vic and I named them: Peter Pan and Wendy, because we'd been taken to see the film by Mr Green. I blinked, pushing the memory away.

'I saw her before,' I said. 'I was walking through the grounds, the day after we arrived, and she fell out of the sky, exactly like today. I hope she's all right.'

'The fox caught her and she escaped, I expect, but she's weak. He got her father back in the spring. Tore half his wing off, had a go at his body. He limped on for a few more days and I hoped he might . . . but no.'

'Oh, that's awful. What happened?'

'I – I had to kill him,' he said with an agonised expression on his long, pale face. 'I broke his neck. Dr Brooke showed me how.'

'I hate foxes,' I said, because I did, with a passion, even though my surname was Fox and to loathe them as strongly as I did seemed like a betrayal in some way of the father I'd never known. I wanted so much to like them but I couldn't. There was something reptilian about them, the blank green eyes, long face: I'd never encountered a fox before I came to Fane. I had seen them creeping up to the stables, stealthy but bold, looking around and there was, to me, something evil about the way they did it that gave me nightmares.

'I don't like them either,' he said seriously, biting the skin around his fingers. 'Lots of things about the countryside I'm not sure about, if I'm perfectly honest.'

'A lot of dark.'

'A lot of sounds after dark.'

'No one's very friendly.'

'No. You can get on a bus in London and go anywhere.'

'Yes, exactly,' I said. London, for me, was freedom, a place where I could vanish and become myself and I longed to be back there more with every passing day. 'I'm going to live there again one day.'

'Me too,' said the Bird Boy.

Stella made a perfectly disgusting sound on my lap and we both flinched and then laughed. 'So you live with Mrs Boundy?' I said.

'Yes,' he said, rather flatly. 'She's been awfully good to me.'

'And how old are you?'

'I'm seventeen. I left the Petworth school last year.'

'Oh why?'

'I didn't like it. Some jolly unpleasant chaps there. Besides,' he said quickly, and I knew he didn't want me to ask any more about it, 'I can help Mrs Boundy. I deliver telegrams and things on my bike for her, although often it's to give terrible news and that's rather hard. I've done my school cert. Dr Brooke's been ever so kind, giving me extra lessons.' He shifted himself on the ground. 'Are you all right? It's rather damp here.'

'I'm fine, thanks. You're studying with Dr Brooke, then?'

'He thinks I could go to Cambridge if I study properly. He's making enquiries. Do you know him?'

'I don't really know anyone.' He laughed. 'No, honestly,' I said, anxious he should understand. 'You're the only other person I've spoken to apart from my family and Mrs Boyes and Mrs Boundy. And we're off to boarding school in a few weeks.'

'Do you mind me asking something?' I shrugged assent. 'Why did you come here?'

'What have you heard?' I said sharply. 'If you're interested enough to ask, you must have heard some theories about it.'

'Well.' He looked down, his face reddening. 'Mrs Boundy says it's because your mother wants to get rid of the old man.'

'She's probably right,' I said, trying to sound nonchalant. I looked down at Stella, on the grass, pecking at the final piece of meat.

'Sorry,' he said, rubbing his face. 'That was terribly rude of me. I really don't know the ins and outs, Victoria. I do apologise.'

'My name's Sarah,' I said, mortified. 'Victoria is my older sister.'

'Oh hell.' He rubbed his face again. 'Sorry again. I haven't heard much that's good about Lord Ashley. Or – dash it, I'm sorry. Or your mother. I wondered. If you were all right. If everything's all right for you . . . there.'

'Oh.' His concern was overwhelming, as if he'd slapped me in the face. I could feel heat, building up behind my eyes, my head aching, like when someone touches a raw nerve, or presses on a twisted ankle. I shrank back, wondering how to get away. 'Uncle Clive is a dear man. It's wonderful to be here again.' I stood up, scrambling to my feet, holding my skirt with the owl in it rather awkwardly.

'I'm awfully sorry again.'

I shrugged. 'I have to go now.'

'You're taking her with you?'

'You said yourself, she's starving, and she might be fighting with her siblings. I'll find her somewhere in the stables. They had barn owls there, my great-uncle told me.'

'Don't get too attached,' he said, his face still stained red. 'You have to train her to leave you. Let her comb herself, one of her talons has a serrated comb on it.'

'I know that,' I said. He was rather a know-it-all. I wanted him to understand *I* knew what was best for her.

'Oh good!' He didn't seem quashed. 'Take her out at night to see the stars. Let her fly, but remember she has to be free to go, eventually.'

'I'll go to the stables and see. Thanks for your help.' We shook hands. 'Goodbye.' Then I turned round and walked away.

'Good luck,' I heard him call after me.

You have to train her to leave you. I heard his voice all the way back to the house, his kindness, like a shadow, following me. It made me uneasy.

It was warm in the barn, and quiet. The scent of old, dry, grassy hay permeated, and I liked it. Uncle Clive was right – up on the wall, at the other end of the long stable block, was a box, for barn owls, I assumed. I started moving hay out of the way, so I could climb up and put her in.

But the owl did not move when I held her, carefully showing her her new surroundings. She dug her talons into my hand, and it hurt, but she kept her eyes firmly shut, making that strange snoring sound, *whoosh*, *whoosh*, like waves crashing onto a shingled beach.

'She'll be fine,' said a voice behind me, briskly, and I nearly fell off the stool I was on. It was my great-uncle in his long, waxed coat, standing behind me, like a scarecrow. 'We've had barn owls nesting in that box for years. Centuries. Pop her out. Don't coddle her. They're awfully lazy, Sarah. Come on, do it.'

I thought of her all alone in here. She hopped along on my arm, her sharp talons digging through my jumper, eyes closed, then opened them and looked around, at Clive, and then me.

Her eyes were gleaming in the gloom of the barn. I didn't feel I could go. I don't know why, but that moment of connection we had shared, the morning after I'd arrived at Fane, still resonated with me. I thought I understood her. Her talons pierced my forearm.

I said slowly, 'I thought I'd take her up to my room.'

'Idiot child,' said Clive shortly, with a hateful laugh, and I felt tears prick my eyes. 'Where will she sleep in your room, on a little silk pillow?'

'Th-there's a shelf, up high, next to the window. I can put a box on it.' I'd found a small wooden crate tidying up the Star Study. 'She can fly in and out of the window there. We sleep with the window open.'

'She's not a pet.' I didn't understand why he was so angry.

'She's not well. And the fox is round here every night,' I said. 'You know he is. I can hear him. And smell him.'

'It's a vixen,' he said. 'She's looking for food.'

I saw my opening, and pressed home the point. 'You said barn owls are pretty lazy. If you leave her there, she'll either fall off again, or she'll hop down onto the ground to pick something up and the fox will get her either way. I'm taking her,' I said now with a firmness I did not feel, and I hopped off the stool, brushing past Clive. I realised, with a surge of something approaching hope, that I didn't care what he thought. 'We can keep an eye on her.' I felt almost cheerful. Vic won't mind.'

Vic *did* mind, a lot, and said so, frequently. Unspoken between us was the understanding that we would always try to find agreement, aware we had to stick together. But this time I didn't care.

'His claws are so sharp. I hate the way they scrape along everything,' she said again when we lay in bed, several days after Stella had begun lodging with us. 'I don't like him, Sarah.'

'Her,' I corrected. 'And they're talons, not claws. They have to be sharp. She has one specially serrated talon like a comb, to groom her feathers, keep them clean and fluffy. Isn't that jolly incredible.' I don't know why I didn't want to tell her about the Bird Boy, but I didn't.

Vic put her horsey storybook down, and turned over in the narrow, creaking bed, pulling the blanket over her head. Her voice was muffled. 'He sits there and watches us.'

'She, Vic. She has spots on her chest. Males don't. She's

young, look. We think only about four months old. They hatch in April.'

'Stop pretending you *know* things,' said Vic in a sneering tone. 'It's awful, how you suck up to Uncle Clive. "I'm fascinated by birds."' She looked up at me, her thin face intense with some emotion I couldn't read. 'They hate that at school, you know. Girls who swank and sneak to the teachers.'

'I'm not doing any of that.' I hugged my knees. Arguing with Vic made my tummy hurt. 'I want to look after her. She's already much more confident than she was. She flies out for hours. She comes when I ring a bell and I give her a mouse.'

'You'll be giving her a name next. Something you think is terribly romantic like Zuleika or Allegra.'

'Oh, go and boil your head,' I said, crossly.

'You want to save her. And you can't. We're going to school. They won't change their minds about *that*.'

Vic did not like Stella, because she was not the sensible outside she liked, which was about mucking out horses and carefully pressing wildflowers into a book, but wild, strange outside, the ghostly screech of owls, the howl of dying animals, the ivy shooting up the side of Fane and getting into the cracks, the full moon veiled in wisps of cloud casting liquid silvery light that spoke of other worlds, of night becoming day, of magic in the world.

'Those boarding-school books you read are giving you silly ideas, Vic. The school sounds dreadful. You know it does. The prospectus was full of spelling mistakes. Remember what Hannah Rose Wilde said about it.'

Hannah Rose Wilde was the kind girl who had been at Minas House, our old school, who used to bring me an apple. Her cousin Celia had gone to Haresfield for a term. When we had told her we were leaving, and moving to Haresfield, she had slapped her hands to her cheeks. 'Oh gosh, girls,' she had said gravely. 'Do you have to go there? My Aunt Joan said it was the kind of place you'd only send a girl you *really* didn't like.'

'Oh, that's so like you, Sarah! What utter rot.' Vic sat up in bed, her thin face glowering at me. 'Hannah Rose Wilde doesn't know what she's talking about. She's a liar, always has been.'

'She's the last person on earth to lie,' I said hotly. 'You know she is.'

'I hate her! She was an idiot! She had . . .' Vic cast around, wildly. 'She had common parents!'

I think I'd have laughed if it wasn't so serious. 'You sound ridiculous. In fact, you sound like Iris.'

There was a silence.

Vic peered out of the window into the gathering darkness. 'I need to be up first thing to muck out otherwise I'm not allowed to ride the horses,' she said eventually in a small, tight voice. 'And I can't sleep with *her* staring down at me, those awful clattering claws like the devil . . . Flying in, flying out . . .' She shuddered. 'Scratching, clawing . . .'

'She just wants food. She's not interested in you, I promise. She's not interested in me, either.'

'What about when we go to school? Who'll look after her? What if Iris finds out?'

'Iris wouldn't care. She wouldn't hurt her.'

Vic took a deep breath. 'The kittens, Sarah,' she said.

I didn't reply. My eyes hurt, and I shook my head. 'You promised.'

'I didn't say anything about them. I just want to remind you of what she does.'

'Shut up, Vic.'

I rubbed my eyes, trying to stop myself from remembering.

There had been two kittens, a gift from our milkman, whose cat had had a litter of eight; he was desperate to get rid of them. I called mine Wendy. Vic called hers Peter Pan. Wendy was black with white paws. Peter Pan was grey-brown with white paws and cheeky blue eyes.

Iris had drowned them in a bucket out on the balcony, whilst we jammed our fingers in our ears to block out the noises. 'We don't have enough money to feed ourselves, let alone two cats,' was all she said afterwards as she wrapped their soft, still little bodies in newspaper.

I blinked, and shook my head. 'Don't, Vic. Please don't.'

'No,' Vic said. 'Sorry. Sorry, Sarah.'

And she reached across and took my hand, and we clutched at each other for a few seconds.

Then she said, softly, 'All right. But just for a bit.'

'Oh, Vic. Thank you.' I pursed up my mouth, to stop myself crying. 'I actually thought about calling her Stella. What do you you think?'

'Stella.'

'It means star.'

'I know that – I'm not stupid.' She leaned forward and shut the curtain, leaving a small gap for Stella. I looked at Stella's snowy, flat, heart-shaped face, cocked on one side, watching us both from the shelf.

We were silent, the three of us, and when I finally turned away and switched off the light, it was only after a few minutes I heard Stella's wings beating, fluttering, and knew that she had gone hunting.

Adrenalin pumped through me. I hated remembering about the kittens. My throat felt thick with emotion. I knelt up and opened the curtains, inserting myself between them and the window. Out in the wide, vast open of the parkland, an odd light rippled over everything. The late summer grasses swayed in the night air.

I could hear her calling out in the night, a light, insistent screech.

I looked up, away from the stench, the crumbling walls – another chunk had fallen out of the kitchen wing only the day before. I spread the curtain around me to block out the light from the bedroom, and saw the stars. I held my breath. I was utterly still, as if turned to stone, for a minute.

There was no moon, yet the whole sky was alight. In London, the smog and the buildings made it hard to see anything beyond the moon. Here, everything was clear, so clear the stars lit up the countryside.

As my eyes grew accustomed to the dark, I started to see more, and more. Stars that twinkled and glittered, ones that remained steady. Some red, some so distant, some gathered together in tiny blobby pinpricks of light. And, below it all, the black of the woods, and the sound of the owls calling.

When I drew the curtain and came back into the room, as if I were Peter Pan, returning from an adventure outside, Vic was already fast asleep, curled into a ball, childlike, earthbound. I could still hear Stella calling me. The particular long, thin wail that was hers and hers alone.

Come. Come outside.

The house was dying, perhaps it was dead already. Just as after our first night here when I had run out into the summer dawn, unable to stay in the house, I saw I had to find a way to escape. To reject what I had been told. I often think it was my ancestors, telling me to look up. To start to see the truth. But this time it stuck.

Chapter Nine

I slipped my bare feet into my brogues, pulled a jumper over my nightgown, and crept downstairs, through the silent house, listening for sounds. A creaking, like a branch in the wind. Something rustling, like crumpled paper. I made my way through the dark hall, hugging myself. It was cold and I was scared. Outside, having carefully opened the great entrance door, I looked up. In the distance, I could hear a wireless radio at the other end of the house, and a light, burning in the window. I could just about hear my mother, talking to herself, her voice rising and falling.

My shoes squeaked on the dewy grass. Stella circled as I crossed the parkland, walking towards the Burnt Oak. I felt like King Arthur, or a Roman emperor with eagles flying overhead. I was invincible. I was the girl who walked out at night to look at the stars. The further I advanced into the darkness, the clearer they became.

When I reached the Burnt Oak, I looked up. Beside it was the black stump of the original oak tree that Rodderick Fane had climbed, many years ago. I stepped back, wondering if there was a particular way up. The oak was in the centre of the landscaped parkland. The house was the only building visible. There was no other light besides the faint lamp from my mother's room, and that was two hundred or so yards away now.

And then suddenly, I was not brave any more. I was twelve, and alone, and terrified. The dark covered me, the sky swamping me: I felt despair like a wing, swooping across me, and all of a sudden I could not move. It was as if I was possessed by something, fear, pouring itself into me. I could feel my legs starting to shake.

'Stella?' I called softly. 'Stella, can you hear me?'

I heard something, rustling above, and then I was really scared. I suppose I had always known I was alone, really. I knew

Vic could not help me. I had no father – I didn't even know what he'd looked like, since the one photo of him we had in Pelham Mansions, in a round silver frame the size of a bottletop, was so small he could have been anyone. I couldn't remember what his parents, our grandparents, who had figured very briefly in our early lives before my mother drove them away, looked like. I had, to all intents and purposes, no other family than Vic.

It is strange to realise that you are alone. That if you vanished, no one would care. That you are invisible. I saw then that if I died my mother would not care. My schoolmates from Minas House might be a little sad, but not for more than a morning. There was no one else. Vic would be the most affected. But the way it was going with us was that we'd each started to behave as though to survive we had to grow apart from each other.

I thought about Elizabeth's mother, the one who had picked her up from the party that day, how Elizabeth had held her arms out to her, how she'd known she was loved. I thought about Mrs Boundy, how she patted the Bird Boy's arm sometimes, even though he was not her son, just so he felt love, so she could remember the sensation of soothing her own child. I thought of the mothers in Hyde Park, how Vic and I would stare at them hungrily, watching them comforting their babies, holding on to staggering little toddler hands as they walked. One summer we'd both gazed, transfixed, at a mother lying on the grass with a small baby on her chest, the two of them gurgling and laughing. Had I cried as a child? Who had hugged me, other than Vic? My earliest memory was the distempered back bedroom at Pelham Mansions, standing up in my cot after a nightmare, and Vic coming in with her fingers pressed to her mouth, censorious, bossy, motherly.

I don't know why I started crying then. Why was it in that particular moment that it all seemed too much? I covered my face with my hands; the future felt brutal and terrifying. I didn't want to go to school. I desperately wanted to get away from here. Stella was the only one who cared, and soon I would leave her: I knew that she was already preparing to leave me. I have felt low, sometimes, but never as low as that moment on that night.

Then I heard the noise again. Scratching, rustling, louder

than before. I froze. Someone was speaking: a small, certain voice, above me.

'*The full moon occurs on August fourteenth, eleven hours and three minutes, and the new moon on August twenty-eighth.*'

I called out, almost angrily: 'Hey. I say, who's that?'

'Hello, Sarah.' Something moved in the darkness above me, and I jumped. 'It's only me – don't worry. Please don't cry. Listen. *The Perseid meteor showers attain a maximum about August tenth, but bright moonlight will interfere with their observation. Venus is in conjunction with the moon . . .*'

It was the Bird Boy. I knew his voice. I couldn't see his face.

'You.' I took a step closer. 'What's that you're reading?'

'Oh, it's a magazine. Mrs Boundy gets it for me. It's called *Nature*. It's awfully good. Funny, though, last month my copy of *Nature* got mixed up with Mrs Woodsome's *Good Housekeeping* – they both had turquoise covers.' I put my hand on the bottom of the Burnt Oak, to steady myself. 'Are you all right, Sarah?'

'I'm – oh, yes.'

'I say, would you like to come up? I've got some food. There's a rope ladder.'

'A what?'

'I'm sorry. I put it up here myself last year. I throw it over the top every time. Your uncle doesn't seem to notice. He never comes this way. I come here when I need to be alone. To remember. It's a good spot for that. Here.' There was a shuffling sound, and something fell to the ground, scuffing my shoulder. 'Let me know if you need a hand.'

I clambered up the rope ladder onto the Burnt Oak, and the Bird Boy hauled me over the edge. His hands were warm, and his eyes shone in the darkness. 'How can you read in this dark?' I said.

He pointed to a hurricane lamp, on the edge of the viewing platform, and turned the dial so the flame burnt brighter. 'Mrs Boundy gave it to me for my birthday. Wasn't that kind of her? Well, Sarah Fox,' he said, as I sat down next to him, crossing my legs. 'It's very nice to have you up here.'

'Thank you,' I said, gazing out at the stars. 'It's lovely to be here.'

To go from terror to safety in a couple of minutes was discombobulating. I was silent for a moment, looking around, breathing heavily.

'How's the owl?'

'Stella? She's very well, thank you.'

'How long since you started looking after her?'

'I'd say a week. I go out with her and drop mice in the park. I ring a bell and she comes flying. It's incredible. But she's started hunting, staying out all night. She flew out tonight.'

'Oh, that is good news. I say – you're shaking,' he said. 'Sarah, have you been crying?'

I rubbed my nose on my sleeve. 'A bit.'

He didn't make a fuss. He looked at me carefully.

'Here. Mrs Boundy packs me a meal when I go out stargazing,' he said. He handed me a twist of waxed paper. I opened it. It had tomatoes and bread and some hard cheese. 'Have it all,' he said. 'I've eaten enough. She grows everything and gives me too much food, that woman. She is wonderful.'

I was hungry – I was always hungry. I wolfed down the food, barely chewing it, and he went back to looking at his charts and maps, which were spread out over the rusting floor. After a while he said:

'Look. You can see Andromeda. Isn't it beautiful?'

He pointed, and very faintly, high up and over to the right, was a pinkish, disk-shaped cluster of light. 'That's it,' he said. 'It's a galaxy. It's easiest to spot in August, but I haven't seen it yet. Bit too cloudy. We're very lucky to be able to make it out, though.' He handed me a pair of binoculars. 'Look through there. Take your time. It's really something.'

I looked, and could see nothing, but as my hands stilled and my breathing calmed I started to see more. A discus-shaped swirl of white, tinged with pink. 'It's bigger than the Milky Way,' the Bird Boy said. 'There's millions of stars in it. At Jodrell Bank, near Manchester, they've built a telescope – it's twenty-seven yards wide! Can you imagine. And they've worked out a way to hear sounds from the Milky Way. Hear sounds!' I could see his smile, even in the darkness.

'Really? How do they do that?'

'Well – Never mind.' He stopped.

'I'm interested, honestly.'

'Oh!' He looked amazed, and frightfully pleased. 'Well, I don't understand it all, but they use radio waves to detect if something's in the way. Then they can work out how far off it is. Look at this tree. If I send radio waves from the house to the woods, the Burnt Oak gets in the way, see? And the sound of it getting in the way tells me what I need to know. Does that make sense?'

'Sort of.'

'Sort of is good enough. You know, at Jodrell Bank, they heard a supernova. Do you know what a supernova is?'

'A star?'

'A star that's exploded. Its core, the white hot centre, it simply . . . collapses in on itself. And that makes a sort of terrible nuclear reaction.'

'Like the atomic bomb. Goodness.'

'Yes, like that.' He hugged himself, his face long in the shadows. 'Do you know Betelgeuse?'

'Pardon me?'

'Betelgeuse. Some people call it Beetlejuice. It's a huge red star. You can't see it now – you'll see it in January. It's Orion's right shoulder. You know, Orion the hunter, with the three stars in a row that are his belt?' I shook my head. 'Well, you'll see it one day, and you'll remember. Betelgeuse. They say it's going to explode. It's getting bigger, and redder, and one day it will simply burst. Imagine that.'

'Would we see it?'

'Absolutely. We'd see it in the daytime, even. They had a piece about it in *Nature* magazine, and then I read up on it in the library. Do you know, Sarah, it *might already have exploded*. We just haven't seen it yet. It's so far away from Earth the light won't reach us for a while. Years.'

'How far away?'

He stretched out his arms, wide. His enthusiasm was totally infectious. 'So far away it might have exploded and we don't know yet! I don't know!'

We both laughed loudly, and then quietly, our voices bouncing around the open area of the park.

'You know an awful lot about it,' I said. The relief of being with someone who had things to say, who wanted to talk to you about something new, was exhilarating.

'Well . . . I have a lot of free time,' he said simply. 'And it's fascinating, isn't it? All of it. We're awfully lucky, despite everything. All these amazing facts being discovered, something new every day. Don't you think that?'

'I –' I didn't know what to say, and then I stared at him, at his smiling face. 'Maybe.'

'I think it's a wonderful time to be alive.' He rubbed his cheeks, joyfully.

'It is fascinating – you're right,' I said slowly. 'Beetlejuice, eh. A star that might already have exploded.'

We both stared up at the sky.

'When I was little, before the war, my mother used to take me stargazing. You couldn't see anything where I lived. There was too much light, and the buildings were too close together. And –' He gave a big shout of laughter. 'The one time I tried, with some binoculars she'd got me for my birthday, the lady opposite complained to my mother! Said I was a peeping Tom. I don't expect you know what that is,' he added as an afterthought.

'We had one of those,' I said sagely. 'Don't worry. He was a colonel, actually. Horrible old man. He used to watch my mother from his flat in the courtyard opposite ours.'

'Watch her?'

'Oh yes,' I said. She'd gone round, banged on his door, called him a filthy old man. Said she would have him up in court. He'd told her she was insane, that he'd have us taken away, that his friend was the chief inspector. We heard all this, crouching behind the door, including a description of what she'd seen him do. Not much of it had made sense to me at the time. But when I thought about it now it made me feel rather sick.

'Well, there's not much chance of being spied on here,' said the Bird Boy. 'I hope she feels safe.'

I had never thought of my mother as someone needing safety, or quiet, or somewhere to retreat. I didn't think of her as a human like other humans at all, in fact. And when I started to wonder about it, whether she had ever been scared, or sad, my brain hurt. *A supernova is a star that might already have exploded.*

'Is your mother here?' I said, knowing the answer, but I wanted to change the subject, to move away from me, to know more about him, this boy who wasn't really a boy, but not yet a man. I edged closer to him, though it wasn't that cold.

'Oh, well, no,' said the Bird Boy, rubbing his hair. 'She died in 1945. The war was nearly over. If she'd been out that evening, if she'd survived just a few more months, I'd have been back with her in Cable Street. I think about that, sometimes. I think about how it might have been. One moment, one night.'

'I'm sorry,' I said. 'That's absolutely awful.'

'Thank you. It is. Most people don't say anything. Or they nod. We do spend a lot of time telling ourselves we mustn't cry in this country, don't we?'

'I've never thought about it.'

'*Keep Calm and Carry On*, they kept saying to me after she died. But one side of me, he wanted to tear his clothes apart. To sob all night, run completely mad. You know, the Greeks used to say it was madness. Love, and Grief. Did you know that?'

'No,' I said, bewildered at the amount of information challenging everything I knew to be true. But the Bird Boy was right. As children growing up after the war, we were all constantly told we mustn't cry. Don't let the side down. Keep control of one's emotions. Put on a brave face.

The Bird Boy peered at me through the dark, and hugged his knees. 'Well, I don't see why I should keep calm. I felt mad. It was awful. It *is* awful.' He gave a half-bow, almost formal. 'Do you know, she gets fainter and fainter to me as a person and that's what I hate. I used to be able to recall a certain twist of her mouth, a catch in her voice. And I'd think to myself, *Oh, I'll never forget that now. I have to remember it. To preserve it.* But time goes on and on and I find myself forgetting her. I will forget her, one day. She had such beautiful brown eyes, and cheeks that were round when she smiled. And she was interested in everything!'

I could hear the smile in his voice. I put down the binoculars. 'Have you been back to London since it happened?'

'I went back the day after. I didn't know it had happened. Mrs

Boundy took me back. It was her day off and she said she'd like to see . . .' His voice cracked. 'It was the kindness, that was the worst, in a way. It was freezing, utterly wretched weather. We walked for about three miles. The Tube wasn't working. I knew where to go, even though all the buildings I knew had gone . . . I showed Mrs Boundy – only I felt guilty that it wasn't much of a day out for her, what with it being her day off – and I remember she said as we went round the corner: "I'm so glad to be able to see where you live."

'But none of it was there. Absolutely none of it. It's very strange. Just – one moment it's there and next it's air. And the violence that must have taken place for it to have vanished.' He was staring up at the sky.

'They never found her. So sometimes I wonder if she wasn't there. If she'll come back one day. If she might have forgotten the name of the village I was evacuated to. Perhaps she hurt her head, forgot who she was.'

'I know,' I said softly. I was used to bargaining with myself.

'I think sometimes she might have got lost somewhere, and she's waiting for me.' He coughed. 'By the way, I know these are all very silly things to think. I know she's dead. I know she – she died. But then I remember her apron – it was yellow-and-white checks, with frills round the edge, and she'd put it on and she'd wipe her hands on it when she held her arms out to hug me. I think about that, and her smell, and her hairclips – round, tortoiseshell – you know?' He patted his head slowly. 'I remember her hairclips.'

I didn't know how to say what I wanted to, which was:

She sounds like a lovely mother. I don't know how to say how sorry I am.

I am sad. I am sad all the time. I cannot explain it to people who don't understand, but you'd understand.

I didn't know her but I know she must have been awfully proud of you.

Slowly I lay down, looking up at the stars. We were both silent.

'I am very sorry about your mother,' I said quietly.

'Well, if this doesn't sound dreadfully rude, I'm sorry about *your* mother.'

'It doesn't sound rude,' I told him. 'Thank you.'

'What will you do next?'

'Me? I want to go to America first, though I want to see everywhere. Then I'll come back, go up to Cambridge, get my degree, and then I'll move back to London again. And I'll be a *flaneur*,' he added.

'What's that?'

'A – a man who is sort of a poet of the streets, a wanderer,' he said, somewhat vaguely. 'He walks through London, observing life. Keeping himself separate from humanity. And so forth.'

I thought this sounded very funny. 'Oh goodness. Is that a job?'

'I'm not sure! But I'll work all day and then go out in the evening.' He hugged himself. 'Doesn't it sound like fun? That's what I miss about London – eating out. Cups of tea in warm cafés. I miss Lyons. Someone should open a café on the high street. Don't you think?'

All these ideas! All this passion! He had lost everything – he had lost his home. He had no one. And here he was talking about supernovas, and ancient Greece, and birds, and cafés. He was unlike anyone I had met, in my narrow, ossified existence. I saw this as clearly as gazing at the stars and seeing them for the first time.

'Sounds extremely exciting. But I thought you said you were lonely.'

'Oh, of course. I'll work dreadfully hard and then, when it's right, I'll get married.'

'Jolly romantic of you.'

He gave a great guffaw of laughter, which, since he was on his back, turned into a cough. He sat up. 'You are funny, Sarah.'

'I'm not.'

'You are, you're just funny. You're dry.'

'I just mean love doesn't happen like that. Or – Well, I don't know,' I said, blushing. I was twelve and my experience of love came from the very rare occasions we had managed to sneak into films – the kittens were called Peter Pan and Wendy because we'd been taken by kind Mr Green to see *Peter Pan*, and both became utterly obsessed with it. The magic of it. We coveted the illustrated Disney edition a girl at school had brought in, complete with pictures from the film – I was transfixed by Tinkerbell, who I thought looked rather like our mother, and wanted to be Wendy, kind and motherly. But we had also managed to creep into *Singin' in the Rain* and it had been marvellous, watching Gene Kelly kiss Debbie Reynolds, and music made me think of love. I felt love when I heard music, very definitely.

'I mean more that what I really want is to make my *own* home.' He cleared his throat. 'Mrs Boundy is so kind, but I live in the room above the shop where she keeps the stationery, and the parcels when there's not room downstairs. I'm not her son, and I won't ever be her family. I want a house, with a roof that doesn't leak, and walls that don't crumble to dust, safe from the outside. A home to make my mother proud. And a wife I can take care of and children I can take care of, and – oh, everything.' He looked down at the platform.

'You're awfully young to be thinking along those lines,' I said.

'You're twelve, Sarah! I'm years older than you. Trust me,' he said, in what I thought was an incredibly patronising way. 'I've been thinking about all this for ever so long. Before my mother died.' Then I felt like a worm.

'Well, I know I don't want any children,' I said. 'I'm too worried I'd be like my mother.'

'Yes,' he said. 'I bet you wouldn't, though.'

'I think it would always be there. At the back of my mind, you see. And a mother ought to give everything up for her children.'

'My mother didn't. She ran a factory making clothes. Her boss said she was the one in charge. He said he'd be out of business if it wasn't for her. She made the money and she was a wonderful mother. I'd go there after school and read while I was waiting for her to finish.' His eyes shone. 'The seamstresses used to give me sweets. It was jolly nice. Anyway, she had to support us both, and she did.'

'My mother's not like that,' I said shortly.

We were silent again, knees up under our chins, hugging ourselves, and staring up at the sky. My eyes were now fully accustomed to the darkness. Galaxies, constellations, groups of stars, clusters that formed themselves into triangles and rectangles and pinpricks of light across the sky that gradually revealed themselves the more you looked, the more you understood how to look.

'What do *you* want to do, Sarah?' he said. 'What do you dream about?'

'I don't dream,' I said frankly. 'I never have dreams.'

'That's impossible.'

'It's not!' I laughed. 'I very occasionally have nightmares. That's it.'

'Everyone has dreams. Every night.'

'Well, I don't remember mine.' I could see a joined triangle of stars above me, like a daddy long-legs. 'What's that?' I pointed.

The Bird Boy sat up, moved the food out of the way and fumbled with his torch for a few minutes, looking at his map. 'Sorry . . . I still don't know half of them . . . Let me see . . . Oh!' He knelt and held up the map, slanting it so the light from the stars shone on it. 'It's Cygnus. The swan. It's rather fine, isn't it?'

'There's a beautiful cello piece about a swan. I used to play it,' I said.

'You played the cello?' He swivelled round towards me on his knees. 'How funny. It's my favourite instrument. I've always loved the cello. The sound it makes.'

'I did too. My teacher said it was the sound of longing. Isn't that lovely? Our mother used to take us to concerts at Wigmore Hall when I was very little. I don't know why always there, and always the cello, but she did. And I just knew I wanted to play it.' I gave a shuddering sigh. 'I don't really talk about it much because I don't learn any more.'

'Why don't you have . . .' He trailed off. He knew the answer. 'How did you know?'

'Know that I wanted to play it? I can't put it into words. Just that it clicked. They had a very posh lady on the Home Service once, talking about being a nun. She simply knew that's what she was supposed to do. And I know –' I stopped, and cleared my throat, and tucked my hair behind my ears, forcing myself to say this, what I believed to be true more than anything else.

'I know that's what I'm supposed to do, but it seems so ridiculous, when you consider our lives. So I try not to think about it.'

'Were you good?'

'I was,' I said, and I shrugged. 'My teacher knew I was. I found it . . . not *easy* – it's a hard instrument – but it sounds wonderful, even when you're not wonderful. It resonates inside you. You have to hold it to play it. It makes one feel – warm. Awfully silly I know, but it's rather comforting.'

'Your mother wanted you to play?'

'I don't know. Perhaps.' I shivered. 'Sometimes I – no.'

'What?'

I shifted around, and lowered my voice. Out in the wildness of the August night, I said, as softly as possible: 'Sometimes I think she was trying to show me a way out. A way to get away from her. But I think that's mad. She's not like that.'

We were both quiet for a long time.

'You should play the cello again,' the Bird Boy said. 'You light up when you're talking about it. Like an empty house, when people come back and start turning the lamps on and drawing back the curtains.'

I gave a dismissive snort, to hide what I really felt. Suddenly, to the east, a glittering line of silver fire seemed to fall from the sky. 'Look!' I shouted. 'What was that!'

'A shooting star,' he said. 'You get them in August; I can't remember the name. I read it earlier, it was in the magazine – oh, where is it? But you're supposed to wish on them.'

'You don't know very much about stars, do you?'

'No, hardly anything! Everything's there to learn, Sarah! But this map, you see.' He held it up. '*Stargazing: A Guide for Beginners*. It's fascinating. I like new facts. That's what's so exciting. That's what makes life bearable. Listen, Sarah: you have to make a wish and it'll definitely come true.'

'The idea of getting something in return for seeing that is very strange,' I said. 'I'm glad just to have seen it.'

He threw his head back and laughed again. 'Fine. Don't wish, then.'

But I did wish. I clenched my fists together and said a silent prayer in my head.

'Thank you. I'll never forget this,' I said.

He turned and smiled in that quick way he had. 'Me too. Don't you think there should be a name for people like us?' he said. 'Who look up and who dream of more, who dream of escaping? Who never lose faith, no matter how hard it becomes?'

'Stargazers,' I said. 'That's what we are.'

'There.' And he smiled at me, and in his smile was warmth, and kindness, and understanding. 'Are we friends? I hope we're friends.'

'Yes,' I said. 'We are. I think we have to be now, don't you? I say – when shall we meet up here again, then?'

He frowned. 'I'm away with Mrs Boundy for two weeks. She's taking me to –' he said it with a grimace – 'the seaside. I keep telling her I'd rather just stay here and look out for birds and take the bus into Chichester to change my library books, but she's insisting.'

I laughed, trying to hide that I felt embarrassed to have asked him to meet again. 'I've never been to the seaside, apart from a daytrip. I'm sure it'll be lovely.'

'I don't know. I'm not sure,' he said with a doubtful expression. 'I said I wanted to go to London, but she said no, London wasn't a holiday place.'

A night wind, rustling the distant trees in the woods, made me shiver. It was so huge and silent out here.

'Well, we might not meet again, then,' he said.

'No,' I said. 'But – perhaps it doesn't matter. Does that make sense?'

'Everything you say makes sense, Sarah,' he said. 'Just remember that. The one true fact I've learned being down here, losing my family, losing everything, is you're probably right about lots of things. But when you're on your own there's no one to tell you, and you get used to feeling you're alone. It makes you doubt yourself. I say don't doubt yourself. It's all rot, being grown up, isn't it.'

'Jolly well is.'

The Bird Boy had packed up the map, the waxed paper that had contained the sandwiches, the Thermos and his magazines. He stuffed them into his blazer pockets and caught the rope ladder in his hands, then climbed over the side of the platform so only his head was visible.

'Rum thing, this Burnt Oak, isn't it?' he said. 'How would you explain it to someone?'

I held out my hands. 'Honestly, I don't know how I'd explain any of it. So I don't.'

'Good tactic.' He jumped off the rope ladder. 'I'll hold it steady for you.'

'Thank you.' I scrambled to the edge of the platform, and lowered myself onto the rope. I heard another owl hooting in the distance. I looked up and I only saw the stars now, not the dark. Carefully, I lowered myself to the ground as the Bird Boy held the rope ladder steady.

'Listen,' I said, brushing the rust from the Burnt Oak off my hands and knees. 'Good luck. Thank you.' I held out my hand. We shook hands. He pressed something into my hand.

'Good luck, Sarah,' the Bird Boy said.

'Thank you,' I said. 'You understand. No one understands, but you do.' I cleared my throat. It was all I could say.

'Yes, I know,' he said, and raised his hand. And as I was blinking, pulling my jumper around me, eyes adjusting to the dark on the ground, I looked and he had gone, and the stargazing pamphlet was still in my hand.

Chapter Ten

I was up on the top floor, sorting and tidying, when I heard the car draw up. It was early September, and we were leaving the next day.

For the last week an unreal, slightly hollow sensation of impending doom hung over me. I hadn't packed – there was nothing to pack, really. We had so little bar the uniform we wore all the time already. My mother said we would wait to see what we needed. I couldn't tell her that Vic's school stories told us one had to arrive at school with the right items, ticked off a list, neatly packed into a trunk. That she was finding out how to be a normal fourteen-year-old girl from books, in the absence of any other information. I knew we would get into trouble, so did she, but what was the point in talking back? She was more unpredictable and on edge than ever – she had actually slapped my face two days ago, when I'd said I didn't have a lacrosse stick.

I'd spent the day clearing out the bedroom next to the Star Study. It was a lovely room, though the window panes were cracked, the walls were swollen with damp and the wallpaper, delicate turquoise toile de Jouy, was peeling away. I opened the windows, drew back the shutters to let the light in, and started doing what I'd done in the Star Study: stacking books, sorting items into piles – photographs, papers, broken crockery, scraps of material and odds and ends – hairbrushes with no bristles, and silk bags filled with hooks and eyes.

Some marbles rolled away and I reached under the bed to pull them out and screamed as my hand closed over something bristly, yet soft.

I drew it out slowly, half turning away from it as I did. It was a dead ginger cat, mummified, stiff, its blue eyes open.

My throat constricted. I didn't know how it had got there, or why. Had it come from one of the glass cases downstairs, a beloved pet preserved forever, taken out of the case for a joke? Or had one of the soldiers frightened it or had it frozen to death? Its fur was flecked with white, and it reminded me of a book about a cathedral cat that we'd had at my old school. I wondered how many mice it had caught when it was alive.

For a few moments, our eyes met, and then, not really knowing what to do, I covered it with a length of folded silk damask I'd found by the window, and slid it back under the bed again. As I stood up, I heard the sound of a vehicle and I knew who it would be.

I peered out of the window, chewing a piece of grass I'd collected that morning whilst out with Stella, and watched as the small black car wound its way along the driveway. It's fair to say that I rather fancied myself then as something of a latter-day female Gabriel Oak after only seven weeks living away from London. Since the night with the Bird Boy I wore an old shirt and trousers embroided with my grandfather's name on them which I'd found in a trunk of school clothes. I had the Bird Boy's map with me and would sit out on the Burnt Oak platform, listening to Stella, and watching the stars. I could now identify the Pleiades, the Plough, Lyra and Sirius and several planets: Jupiter and Mars were easy to spot now. But most of the time I just lay there, looking up, thinking. I would return to our room in the middle of the night, creeping in silently – I learned to walk quietly in those dog days of summer. At some point, Stella would return too: if I was lucky, and happened to be looking out of the window, I'd see her approach, like a golden-white shooting star pelting through the night, utterly silent, until she landed on the window casement with a loud thud, talons curling round the rotting wood, bringing with her a rush of fresh, sweet air into the decaying stench of the house.

Stella made things better. It wasn't just that she was another creature, exotic and bewildering as anything I had ever seen. It was that she needed me, and I needed her. I had to be good for her, to hold out my arm for her to land on me – I was still collecting mice for her from Uncle Clive, although as summer went on and she grew in confidence she caught more and more small animals, stayed out longer and longer. Without her, Fane was a grim place, devoid of any joy at all: our mother almost invisible at one end of the house; Uncle Clive trapped in the other, growing thinner, wilder and smellier every time I saw him and Vic and I in the middle, growing further apart every day. Sometimes I resented the Bird Boy, for showing himself to me, giving me hope that a friend was there, and then vanishing.

There was no doubting Uncle Clive *was* getting more odd. His memory was strange, and he picked methodically at the yellow-clear skin at the side of his nails, tearing it into long strips that swelled up around the nail, one at a time. He didn't wash. His hair, which was white, grew more and more yellow. By September, I don't think he'd seen anyone but me for several weeks.

In the mornings after Vic had vanished to go riding, I'd often reluctantly take myself off to the kitchen of the East Wing, listening to him rave about changes to society since the war, how hard he had worked for the estate and how everyone had deserted him. He was increasingly unpredictable: one day he threatened me with a poker when I went round with Stella to see if he had any spare mice. I have not described how often he made me cry with cruel words, brusque, angry dismissals, yet I kept trying. I suppose I thought something might come of it.

He had called his solicitor down from London, he'd told me two days ago. 'He'll see what's going on. Old Murbles. He'll see me right, Sally. After all I've done for this damned place. He knows what she's up to.'

As the small, black car drew up to the portico, I shrank away from the window, but kept myself close so I could see. A short, neat-looking man climbed out and looked around him as if not sure whether anyone was waiting to greet him or not. I could see him glancing up and down, taking in the state of the house before fixing his trilby on his head and ringing the bell.

I didn't want to answer the door. I crept along the top corridor to the stairwell, staying out of sight, and peered down into the hallway. Footsteps sounded and my mother appeared with a bright silk headscarf tied over her shining hair and one of the ancient, broken ostrich feather dusters in her hands, as though she had been cleaning the windows. She threw her hands up in surprise as she opened the door and let the stranger in, ushering him into the hall.

'I'm so sorry! I didn't know we had guests today. I should have – oh forgive me. Please excuse me. I'm Iris Fane – Lord Ashley's niece, you know. You're George Murbles, aren't you? I remember your father.' She wiped a dirt mark off her cheek, one slim finger denting her apple cheek. Then, slowly, she pulled off her cleaning gloves and shook his hand, smiling and saying: 'Your colleague visited me last year in London. Thank you for coming to see us now yourself. Such a pleasure.'

'The pleasure is all mine, Lady Iris,' Mr Murbles replied courteously. From my vantage point behind the balustrades on the first floor, I watched as he bent over, kissed her hand. For a split second, her eyes glinted with a steely gaze as she stared down at his balding pate. He stood up, and she smiled at him again.

'You've come at the behest of my uncle, I assume?' She looked away, running her hand over a collection of the glass cases stuffed with little birds, robins and wrens and linnets, that huddled together in the corner of the hall. 'I'm not sure where he is – I'm so sorry. Won't you come this way?'

'In fact, I should be glad of a word with you before I see Lord Ashley, Lady Iris. He has made some extremely wild accusations, Lady Iris.' Mr Murbles cleared his throat, delicately. 'Forgive me, before we go any further. You called yourself Iris Fane – have you given up your married name? I understood your surname to be Fox, that of Major Henry Fox, your late husband.'

Henry Fox, my father, the invisible man.

'Oh, yes,' said my mother, not missing a beat. 'I reverted to Fane when we moved back here. The girls will keep Fox, if they want.'

Mr Murbles said after a few more moments' heavy silence. 'I see. This will have to be noted, you must understand.' She nodded gravely. 'Now, Lady Iris, I must be frank with you. In addition to a communique I received last week from Reverend Thomas about the deteriorating situation here, the earl himself has written to me laying before me accusations of a most serious nature – I have come here to get to the bottom of it. Will you permit me to ask you about it?'

My mother tugged the scarf off her head, shaking it so her hair fell out like shining spun gold. Eventually, she said: 'Oh, I – I can't.'

'Can't what?'

'Mr Murbles – you must understand.' She dragged her eyes up so they met his. 'I don't want to upset him. He – Well, I won't say any more. Sometimes I'm afraid of what he'll do. You must talk to him, not me.'

Mr Murbles pursed his lips. He said shortly, but with feeling, 'My dear child, I only want to find out if his lordship is well, ascertain whether these allegations carry any weight and if you might be in any danger.'

'He doesn't mean any of it,' she said quickly. 'The war, and losing Auntie Dolly – it's all been dreadfully hard for him. I'm *sure* of it. I know he's not a *bad* person. And as for what else they say about what he has planned – well, it's poppycock.'

But Mr Murbles waved his hand impatiently. 'On to that in a minute. What do you mean, what he has planned?'

Oh, she was good.

'You didn't know. Well, it was out soon enough.'

'Out? Do you mean a fire? I hadn't heard about a fire.' The lawyer looked round, briskly. 'What damage was there?'

She gave a bleak, despairing laugh. 'Mr Murbles, it was in the West Wing a couple of weeks ago, in my room, and I had it out in a trice. A hole in the carpet, nothing more. It's him. He never comes to my end of the house, but who else could it be? It was him – I know it was.'

'Lady Iris, what do you mean?'

'He'll take the whole place down.'

'That is a grave accusation.'

'Is it?' She laughed. 'Is it? The developers have been sniffing around – you know what happened with Marple Hall, don't you? Mr Macmillan is saying 200,000 houses must be built and room has to be found for them somewhere.' I peered over, to see her expression. 'None of this is for *me*. But I want to do my *bit.* Bring the village into the twentieth century, and the house . . . The place is falling down around our ears and –' She sniffed delicately, and he nodded, eyes closed, as if unwilling to acknowledge. *It smells of human waste.* 'I didn't want to, but I thought of my darling father, and Grandfather, and I felt they'd want me to.'

'I knew your dear father very well, because of the business of the estate, Lady Iris,' said Mr Murbles, his tone softening. 'A great tragedy. For you all. I didn't know Lord Clive before . . .' and his voice trailed off. 'Your grandfather Arthur, the third earl, was an exceptional man, in great matters of state and other areas such as the expansion of the estates and their management, but his one failing, if I may, was to deny his younger son the opportunity of learning about Fane.'

He cleared his throat, rocked a little on his heels as if regretting his frankness. 'Ahem. The third earl made it his responsibility to see that *your* father was well-prepared when he assumed the title. Yet your father, when his father died, had no heir other than yourself, Lady Iris – and I do feel that if Clive – if the present Earl Ashley had had a chance to become acquainted with the workings of Fane, to know and love the estate as his brother did, he would not have gone to Canada after the war, would not have been so hard to extract – we spent years urging him to come home. But for years there was only silence . . . And of course he was quite different when he came back, you know. A terrible ordeal for him, losing his father and brother, and not being close to either of them. And since then, well, I do not think he has done the job he might have. Forgive me. I have spoken too freely, perhaps.'

I could see my mother, see her lizard-like eyes, flicking from side to side. Some of this was new information to her; I knew it.

She said slowly, 'Thank you, Mr Murbles. My discretion is assured – you may be certain of that. Poor Uncle Clive. I think the war was very hard for him . . . having to come back here, trying to live up to my father's reputation when he was a quite different person. Quite different. Come with me, won't you?'

They vanished through the Rose-Red Drawing Room, their voices more distant. 'That's the portrait of my father . . . Isn't he handsome? Do you see the likeness between us? Do be careful there – and there, Mr Murbles. Yes—'

I heard his faint cry. 'Good God! What has happened here?'

'I'm afraid it was like this when—'

'But, Lady Iris, why was I not . . .'

I could hear no more, beyond the faintest sound of rubble and furniture moving around, creaking doors and windows, and the low rumble of Mr Murbles's voice.

They were gone for ten minutes, and I sat there, leaning against the bannisters, waiting for them to come back, happy to watch at a distance. When they returned, there were two lines, joined like a V, deeply etched between Mr Murbles's brows and he was flushed, with dust on the shoulders of his suit. He cleared his throat.

'Lady Iris, I am most alarmed and astonished that damage of this kind has not been reported. May I speak frankly? How long has the roof been in this state? And the damp? The house is unsafe.'

'For ever so long. Since the war.' My mother thoughtfully tucked a stray lock of corn-coloured hair behind her ear and turned her limpid eyes on him. 'Mr Murbles, all I want is for Fane to remain in our family. To take care of it.'

'I had understood,' said Mr Murbles, watching her carefully, 'that as per the previous Lord Ashley's will, everything your father was able to leave you he did – paintings, jewellery, and so forth – but within the terms of the trust you are not permitted to remove anything from the house.'

'Well, exactly.' Her voice was harsh, too eager. 'And what bloody use is that to me?'

He didn't smile back, and I saw, for a split second, the panic and anger flash into her eyes. 'And since all this business in the press about houses being torn down – Bowood, Ashburnham – you know, I have to tell you that both the Georgian Society and the Ministry of Works are awfully persistent. They've tried to gain access to the house, and now they've both written to say we *have* to make repairs. Uncle Clive doesn't pay them any attention. He merely gets angrier and angrier when I try to talk to him. I'm awfully afraid of what he might do next.'

This was, of course, a lie; she had not spoken to him for weeks.

Mr Murbles made a tutting sound. 'My dear Lady Iris, it's a scandal what's happening at the moment. One year on from our gracious queen's coronation and we find ourselves in this situation. Most perilous, most perilous. Oh dear. Oh dear . . .'

He tutted again. I was increasingly uncomfortable in my position, but I leaned forward, and saw my mother's hands, clenched so tightly that the bony knuckles gleamed in the gloom. Mr Murbles was fussing with his fob watch, looking around the dusty black-and-white hall.

'Oh dear,' he said again, and I moved, unable to keep my cramped legs still any more, and his eyes followed, narrowing. I retreated, but it was too late, and he said rather sharply, 'Aha. What have we here?'

'Hello,' I said, standing up and leaning over the balustrade.

'You must be Susan.'

'Sarah.'

'Good afternoon,' Mr Murbles said as I walked down the stairs, rubbing my eyes.

'Are you the man from the taxidermist's?' I said, feigning ignorance.

'No, my dear!' He smiled at me. He had kind eyes. 'I'm your great-uncle's lawyer.'

'Oh.'

'I expect you're loving living here, aren't you?'

I looked over at our mother then back at him and at my feet. Mr Murbles raised his eyebrows, and glanced at her, and I saw her pupils dilate, the tiniest flicker of fear.

'I'm afraid I've rather neglected the girls since we arrived – I've been so awfully busy. But they've been marvellous, exploring the place – it's paradise for children. Isn't it, Sarah?'

'Oh, I'm absolutely loving it here, Mr Murbles,' I said enthusiastically. 'Mummy's done so much to make it welcoming for us. I'm terrifically excited about school, though, too.'

'Ah. Of course!' Mr Murbles was delighted at all this, and nodded, his whiskers waggling. But then his expression changed: 'Lady Iris – I must attend to your uncle.'

'I've said too much, Mr Murbles. Go and see him. Listen to what he says. I'm only trying to make sure Fane is here in the future. For my girls. You understand. He can be a rather stubborn old so-and-so, can't he?' She blinked heavily and fixed her eyes on him, pools of blue framed with the white lashes in her glowing, heart-shaped face.

'He's fortunate to have you here, Lady Iris. We will talk again, I am certain.'

'I'd much rather we didn't, Mr Murbles,' she said. 'Please *don't* mention you discussed it with me. I beg of you. For my own peace of mind, shall we say. It's remote here, and I'm very silly I know, but I'm often rather frightened. Thank you.' She squeezed his tweed-clad forearm, and nodded, then walked away, back to the things that kept her busy all day, that she never let us see.

Mr Murbles gave me a short, non-committal grunt, and a smile. 'May I show you the way?' I asked politely.

'Don't worry, my dear. I know it. Thank you very much.'

He made his way carefully across the cracked tiles, opening the door onto the East Wing. I could hear his tut-tutting as he picked his way down the long, cluttered corridor. He would have to step over broken floorboards and past cracked windows and rotten doors.

He had been here in the glory days when my mother was a child. I wondered about Fane then, the one I'd seen in photographs up in the Star Study of the glorious Edwardian era. Lavish parties, cars and carriages queuing up the drive, my great-grandparents hosts, my grandfather – Iris's father – the true host, leading the games, dressed in fancy dress, tea on the lawn, parasols, lace dresses and servants at a distance. The house was always immaculate in these pictures, opulent and gleaming, everything just so, from the pictures on the walls to the shining brocade curtains, the flowers on every surface.

I stood watching him then crept upstairs. After a few moments I heard her shoes on the chequered floor. She had come back to make sure Mr Murbles had gone.

'Sarah,' she said very softly, but I was so still she could not hear me.

'Sarah,' she called again. I held my breath.

Sometimes, I felt she was like the owl, could see and hear everything. She stood for a moment in the centre of the hall, silent, then she sniffed, and gave a little laugh, tapping and scraping her feet along the ground. Then she scratched her neck, looking up to the cupola where the light got in, raking long thin red lines down her throat with her sharp nails.

I thought about the dead cat upstairs, pushed out of sight under the bed. Was it real? My mother did not seem human to me any more, scratching at herself, scraping her shoes along the floor, muttering to herself. A door slammed at the other end of the house, voices were raised – I could hear Uncle Clive's voice, louder and louder, in waves. Iris looked up, and laughed, and then walked away, towards her wing. 'Soon,' I heard her say. 'It must be soon.'

As soon as she'd gone, I heard someone crying. I peered through the window above the front door and saw my sister, creeping up the steps, stopping under the portico, leaving a trail of mud and straw behind her. Swiftly I ran downstairs again and opened the front door.

Vic was standing there, sobbing and stuttering quietly. Her face, her shirt, the ancient jodhpurs, were covered in inky-brown swill. Her beloved copy of *Jill's Gymkhana*, which she had bought for her birthday two years ago and was nearly always wedged under her arm, was covered in the stuff. She smelt, even by the standards of the house, awful.

'Vic? What happened?'

A wave of bitter ammonia aroma hit me. I clutched her arm to take her up to our bedroom where we could speak.

'They were waiting for me at the gates when I came by on Lucky,' she said, her small face white under the slurry marks. I shut the great door behind her. 'They threw it at me, from a bucket. Lucky got covered in it. They shouted all these things. About Mother. About Uncle Clive. They said she was a witch. They said he was . . . a something about a pedagogue. Or *something.* That we shouldn't be here. They told us to get out. Go home.'

'Who's "they"?' I said, folding my arms. I wanted to give her a hug, but I also didn't.

'Some children. From the village.'

'Did you know them?'

She said, 'That awful Bobbie Thomas. And – the others. They – they were laughing.'

'Oh gosh. Vic.'

'That strange boy from London, that Bird Boy – he tried to help, but they pushed him over too.' Tears rolled through the dirt on her face. 'I thought – they liked me.'

'The Bird Boy is back?' I said, eagerly.

'Why do you care?' she said suspiciously.

'Oh – I met him one evening. He's all right,' I said.

She stared at me, her face overcome with anger.

'He's not all right. Bobbie says so. He's the lowest of the low. He peers in on them when they're eating. He is queer. And different. He ought to leave, go back home.'

'Oh goodness, Vic,' I said with irritation. 'What rubbish. They're awful, the Thomases. Just awful. They're the vicar's children – they can't just go around throwing horse whatever it is at you, and making these dreadful accusations about people. He's a nice boy. I've spoken to him. He's lost his mother. He's lost everything. We're friends, anyway.'

'He grew up in a *slum*, Sarah. And he's wrapped Mrs Boundy round his little finger – it's disgusting. The vicar says she's given him money, all of that. He's played a confidence trick on you, on her, on Dr Brooke, and now he's taken off, gone to London, all paid for by Dr Brooke. Don't be so naive.'

I took a step back, as if I'd been winded. 'You're just making all this up. You're upset because the awful Thomases have turned on you. They're horrible, Vic. Forget about them.'

'You don't get it, do you?' Vic said, shrugging her shoulders. 'There's no one to help us, Sarah. No one.'

We were standing outside our bedroom. I kicked open the door.

'The Bird Boy tried to help you.'

'Gosh, Sarah, you're frightfully dim. Only because he's got no friends, either. They kicked him and called him a filthy name.' She wiped her face on her sleeve. Underneath the mud, she was bone-pale. Several weeks of roaming outside had turned my skin a light caramel, popping moles and freckles on my skin. Vic was either under her velvet helmet, riding, or in bed, reading. I noticed now she was crying softly.

'We leave tomorrow, Vic,' I said, trying to cheer her up, to remind her that her uniform was packed, neatly folded, her pyjamas and toys placed neatly on top of them under the narrow rusting bedstead, ready for her departure. 'I know it's been jolly odd, but we can be different there. It doesn't have to be like this. We should stick together.'

'It will always be like this,' she said, and I never forgot the way she said it, as if that was how it was.

I watched Vic as she washed herself with ice-cold water from the sink – there was no hot water up there, and the bath had always been blocked. We didn't seem to have anything else to say to each other. Afterwards we both lay on our narrow beds, staring up at the peeling paint on the ceiling. It wasn't yet lunchtime, but there was no point in doing anything else now, nothing at all. After a while I heard Mr Murbles's car starting up and juddering away, down the long drive fringed with grasses bleached white by the late summer sun.

Tomorrow, that would be us, leaving Fane behind to go to school. I stared up at the box on the shelf where Stella was sleeping, waiting for night-time, until she could fly out and be free. Below us, the clock ticked in the hall, slowly, it seemed, counting down the time.

Iris

1924

They arrive when no one expects them.

It is the end of summer, and the hall and grounds are quiet, slumbering in the heat. Bees work busily at the honeysuckle that smothers the old gold stone wall leading to the stables. She is sitting on a terrace next to the ornamental pond beside the East Wing, pushing a wooden toy boat. It is cool here, the monumental bulk of the house casting a wide shadow. Her satchel is slung across her body. It contains binoculars in their own hard case, which belonged to her father, a portable telescope, a compass, a lined notebook and pencil, a sheaf of the letters Daddy wrote to Mother about the management of the estate, a hunk of bread and some cheese, and one of the first peaches. She eats a peach, watching the water boatmen skit across the cold surface of the pond, out of the way of the boat. The lily pads glint in the sun, reflecting heat at her. Her shoes and stockings are neatly placed beside her and her feet are submerged in the water. She can feel slimy, silty sand and mud between her little toes.

This morning Miss Gulling talked about the tenth anniversary of the outbreak of the Great War, which is tomorrow. She tells Iris we must have peace at all costs, to avoid people like her dear father dying. Her mother gets up and leaves the room.

Iris feels sad about her father, though she barely remembers him. She is proud of him, proud to be his daughter. More than anything she likes it when she does something plucky, or rather outrageous, and people's eyes light up, and they exclaim: 'Aha, I say! Arthur's daughter to the life!'

She keeps her father's letters close by.

Tell Mama old Noyes mustn't be allowed to have his 12th August party at the house – the fellow will make a terrible mess, drink too much and wreak havoc. He's a good man but for this one weakness.

Ask Mama to dry her tears and not let them ruin her pretty face. Tell her to teach herself a new piece to play me, and ready herself for my return for I miss her and you, my little owl, very much.

Trees: I am concerned the oaks need coppicing again, as it is three years I've been away. Would you, dearest Iris, ask Fordham to visit Mama and discuss it with her.

Your mother wrote to me about the damp in the West Wing and the dry rot which she fears has taken over. Tell her not to fret, but ask her to mind and see that Noyes examines it most carefully. It was a problem many years ago, and dear Clive had a man over to address it. Donald Chalk was his name. Perhaps he has gone to war. Find out. He was an odd chap, an old drinking friend of Clive's, I believe: not altogether savoury, very like Clive and the sort dear trusting Clive gave his time and money to: my father was most angry with my brother for bringing him to Fane, but I am happy to say thanks to him it was brought under control. But it must be attacked if the house is to survive.

Letters full of lists, advice, jokes, concern: a how-to guide to running the estate, and she remembers it all, every last bit of it, and she and Mama laugh and sigh over it together, and she asks her mother to tell her about her father, how they met and fell in love quite instantly, how he gave her a diamond brooch of a bird in flight with a clasp that was part of a set, and gave her the rest on her wedding day, birds flying across the sky.

She knows all this and keeps the letters close, in case her Mama needs to see them again, in case there is something she needs to remember about the house, to keep it going. Mrs Boyes is very good, of course, but Mrs Boyes is *new*. She, Lady Iris Fane is the daughter of a man whose fathers and forefathers have lived here for over four hundred years, first as gentlemen in their manor house, then as lords in their stately home.

She hears the phuttering, roaring sound of a car and, eager for something new to do, clambers out of the pond and hurriedly puts on her stockings and shoes. It is hard; the stockings stick to her feet and she curses and wishes once again she was a proper young lady. She snatches up her satchel, and runs round the side of the house towards the front terrace. At the corner of the West Wing, she pauses, trapped between the world at the back of the house and the front. She does not move. She watches.

In the distance, a maroon car gleams in the midday sun. For the rest of her life, she will hear that engine, which purrs like an animal, punctuated with growling stops and starts, whenever she closes her eyes.

Eventually, it draws to a halt, right outside the front steps. She observes them, in the car, talking to each other. The woman waves her hands. Small, jerky movements, her mouth and eyes open wide. Iris draws back, afraid she might be seen.

After only a few seconds – but it is long enough for fear to sow seeds inside her – the doors suddenly swing outwards. From the driver seat a man emerges, long limbs, long, twitching fingers, long face, almost hidden by his tweed deerstalker.

He wiggles his fingers, flexing them as if they are stiff. He stretches himself, and waggles his jaw. He is tall, very tall. Too tall. He wears a three-piece suit in biscuit-coloured tweed. A watch chain hangs from a pocket and he keeps touching it, clutching it tightly between long, bony fingers. Iris recognises the watch chain, from the portraits in the Robert Adam panelled library. She notices things.

The woman is short, even when sitting in the car. She wears a similar jacket in tweed, beautifully fitted, with a high-necked ruffled shirt, a black brooch at her throat. On top of her soft auburn curls is a beautiful pea-green hat in plush velvet, trimmed with a feather – a dancing, fluffy, white curling feather that gives way to caramel. Iris freezes; she knows the toffee-coloured stripes and spots on the feather's tip. It is so soft she wants to reach up and run her fingers through it. The two visitors look at each other, and the man says something, his lips hardly moving. Then he moves to the other side of the car as she gets out. He says: 'No! Not like that! I hold the door for you. Or a servant. You wait, next time. You see?'

She nods, and shrugs. 'Sure.'

'Remember,' he says to her, and Iris hears the voice he uses.

Slowly, they walk up the steps together. He pulls at the heavy, clanging bell. It echoes through the empty rooms.

She knows she is not supposed to rush up to people, that Nanny will spank her if she repeats what happened when Lady Amesbury came for tea last month. She knows she must be seen and not heard, must smile and bob. She knows all this, yet something makes her dart forward as they stand there on the steps. They turn at her approach. The tall man frowns.

'Well, hello! How splendid. What have we got here? Now, I wonder if I could put a name to you – though you won't remember me, of course.'

He has a gruff, croaking voice, as though he needs to clear his throat. It disturbs her, as do the lines on his face, the way she can't quite see his eyes under his hat.

'Go on,' she says boldly.

He bends down, his long legs sticking outwards. They are looking at each other. She sees his eyes now. Grey. He does not have pale eyelashes, like her father had told her he did, the same as hers. They are short and stubby and black. 'I say I'm right, aren't I? I'm your uncle. Clive.' He holds out his hand. 'What curious eyelashes you have, my dear. Almost white.'

He smiles, and it does not reach his eyes.

We must be very kind to him, Mama has said.

He straightens himself out as the door swings open, and Mrs Boyes is standing there, a blank look on her face.

'Mrs Boyes?' he says.

'Yes,' she says, her tone flat.

'Lord Ashley. Charmed.' He lifts his hat, briefly, then gives a small bow. 'And this is my wife, Lady Ashley.'

'We have corresponded,' says Lady Ashley. She has a strange accent. It is thick, and halting. 'Thank you for all your help, Mrs Boyes.'

'It's my pleasure, Lady Ashley.' Mrs Boyes twitches her nose. 'We're most thankful you're here now. Everyone will be. This place needs someone in charge again.'

Iris stares at the man who is her uncle and this woman who is her aunt. He drops his gloves onto the plinth of the black marble statue.

'Have someone bring our bags in, would you?'

'Yes, sir – can I fetch you some refreshment? Some tea, in the library, or the Rose-Red Drawing Room?'

Iris is embarrassed at Mrs Boyes, that she doesn't know the correct way to address an earl. This is all wrong. She wants them to feel welcome.

'Oh God, these names again, after all these years.' He stands quite still, blinking brightly, and shakes himself. 'I can't quite believe I'm here. Dolly, can you believe it?'

'No, dearest.' She turns and gives Iris a little smile. 'It is like a fairy tale.'

'I won't take tea just yet.'

'Then, sir, would you like to inspect the house? Or meet the rest of the staff?'

'I'd like to meet my sister-in-law again.' He puts his arm round Iris, and squeezes her shoulder. 'It's been so very – ah! There she is. Charming. Jacquetta, my dear girl. How wonderful to see you again.'

Her mother stands at the top of the stairs, looking down, the halo of her wispy blond hair shimmering in the afternoon sun. She gives a gentle wave. 'Clive – my goodness. Is it really you?'

Iris's mother runs downstairs. They embrace. She clutches his upper arms with her slim fingers, almost fiercely.

Next to her, Dolly waits patiently. She smiles at Iris again.

'Ten years . . . I didn't think you'd come back, Clive.' Her mother is crying now. Mrs Boyes looks awkward. Uncle Clive looks awkward. 'I'd forgotten how tall you are. You were taller than Arthur, weren't you – Oh dear. Oh dear.' She gives a small sob. 'You are so very different, Clive – I thought you might remind me of – Oh, I'm so sorry. It's just rather a shock.'

'I am the same, as you will see.'

'Of course. You're so much older!' She gives a little laugh.

'I'm sorry once again that Canada detained me longer than I thought. I should have come back when I heard Arthur was dead. I was scared, I suppose.'

'Was there gold there?'

They turn at the sound of Iris's voice, childish and high in the echoing hall.

'No,' he says shortly. 'No gold. I looked everywhere. Everywhere.'

She looks at him, and rubs her eyes but he does not smile. He watches her.

'Dear Clive,' her mother is saying. 'I have the Blue Bedroom, you know, and by rights it is yours – I would be of course most willing to move to whatever room you think best – immediately if so!'

He misunderstands her, and says, 'We need not discuss your future as yet, Jacquetta. You and the child are both most welcome to stay here; for the moment, whilst you make your plans.'

Iris knows the idea they would *not* be welcome to stay has not once occurred to her poor mother, and to have this raised so swiftly is mortifying. Red spreads along her mother's neck, up towards her jaw. 'Oh. Thank you – I – I'll help you – whatever you need assistance with, Clive, dear. It must be awfully strange. I know how close you and Arthur were – I suppose you will want to carry on the work he did. I have all his letters, all the notes we've made—'

But he waves this away. 'You're not to worry about any of that now, my dear. Concentrate on bringing up your child. Leave the running of Fane Hall to me.' He makes as if to pray, then brings the tips of his fingers up under his chin. 'It's my house now.'

She watches her mother's expression change, very slightly. But, still, she doesn't really understand what he means. Iris thinks perhaps she will tease him about it one day, her strange, gruff uncle who doesn't fit in here. Then she thinks about teasing him about anything and shivers. She stares at him, in confusion, and with growing panic.

Over the next few days, it is even worse than she thought. Uncle Clive does not want to be their friend. Aunt Dolly does not want their help. She and her mother are moved out of their bedrooms. She does not sleep in the dear little room with the embroidered curtains of children playing, and the slippery duck eiderdowns, the colour of oysters. It is needed for Aunt Dolly's maid, who will be arriving soon, but then does not arrive. Her mother's possessions are moved up to the top floor by Mrs Boyes, quite without her mother being asked. Some are sold.

Uncle Clive orders the West Wing to be shut up – her father's wing, where they had lived. He says the dry rot has set in and it is unsafe. He has a lock and bolt put on the door to the Rose-Red Drawing Room and after that no one goes there.

He sells the Turkish diamonds that were given to the second earl. He says it is to pay for the dry rot, the damp, the blooming orange fungus and the damage done from storing the grain in the ballroom. He and Aunt Dolly take a house behind Piccadilly and decamp to London. They do not invite Iris and her mother. But she sees a photograph of him, one day, in *The Times*.

'There,' says Miss Gulling, jabbing a thick finger at the newspaper the following December as wind whistles around the house, rattling the windows, and the blasted oak on the lawn is not visible in the sleeting snow. 'That's what all the money is going on.'

'Shhh,' says Nanny Pargeter. 'Not for small ears.'

She pretends she didn't hear and carries on practising her handwriting.

How small she had grown – and how brown! And covered with PRICKLES!

Why! Mrs Tiggy-Winkle was nothing but a HEDGEHOG.

'Hello, dears!' Jacquetta, Lady Ashley, says, bustling into the room, fake gaiety in her voice. It is draped around her like a cloak these days, and as a result she cannot be trusted, because she has taken their side. She clutches a letter. Her fingers are raw, purple and swollen with chilblains, her eyes are red from crying, she is thinner than ever. Aunt Dolly, a plain dumpling of a woman, who says so little but accomplishes so much, has asked that Arthur's widow and child eat in the nursery from now on. The request is relayed via Mrs Boyes, with no emotion. ('*She's* in it with both of them, up to her neck,' she has heard Nanny say to Miss Gulling.)

'Well, it's time for a super adventure now. A *super* adventure. Uncle Clive feels it is not really a suitable place for a small child, and he's suggested we move out of Fane and start afresh. There's an old flat, belonging to Daddy's aunt, in South Kensington, and we will have a bedroom each, and room for the cello! Perhaps I'll start playing again.' She crouches down in front of Iris, her thin, kind face split into a too-large smile, and takes Iris's hands in her own. Her mother's skin is rough like sandpaper. Iris catches a whiff of the rotting tooth at the back of her mother's mouth. She recoils. She loves her mother so much it is painful. But she hates her for being weak too.

'We have a bedroom each here. This is our house,' Iris says. She doesn't understand.

'Oh, I know, but it'll be a tremendous adventure!'

'Will he give us some money?'

'It's vulgar to talk about money.' Her mother kisses her head. 'You mustn't worry about any of that, my darling. Daddy wouldn't want you fretting. Uncle Clive will see us right. Don't you worry about that at all.'

But Iris knows that he won't. She knows how it goes; she isn't stupid. She sees now that her mother is a fool, that she can't understand that they want them out. She sees what no one else does. It is very strange.

Two days after her mother has told Iris that they will be leaving Fane there is a row. She hears them, shouting. It is very unlike her mother to shout. Iris hides behind the balustrade above the great hall, looking at the black marble statues, listening to her mother sobbing.

'Stupid, stupid woman,' she hears her uncle say as he strides into the hallway. 'It's over, can't she see that?'

He glances up at the statues. And that is when she first notices it.

She sees his head, tilted on one side, the arms in his country gentleman's tweeds folded tight. She sees the way he stares at Cassandra, raising her arms to heaven. Confused, as if he doesn't know what to make of it.

'All all right, my ducks?' Aunt Dolly appears in the hall, wiping her hands on something: she is a very housewifely sort of woman, happiest when up to her arms in potato peelings, or making raspberry jam. Iris has seen her once in the kitchen with a tankard in her hand. It is so unexpected, the idea her own aunt would drink beer from a tankard, that she stares, and for her staring gets a smack around the head from her uncle, who tells her she is a sly, rude child. 'She is Countess Ashley, and you don't stare.'

Iris watches the two of them stand in silence, staring at each other in the hall. Rain is falling on the great dome, against the long windows.

'She is a stupid woman,' Uncle Clive says. 'She bleats, and whines, and I don't care. I don't care about her stories of dear Arthur and some tea party with Queen Mary. I want to say to her, when she starts up again, twisting her fingers around and pleading, I want to say, your husband died of an infection. That isn't bravery.'

'It's hard for her to accept she has to leave. But they'll be gone soon. Be patient, love.'

When Uncle Clive talks to his wife, his voice is rougher. She knows she is seeing the real him, and she hates him. 'You're not stupid, Dolly. She is stupid. And the daughter is a nasty little thing. I don't like her. She unsettles me. It's best they're gone.'

'It will take time,' Dolly says, and she shrugs. 'These things, they all take time.'

They stare at each other, no emotion, she short and round, looking up at him. He is tall, and bends down. He drops a kiss on her nose. 'You're right.'

Uncle Clive does not care for visitors. He does not have the Harvest Festival that year, where formerly the villagers were invited up to the house for cider and a feast in the giant ballroom in the East Wing. This Christmas, instead of carols with the villagers around the Christmas tree, hamper after hamper from Fortnum and Mason arrives, and he and Dolly hole themselves up in the East Wing eating duck and marrons glacé, drinking wine. Iris can hear them.

He doesn't even trouble to come and say goodbye when they leave, a few days after Christmas, to move into the hastily furnished flat in Kensington, where she will live for the next thirty years until she finally returns to Fane. Her mother stands on the platform, her shoulders slumped, staring into space, occasionally remembering where she is and fidgeting herself into action. They have to haul her mother's cello onto the train themselves as the porter does not appear. Mrs Pargeter and Miss Gulling, both summarily despatched, sobbing, take the train with them into London.

'It's not right, Lady Ashley,' Nanny keeps saying. 'This isn't right, none of it. I don't understand how it can be right.'

'If she was a boy,' says Miss Gulling grimly, 'if she'd been a boy, none of this would have happened.'

Iris watches them all turn slowly towards her. What a disappointment she is, for if she had been born male everything would have been all right. She would have saved the family, saved Fane Hall from Uncle Clive. This is not how it should have been. Because it is her house.

Part Three
1954

Chapter Eleven

December 1954

'Lorna, you stand here. Anne? Are you in? Well, you're there, then. Judy, next to Anne.'

Susan Cowper stood back on one slim leg, considering. I sat beside her, perched on Miss Trubshawe's desk. In front of me were two straight lines of girls, facing each other. They were 'the guard'.

It was ten days before Christmas. Whorls of ice lined the inside of the casement windows. Haresfield had once been a home of an earl, and it was considered a tremendous rag to say, 'Gosh, I'm frightfully hot – someone open a window! How did the nuns bear this heat!'

At first Vic and I thought we were missing some vital component of the joke, before realising that there was no joke to get. Haresfield was that sort of place – it took a few weeks before you realised the jokes weren't funny, the girls weren't clever or interesting, the staff wasn't dedicated or particularly bright. Everything was third or fourth rate.

Now Susan Cowper pointed at the tallest girl, and jerked her head to one side. 'Diana, can you budge up that way? Give Margaret and Anne some more room. I say, do hurry. Lorna, Judy? Come on, do. Where's Monica? Let's get on with it, shall we? Miss Trubshawe will be back to collect the dusters soon.'

'Susan,' Anne said, timidly, 'Judy and I have to go in a min. It's the final rehearsal for the carol concert.'

'Oh, I am so sorry,' said Susan, her hands flying to her cheeks. (Susan Cowper had been told, by one of the new queen's ladies-in-waiting, no less, that she had elegant hands. Discretion, as she often reminded us, meant she was unable to disclose where or when this encounter had taken place, but also meant she took every opportunity to display her hands thereafter, doing things like ostentatiously hugging the water jug, sliding her hands around it, before lifting it up and passing it down the table at lunch. 'It's like she's having a passionate affair with a jug,' Vic had hissed to me, and I'd laughed, and got into trouble for laughing.) '*So sorry*, Anne.' She banged a duster from the board hard down onto the teacher's desk. Clouds of purplish-grey dust flew into the air. Monica started coughing, but otherwise there was silence.

'You don't care, it would seem, that Sarah Fox threatens everything about the school and that which we hold dear? You think carols are more important. So go, Anne. And you too, Judy.'

'Susan, I don't want to. I really don't. It's only that the Old Dear said if I was late a-again I'd have to sit in front of Founder's tonight, Susan, and I can't –' Anne's eyes were huge, and she shivered in the freezing chill of the dimly lit room. The other girls said nothing; they knew what had happened the time Caroline Powell had been late for Evensong and had to spend the night in front of Founder's. The school had to call her parents when she was taken to the cottage hospital four days later with pneumonia.

Boxers, the long-established venerable boys' public school, was only a couple of miles away, a bleak windswept building high on a hill, a place designed to turn out new generations of Englishmen to replace those who'd died in wars or in the colonies. Haresfield had been founded fifty years ago, by a sister of Boxers' then-headmaster but unlike Boxers it was a school for parents who didn't want their girls developing a thirst for knowledge: heaven forbid. Of course it was important girls were educated so they could read basic instructions, write polite thank-you letters and keep up their side of a conversation without becoming tongue-tied. It was a school for those who didn't have the right connections to get their daughters into one of the really smart girls' boarding schools where one's mother had a tiara in the family vault and a chauffeur dropped one at school. Sometimes it was simply a school to get one's daughter out of the way. Many girls from colonial families came here, sight unseen in most cases, arriving back on boats from Dar-es-Salaam or Bombay to a country they'd never visited but called home, shivering into a British autumn.

It had been an unimaginably long first term. Perhaps what made it worse was the thought of nothing to look forward to: the girls who sobbed at night, freezing under the frayed blankets, had parents, pets and siblings they actually missed. But Christmas was nearly here, and school broke up in two days' time. It was the headmistress Miss Dearlove's final week at the school: it had been announced, rather abruptly, that she would be leaving at Christmas, rumour had it to have her hump operated upon. Whatever the reason, her impending departure had done nothing for her temper. When Vic and I had arrived on the first day, dripping wet from a downpour that followed us all the way from the train station to the school gate, she had at least nodded and met our eyes.

'New girls, eh? Hygiene is very important – remember that, please,' she'd mumbled mysteriously, and then rolled her shoulders up and down so that the aforementioned hump had reared up behind her, and Vic had involuntarily taken a step back in alarm.

However, over the course of our first term, Miss Dearlove had progressed from being stern and uninterested to being deranged and uninterested, her hair growing wilder, her gait more unpredictable. She walked so wildly that after the exeat weekend in November she had veered suddenly to the right and squashed one of the youngest girls against the wall, wrenching her shoulder out. I naively supposed that would be the last straw. But she was found in the dorm next to ours the following night, stroking a third-former's ankle and muttering, and I think she might have tried to pull her out of bed onto the floor had not the Loon appeared and beckoned her away.

'Miss Dearlove! Oh dear me . . . I say! Miss Dearlove! Would you like a biscuit? Miss Dearlove, move away! Move *away*!'

We had watched in the corridor, Monica Powlett and I – Monica had the bed next to mine and was the only girl who seemed even half-normal. 'Have you been to the zoo?' she said to me, in an undertone. 'I was there last Easter when one of the lions got hold of a keeper's leg and had to be lured away with a wildebeest carcass.'

'Right, go, then. Just go.' Susan Cowper waggled her fingers now at Anne and Judy, who skedaddled unhappily out of the room. I had thought that Anne was my closest friend at Haresfield, but she didn't even look at me as she left. Judy flicked me a glance, dead-eyed, mute, then turned away. The life of the acolyte was a wretched one, acting unnaturally, glancing over one's shoulder for the queen bee, living in fear that the axe will suddenly start to hover above you, as it eventually always does.

Susan put her hands on her hips, her fingertips delicately resting atop her ribcage, and tossed her hair. She glanced at the guard of honour in front of us, about ten girls. Her green eyes seemed to flash, as she said:

'Here we go then. Girls. Sarah Fox drags the name of Haresfield into the mud. She is uncouth and vulgar and shouldn't have been allowed at the school. She's not for us. Are we agreed?'

Diana stood up from the table, shoulders back, voice trembling. 'Yes, Susan. I'll stand with you.'

'And I,' said Margaret, and Lorna, and the rest of the girls. They said it passionately, as if they were defending something noble, for it was practically the law that every girl our age must still be in love with Olivier as Henry V.

'And I.'

'And I.'

'And I, Susan.'

'And I.'

'And I, Susan.'

'And I.'

'Me too.' This was from little Amanda Colston, known as 'Minnie' and a pet to everyone, being the youngest member of school. She reminded me of a ferret. Susan smiled indulgently at her.

'That's all right, Minnie. Jolly good to have you with us.'

Only one girl, at the end, was still.

'And you?' said Susan. 'Are you with us?'

'Aha,' said Monica Powlett in her soft, amused voice. She closed her eyes for a split second. 'Actually, I'm not sure I am.'

Susan flinched, very slightly, then said in mellifluous tones – another thing she had been told, this time by her brother's best friend, an ex-Boxer boy who was not only a marquis but now also at Sandhurst, was that she had a beautiful speaking voice, rather like Jean Simmons.

'You say that you are *not* with us?'

'Well, honestly, Susan. Isn't it all rather silly?' Monica folded her arms. I was used to the sound of her breathing at night. She had asthma, and no one at school seemed to take any notice. Conversely, I think she liked this lack of fuss, but I saw how she suffered with it.

Susan's voice rose slightly. 'She *cheeked* me, Monica. She said my new hat made me look like – like – Well, you heard her. Then – *then* she laughed.'

'Well, it was rather funny, wasn't it?' There was a sharp exhalation of breath. 'Your hat does look like a can of upturned Spam and with that lipstick and everything, well, I'm sorry, you did look rather ridiculous. You're twelve, Susan, not twenty. Not that I care. You seem to think I care.' Monica paused for a moment, breathing deeply, as the rest of the room gaped at her. 'I'm off now anyway. Got to sit it out for a bit. Sarah, are you coming with me?' I shook my head dumbly. 'No? Well, come and find me afterwards. Cheerio.'

I tried to give her a small sign of gratitude, but she avoided my gaze, her hand on her breastbone, her breath ragged. Just then there was a noise in the corridor and the girls swivelled round, as one. We were afraid of Miss Trubshawe, who was strict, sarcastic and spiteful.

'You must leave now, please, Monica,' said Susan calmly, as if Monica hadn't just announced she was going to leave. 'Everyone knows you put on your eczema, or whatever it is. You could breathe perfectly well if you just tried. It's because your posture is so terrible and your shoulders are hunched. Matron told my mother so. On we go. Sarah Fox. You are accused of heenious – hoonyus – terrible crimes against schoolfellows, of cruelty and derision and – and besmirching the noble name of Haresfield. What do you have to say?'

'Susan, I didn't mean to be rude about you.' I stood up. 'I was trying to make a silly joke to my sister about something to do with home. It wasn't for other people to hear.' I stood up. I knew my cheeks were red and I twisted my fingers together. I hated myself for letting it matter to me.

There was total silence as the group of girls stared down at their shoes. 'Here, Sarah. Come.' She admired her hand for a moment, as I took it, cautiously. 'Oh, Sarah. We're all so awfully *sorry* this has to happen, but the group feels – as one, you understand – that you must be Released.'

Minnie gave a small squeak, and the others inhaled. Being Released was the worst thing that could happen to you at Haresfield. I knew because I had partaken in a Releasing ceremony only a few weeks into my time there, when I was new and interesting, and Susan had heard Vic and I lived in a stately home and had an uncle who was a lord.

'Oh, Susan, please no,' I begged. 'Please.'

'I'm afraid so, Sarah.' Susan's voice was gentle. 'It's awfully sad, but we were mistaken in you. You're not right for our group.'

'Why? Just tell me why. I'll change.'

'Change.' Margaret giggled. I could see her looking me up and down, at my thin arms, at the uniform that was faded and frayed after being worn through a whole summer at Fane because we had so few other clothes, my untidy ponytail falling out of its ribbon. Other girls had neat ribbons and hair clips, and new lacrosse sticks and sponge bags. We had arrived with our possessions in my uncle's old trunk, and had to share the lacrosse stick, which was being eaten away by some fungal disease that caused the wood to warp and turn green at one end. 'You can't change who you *are,* Sarah.'

'Vic has,' I said, before realising what a terrible error that was.

'Do you mean your sister? Why, how cruel. Victoria is nothing like you,' Susan said, but I saw her hesitate. Victoria had cachet in the school. I didn't know why, but she did. 'Victoria isn't a sneak, and a coward, and – and a thief.'

'No, Sarah,' said Minnie, her small shining face turned upwards.

I reminded myself what Anne had told me a week after I'd arrived in hushed, urgent tones, that Minnie's mother had driven her to the school when she was seven and dropped her off, then told them to return her when she was sixteen and not to bother her about Minnie until that time unless it was an emergency. She had no family and often had to spend the holidays at school with the Loon, as we called Miss Dunoon. 'She's ghastly – an absolute sneak, a little – Ooh, I hate her,' Anne had hissed. 'But you *mustn't annoy her. Everything* she sees goes straight back to Susan.'

I felt sorry for Minnie, this half-life in this dreadful place. I had seen things and dreamed things that would never cross her path, I understood already, albeit obscurely, how infantilised these girls were and how Vic and I were a fair way to being fully formed, forging ourselves as the people we had to be to survive, and I would not have wished that experience on anyone – nevertheless, I frequently had to press my arms to my side to stop myself slapping Minnie.

'Shush,' said Susan reprovingly. 'Thank you, Minnie. Thank you, Margaret. You're real bricks. The decision has been reached and—'

'I'll do anything,' I said suddenly, my voice low, and urgent. I couldn't tell Vic. I couldn't bear for her to know. 'You know I will. Please don't Release me, Susan. *Susan.*'

'No.' And she pushed me, suddenly, so I tumbled from the table, righting myself as quickly as possible so I was at the head of the honour guard of girls.

She flexed her fingers and began clicking them, and the sound echoed like gun cracks in the silent classroom, as in the distance girls' voices singing 'God Rest Ye Merry Gentlemen' floated in through the frowzy window. It was snowing fast outside now, blurred swirls against black. I sniffed the dreadful smell of boiled vegetables, Jeyes fluid, mouldy books, the smell of school, the smell of despair.

As ever at times like this, I let my mind soar away, floating on silent wings that drove through the night air to wherever

Stella was. I had seen her once since the summer, our October exeat, or weekend back from school. There had been no one to meet us at the station, and in the end Dr Brooke, who happened to be on the next train coming in from London, gave us a lift to Fane. He had a tiny car, and he let Vic sit in the front. I climbed into the back, and a couple of times when I looked in the rear-view mirror throughout the drive, his kind eyes were fixed on me, steadily, and he would smile, and say something to Vic, who by contrast barely gave him the time of day.

'Thank you,' I'd said as the car rolled up to the house and my stomach lurched, the wet smell of autumn and the chill in the air bringing a new energy to Fane. 'You're very kind. I'm sorry if we put you out.'

'It wasn't putting me out,' he'd said. 'I'm glad to see you both back here.'

'Dr Brooke, how is –' I was embarrassed I didn't even know his name.

'Oh yes, you were friends with my pet student, weren't you?' he said. 'He's left the school I spent months arranging for him. Went to America after three weeks, would you believe.'

'Oh,' I said, feeling a sharp pinch in my heart, though I wasn't surprised. I'd been at a boarding school for six weeks now and if it wasn't for me it really wasn't for him.

'"Wrong crowd", is how he termed it in his letter. Says he wants to be in on the action, whatever that means. He was staying with an old friend of mine in Brooklyn, a chap I met in the war, but I've no idea where he is now. He's nearly eighteen; he can make his own mind up now, I suppose.'

'You don't have an address for him?'

'No. You were friends, weren't you?' He'd looked at me again, those keen eyes. 'He mentioned you a couple of times. I'm glad. He's a remarkable boy.'

'We weren't really friends,' I said. Vic, next to him, cleared her throat. *Shut up*, it meant. 'But I liked him enormously. We were . . .'

I didn't know how to say what we were. We were stargazers,

I wanted to say. But it sounded so silly. Still, I had to say it, so I said it under my breath.

'I'll mention I saw you, when I hear from him. I'm sure I will.'

Back at Fane, we'd trudged upstairs to the Thin Room in the ringing silence of the house. There were mouse droppings all over the quilts; the room was coated with dust. After ten minutes our mother had appeared.

It was the longest I'd ever been away from her and at first I simply stared at her, her fine, pale lashes, the blankness in her pale-blue eyes. Her gathered silk dress, one of four or five she always wore, this one in sage green, was cinched at the waist, and she was thinner than ever. Over it she wore an man's old shirt, covered in dust and marks. Her jaw was working, her eyes moving, rolling in their sockets and her bony hands scrabbled at whatever she touched. She seemed dried out, even more dusty and desiccated than before. I wondered when she'd last left the estate.

'There's no real food.' She flung some dry water biscuits down on Vic's bed, took two wrinkled apples out of her pockets, and a scattering of aniseed sweets. 'I'm very busy with the house at the moment, girls. I'm writing letters, enlisting support for our position. You'll have to fend for yourselves this weekend.'

It's funny, people usually use this expression as . . . an expression. With my mother it was literal. We really did have to defend ourselves, keep ourselves, and each other, safe, to survive. She'd glanced over our uniforms.

'Victoria, you're getting fat, darling. Stop eating the tapioca pudding, would you?'

'Yes, Mother.'

'Come and get some clothes from my side,' she'd said. 'Don't ruin your uniforms. I'm not bloody buying any more.'

This was in contrast to when she'd refused to buy us new clothes in the summer because we had our school uniform, but she was never consistent. She'd let us into the two rooms beyond the Rose-Red Drawing Room which we hadn't been into more than twice before. I'd forgotten how it was. Piles of rags heaped in a corner, crates of shattered glass and twisted filigrees of metal lamps, chandeliers lying dark on the floor like a nest of glass snakes, the rotten smell draped over everything.

It was unseasonably hot. We picked, from the trunk she directed us to that was full of old clothes, two Edwardian smock dresses. She was delighted. 'You look like young ladies. The house should have young ladies in it.'

I started to say how stupid this was, but Vic nudged me, hard, in the ribs. Our mother turned on her heel and went out through the rest of the West Wing, up to her room. A minute later we heard the radio start up again.

Feeling like idiots, encased in flowery too-long muslin dresses that clung to our legs, we left to walk to the village to buy food.

On the way there, I insisted we went round to see Uncle Clive, poking around in the stables, the back door to his wing open. 'Oh! You two, then. I've been wondering when you'd come back,' he'd said. He was wilder, and smellier, than ever. A dried pea, yellow and wrinkled, was lodged in a fold of skin by his mouth. He held a mousetrap in his hand.

Vic stood at a distance, arms folded.

'How's Stella been?' I said, not knowing what to say to him.

'She doesn't come back now,' he said. 'Why should she?'

'Come on, Sarah. Let's go,' said Vic.

He glanced up at her, his face creased with ugly, barely restrained fury. 'Ah, you can't even stay to talk to me. To be even slightly polite.'

'Uncle Clive, we need to—' I began, but he cut me off.

'You going into the village, you said? Get me a bottle of whisky, would you? Put it on my account.'

And he walked away into the stables again. His corduroy suit was simply worn away in places, great gaping holes where the elbows, or knees, should be. He was stooped and wizened, yet still taller than most men. As we let ourselves out of the tall rusting gates at the bottom of the drive and emerged onto the high street we spotted Bobbie Thomas, the vicar's middle daughter, lounging by the War Memorial, eating an apple.

'Look at you two, Little Lord Fauntleroy and the Little Princess,' she said in a jeering tone. 'Hah! Hah!'

'Go and boil your head,' I said wittily.

'Your mother's madder than ever, your great-uncle smells of something disgusting and you two look like beggars. *My* sister and I are getting roller-skates for our birthdays, did you know?'

'I can't imagine anything worse than roller-skates,' I said hotly. 'I know a girl who died, knocked down by a car. She was on roller-skates and she didn't look out before she skated into the road. But now I wish I hadn't told you,' I said to an astounded Bobbie. 'Because you might have been killed too and now you won't be.'

It's to my credit that this entirely vile speech did, temporarily, shut Bobbie up.

'Ignore her, Sarah,' said Vic in a superior tone. 'She's riff-raff.'

I obeyed her and walked past Bobbie, my nose in the air. She stuck her foot out and I went over it, falling into Vic, who tripped, so we lay on the dusty gravel, entwined and furious. We got up in silence as she laughed and ran away.

At the post office, Mrs Boundy smiled at us. 'Hello, girls,' she said.

Vic gave her an icy stare, but I smiled back. 'Hello, Mrs Boundy.'

She was tall, and heavy, with sensible short hair, and dark shadows under her eyes. Her eyeballs were slightly yellow, and she breathed heavily. 'Would you mind . . . which one of you young ladies is my boy's little friend?'

Vic turned to me in horror, but I said simply, 'It's me, Mrs Boundy. How is he?'

'Well, I don't know I'm afraid. But I'm glad he's out of here, and that's all I'll say.' Her blue eyes filled slowly with tears. 'No place for a brilliant young man like him, that's for certain. He was a ray of sunshine to me, after all my troubles.' She gazed at me imploringly. 'You'll understand.'

'I do,' I said quietly. I put my hand on her arm, and nodded.

'Oh, I do miss him,' Mrs Boundy began. 'Something dreadful.' Tears trembled in her eyes.

'I'm sure you do—' I said.

'Sarah!' Victoria interrupted me. 'We must be going. Come on now.' When we were outside, she gripped my shoulder. 'You mustn't talk to people like that, Sarah.'

'Oh honestly, Vic,' I said, hunger getting the better of me. I looked in through the window of the little shop and waved at Mrs Boundy, smiling at her. 'Do shut up. You haven't the faintest idea. You're as bad as *her* sometimes.'

She didn't speak to me for the rest of the weekend. We didn't get Uncle Clive the bottle of whisky. We simply avoided him.

Click.

Click. Click. Click.

Susan began clicking her fingers, louder, and louder. I could feel my vision blurring. I wanted to laugh, to shout, to tell them all I simply didn't care, that they were all ridiculous. One by one, the girls joined in

'Sarah, you have to walk between us now,' Minnie said in a high, soft whisper. 'You remember?'

Slowly, I started the walk down between the two rows of girls as they clicked their fingers. Behind me, Susan was whispering.

'Release.'

'Release.'

As I walked through them, they hissed on 'Release', and each girl would click and then tap me on the shoulder. The sound of it was like rustling, like the mice in the cupboards, like the grasses in the fields.

'Release.'

'Release.'

'Release.'

'Release.'

'Release.'

'Release.'

Vic had wanted us to believe we might end up at one of the schools in her books, a thriving community of young women mad about lessons and fun and service to our new queen and the Commonwealth. But I had known, the moment the cab drew in from the station and I saw the weeds growing high and luxuriant in the driveway, saw the cracked stone stairs up to the front door, that we had exchanged one crumbling old home for another, that we would be shuffled and shunted around, marking time until we could get out ourselves. I understood it, in fact, and it was something of a relief for once to be right. I knew Vic didn't see this, not yet.

At the end of the line, Susan pushed me gently so I was facing the wall. I bit my lip furiously, certain of one thing. Now the act had happened, they must not ever see me cry. Ever. I thought of the Burnt Oak, of the sky, with stars extravagantly sprinkled overhead, of looking up and seeing other worlds. This will be over soon, I told myself, and just like that the clicking stopped.

'Tie, please,' said Susan, walking between the girls.

'Susan – please no – I won't be able to—'

'Shut up!' Susan said furiously. 'How dare you plead for special treatment! Give me your tie.'

So I handed the tie over, watched in silence as Susan took Miss Trubshawe's shears from the pot on the table, and cut the tie below the knot.

'Now,' said Susan grandly in that clear, cool voice, handing the tie back to me. 'You are Released. Henceforth no girl from our group will acknowledge you. Henceforth you are not our friend. Henceforth you will have to go about with other girls. You must not attempt to talk to us and you must accept you are not one of us.' She gave an almost regretful smile. 'Thank you, Sarah. You are Released.'

As I walked away, along the squeaking linoleum floor, I found I was shaking with some sense of liberation, though I didn't understand why when there was no hope for me now. I'd seen it with Lavinia when she'd been Released. No one had sat with her at lunch. Every evening she had an apple-pie bed. The girls refused to walk with her into the village, and she had to walk with the Loon. She was accused of cheating and vandalism – no one could outmatch Susan in duplicity and outraged innocence. No one could ever pin anything on her. And all because, on her first evening at Haresfield, Lavinia had swanked about her father having a Bentley.

'I'm afraid it serves her right,' Susan had said regretfully over breakfast. 'She really was a bad egg.' And, as her parents removed her abruptly from the school, Lavinia was never mentioned again. I have already lived a life, I would tell myself as I circled the hated boundary walls and fences of the school during break and the evening strolls. They have no idea, these milky, foolish girls. But I didn't say anything about Fane. I had promised Vic we would never talk about home life.

The choir had stopped rehearsing 'God Rest Ye Merry Gentlemen' and had moved onto 'Lead, Kindly Light', Miss Dearlove's favourite hymn, not suitable for Christmas, but strangely suitable for Haresfield, which operated within its own rules, a microcosm of real life.

'The night is dark, and I am far from home.'

I scuttled back to the dorm to wait for bedtime.

Vic loved the rules and restrictions. She was happy. Her hair shone. She was even good at lacrosse, whereas I kept hitting my knees and those of other girls with the stupid stick.

Haresfield Hall had been the home of an earl who had sold up after the Great War, presumably because he could no longer bear to live in the dark, echoing Gothic house where the wind from the fens came at you horizontally, where every room was vast and freezing. It had too many staircases that seemed never to connect one section of the school with another; to get from the dorms to the refectory on the other side of the house one had to take three different staircases. The kitchen was at the end of another block, so by the time the mostly inedible food reached the dining hall it was cold. In the long, high-ceilinged dormitories, which had once been a duchess's bedroom or dressing room and which were now bare, disinfected cubicles where the water in the basins froze solid in winter, I heard sobbing every night, but no one owned up to it. I didn't cry, of course: I had learned long ago there was no point.

The rules. Later, I would wonder what it was about women that when they were together they insisted on putting in place so many rules. Was it the absence of men making rules for them? No wristwatches. No using the front staircase. No scented soap, only the stuff from the chemist that smelt of oil and fat. No leaving food, because of the starving children around the world, so you stayed behind until you had choked down gristly turkey, and cold, gelatinous rice pudding. The doughnuts – a Friday treat when there was a birthday – were fried in the oil used for frying fish. They tasted like rotten cod, so even a treat became something to dread. No asking questions in class – so if you didn't understand something, it just went over your head, and no correcting mistakes, of course.

Then there were the other rules, made up by the girls, unwritten. No swanking. No sneaking. No cheeking. No big-headedness. No showing off about one's 'people', one's house and car and what one's daddy did for a job and how many servants one had at home. But they all did, of course. Susan and all the others were constantly harping on about their mother's furs and their father's new Rolls. But the rules said you could rag another girl, and play horrible tricks on her, like leaving beetles in her pillow after she'd specifically said she hated beetles, or shaking hands with her and leaving a dollop of porridge behind, smearing porridge into her hair as you left and if she complained she was a sneak, because it was all good fun.

I sat on my creaking narrow iron bed, swinging my legs. The sound of feet came from further down the corridor. I froze, not certain whether to hide or not.

'Hello,' said Monica from the doorway, hands in her blazer pockets. 'I thought I'd come and see if you were all right.'

'Thanks,' I said. 'I'm fine.' I didn't want to appear a drip in front of Monica, who spent days in the san when her asthma was bad, and still had to do sports, and never complained.

'Running away?' said Monica drily, looking at the bundle of clothes at my side. I had, in fact, taken a spare jumper and pants and socks and put them into one of Uncle Clive's large handkerchiefs, with what aim I wasn't quite sure.

'Might do,' I said, and shrugged.

She leaned against my bed. 'Listen, Susan will change her mind. She did it to me last term. It was awful, but it passes.'

'You were Released?'

She nodded. 'But they couldn't be *that* cruel to me because of the asthma. They'd get into trouble. And the main thing that changed their minds was I obviously didn't care that much.' Her merry eyes smiled. 'They're cowards. I'd have had a jolly sight more respect for Susan if she'd really gone for me.' She put her hand on my arm. 'All's well that ends well, Sarah. You just have to let the ragging and jokes fall flat, then they get bored and start to look amongst themselves. That's the way the pack hunts.'

'Thanks. It's more the whole show of it.'

'I know. It's rotten. It's a rotten school too. I keep telling Father, but he doesn't listen, and Mummy loves it because Susan Cowper's mother was a deb with her and she thinks everything she does must be all right. Mummy's usually so sensible too.'

'Can't you tell them what it's really like when you're ill?'

She gave a small wince. 'Ah . . . but I like being at school. I don't have any brothers and sisters and Daddy's away in London most of the week. I was so bored at home with just Mummy. It's hardly like they work us particularly hard. My cousin's at Roedean. She has to pass a test on Latin subjunctives, otherwise she can't go into the upper fourth. Can you imagine anything so dire? When it's bad, I just do what I do with the asthma: pretend I'm somewhere else and wait for time to pass. Then I'm going to go and have an adventure.'

'An adventure?'

'Yes,' said Monica, her eyes shining. 'I'm going to jolly well go to Paris after my A levels, and learn to make quiches and puddings and pastries, and then I'm going to write a novel that sells like hot cakes. Some bosh about a girl dying young in the arms of her lover. I've got some money from Mummy's parents, enough for the boat train and hotels. I'm going to change my name.'

This was exactly the kind of conversation I liked. 'To what?'

'Oh, Cleone St Clair or Vivien Sheridan, something glamorous like that. Then I'll probably get the train to Italy.'

'I say, how brave.'

'Not really,' Monica said. 'I've spent so much time in bed that when I'm well being with Susan and her crowd just makes me feel hollow. What will you do when you leave school?'

'Oh! I haven't the faintest idea.'

'Come on. You must want to do *something*.'

I gestured to the instrument in the hard case, propped up against the wall.

'Well – it's funny, because I've trained myself like you've trained yourself. I try not to think about it too much. But if I could I – I'd like to do music again.'

'What kind of music? Mummy asks me to stop when I start singing,' said Monica, her eyes half-moons of mirth.

'I learned the cello. At my old school. Just for a short while, and I wasn't any good I'm sure.' I'd learned to hide the passion, the fierce, white-hot certainty I had about it. 'But I loved it.' I swallowed. 'I'd like to learn again.'

'Gosh. How clever you are,' said Monica admiringly. 'I'm no good at anything like that – lessons, music. Is that yours?'

'No, it's Susan's, worst luck.' The fact that Susan Cowper, of all people, was the person who learned the cello was especially galling. I'd hear her skip off to cello with Mr Williams, giggling because he was a young man and she was very silly. She had played in assembly once, two weeks into term, and had yanked her bow across the instrument like she was slicing stale bread. It had been painful to watch.

'Are you learning?'

I shook my head. 'Not at the moment.'

'How do you know you want to play, then?'

'My mother used to take us to concerts. Cello recitals. I – I just knew, when I saw the cellist; I understood it. Doesn't that sound silly?' I rubbed my cold nose, slightly mortified at having to explain it. 'And then I went to the Proms, and they had a cello solo . . . some Brahms and then Henry Wood . . .' Monica looked blank. 'I heard the sounds and I remembered, right away.'

'How to play again, you mean?'

'Oh, yes! I had lessons at my old school, but it was a year or so ago. Another lifetime. My teacher was lovely. And I was good. I knew I would be. I'm not boasting,' I said, thinking of the unwritten rules. 'But that's all stopped and I try not to think about it too much, because it's rather difficult at home, and it's all I want to do.'

'Why?'

'It's hard to put into words,' I said. 'When I'm . . .'

I trailed off. I didn't know her well enough to explain it. There was only one person who would understand.

When I'm walking across the fields at twilight, and Stella is soaring overhead and the stars are coming out I hear music. Soaring, soulful music that seems to run through me.

When I am sitting on the train back to school, feeling the unfamiliar, sickening motion of the engine, hearing the chatter of other girls who have friends, who have been kissed goodbye by a parent that morning, patted a family pet, I hear the bow, moving across the strings, low and sad, sweet, sublime. The feeling of the instrument against me, how I embrace it, hold it close.

When I am lying in this cold, creaking bed, the night chill on my face and the heavy, slightly damp blanket weighing me down, I hear a deep, haunting refrain, trembling notes coaxed from the chestnut-coloured wood that resonate inside me.

When I play the cello, I am entirely myself.

I'd only had a year's worth of lessons, but Mrs Marshall-Wessendorf, my old cello teacher, understood. She told me once her own mother had trained to be a seamstress, but there was a problem: she was left-handed. She couldn't use scissors. Her husband was a blacksmith. He made her a special pair of back-to-front scissors and when she held them, suddenly everything made sense: the material slid through the scissors. When I sat with the cello, it felt right. It made sense.

'We have a tree at home,' I began. 'It's called the Burnt Oak.'

'A burnt oak tree?'

'It's a family joke,' I said, thinking how strange it was this passed for humour. 'It's not a tree. But one has to see it to quite understand it. My grandfather built it. It has a platform, one can climb up onto it and view the stars. It's hard to explain, but whenever I'm there I hear music. I didn't see it for a long time, that loving music and loving playing the cello, they could be things . . . for me. I have to find a way to get away from here, but the trouble is I want to get away from home too.'

'Oh,' said Monica, looking at me with her intelligent eyes. 'That's rather grim.'

I remembered too late my promise to Vic about not talking about home, but I decided to trust Monica. 'Well, I'm looking forward to growing up too.'

'Come to Paris with me.'

'All right!' I said. 'I'll study music there. We can share an apartment.'

'Have you seen *An American in Paris*?'

'I've seen *Peter Pan*,' I said.

'Well, that's not the same thing.' She poked me, with a grin.

'No. I'm sorry, I like to mention it, 'cause the truth is I've barely seen any films, just that one. I've been virtually nowhere. I'm not very interesting.'

'Oh! That's not true. I'd say you're one of the most interesting people I know. Don't squirm. Anyway, it's awfully good. Gene Kelly is an absolute dream, if you ask me. There's a scene in it,' Monica said, and she leaned forward, 'he wears these trousers, and he dances, and you can see –' she whispered in my ear – '*a large bulge.*'

Her breath tickled my neck, and I snorted with laughter, which surprised us both. We collapsed on the bed, half giggling, half gasping.

'I say,' I said, after a minute, 'thanks for coming to see me.'

'No, Susan's awful. I wholly sympathise. It's bad luck about the cello, too. I wanted to say, do be careful around her. Lots of girls don't understand her, how she works.'

'Well, don't worry about me. I'm used to people like her.'

'Really? Well, poor you. She's absolute poison. Do you remember the Loon's cat?'

'The one who died?'

Monica gave a significant look. 'I hear Susan did it. Fed it yew berries, mashed up into bits of chicken. Because it scratched her.'

I clutched the blanket, genuinely shocked. 'She couldn't.'

'She could, and she did. She's just awful.' Monica stared at me. 'I say, how does she get on with Victoria?'

'Oh! Fine, I think.'

'Your sister is everyone's new crush.'

'Well – she's popular,' I said unwillingly. 'I'm glad she's settled in.'

'Settled in!' Monica's bright eyes sparkled. 'Gosh, there's never been a hit quite like Victoria Fox. It's strange to think you're sisters.'

I knew what she was trying to say, and at that very moment, as if conjured up by magic, there was the sound of a gaggle of girls clattering along the corridor and we froze. They appeared in the dorm doorway. It was Vic, and she was with three or four other girls, and they were arm in arm.

'Vic! Hi!' I called, anxious to prove some point suddenly – why on earth!

'Oh, hello, Sarah,' said Vic, stopping and waving at me. She gave me a quick, bright smile. Around her, the other girls watched, giving each other sidelong glances. They weren't sure what to make of me. I was her sister, but I had been Released. 'I heard about the incident earlier.'

'It's fine.' I stole a direct glance at her. 'Nice to see you.'

She was already turning away. 'Oh well. See you for the journey home. Bye! Bye, Monica.'

And she walked off. I saw the briefest, smallest flicker of a glance at me as she turned back to the corridor, the white light.

I sat on the end of the bed, considering.

Eventually, Monica said, 'Listen, next term will be better. Winter will be over. And Dearlove's going. Miss Parker's the new head. She can't be worse, can she?'

'You're right.'

'I ought to go. I write to Mummy every Wednesday. She's furious if I don't. I want to make sure she's got my most updated Christmas request. Oh –' She stopped.

'What?'

'I wish you were coming to us for Christmas. Isn't that rather forward of me? But we'd have so much fun, Sarah Fox. Let's be friends, do.'

'Let's,' I said, and warmth stole through me. I smiled, and the effect of smiling on my body was strange. I felt better already. 'Bye, Monica. And – thanks.'

The dorm was silent. Snow muffled the noise from elsewhere in the school. I was alone. I stood and walked up and down the dorm, touching each of the rough iron bedsteads. Each bed had its small variants – the rag doll with a missing eye, the dog-eared photograph of a mother holding a new baby sibling propped up against a toothmug, a crucifix necklace, a small scrapbook of pressed wildflowers.

'I release you,' I murmured, as I touched each one, imagining myself to be awfully dramatic.

Next to my bed was a Ruby Ferguson book Vic had given me – she didn't like horses any more – and two feathers from Stella's tail. They were wide, snow-white and edged with dark gold.

Opposite my bed, in the corner of the dorm was Susan Cowper's bed, nearest the sink and the radiator, and next to it was her cello. I remembered her saying she'd played at a summer fête and the Duke of something had told her mother she ought to be professional. And I smiled. I don't think I was ready, before. I don't think I was desperate enough to Be Good at something. Because sometimes, that is how it works.

I knew I shouldn't have played Susan's cello. I didn't care. I had to. It's as simple as that. Perhaps Susan caused it all, everything that followed, and instead of backing away from her in Peter Jones I should have followed her, and thanked her. If she hadn't decided to torment me, I wouldn't have been in the dorm room. If she hadn't isolated me, Monica wouldn't have come to check on me, and we wouldn't have talked. My darling Mon would know what happened to Susan after school. She was good at keeping up with things like the Old Girls' Association. Certainly, despite her assurances to us all that she was Someone, I never heard of Susan again: she wasn't married off to a duke, or voted the finest foreign secretary we'd ever had. I never heard her name in conversation, either, as someone who was a kind friend, a member of the community, like Monica back in Surrey, with her soup lunches and Meals on Wheels and prison visits. What a successful life really means looks quite different, I realise, the older you get.

Life is timing. The cello lessons had stopped because my mother had decided on a whim that they would, and I was extremely upset, but there was so much she ruined that it was just another piece of patchwork on the quilt. The drowning sounds the kittens made. The feel of her bony hand as she slapped our cheeks.

But I was older now, and something had happened to me that summer's night on the Burnt Oak. I'd learned to look up. To see what I wanted. There was a cello in the room upstairs at Fane, and I hadn't been ready for it. I knew it was Iris's mother's – I knew nothing about her other than that she'd met our grandfather at Wigmore Hall – and I hadn't wanted to touch it.

I picked up the cello, and took it out of its dusty case. Susan didn't practise much, because she said her hands mustn't be damaged. I picked it up.

Now, now, I was ready. I settled my shoulders, squeezed the bow between my fingers. I paused. Then I started to play 'The Swan', from *The Carnival of the Animals*, because I remembered it, note for note.

Mrs Marshall-Wessendorf would fold her arms and sigh when I played the scratched, chipped cello she'd taken when she fled Berlin, carrying her baby son Rudi in one hand and her cello over her back in the other. She never saw her husband again: he was a Black American she had met at the Berlin conservatory where they were both studying cello, and had been 'detained' by the Nazis.

'Ze vibrato, Sarrah, ze vibrrrrrato!' she would hum. 'Ach, but you are young . . .'

I smiled as I played, remembering her kind face, the round glasses, the shapeless floral dresses she wore in summer and winter. How when she picked up a cello and played it sounded different. Like longing, like the wind through the trees, like sadness and beauty.

For several minutes I played, and my back started to ache because the beds were high off the ground and my posture was uncomfortable. But I was barely aware of it. I don't recall what happened next, whether Susan found me, or Mr Williams. I only remember that I turned, and he was there, arms folded, leaning against the open door. He had leather patches on his tweed jacket, though he was young. I remember that, and that Susan was screaming – actually screaming, her potatoey face bright red and her eyes even more like currants than before. I remember thinking as I played on, finishing the piece and starting it again, that she was very plain. I assumed she'd fetched Mr Williams. I was wrong, though.

He stood at the open door, with a curious, intense expression on his kind face and when Susan stopped shouting he merely nodded.

'Are you listening to me, Mr Williams?' Susan demanded. She was out of breath. A crowd of girls had by this time gathered around her.

'I am listening,' Mr Williams said quietly. 'Susan, please report to the headmistress, and tell her I sent you to her for unscholarly conduct towards a fellow pupil.'

Susan opened and shut her mouth several times. 'But that's *my* cello, and Sarah Fox has stolen it!' she said eventually.

'I picked it up to try it,' I said, putting the cello down. 'I'm awfully sorry, Susan. I couldn't help it. Here.'

She turned away, horrified that she had to talk to me, acknowledge me. But Mr Williams raised his hand. 'Susan, listen to her. Your attitude is disgraceful,' he said, but because he spoke in a mild, calm way, it merely sounded as though he were commenting on the weather. He waved her objections away. 'Off you go,' he said.

'You will be hearing from my mother that I do not wish to continue with lessons!' Susan said, shaking. 'You'll hear from her – Oh, yes—'

But Mr Williams raised his hand again, and in the same level voice said: 'Righty-ho, Susan.'

Susan turned with a little sob. There was a brief inhalation from the girls gathered around her. How terrible! How embarrassing for her too! I saw one of them, on the edges of the group, shimmering behind the others, always visible to me. It was Vic. She blinked, slowly. I knew, from the way she inhaled quietly, she was trying not to cry. Mr Williams silenced them all, and then he turned to Vic.

'Thank you for sending me up here,' he said quickly, so quickly I might not have heard it. She flinched.

Later, she would never admit it, but I know that she did. I know she found him and told him to come and listen and that he walked away from the rehearsal rooms to the dorms where, as a music master, he usually didn't venture. I wonder if other teachers would have made the effort. But he did. She did it for me, and perhaps he saw that.

He folded his arms again. 'I see you've mastered first position, and fourth.' He was watching me, closely. 'How old are you?'

'I'm twelve.'

'It's a good time to start learning properly, if you're ready.'

'I am ready.' I nodded.

I had never been conspicuous, been praised, been noteworthy. I could write a short story, but it wasn't very interesting. I knew algebra, but I never got the answers all right. I was hopeless at sports. This was what I could do.

As the sound of Susan Cowper's heavy tread thundering along the creaking floorboards receded, Mr Williams held up his hand.

'Move along, girls.' His eyes twinkled. 'The show's over. Let her play on. This is very interesting, very interesting indeed.' He turned back to me as the crowd of disgruntled, vaguely curious girls dispersed, muttering amongst themselves like a host of sparrows in late summer. 'Now, Miss Fox,' he said. 'Play on.' I hesitated.

'I ought to find Susan, give the cello back to her.'

'Eventually,' Mr Williams said. 'But we have a saying in my family: you have to make a noise to be heard.'

And so I played on. When I looked up, Vic had vanished. But I played on.

Chapter Twelve

I have no idea why Mrs Boyes thought it would be a good idea to roast a chicken for Christmas dinner. Perhaps she thought something had to change. Perhaps, like everyone, she wanted to break the stalemate in the war between my mother and great-uncle. Perhaps she thought something had to change. Perhaps she was sentimental. Christmas is funny like that.

Christmas Day passed slowly. It was too cold to go outside; we only had macintoshes and besides, Vic and I did not want to gambol in the snow-covered parkland, throw snowballs, make snowmen, like children in a Victorian scene. Vic lay on her bed and read school stories she had acquired from somewhere, I didn't know where. I practised the cello music Mr Williams had given me, the fingering, the positions, lying on my bed. My fingers were already hardening, ten days into picking up the cello again. I remembered it all with ease.

There was soup for lunch, left in Uncle Clive's kitchen, and we wished him a happy Christmas then returned to our part of the house. In the afternoon, I went up to the Star Study, looking at the old photos, sorting out what I could.

My mother and Uncle Clive did not feel the cold. The stench of the house in winter combined with the damp, inferior-quality coke Uncle Clive burnt in the few grates that worked made it hard to breathe sometimes. We wore the dresses my mother had found for us in the autumn. I hated mine. It was like being made to dress up as a doll.

Uncle Clive appeared in his disintegrating tweed jacket and trousers, an improvement on his now usual costume of long johns and a grubby old shirt. And then, finally, my mother, in the pale gold dress she had worn at her wedding, made by Worth. It was thirties, and out of date, but she wore it with a wide duck-egg blue belt, baby blue shoes and a blue jacket with fur collar. This was her smart outfit; I had seen it periodically over the years, and couldn't help but gaze at her glacial, aristocratic beauty when she wore it. The fine cast of her shoulders and collarbone. Her high cheekbones, pale yellow hair. She sat down carefully, spreading her skirts about her, her eyes twitching, only slightly. Snow floated past the windows; the night was bitterly cold. I glanced out now and then, every drifting shape reminding me of birds' wings.

I had not really seen Stella since we'd come back. 'She's not here, your little project,' Clive had informed me, when we'd arrived two days before. 'I've looked out for her. She's probably dead. Found a tawny owl in the snow this morning. This weather's killing them. They can't see the animals on the ground for the snow.'

The cold was killing everything; only yesterday, an old man in the village had been found dead in his garden, curled up next to the bird table. He had fought in the First World War.

Mrs Boyes produced the chicken and potatoes, and some green vegetable boiled to a puree. She'd unearthed table linen from somewhere. There was bread sauce, and a sticky-sweet Christmas pudding. Vic and I sat next to each other. My stomach ached the whole way through as we picked at the food. I couldn't relax – experience told me it wasn't safe to relax.

Halfway through the meal, our mother raised her glass to Uncle Clive. 'Well,' she said. 'Here's to Christmas together. One *big, happy* family. Wouldn't you say, *Uncle Clive*?' She said his name in a high-pitched, baby voice. 'Isn't it lovely, having your family here?'

Uncle Clive was slumped in the large mahogany dining chair at the other end of the table. The other dining chairs had long gone, and we sat on an assortment Mrs Boyes had dragged in from other ends of the house. I watched Clive scratching his face, curved uncomfortably in the too-low chair, gazing anywhere but at my mother, his grey face, the lines deeper than ever, the strange inscrutability of him, timeless and harsh. And she, at the other end, like a Christmas angel, her smooth almond-shaped nails gleaming as her slender hand clutched the cut glass, her face glowing in the soft candlelight.

Uncle Clive took a sip of wine. 'Shut up, you stupid bitch,' he replied, and, picking up a spindly chicken leg, tore into it with his rotting teeth.

I knew she was goading him, playing him like a cat bats a mouse around. The power of his anger was frightening to me, she wasn't afraid of him. I think once she had been, but not now.

'I knew they'd ruin it. I said to Mrs Boundy, they'll have a row. But I always make Christmas dinner in my house,' Mrs Boyes said, bristling, when Vic and I appeared in the kitchen, carrying the plates uncertainly between us. She snatched them from us and placed them heavily in the vast cracked porcelain butler's sink, then turned on the juddering, clanking tap. 'If I'm to work here, I make Christmas dinner. And after what I've seen, and what I've had to put up with . . .'

Vic and I both backed away wearily. We couldn't take any more of it. I had no idea why Uncle Clive had agreed to come to the Christmas dinner, and that night back in the Thin Room I'd asked Vic what she thought.

Vic put down one of the battered old school stories she was rereading for the umpteenth time that was now falling apart. She looked thoughtful for a moment. 'It's food, isn't it? Mrs Boyes roasted a chicken. God knows there's no proper food here. I should think both of them came for the roast chicken, and the potatoes, and Mrs Boyes is heartily sick of them and wants them to either murder each other, or come to some agreement.'

She was right, of course. The potatoes had, in fact, been delicious.

I couldn't let myself think of other families, of children eagerly burrowing into knitted stockings for oranges, sitting around small tables in cosy houses pulling crackers and listening to the radio, or eagerly turning to their Christmas presents – books, dolls, bows and arrows, jumpers, or watching their new television sets. I knew Monica's family had a set. I knew they would be taking a walk on Boxing Day, up in the ancient woods of the Surrey hills. I couldn't think about that, or about her cheery parents who collected her in their shiny wine-red Rolls from school, both holding their arms out for her to run towards them and Monica having to choose whom to hug first, all of them absolutely beaming with joy.

Vic pulled the thin duvet up over her and rolled over.

'Happy Christmas,' I said, but there was no reply. I sat in bed, watching her still form, then I lay down and tried to sleep myself. But I knew I wouldn't be able to. I turned over, and over again, twisting myself in the sheets. Since I'd been back, something had been worrying away at me. Every night I'd lie there, twisting the sheets into whorls, biting my nails.

'Of course I will teach you,' Mr Williams had said back at school. 'But while I'm happy to give you a few free lessons I can't formally teach you without your parent's consent. I'm paid by the parents, not the school. I invoice them via the school.' He had looked at me, intently. 'You must find a way to persuade your mother, Sarah. No matter what it takes.' Outside, I heard the call of an owl. As though it were a sign, a message, I sat up again, pulled on my socks and school jumper and left the dark little room quietly.

I paused at the small round window further down the corridor. The land around was utterly silent, moonlight coating the trees, glittering the frost. Upstairs, amongst the detritus of the top floor, I found what I was looking for: the cello I'd remembered. It was stuffed in the corner of a room along with rags and dirt and bricks and other rubbish. I crawled over to extract it, scraping my knee on a rusting nail as I did so.

Hugging it close to me, I put it gently against the wall then crept downstairs, through the Rose-Red Drawing Room, where the smell really was at its worst, then up the stairs of the West Wing. Up I climbed to my mother's room, and knocked on the door. There was no answer. I knocked again. I could hear breathing, a very slight rocking sound.

I pushed the door open. She was pacing up and down, her arms wrapped round her frame, pale eyes unreadable. 'What?' she said, head jerking up. 'What do you want? I'm thinking. Don't come in.'

But I folded my arms and stepped inside, and she gave a long, low hiss. I looked around. It was dimly lit, a candle in the corner, but it was warm and relatively cosy – an old patchwork quilt on the brass bedstead, an oddly cheery lemon-coloured Lloyd Loom basket chair, a wardrobe, a huge chest of drawers. A fire burnt in the grate. An actual fire. I turned towards it, feeling the very edge of its heat.

'I wanted to ask if I could have the cello upstairs. Your mother's cello.'

'What do you want with it?'

'I want to learn again.'

Her thin face was skull-like in the shadows. She stretched out her arms and waggled her fingers. The gold dress glowed in the soft light.

'You? You're no good. They said you were no good. I'm sorry, but that's what they said.'

'I am good,' I said, suddenly losing my patience. 'Stop being so boring. It's *so* boring, the way you say the most cruel or untrue or coarse thing you can. Every time. Can't you see it means we simply don't listen when you talk any more. *You're* boring.' I didn't know I was going to come out with it, and I put my hand over my mouth.

She just laughed, and laughed, pealing gales of mirth ringing out over the silent house until I heard Uncle Clive swearing and slamming a door, far away. She stepped forward. 'Brave. That's what your father said about you. He said you were brave.'

'My father?'

'He only saw you once.' She was chewing her lip, as if trying to remember. 'At the nursing home. They patched him up and he went back to France the next day. He said – Oh, I can't remember now. Said you were plucky. Come here, Sarah.' Her eyes glittered, and I moved towards her, obediently. 'See if this is – what did you say? – boring.'

She reached forward, and slapped the right side of my face so hard my neck clicked. Then she hit me on the jaw, forcing my head upwards. The force of it made my bones ache, my skin sting. She had slammed the fine cartilage so hard a whistling sound started in my ear.

I gave a cry of pain, and staggered back, but she stepped

towards me again, without any expression, still chewing her lip. I felt cold air whistling through the gap in the windows, and her hot breath on my cheek as she slapped me again, on the other side of my face. But *slap* isn't quite the right word – it was with her open palm, but it felt like a punch. Both of my ears rang with sharp, bone-deep pain. My cheeks and jawline started to smart, my neck aching. As I righted myself, she hit me again, and then again, and I was backing away, and fell onto the bed. But she kept coming for me, slapping my whole face, so my nose twisted to one side, like a sail, and my bottom lip was caught on a ring of hers, until eventually I stuck out one hand, blindly, and caught her wrist. I held it, wondering if I could snap it in two, if that was what would be necessary to stop her hitting me. I thought I probably could. She was so thin. She raised the other hand and I took that too, then I pulled myself up, and we were face to face.

I was almost the same height as her now. She was breathing hard, small panting gasps. Her breath was sour.

'I'll kill you,' I said in a low voice. 'I will kill you if you hit me again.'

I meant it. I can still feel the weight of the words. My cheekbones felt raw, and my eyes seemed loose, my vision hazy, as if the eyeballs might simply drop out. I still wasn't crying. I think I was in shock.

'You made me cross, Sarah,' she said blankly. 'I'm doing this for you, and Vic. For both of you.' I gaped at her. 'Why did you come? Oh . . . yes. Listen.' She pulled her wrists free, sharply, and slapped me again, just once, then danced to the other end of the room, away from me. 'It's quite simple, Sarah. You live here, you go to school there. One day, you'll come back here and live here again. Why do you imagine you'd need to know how to play a cello for that?'

I flattened myself against the opposite wall, edging towards the door. 'Do you think that's what'll happen?'

She didn't answer. 'You can't play that old thing. It's terrible. She hated it.' She swallowed again. 'It needs new strings. It's got woodworm. She was mad by the end. Quite mad. I tried so hard to get her to understand – she didn't understand! She never believed me, Sarah. I've never lied. I'm not a liar. I've only told the truth.'

'Believed you about what?' She was beginning to rant.

Her eyes darted from side to side, and she licked her lips. 'Important matters. To do with my inheritance. But you're here. I've given up on Victoria. You'll help me sort the place out, and we'll make it wonderful again. Look.' She swept her arm around. 'Look at what I've done.' She came closer towards me, her eyes sunken in the dim light from the lamp. I backed away towards the open door. 'I went into the Star Study a few times while you were away. You've done a grand job, Sarah. Tidying it, sorting it, ordering it all.' She swallowed, her blue eyes gleaming, the pale lashes fluttering. As she came towards me, I fumbled for the door handle. 'Vic's done. Vic's not it any more. She's lost herself – school and boys, no doubt – and – oh, she looks at me and judges me. I see it! But *Sarah*.' She reached across and took my hand. She had not touched me with tenderness for – I couldn't remember when, actually. It was very strange. 'Sarah, I think you're *right* for Fane. You understand what needs to be done with the house. I see you understand.'

Desperation made me truthful. 'I don't want to live here. I want to learn the cello. That's all.'

Her eyelids fluttered. 'Don't be an imbecile. I want you to understand what an *honour* this is for you. It's my house. Soon, it will *all* be my house.'

The close, perfumed smell of the room had masked the stench of the house. I took a step back into the cold corridor and it hit me again. I will never forget how her touch felt. I knew she might drag me down with her, into the madness. I knew I had to keep looking upwards.

Look up at the stars.

I said what Vic had told me to say only that morning, Christmas morning, when I'd been crying about the cello lessons in bed and telling her it was all I asked for. She somehow knew how I felt.

'I'll tell Murbles if you don't let me,' I said.

'What?' She was smiling, a ghastly rictus smile, and I was

desperately afraid she'd shut the door, and I'd be trapped in there, with her.

'I'll write to Mr Murbles. I'll tell him how you've treated us, your cruelty. I'll tell him about the slaps. The hunger. How you've as good as said you want Uncle Clive to die, how you talk about demolishing the place, how you're plotting to snatch it out from under him. "*I'll huff and I'll puff and I'll blow your house down.*" That's what you said to him when we'd just moved in. I'll tell him what they say about you in the village.' I took a deep, shuddering breath, surprised at my own momentum. 'I'll tell him everything.' She did not move. 'Give me the lessons, and I won't say anything,' I said. 'And give us some money, and then we won't ask you for more. You won't need to bother with us again.'

'Yes . . .' She exhaled slowly, turning to the narrow double bed, lifting up the mattress. She took four five-pound notes out of a large wallet, and handed them over to me. I saw my hands were shaking. My ears rang with the force of her punches. I felt dazed, as if I'd fallen a long way, and was still falling.

'I don't like threats,' she said quietly. 'I thought you were different.'

'Well, I'm not,' I said. I folded the money and put it away in my pocket, looking around the room again. 'Was this your room?'

'My governess,' she said. 'Miss Gulling.' She gestured to a wooden crate on the floor filled with broken, or cracked, willow-pattern plates. The radio that she'd listened to all through summer was on the windowsill; the aerial was broken. 'I'm very busy, trying to save the house. And it's not very nice, what you've done. It's blackmail. Take the money, then. So I'm free of you, is that what you're saying?'

This was the longest conversation we'd had for some time. The adrenalin that had flooded me was draining away, and I felt exhausted, unable to speak. I turned away, and didn't answer.

I closed the door behind me and went back downstairs and over to the central part of the house, clutching the bank notes tight between my fingers. Ice and snow glittered across the parkland in the stillness of that black night.

I went back to our bedroom. My head, face and neck were all

aching. Tears rolled freely down my cheeks. My skin stung in the sharp, cold air. I would have marks and bruises all over my face, but who would see? Who would care?

Outside our room, in the corridor, the cello stood, propped up where I had left it. I stared at it. And softly, instead of the ringing in my ears, I gradually started to hear the opening notes of 'The Swan', which was the last piece of music I'd begun to learn again. The elegiac, beautiful melody, echoing through the cold, empty rooms. I could hear it calling to me. I know it sounds utterly mad, but it was real, that moment. It was the best Christmas present. I heard music. I stepped forward.

'Happy Christmas,' I said, and I hugged the cello to myself, alone in the corridor.

Two days later, following advice from Mrs Boundy, I took the cello on the bus to Chichester to a music instrument shop where the owner restrung it. I wrapped my head in a scarf, ostensibly guarding against the cold, but also against the bruises that had bloomed, a virulent raspberry pink over my pale face.

'That's a fine instrument you've got there,' the owner said, running his hands over it. He did not meet my gaze. 'It's a Matteo Goffriller.' He tapped on the wood. 'Exceptional luthier, Goffriller. Never thought I'd see one myself. Fetch a pretty price if you ever sold it. Best take care of it.'

'Thank you,' I said as he put the cello carefully back in its canvas case. 'I will. I promise.'

As I left the shop, I heard his assistant, leaning towards him to say, 'I say, what was wrong—'

'Sshhh,' he said sharply. 'None of our business,' and the door banged behind them.

On the day we went back to school, a week later, I looked for Stella. The treat I'd left for her – a dead mouse for, as Monica liked to say, there's a lid for every pot – was still there, untouched. I knew in my heart that she was nesting somewhere else, hopefully a barn. It was good. It meant she could hunt for herself. But it was painful to know she had left me. I felt she had been the music inside me, for the months when I didn't have any, in that time when I started to see I had to have it, had to find something for myself, or lose myself entirely.

I gave half the money our mother had given me to Vic.

'Thank you for telling Mr Williams to come up and listen to me,' I said as the train drew away from the station and we sank back into our seats, glad of the temporary respite – from home and from school. 'I've got money from her for lessons. Here, the other half is for you.'

Vic looked up at me from under her long lashes and took the notes I handed her without comment. I had openly defied our mother now, gone against her, and I didn't know how she'd respond. But for a while I didn't care. I had the money for lessons, and I had the cello, and Monica, and I was determined to believe that would be enough.

Chapter Thirteen

I'd thought I couldn't be as cold as I was that first winter at Haresfield, but I was wrong: the slicing, cruel sharpness of spring in Rutlandshire was something else entirely, not least because we were obliged to wear summer uniform from half term onwards, even though the ground was still frozen stiff and remained so, up to April 1955. It was one of the coldest winters on record, with thirty feet of snow in the Highlands, thousands of sheep frozen to death only a few miles north of us. Our Home Economics teacher, Miss Babbacombe, went home to Lincoln, ninety miles away, to nurse her mother after an operation and couldn't get back to school for a fortnight.

My hands were by now permanently red and chapped, my lips were always broken and sore, the chilblains on my legs and feet like raw patches of fire. The callouses on my fingers from constant practice grew ever more red. Sometimes, when I came to play, my hands were so cold I couldn't move my fingers for several minutes. We leaned against the tepid radiators that peppered the draughty building when we could, but covertly, knowing we would be punished if a teacher caught us. In any case, they were rarely on. We each had hot-water bottles, but only a small amount of water was permitted – why, I have no idea.

At first, on my return to Haresfield, things appeared to be getting better. Miss Parker, the new head, was young – she still seemed immensely old to us, but younger than the other teachers. About half the school was in love with her within a week. She had come from a girls' school in Cornwall, but Vic told us she had grown up in London. She was neatly dressed, with a crisp, low voice. She had short hair, a brisk manner and a very slight twitch under her right eye when she looked at you.

'I have such a pash on Miss Parker,' I overheard Susan Cowper saying as Monica and I walked past her, pressing her flattened palm onto her breastbone as a horseshoe of girls around her swooned and giggled. 'Wasn't she wonderful today in assembly, talking about duty? We must support our new queen, however we can. I was lucky enough to meet her, you know—'

'Oh *yawn*,' said Mon in a loud, exaggerated voice. I nudged her, shocked and delighted as Susan Cowper's gang turned to us, confused. I, after our run-in at Christmas, was Susan's sworn enemy. Susan opened her mouth to say something, but Monica just opened hers too, gulping like a goldfish.

'Stay away from Sarah Fox, Monica. She is heading for disaster,' Susan called after us, but we merely laughed and linked arms, then turned and walked on.

Monica and I loved our new role as outsiders. Since returning to school after Christmas, we had formed a unit of two, and I found in her a true friend, whose kindness and sense of fun brought sunlight into every day for me, no matter how bleak. All one needs is one friend at school for things to look much brighter. Of course I ached for Vic, but what could I do? We had each chosen to survive in our own way, and now I had Monica, who was interested in everything around her, who properly listened when people talked. She looked forward, always, with joy: she had been confined to bed for so long as a child and wanted to get out and start living. After a while, this attitude rubbed off on me, only a small amount, but enough.

'One had to just keep on going, with a smile on one's face,' she'd say.

It's a mouldy day and it's boiled fish and horrific mash like concrete for lunch, but the snowdrops are out and there's a beautiful crisp smell in the air, Sarah. Let's walk outside, just for a few minutes.'

Monica aside, the main reason school was bearable was that I had the cello. And I came to see that the break from it was vital. Learning now wasn't like those first lessons with dear Mrs Marshall-Wessendorf in London. I had enjoyed it, but I was too young then to know how much I wanted it, had to have it.

This time it was like falling in love, waking up every morning knowing it was there, it was yours, that no one could take it away from you. School was dreadful, but it wasn't as unstable as life at Fane where one wasn't quite sure what might happen next. This was what I had to do, and I wonder if I hadn't had the uncertainties of my home life whether I would have worked as hard as I did. Certainly there were students at the Royal College of Music later on who were there because they'd been cosseted and supported every inch of the way, but when it came to grit and determination, steeling yourself for auditions, practising so hard your fingertips throbbed, living out of suitcases for weeks on end, they peeled off, one by one. They became interior decorators, stockbrokers, waiters, housewives, even teachers. I outlasted them all, because I was talented, but also because I wanted it. I wanted to play more than anything. That evening under the stars with the Bird Boy had made me believe I was worth something. My cello-playing progressed quickly: I was twelve and utterly ready to learn, and I practised hard, and I had Mr Williams.

Mr Williams did not live at the school. He taught the cello in and around Cambridge, and drove up once a week to teach the four girls who learned with him at Haresfield. Thus he seemed to be part of a world unconnected with school, and Fane.

I longed for my lessons with him. I liked his stories of life at Cambridge, of punting on the Cam, of the thick black gowns you wore to lectures, of the library at Trinity, built by Christopher Wren, of the time the master fell asleep in his soup. He had a long, kind face, and a tuft of hair at the top of his head and no matter how many times he smoothed it down it invariably stood back up again within seconds. He was a little awkward in person, but with large, gentle hands and square-edged fingers that moved rapidly and precisely over piano keys, across cello strings, adeptly catching a pencil he'd tossed in the air. He always wore hand-knitted Fair Isle jumpers. He came from a big, happy family he liked to talk about.

I was shivering one day in early March, and he lent me a jumper. 'My mother knits a new one every year for Christmas,' he said. 'This is this year's version.'

I hugged it gratefully to me. It was beautiful work, the twisting lime-green and red pattern weaving in and out of the teal-blue background. 'Imagine doing anything as clever as that.'

'She's one of those people,' he said, with a laugh in his voice. 'She can knit a jumper, bounce a baby on her knee *and* cook a meal for ten people including a couple of strays. She had twins, you know, when I was fifteen. Quite a surprise. I came down one morning and there she was, rocking in her chair next to the range, a baby in each arm and my father had to get the breakfast! But, you know, our kitchen is rather like that,' he said, folding his arms, and looking rather wistful. 'It's the sort of home where people have babies and eat meals and argue and fall in love and all of that. You know what I mean.'

I wanted to say that the only thing my mother had given me for Christmas this year was tinnitus, but I didn't. I loved to picture his family home. I could see the kitchen, the range, the rocking chair. I could see the scrubbed pine table and the kettle boiling and the rug on the floor and a group of Mr Williamses of varying ages and sexes gathered around the table. I opened my mouth to ask something, but couldn't speak.

He smiled at my expression. 'Cat got your tongue?'

'Can I ask you something?'

He turned a page of music over. 'Of course.'

'How did she have the babies in the kitchen?' I asked him. 'Didn't she have to be in hospital?'

'No, you can have a baby at home,' he said. 'How do you think they had babies in the years before there were hospitals?' He was smiling. 'Come on, let's turn to the Fauré—'

I interrupted him. 'I don't understand. Don't they give you the baby when you go into the hospital?'

Mr Williams laid down his pencil. 'Oh my goodness, no. You grow inside your mother, Sarah,' he said, seeing my bemusement now. 'Didn't you know that? You're twelve.'

I stood still, staring at him, appalled. The conversation had come out of nowhere! I dropped the bow I was holding, my hand slick with perspiration.

I'd seen women with distended stomachs, and known they were going to have babies, but somehow I didn't think that was where the baby came from. 'I thought a doctor gave them to the mother at the hospital and then she took it home.'

'No, Sarah. They're inside the mother already,' said Mr Williams. I wanted to ask: how? How did they get inside the mother? But he said, rather brusquely for him: 'Can we move on? I don't think this is an appropriate . . . Do you have the Fauré music there?'

'Of course.' I swallowed, still slightly stunned at what I'd learned. My mind was still on his mother in the rocking chair, babies appearing – from where? How? How on earth did a baby get in there, and then get out? I knew the old headmistress, Miss Dearlove, invited girls to tea in her study before they left and gave them a Talk, but no one ever said what the Talk was about. Perhaps it was too horrific for us to know about. Perhaps that was why our mother hated being a mother so much.

With a huge effort, I tore my mind away again, and picked up the bow just as there was a loud knock at the door. We both jumped. Without waiting for an answer, the door opened.

'Mr Williams? Um, sorry. I was looking for my flute. I wanted to do some practice.'

'We're in the middle of a lesson, Susan,' said Mr Williams politely. 'I haven't seen a flute. How are you?'

Susan Cowper inserted herself into the room, leaving the door open only a crack, as if she didn't want us to see the corridor behind us. 'I'm fine. Thank you. You see I'm learning the flute now, and my mother says I can go to a conservatoire in Paris if I want to when I leave school.'

'How wonderful,' said Mr Williams kindly. 'I'm so glad. But the flute's not here.'

'No, I can see that,' said Susan, who hadn't once glanced around the room. 'What were you talking about when I knocked on the door?' she said. She put her head on one side, finger poking into her chin, and brushed her wavy fringe out of her eyes.

'Oh, family,' said Mr Williams. 'Thank you very much, Susan—'

'It didn't *sound* like people talking about their family. It sounded much more interesting than that.'

'It's none of your business, Susan,' said Mr Williams sharply, as if goaded beyond endurance by these foolish girls. 'You can report the flute to lost property. Be on your way, why don't you?'

Susan opened her mouth, as if to say something, and then shut it. I noticed she had a spot on her nose. I remember feeling really glad. Her small green round eyes glared intently at Mr Williams.

'Yes, Mr Williams,' she said with her chin jerked out. 'Goodbye, then.'

She slammed the door behind her.

'She's awful. She's used to having everything her own way,' I said, rolling my eyes. But Mr Williams didn't rise to the bait, to my disappointment.

'Yes, perhaps. Now, let's get on. Where are you on the Fauré?' he asked. 'Well, come on, then. Play some for me.'

I played the first few bars for him, and he clicked his tongue.

'Was it that bad?' I said, laying the cello down and rubbing my sore hands.

'No,' he said. He nodded. 'Quite the opposite. But remember your fingering. Just relax, and if you've practised enough the fingering takes over. Trust me.'

I picked up the cello again. I rested it between my knees, holding the bow, feeling the slight callous on my breastbone where the scroll of the cello rubbed against my skin. I drummed my left hand on the strings, proud that my fingertips were hardening the more I played.

'It really is a beautiful cello, Sarah,' he said. 'It makes a lovely sound. It's – oh, it reminds me of many things. Autumn. Beatrice Harrison at the Proms. My mother, listening to the wireless in her kitchen. Now listen, we don't have long. As my grandfather likes to say: *But at my back I always hear Time's wingèd chariot hurrying near.*'

As I played I thought about how I hadn't said what I wanted to, which was that this lesson was the highlight of my week. I loved hearing about his family too, about the stray cat they'd adopted, about his grandmother who had been given a rose by Millais, about hot, lazy days in the gardens opposite. The Summer Exhibition every year, the Proms, the walk to school – I loved all his stories, which were so exotic to me because of their normalcy, bringing a tang of the London I missed so much.

Most of all, I loved it when he took the cello to show me what he meant, and his careful, kind face screwed up in concentration and his square-tipped fingers patted the fingerboard of the cello.

'I want you to practise these holidays,' he said gently. 'I know you do already. But the kind of practise I mean is the dedication one requires to be a real musician.' He took the bow from me, and lifted up the cello, resting it on its side, deftly twirling it towards him. He played only a few bars, but they were haunting, lilting notes that seemed to soar and swoop, to speak of pain, and I closed my eyes, surprised at the intensity of the feeling it always evoked in me.

'What's that?'

'Elgar,' he said simply, handing it back to me. 'While he was dying, he was asked what memorial he wanted and he said: "I need no memorial. Go up to the Malvern Hills, and listen, and you will hear me up there. That is where I am. I am always there."'

'Beautiful,' said a dry voice from the doorway and we both jumped in our seats.

Miss Parker, the new head, stood on the threshold. She smiled, and I saw a slight smudge of red lipstick on her teeth.

It was the Thing at Haresfield to treat her arrival as the equivalent of the Coronation – that she was a new broom, a simply super young headmistress who embodied what we most wanted from our school – young, stylish, full of lofty ideals, but looking both to the past and the future. The majority of the girls, like Susan Cowper and Vic, who had become worryingly friendly this term, worshipped her, and loudly proclaimed they did to anyone who'd listen. But I did not like her and I didn't know why.

Haresfield had been failing as a school for a while – the fees from fifty girls in their uneven rows in our infrequent assemblies was not financially sustainable and, in fact, it would close two years after I left, Miss Parker dismissed in disgrace for financial mismanagement. The Haresfield estate did not sell, and was allowed to fall into ruin, the lacrosse pitch churned up for new houses, the main house demolished a few years after, the whole place simply erased.

Now I looked at Miss Parker, at her folded arms in her neat black jacket and her neat grey wool skirt. She met my gaze and my eyes fell to the floor, to her scuffed black shoes, with one sole coming away, the toes bulging at each side. The lace on the left shoe had broken, and was tied back with a knot. I raised my eyes to her again, so she wouldn't think I'd noticed. Why did she have immaculate, expensive new clothes, yet wear shoes that were virtually falling apart?

'Another visitor! How may I help you, Miss Parker?' said Mr Williams easily.

'Oh, hello!' she said brightly. 'I wondered if I could have a word.'

'Yes, when I'm not teaching,' he said reasonably, and she gave a small, hissing sniff.

'Of course. Come to my study, after the lesson.' He nodded.

'Thank you.' Her dark gaze landed on me.

She shut the door and we glanced at each other, conspiratorial, and then Mr Williams shrugged with a merry smile. 'So that's your new head.'

'Yup.'

'She reminds me of a flapper in a detective story I read as a kid. Goes mad and shoots everyone with a pearl revolver.'

Being taught by Mr Williams was like being in another world, so that when I stepped out of the lesson and Miss Trubshawe shouted at me for walking on the floorboards not the carpet, or someone hid my toothbrush, or Susan Cowper pushed past me so hard I fell against the wall and walked away, whispering with her gang and I noticed Vic was one of them, I could right myself and keep on going, even if my eyes stung with tears.

Because of the cello, I was not worried about the academic lessons I didn't understand, whether because the teaching was so terrible or the blackboard was so ancient often one couldn't read the warped letters and I needed glasses, but wouldn't realise until I was at music college, or the sensation, not understood but vaguely noticed by me, day after day, of being a pubescent girl with barely enough food to eat, and what we were given to eat never being healthy or nourishing. In other ways, too, we were neglected: our beds were poorly bolted together, and they swayed – a girl in the third form had broken two ribs when her bed collapsed in the night – the mattresses too thin so springs caught you, our lives regimented and dull, with no hope or reason to aspire to anything.

There were some girls who suffered more than I did – beaten with slippers, tormented by teachers and by the other girls. But I was protected in part because of the cello, so I didn't really care, in part because nothing now was as bad as life at Fane and the threat my mother posed to us, in part because of my friendship with Monica and finally because I was Victoria Fox's sister. Miss Parker never remembered who I was, but she had taken a shine to Vic: she called her 'the best of her kind' and had made her a prefect, though she was only fourteen.

'Well done,' said Mr Williams, as I was packing up. 'I want you to really practise the Elgar for next week.'

'Oh Lord,' I said. 'It's terribly hard.'

'Not for you, Sarah, surely,' he said. 'If you really want to get better, you'll do anything. Won't you?'

'Yes,' I said, rather faintly. 'I suppose so.'

'Listen to me,' he said. 'I wasn't good enough. I was good, but I wasn't the best. You have to tell yourself you want to be the best. Perhaps you won't be – I don't know – Rostropovich. But if you work hard you might be one of the finest cellists in the country.'

'Me?' I said in disbelief. I shook my hair in front of my face, to hide my embarrassment.

'Oh yes. You.' He pointed the pencil at me. 'But if that's what you want, the cello has to come first. Always.'

I nodded, shivering in the cold. Mr Williams paused for a moment, then he said: 'This school won't help you with your playing. If it's something you take seriously, you'll need more lessons than I can give you and you'll need to think about applying to music college. You'll have to speak to your mother. I know from what you've said your home life is difficult, but there must be a way. You should have teachers who can advise you—'

'I can't.'

'Your mother will understand.'

It was my turn to laugh. 'My mother wouldn't understand,' I said, my hand on the open door, the cello on my back. 'I'll have to stay at this school, and the most I can hope for is that she'll leave us alone. Or . . . vanish one day. I don't have any other choice, you see.'

'I might be able to help with that. In the future.'

'What do you mean?'

'My grandfather is interested in the school and is a man of influence. And in you. I've told him about you. He might be able to help. Now, I'd better go and see what that murderous flapper Miss Parker wants, and to give her a gentle warning about this place.' He shook his head, seriously. 'Do your practice. Remember what we say in my family?'

'*You have to make a noise to be heard.*'

'Exactly. And you will make a noise, Sarah. I'm sure of that.'

Towards the end of term, Mr Williams gave me a fiendish piece of Brahms to learn. In the evenings, the music room wasn't used by anyone else and some of my happiest times were walking down the chilly corridor, the leaded windows rattling with the force of the screeching, wailing winds buffeting the old building, towards the room at the end, where I could sit for two hours at a time, practising until my back ached, my fingers on my left hand felt almost raw to the touch, my eyes stung, but the notes were there.

No one disturbed me. The teachers left me alone, not through any desire to see me improve or to encourage me, but because it didn't occur to any of them I might be there. Once Miss Babbacombe, one of the more human teachers, opened the door and I jumped out of my seat, banging my jaw on the scroll of the cello, but when I explained, and begged her not to get me into trouble, she said, wearily, 'Fine, Sarah. Put away your things and get ready for bed.'

Two days before we broke up for the Easter holidays, I was walking down the corridor on my way to my cello lesson. I wasn't looking where I was going, my head bent, back slightly bowed with the weight of the cello on my back, arms folded, thinking. Suddenly I felt a hard thud, then a sharp tweak as I caught my hair in the strap and fell against the wall. Someone had crashed into me.

'Get out of my way – Oh! Hello!'

I looked up. It was Vic with her arm through Susan Cowper's. 'Hello, Vic.' I coughed. 'Toria.'

The other girls with them giggled.

'Hello, Sarah,' Susan Cowper said, and she darted a glance at Vic, then nudged her.

'Where on earth are you going with that thing?' Vic said.

She had her hands in her pockets, which was utterly forbidden, and her hair, which should have been tied back, was loose around her shoulders. Her cheeks were glowing; she exuded confidence.

'I'm running away with Dirk Bogarde,' I said. 'Don't tell anyone.'

Vic was not good at jokes at the best of times and her eyes narrowed. 'I mean, I'm assuming you don't have a cello lesson, so where are you going?'

Something in me was riled enough by the superiority of her tone not to respond and point out that yes, I did have a lesson, and she didn't know what she was talking about. Instead, I said: 'I'm late. I'd better go.'

Susan leaned over, and whispered something to Vic. 'She hasn't heard yet, has she?'

I pretended not to listen, and adjusted the strap on my cello. But Vic shook her head, and made to move off.

'Good luck, Sarah,' she said. A tiny frown puckered the space between her brows, but cleared, and she and Susan gestured to the others to walk on behind her, like horses in a slow trot.

'What do you mean, good luck?' I started walking with her, bowed over with the weight of the cello. I felt rather like a servile henchman.

'Just that. Good luck.'

'See you tomorrow, on the train,' I said, loudly, to remind her she couldn't push me away like that.

But she just said: 'I'm not coming back for the holidays – didn't you know?'

I put my arm out to stop her. 'What? Where are you going?'

'I'm going away with Miss Parker. She's having a reading holiday with a group of girls at a friend's house in Devon.' She gave me a friendly smile. 'I'm awfully sorry if you hadn't heard.'

I thought of the Easter holidays with just me, our mother and Uncle Clive. 'No,' I said. 'You can't.' I was trying very hard to keep the wobble in my voice under control.

'Sorry, Sarah. We're off to the common room. It's Libby's birthday, and I promised her I'd watch her open her present. Then Susan and I are taking it in turns to read aloud to each other.'

Libby, behind me, gave a simpering nod of pure happiness. I shot her a pitying glance. 'You can come too, Sarah! I'd love to have you,' she said.

'Sarah's busy,' Vic said. 'She doesn't want to go about with us in any case. Well, Sarah, I suppose I'll see you next term—'

I heard myself say, 'You *have* to come back with me. You can't leave me there. I'll tell everyone.'

'What?'

'Everything.' I gave a laugh. 'There. At Fane.'

Vic lowered her voice. 'Be quiet,' she hissed. 'You wouldn't.'

'*I* don't care.' I hoiked the cello up over my shoulder and stood up straight, suddenly feeling furious. I gave Susan an up and down glare, turning to Vic. 'I won't have it. You flitting off to other people.'

'What does she mean, Victoria?' Monica said curiously. I hadn't noticed she had appeared. She must have been looking for me. 'Where do you live, then? You've always said your house was a stately home, one of the largest in the country. Is that not true then?'

'Of course it's true,' said Susan. 'Victoria's a Fane, of Fane Hall, in case you didn't know.' As if I weren't there.

'Well,' Vic said. 'Our house is rather large, she's quite right. But let's not go on about it.'

'Do you want me to start telling the truth?' I said. I moved towards her. We were facing each other. 'Do you?'

'Victoria, what does Sarah mean?' Susan asked Vic, total confusion on her face.

The rest of the pack were glancing at one another. We had been to London Zoo many years ago with our father's mother, our little-known grandmother, and I remembered the flamingos now. They moved in a pack, entirely together, their necks swivelling around in a rather pathetic attempt to assert their individuality, when they were essentially bound together.

I stared out of the windows over the grim, still-bare Rutlandshire flats, the endless mud, the clean, clear sky with shivering white clouds.

'I'll come back for a few days,' Vic said quickly. The girls swivelled to look at her. 'I want to make sure you're all right, Sarah. And check on Inigo. My horse, you know,' she said casually to the girls behind her, though Inigo belonged to the stables and Vic hadn't been allowed to ride her at Christmas because our mother said Inigo had given Vic ringworm again during our weekend in October, a fact we had kept secret from school.

'Vic, you're a brick,' I said, smiling at the rhyme and shifting my cello.

'You'll wish I'd stayed away,' she said, quietly. 'Enjoy your lesson.'

As they moved off, chattering and giggling, I patted the cello case, as if it were an old friend. Vic was fourteen now, and I knew that, underneath, she'd be tired of it all. I knew she didn't like Susan, nor Miss Parker. I knew her escape to the holiday reading club was her looking, simply, for a way out. We both were. I didn't blame her. I opened the door to the music room.

It creaked, satisfyingly, as it always did. 'Hello,' I said, putting the cello down on the floor. Mr Williams turned round.

'Ah, Sarah,' he said, and his expression was strange but I didn't notice it then, not till afterwards. 'I wasn't sure if you'd come.'

'Wasn't sure!' I thought he must be joking.

'Very good. Right, let's get on. We don't have long.'

If I'd known it was the last lesson, what would I have asked him?

If I'd known it was the last time I'd see him, how would I have thanked him for changing my life? For making me understand you have to make a noise to be heard? I had always thought I was someone crushed by circumstances beyond my control, that life would never amount to much for a girl like me. The Bird Boy made me see I should look up, look around me. But Mr Williams made me see the way out. I'd fight, and fight, to keep on going, to get to where I had to be. If I'd have known, I'd have shaken his hand. I'd have thanked him for making me see how lucky I was. Because I was lucky, after all.

I played the Brahms cello sonata that last time, and Mr Williams accompanied me on the piano.

You search for a person who understands you musically, in a bone-deep way in which other people don't. He was a great teacher, but there was something between the two of us, a weird-musical-child alchemy that meant we just knew each other. As I played the first low, scraping minor notes of the first movement, I knew it. The acoustic of that room was peculiarly intense. It held the music so the notes sat suspended, shimmering in the chill of the room. It was the first time that I utterly lost myself in a piece. I have played the Brahms many times since, but every time it is as if I am replaying the memory of that first time.

Afterwards, he marked up the score in pencil, reminding me, as ever, to keep my bow straight. We discussed dynamics, and a particularly knotty bit I couldn't play. It was technically too hard for me, he said, but he had wanted me to give it a go, to see how far I could stretch myself, and he was glad. We were completely absorbed in the music in front of us, heads bent over the sheets. At one point there was a thud from the floor below and I jumped, having to remind myself where we were – I could not have told you. I only noticed we'd overrun by fifteen minutes when I looked at his wristwatch, lying on top of the piano.

It was almost still light outside. The evenings were getting longer. I said something cheery as I was packing up, like:

'Righty-ho, Mr Williams, thank you ever so much. Have a wonderful holiday.'

'Yes,' he said. 'Listen, Sarah.' He looked down at his feet. 'It's rather difficult, telling you this, but I'm afraid I won't be back next term.'

I didn't understand what he meant. I swung the cello onto my back and said: 'When will you be back, then?'

'Well, never,' he said. 'I'm afraid I've been dismissed.'

'Dismissed?'

'Yes. Sacked. Fired. I'm leaving today.'

The cello was heavy and I shifted my weight from side to side.

'Mr Williams, don't joke,' I said, praying he was, in fact, joking. 'Tell me what you're really doing this holiday.'

'Sarah.' He pulled up a chair, and unhooked the straps of my cello case from my shoulders. He leaned it gently against the chair. 'I would never joke about something like this.'

I couldn't breathe properly, couldn't catch any air in my lungs. I pressed my lips together, staring at him. 'But we've only just started. I don't understand. Why are you going?'

He didn't answer, so I shouted. 'Why are you leaving me?'

When I replay the scene as an adult, I can see how his hand-knitted jumper hung loosely on his shoulders, how his face was unformed, how young he was. He rubbed his forehead. 'Don't make a noise, please, Sarah. They'll hear.'

I said:

'Did you tell your father about the school, how bad it is?'

'My grandfather. Yes, I did, but that's not why I'm leaving.' Someone made a sound, outside the door, and his head jerked round. 'They're spying on us again. Twisting things . . .' His face was taut, his eyes haunted. 'Listen to me – we don't have long. What's most important to say? Where should I start? There's no time.' He leaned forward. 'Sarah, you are very talented, but you doubt yourself. You play as if you don't want people to see you. You can't do that if you want to make music your life. You have to say: I am here, I am visible, I am a person worthy of your attention. Second: straighten your bow. Work on your little finger, stop it buckling. What else – what else—'

'But – I still don't understand what you're talking about,' I said. Tears stung my nose; I rubbed my eyes. 'You can't be leaving. That's just nonsense.'

'I don't want to leave. I haven't done anything wrong. They have twisted something. She – no, no. I won't do that.' He turned to me, and gripped my wrists. 'They'll come soon. They call someone like you gifted. As if it's been given to you, as a present. You're not *gifted*. You were born with it, and you're working for it, and *that's* what matters, Sarah. The graft. The playing. Playing till your fingers bleed. Oh God.' His face was pinched. 'I am so sorry, Sarah.'

'I still don't understand,' I said, not caring that tears were dripping down my face. 'And if you're gone, what am I supposed to do now?'

He gave a small laugh. 'That's my girl. You must find another teacher. Tell Miss Parker you have to go to Boxers, to the boys' school over the way, for your lessons now you've been left without a teacher.'

'She'll never let me go.'

'Oh, she will. She has to. Otherwise questions will be asked. I've scared her enough for that, that's for sure.'

'Is she the one who's done this?'

But he ignored me.

'Mr Williams . . . what has she done?'

'I won't tell you,' he said. 'She has made vile insinuations, that's all.' He rubbed his face, his hair sticking up on end. 'I didn't know how vindictive some people could be. If you back them up against a wall, they come out firing.'

'Oh, yes,' I said, thinking of my mother. And I happened to glance at the piano, and saw my sister's writing on the sheaf of papers there. Vic had lovely handwriting, stylish and italic. 'What's this?' I said.

'Don't read it,' he said. 'It's not important.'

But I ignored him. I crossed over, and picked up the sheet of paper. It was a letter, carefully spaced and in handwriting I knew better than any other.

Dear Miss Parker

Mr Williams is an unsuitable teacher. We believe he is a danger to all of us and we ask that he be removed from the school at the earliest opportunity. As an example we have a transcript of a conversation between him and Victoria Fox's sister Sarah Fox, wherein he discussed subjects unsuitable for a young girl's ears, let alone a cello lesson. Susan Cowper was forced to give up the cello because of his behaviour towards her. We know the school wants to avoid scandal at all costs. We will do anything to protect the good name of the school and the girls it educates.

Yours very sincerely
Victoria Fox and Susan Cowper

'How have you got this?' I turned to ask him, waving it between my fingers.

'They wrote it out twice. Miss Parker gave me a copy. So I understood. How serious it was.'

I stared down at my sister's handwriting. 'I don't know what they're talking about,' I said.

'They were listening at the door one day. You asked me –' His face was pale, but his cheeks burnt red. 'You asked me about my mother, about how babies grow. They must have heard. They told Miss Parker.'

'Who did?'

'Susan.'

Oh my goodness, Sarah, no. You grow inside your mother. Didn't you know that? You're twelve.

'Susan –' But I kept looking at Vic's handwriting. She must have known I'd see the letter, that I'd know she had a hand in it.

'Back to your new teacher,' Mr Williams said. He blinked, rapidly. 'Where was I—'

'But this isn't true, any of it. Why didn't you say that?'

'I did, Sarah. You must understand I did. But sometimes you're outflanked. Miss Parker has had it in for me since I told her I had concerns about the school. This letter helps her. It's almost too good to be true. Now listen—'

'I won't listen!' He reached out towards me but I flung my arm away, lifting the cello and standing with my back to the wall, facing him, my shoulders shaking, tears sliding down my cheeks. My nose ran. 'How could they? How on earth—'

'I don't know. I don't know!' He gave a weary smile, so sad that it haunted my dreams for many years afterwards. There is no hope, it said. 'You must listen to me,' Mr Williams said. 'They'll come any minute. You must have lessons at Boxers. She has agreed to this. You must ask to be taught by Mr Marshall-Wessendorf. He's an excellent man. I knew him at college. He studied with Becker and Casals.'

I was blowing my nose, but at this I stopped. 'My first teacher was called Julia Marshall-Wessendorf. She had a son, Rudi. She always said he was very talented . . .'

For the first time, his face lit up, the old spark in the kind eyes. He straightened himself, and ran his hands through his hair. 'Really? Excellent. Well, this is a stroke of luck. It will help. You'll go to Rudi.' He tilted his head again and listened, like a bird, straining to hear the sounds outside. 'You're thirteen soon, aren't you? There's still lots of time, Sarah.' He put his hand on my shoulder, just as someone knocked sharply on the door, and we froze. I knew it was over then, that this was it.

'Thank you,' I whispered. I swallowed. 'But I don't want you to go.'

But he ignored me. 'Listen,' he said, and the knock came again at the door. 'I want you to remember what I said. Play as if your *life* depended on it. Make sure you live too. Live with passion, and love, and hatred, and rage – all the things life needs to give it spice.'

'Mr Williams,' came a small, piping voice. 'Mr Williams? Miss Parker said to say the car is ready for you.'

I watched him, hands clenched by my sides, my shoulders raised up almost to my ears. He looked at me, but through me, as though I had already gone, and he was talking to himself. 'Have you told your family you're going home?' I asked.

He shook his head. 'What will I say to them? How will I explain? She's told so many people these ugly lies . . .'

'Are you going back to London? Can you tell me that?'

He looked at me, past me, as if I wasn't there. 'Back to London. Yes. That's what I'll do.'

'Mr Williams? What's your address? Can I write to you?'

'No, Sarah. I'm sorry. You can't. Remember about the lessons. And remember: you have to play loudly to be heard, Sarah. Don't ever stop, no matter how hard it is. I'm sorry. I'm so very sorry . . .'

I bowed my head, unable to look at him as he left. The door

banged open then swung shut. All was still in the grey, chilly room. I was alone.

The whispering started as I made my way back through the school corridors and to the dorm. The girls stood in lines, grey pinafore skirts swinging like bells, hands next to mouths, shielding the words they whispered, trying to conceal what was being said, because it was so very shocking. I ignored them, marching with my cello back to our dorm, where I collapsed on the bed.

I think I must have been there for about ten minutes, listening to the creaking of the wind in the trees and the hush of silence as girls walked past the dorm, peering in to see Sarah Fox, lying on the bed, heartbroken.

Suddenly, someone prodded me – hard – in the back, and I cried out in shock.

'Sarah?' said Vic. 'What's happened?'

I sat up and looked at her. 'How could you do that?'

'What?'

'Write the letter. Put your name to those lies.'

'They're not lies. Miss Parker told me.' Vic folded her arms. A girl scurried past the open door, glancing in. Vic clicked her tongue, and leaned in closer. 'Mr Williams has been dismissed for immoral behaviour,' she said as quietly as possible. 'He's a bad man. He's done it before, apparently, using his position and – well, it's vile and we shouldn't talk about it. Miss Parker has had to ask him to leave. They're taking him to the railway station now. They said it was a good thing the police weren't being called in.'

'I hate Miss Parker,' I said, my voice shaking. 'Oh, Vic – how could you believe her? It's not true.'

'Of course it is.'

'It's not, Vic. Susan Cowper is a liar. *She* should be in prison. If she was eavesdropping, she knows it wasn't a conversation like that. I was asking him about how his brother and sister were born. And he wouldn't tell me.'

'He shouldn't even have allowed the conversation. Susan said you were under his influence, Sarah. It's more than time he was got rid of. You should have known better.'

'You put your name to the letter, Vic. To a lie.'

'It's not a lie. It's disgusting, Sarah.' Her eyes were burning, whether with fear or panic or righteous anger, I wasn't sure.

'But, Vic . . .' I stared at her, and understood for the first time that I was right, and Vic and I had grown apart, and were utterly different, but that I'd got it the wrong way round. I'd come to believe she was the one with the power, and I had none. But that wasn't it. Vic wanted to fit in. She wasn't wild, and free. She was deeply conservative; she had to conform to feel safe. Whereas I no longer cared. I didn't want to fit in.

I sat up in bed, looking at my sister, her lovely narrow face, the bobbed hair – when had she had her hair cut? – falling in her eyes, her thin fingers, lined with red-raw strips where she'd torn the skin away from the nail.

'I'm sorry for you,' I said.

She laughed, in complete disbelief.

'Miss Parker's made a pet of you, hasn't she?' I said. 'You and Susan. I wonder what she's giving you both for all this.'

Vic flinched. 'You see everything in such base terms, Sarah. Blackmailing me to come back to Fane with you at Easter. Making a fool of yourself with that man. You can't see how much you've let the side down. Miss Parker's a good egg. And the girls who care about the school want her to do well.'

I heard the sound of a car door slamming, an engine rumbling, stalling, then, slowly, restarting and moving away. We were silent. I stood up. My shoes squeaked on the sticky lino.

'He didn't do anything wrong, Vic,' I said. 'One day, perhaps you'll understand what *you've* done wrong.'

'You're such a child,' she said, and she stood up, brushed down her skirt, and left.

Chapter Fourteen

My mother picked us both up from the station for the Easter holidays. The sun was blinding white in the midday sky, yet it was still extremely cold. She said nothing as I carefully loaded the cello into the tiny boot, anxiously packing it in with a plaid blanket from the back seat. The car was new, as was the blanket.

She didn't ask us how we were, or how term had been. As we rattled through the narrow Sussex lanes, I wondered if Mr Williams was at home, with his family. And, because I was young and selfish, I wondered if the school had contacted Mr Marshall-Wessendorf yet. I had been to see Miss Parker and told her it was what I wanted, that Mr Williams said it had to happen. She had simply nodded then got up from her desk and led me out of her study, like a donkey.

My mother was singing loudly along the lanes:

'Keep the home fires burning!
Though your hearts are yearning
Though your lads are far away
They dream of home!'

She had a beautiful voice. Lilting, swooping, with laughter in it, touched with gold. Such a lovely sound. I wondered, had *she* ever gathered round a piano, with her mother, playing the cello, her father holding her on his knee, and had they sung together? Had she sung with my father, and Vic? Had we ever all been together, the four of us? She'd said not. Was there music, and noise, ever in her childhood? Because I was starting to see that what had not happened to her was as important as what had happened.

'So,' my mother said, her voice brimming with glee, 'there

have been a few changes since you girls were last at Fane. I hope you'll like them.'

'What kind of changes?' I asked.

'For the better. You'll see. I'm much more in *control* of things.' She rolled the word around in her mouth. 'Control. Control. Con. Trol. What a funny word. Cont. Roll.'

'Where's the new car from?' Vic said, cutting across her.

'Oh. I leased it. Used up some money. Vic, you're looking fat again. Too much rice pudding, diddle diddle dumpling.'

I stole a glance at my sister, hands on her knees, her school hat slightly awry and her cheeks flushed. I thought she might be about to cry. But she didn't. She raised her head, her jaw set.

'My name's Victoria now,' she said. 'Don't call me Vic.'

'Oh goodness. You are a twerp, Vic. A twit. An idiot. You're – I'm running out of names for you! You like name changes, don't you? Oh, I could tell you some name changes. You'd never believe me. Twerp. Idiot. Donald. Burnt Oak. Victoria.'

Vic folded her arms. 'Don't talk to me like that.'

My mother started zig-zagging along the road, darting erratically from side to side. I clung to my seat, stomach heaving.

'I'm having fun now,' she said, and she curled her arm in one swoop as we veered into the driveway and began the climb up the drive to the house. I thought I would be sick. I could feel it, sloshing in my stomach, trying to work its way up to my mouth. I swallowed, hard.

'Leave her alone,' I said, my voice shaking with rage. 'Please, just leave her be.' We were in it, back in the mire, the filth, minutes after getting off the train.

'That's enough from both of you,' she shouted. 'It's so close, it's almost mine, and you both . . . He's nearly gone. He knows . . .' She gripped the steering wheel so tightly her elbows stuck out. 'You be quiet, you hear? I will come to you in the night, like a bad, bad witch. I'll twist your hair round the bedframe and tie it there with wire. And you won't be able to move. You'll lie there for days until you starve to death, or pull your own hair out from the scalp. The second earl, Arthur, he lived in Turkey. That's how they punished the women in the harem, the ones who disobeyed. It's good, isn't it?'

I was silent, but Vic looked over at her, and I saw her expression. 'Oh, shut up,' she said. 'Just shut up.'

No child I had come across, in my nearly thirteen years, had told a grown-up to shut up. I rubbed my eyes. Then Vic moved closer to the front seat. Clutching the leather headrest with her slim little fingers, she hissed into our mother's ear:

'Sarah and I are only here this holiday to tell you we've had enough. Miss Parker is our headmistress and I am in her confidence. I've told her some of what goes on here. She is watching you carefully.'

My mother was quiet, for once. 'That's a total bloody lie,' she said eventually.

'It's the truth. I don't know what you're doing this for, but it hasn't worked.'

'Doing what for?'

'The house! This damned house.' Vic's voice rose then, and fell, like a bird falling to earth. 'Why you've had this obsession with coming back here. Us living here. Trying to finish off Uncle Clive. It won't ever work. Who are you doing it for?'

'For you girls.' My mother began rolling the sounds around on her tongue. 'You girlsssss. That's a funny word too. I'm doing it to make it right. I'm doing it for you. For you both.'

Vic shook her head, and folded her arms. 'Oh, be quiet,' she said. We turned the corner, and the great portico of the house came into view, the dull grey pillars each the size of an old tree. 'It's all been a waste, Mother. Sarah came back because of Stella, and I came back because of Sarah.'

My mother cleared her throat, then muttered something under her breath. I heard 'Stella'. Then, quite suddenly, she picked up speed. 'She makes mess, and *he* invites her in,' she said. 'That stupid filthy owl. I'll kill her if I get my hands on her. I got the house back. It's my house. What I've done for you – what I've been through – what I've had to lie and cheat about to get us back here – You've no idea—'

'I said shut up,' said Vic calmly, cutting her off. 'Stop driving like this. Slow down. Stop being like this. Just stop it all.' She opened the car door. 'I've had enough. It wasn't worth it, whatever it is you've done,' Vic said. 'It's just a house.'

The door flung back, as wide as it could. The sound of crunching gravel under the wheels grew louder. And then she simply stepped out of the car.

I gasped and caught at her, but she was gone, thudding on the ground behind us, like tumbleweed, rolling away. There was a sickening crunch, and a snap, and a low, moaning cry. My mother did not look around. I realised I wasn't looking back to see how Vic was. I was watching our mother, watching for her reaction. But there was none. She kept on driving the car, right up to the house.

'How are you, darling? How are you?'

'She doesn't answer any more.' Uncle Clive stood in the doorway to the Thin Room, almost in darkness, the gloom of the corridor.

Downstairs, I could hear Dr Brooke, in the hall, talking to someone. I ignored Uncle Clive. 'Darling Stella – how are you? Come here! Look what I have for you!'

Stella paid no attention. She sat on the edge of the shelf by the window, and closed her eyes, rendering her frontage entirely white. 'Like a newel post, on a staircase,' I said. I made sure to make a little noise as I approached, so she wasn't startled. Still she didn't move. I was tired, and shaken, and afraid for Vic, unable to shake the image of her small, broken body, lying on the driveway like a patchwork doll.

'I should have thought of all people you would have some understanding of animals. Owls aren't puppies, or babies. They're lazy, they like an easy life and they're not particularly intelligent. She doesn't need you any more. I don't think she ever did, really. You gave her five weeks of unremitting attention – you ruined her for the outside world – and then you left.'

I turned towards him, taking in the sight of him, his rail-thin tall frame, his long, square head with the shaggy hair falling in his eyes. 'I had to leave,' I said uncomfortably. He really looked half dead to me, a walking skeleton. It was painful watching him, but always at the edge was that feeling of unease he gave me, the sense that he would, if he had to, reach out and squeeze me to death, crush my skull like a mouse he'd caught.

He closed his eyes gently. 'Listen. I've seen their nest, such as it is. It's in the Fane mausoleum, next to the church. The window's been smashed for some time now, glass blown out years ago. She's in there. She wants to mate. She will lay eggs soon. She's not a pet.'

I heard Mr Williams again. *You grow inside your mother.* I had grown, inside Iris. So had Vic. The idea was utterly crazy. How?

'Did you have any children, Uncle Clive?'

His huge, craggy face loomed into the bedroom. 'Don't be foolish. You know I didn't.'

'How did you meet Aunt Dolly?'

'What's all this about? Why are you asking me? I met her out in Canada. That enough for you?'

'She was Canadian, wasn't she?'

'No, she was from Sydenham. Like me.'

'What do you mean, like you?'

'Sydenham was where I'd trained, you blasted idiot. I joined up and was sent there to barracks. And I met Dolly out in Lakeshore. She was running a bar. Pretty rough place. Such a sweet thing. A lovely, lovely girl. Her family had emigrated, looking for gold, and they'd all died and she was stuck out there in this mining village on the edge of the world. We knew the same parts of London, you see. I promised her, I said we'd come back. I said I'd look after her . . .' He rubbed his face. 'She didn't believe me. Her face . . . oh ho, her face when we drove up towards the house, that first time. "There," I said. "Didn't I tell you?" Now, you don't tell anyone that,' he said, walking towards me, and he grabbed my school blazer and held me up, so that my feet left the floor and my shoulder felt as if it was tearing. 'You do not breathe a word about any of that, you hear?'

'What? Why?'

'Where my training was . . . top secret . . .' He looked as if he couldn't remember why, as if he didn't know why he was there. He set me down again, and my knees buckled. I sat on Vic's bed. 'Secrets, you see. Mustn't talk about our secrets.'

'I won't say anything.' I watched Stella, impenetrable to me now, her dark eyes shut. Clive turned, very slowly, in the doorway.

'Anyway . . . I was coming to say . . . Don't come and see me any more. I don't want to see you again. All right?'

'But you've come to me,' I said, confused.

'I said don't come and see me. Don't be rude. Do you understand?'

I shrugged, to hide how upset I was. 'Why not?'

'I don't like it. Poking your nose in. Interfering. You're on her side anyway.'

'I'm not on her side,' I said. 'I don't have a side. She brought us here.'

'Ah, but you're asking questions. You're her child. She wants to get rid of me. But she doesn't know. She doesn't know what's coming.'

'I don't know what you're talking about.'

'Never mind.' Uncle Clive was expressionless. He stood on the threshold, holding on to the door frame. 'I wonder if it was worth it,' he said after a minute.

'What?' I rolled my aching shoulders, up and down.

'Coming back from Canada. Sometimes I think, what if Dolly and I had stayed out there.' His eyes slid from me to the cornicing to the floor, sly, furtive. 'I often wish the whole lot was gone. Razed to the ground. Flattened like it never existed.' He thumped the door frame with his fist, and a piece of plaster from the cornice crumbled and fell lightly onto us. 'I've said too much now. Leave me be. 'Night.'

I found Vic propped up in bed in the West Wing, in the one good bedroom, near my mother's and directly above the Rose-Red Drawing Room. It had pink floral wallpaper and a white bed with a glossy, oyster-coloured quilt.

I'd run into the house after it happened, and my mother had disappeared straight away. I'd run back to find Vic on the driveway whilst Mrs Boyes had driven to the village and fetched Dr Brooke, and they'd taken her up to the house and we'd all helped her into bed, and I'd left her whilst she was examined. She was all right. She had a bandage placed over one eye, to strangely comical effect, and her right arm was in a sling. She was very pale, almost as white as Stella, but she was eating a sandwich, and reading a book called *Trouble in the Fourth Form*, and at first I was so glad to see her I nearly threw myself at her. I darted forward to hug her, but something stopped me. I patted her foot awkwardly instead.

'Vic . . .' I nestled on the bed, as close to her as I could. 'How are you?' She carried on eating. 'I think you're awfully brave. Thank you,' I said, awkwardly. 'For . . .'

She swallowed, and fastidiously brushed her fingers over the side of the bed, showering me with crumbs in the process.

'For what? I didn't do it for you.'

'Well, I know, but it was jolly exciting anyway,' I said stoutly.

'You thought it was *exciting* seeing me fall out of a car.' She raised one delicate eyebrow.

'I didn't mean it like that.'

'Fine.' She turned a page.

'Vic,' I said, trying one last time, 'I wanted to talk to you. Can't we be friends again?'

She glanced up from her book. 'Oh, Sarah. Do go away and stop bothering me. You forced me to come back here, and I've proved my point. Iris knows I won't put up with it any more. Just forget I'm your sister, forget we're related, forget you know me. Next year, I'll take my O levels and as long as I pass them it doesn't really matter. I'll be able to get away. And everything will be fine!'

And she gave a slightly manic grin. I thought she was joking, and smiled, in return.

'What will you do?'

'I want to be a vet. Or –' She pushed a lock of hair out of the way and said casually, 'I thought I might learn shorthand. Miss Parker says I could even stay on at the school and help her. Be a secretary.'

Astonished, I said: 'You'd stay on to work at Haresfield? *Really?*'

She gave an angry shrug, then winced, and lightly touched

her right shoulder. 'We need to earn a living somehow, Sarah. I don't think you've realised that. How will you get away from here otherwise?'

'It's obvious,' I said. 'The cello.'

She actually laughed.

'It's everything. It's all I think about.' She gave a patronising smirk, but I knew it had hit home. 'It won't be easy, but Mr Williams said I have a chance to play professionally if I work hard enough.'

I saw her mouth clench. 'You mustn't mention him again.'

'How did Susan get you to help her with the letter?' I asked. 'Did she threaten you with something?'

'She didn't *threaten* me. Stop being so dramatic. I was trying to *help* you. She heard what she heard, Sarah.'

'But she didn't hear anything! We were having a conversation about how his sister and brother . . .' I trailed off.

She laughed at my dumbstruck expression. 'Come on, Sarah. You're twelve, not a baby. He's a . . .' She hesitated, and I knew she wasn't sure of the word, but I knew what word she was reaching for. 'He's a pervert.'

I had had nasty experiences, as all girls do – an innocuous bowler-hatted man next to me on a Piccadilly Line Tube train who, under cover of his *Times*, began quite leisurely rummaging around inside my knickers, roughly and impersonally as I sat quite still, trembling and ashamed. And a man on the street one day, who blocked us against a wall and asked Vic to hold something for him, but Vic being Vic had said briskly, 'Oh, go away,' and left him there in the street, his dangling member wagging in the dank air. I remembered these men, and others too, whose behaviour made me uncomfortable. I was quite sure Mr Williams was not one of them.

'Vic, I can't believe you're swallowing all this . . . this bilge. It *is* bilge too. Mr Williams isn't the one who's trouble. Miss Parker is. He's been left without a job.' I thought of the hollow way he rubbed his face, his staring eyes. *How will I tell my family? They won't understand. They won't understand . . . because it's not true.*

But she simply turned a page of her book. 'I think you'd better go now, Sarah.'

I wish now I'd shaken her by her bruised and torn shoulders, told her that she was good but not good enough at being the School Pash, that she should give it up and go back to being the Vic I knew and loved, brusque and direct and kind, and not one to run this sort of affair, not someone who sat with false smiles plastered across their face talking about how things were all Fine. She and I had once watched two foxes doing something together when we had come on a visit to Fane as young children and afterwards Vic had said, in her dry, stiff way, 'Goodness gracious, Sarah. I don't know what that was about, but it looked jolly interesting.'

I wish I'd bound her to me then, so tightly that she had to keep me with her. So tightly that we came first, everyone else second. But the wolves were at the door and I did not. I nodded. 'All right then, Vic.'

I left her reading, went downstairs. It was darker now, the sky that deep cornflower blue you get in spring, and through the porthole in the stairs I stopped and looked up at the stars emerging, and as I did I saw Sirius, the Dog Star, gently appear, and then another star, and another.

At the bottom of the stairs was a side door, and I went out onto the end of the terrace. Something moved, further ahead of me, and I started. My mother was pacing up and down the stone steps, back and forth.

They say with memory that you only remember an event once – and after that you are recalling the memory *of that event* – so every time it is a little more distorted.

When I look back at some moments in my childhood, I wonder if perhaps some of this was not her fault, and if there might have been a way in which she could have been helped. And then I'm not sure, and tell myself she was evil – it is easier to remember it that way. But some little tears in the fabric covering the past leave gaps through which I can clearly see scenes with such intensity that I have to pause. My eyes ache with the sensation of wanting to cry. For me, for us all.

There were five wide, low steps running the length of the front terrace from the drive, and she was walking up and down, muttering to herself. '*One two three four five one two three four five one two three four five*—'

‘What are you doing?’ I said, and she stopped, and her eyes darted over me, as if she were trying to remember who I was.

‘I’m counting,’ she said. ‘It’s so loud sometimes,’ and she touched her head. ‘I can think.’

I went inside, leaving her alone. When I looked out a little while later, she was still going up and down the steps, marking out the seconds, the minutes.

Chapter Fifteen

Two days later, on Good Friday, I was upstairs on the top floor, trying to finish tidying up the little bedroom next to the Star Study, when I heard a bell ringing. It was loud, rather shrill, and I could hear the echo of it across the grounds, as far as the edge of the woods. I realised where it was coming from. It was a telephone on the floor below.

I went down the back stairs that I never used, towards the far end of the West Wing and the sound of the ringing. I flung open my mother's bedroom. In the centre of the room was the telephone, ringing loudly. But there was no telephone at Fane – or at least there had formerly never been one.

I picked the receiver up. 'Hello?' My voice was croaky.

'Who's that?' The line crackled with heavy static and a muffled voice said: 'That Lord Ashley?'

'You can talk to me,' I said, without thinking, and I lowered my voice to sound as grown up as I could. 'Go ahead.'

'Good. Listen. It's happening Monday. I'm just making certain . . . it's the West Wing we start in?'

'Yes. I understand. What time?'

The low, aggressive voice grew closer to the phone. 'First thing, of course. Not a word. You understand? You tell him, yeah? You made sure you'll have cleared out? Got that?'

'Yes,' I said, as firmly as I could. 'I know. Thank you.'

'Listen.' The line crackled. 'You . . . sure about this?'

'Course,' I said.

'Right. G'bye, then.' And with a click the line went dead.

That afternoon, Miss Parker swept up the driveway and, with the engine running, waited for Vic to emerge. I watched, covertly, from our bedroom window. She tapped her cigarette on the walnut dashboard, looking up at the vast façade of the house, her shiny nose wrinkling slightly, wondering – where was that smell coming from? Was it her? I could see she was impressed: Victoria Fox hadn't lied, after all, about the situation of her antecedents; she was definitely someone to be cultivated. I saw her adjusting the little hat she wore with the jaunty feather on it, thinking she was quite marvellous. Her mouth curled into a little smirk. I hopped off the windowsill and went downstairs.

'Good afternoon, Miss Parker,' I said, appearing behind her as she got out of the car.

'Hello – hello – Sarah!' she said. She gave me a bright smile. 'Well! Are you having a nice Easter?'

We were always being told not to use the word 'nice'. *A better word than 'nice'* Miss Trubshawe had written on the board last term, and we'd had to write down substitutes: *Great pretty beautiful fun pleasant cordial.*

I looked at her. 'Very nice, thank you,' I said. 'I've been out looking for my barn owl. She's laid eggs, apparently, but I can't find her. And I've been practising the cello lots.' Her eyes flickered to the side, and around. She could not have been less interested.

'How funny. Aren't you a bit old for that sort of thing? Owls, I mean.'

'I found her, injured, in the summer holidays. They starve when they can't hunt for food. I catch mice for her and I've built her a nesting box she can use in my bedroom. And now she's built a nest in the graveyard, and—'

'Never mind now, dear,' said Miss Parker. 'Where's your sister?'

'She hurt her arm so everything's taking her a bit longer, but she'll be here in a minute.'

There was an awkward silence.

'Have you heard from Mr Williams?' I asked.

'Who?'

'Mr Williams. The – my—'

'Oh! Of course. What do you mean?'

'Is he all right? Do you know if he's found another job?'

'Heavens, Sarah, how should I know? I should hope he thinks very carefully about what he does next.'

'You know as well as I do—' I began, but she shushed me again.

'Ah! Here she is.' The great front door opened with a wheezing creak and Vic appeared, lugging an ancient suitcase with her good arm. The faintest smell of the stench rolled out behind her, and she shut the door hurriedly. It was very silent – just the three of us.

'Let me take that, Victoria,' said Miss Parker with a broad smile. 'What have you been up to, then?'

'Oh,' said Vic with a bashful smile. 'Absolutely ridiculous, entirely my fault – the car door opened and I fell out. I'm fine. It's much better now.'

'Aren't you silly! What a thing to do,' said Miss Parker with a gleam in her eye. She liked belittling people, anyone she could, it was a sort of reflex. 'Come on, then. Get in the car.'

Vic looked at me. She said: 'I didn't get you anything for your birthday, but there's some books in our room you can borrow if you want.'

'I don't care about my birthday,' I said angrily. I had to blink forcefully to bat away tears. I couldn't make her stay, and I knew she was trying to get away, that I had become dead weight.

Miss Parker was waiting, humming to herself, occasionally crouching down and looking in the wing mirror of the car.

'I haven't seen either of them,' Vic said to me quietly. 'I don't know where Iris is. I haven't seen her since yesterday evening. And I just can't find Uncle Clive. I've looked for him.'

'Why?'

Vic looked down at her feet. 'I probably won't be coming back,' she said casually.

'Oh.'

'Sarah,' she said, and she moved her arm in the sling closer against her body, and I realised she still must be in pain. 'Have you seen either of them, the last couple of days?'

I opened my mouth to speak and then shut it again.

'I went up to find her,' Vic said in a low voice, very fast. 'To tell her why. To say . . .' Her voice thickened, and she trailed off. 'All the things I want to say,' she said eventually. Her good hand crept across to mine, in the chilly afternoon spring light. 'I don't know where she is. And I realised . . . I haven't seen her since Wednesday evening.'

'I think she's gone,' I said.

'Gone? Where?'

'No idea. The London flat?' The flat was still in the family, and had never been sold, even though we were hopelessly behind with the bills and management fees.

'Why would she go back there?' said Vic.

I'd seen our mother driving away yesterday lunchtime in her new car. She sometimes did go off in the car, but now I thought about it I hadn't heard her at all since then.

Vic looked at me expectantly. I wanted to tell her about the phone call, the man who'd said they were coming, that they'd start in the West Wing. I wanted to fling my arms around her and tell her about Christmas, when Iris had hit me so hard I couldn't see or hear straight for a few days. Vic had noticed. But she'd never asked.

I shrugged. 'No idea.'

'Hurry up, Victoria!' Miss Parker called. 'What *can* you two be talking about!'

But Vic ignored her. 'So she's gone. What about Clive? I haven't seen him either. Sarah—'

'I saw him yesterday.' I felt nausea pooling in the pit of my stomach.

I'd been out in the churchyard and the woods, looking for Stella and was coming back when I saw him. I didn't say that he hadn't heard me when I called to him, that he was grey, and shuffling like a ghost, his feet wrapped in old rags as his shoes were entirely worn through. He had walked up to the Burnt Oak, very slowly, looking up at it, and I could see his lips moving. His eyes, raised up to the top of the Oak, were hooded and blank. He lifted his arm, shaking his fist at the Oak, and I heard sounds, carried on the wind, but couldn't make out what he was saying.

I didn't say that I'd watched him stumbling, and hadn't gone to help him, that I hadn't seen him since, and that I wouldn't dare go and look for him, because I was too scared, and that I'd be on my own in the house if she left, and it terrified me.

I saw now I had to let her go. I knew that if it was the other way round she'd do the same for me. It occurred to me if I told her I thought our mother had cleared out and Clive had vanished and I was alone that Vic might stay. I wanted her to be safe.

'I'm going to tea with him a bit later,' I added. I sniffed and wrinkled my nose, then looked away, as if I was tired of the conversation.

'Why don't you come with us?' she said suddenly. 'If she's gone and it's just him here . . .'

'I'd rather die,' I said childishly. 'Just go away. Clive and I are fine without you.'

Her face hardened.

'Come on, Victoria!' Miss Parker called. 'It's as if my time isn't important! Do hurry up now.'

'Sorry,' said Vic, putting her case into the boot with her good arm. I saw her adjusting her school beret, turning back to the house once more. She looked up at it. 'Right, then.'

Miss Parker followed her gaze. 'I must say, this is a very impressive house. Susan didn't exaggerate about it. I wonder if I might meet your mother before we go. Is she in? May I say hello to her?'

'No.'

'I beg your pardon?'

'I'm sorry, she's not in. She sends her apologies.'

'Well, it doesn't matter.' She opened the driver's door of the car and got in, but didn't make any effort to help Vic, who lowered herself in, slowly. 'Hurry up, Victoria, do! Sally Farnsworth is joining us later and so you can go in the back. My little click.' Her cold, hard eyes fixed on me.

'It's clique,' I said. 'Not "click".'

'It's *not* very *nice* to point out others' mistakes, Sarah Fox. It shows a second-rate mind. Anyway! Let me just fix my hat and scarf, dear.'

She started fiddling with her scarf, angling the wing mirror towards herself, oblivious of the appearance of it, how she betrayed herself. My mother, with wearisome tedium, was a stickler for correct usage – writing paper not notepaper, that sort of thing.

I leaned in towards Vic, as though giving her a hug. 'I say,' I said, and she turned towards me, I think momentarily disarmed.

'Well . . . Bye, then, Sarah,' she said. 'Happy birthday for Sunday.'

She paused, waiting for me to answer. The bandage was off her eye now, and the bruising had gone down a little bit. But her face had a pinched look.

In reply, I leaned forward, and began slowly clicking my fingers. Then I whispered in her ear.

'We're not sisters any more,' I said. 'I release you.'

Her small body was suddenly rigid; I felt the sharp intake of breath. 'You can't do that.'

'I do,' I said, biting my lip. I couldn't look at her. 'You're not my sister any more. You betrayed me, with the letter. With everything you've done. I release you.'

'Right, then!' said Miss Parker, looking up from the wing mirror. 'Sarah, don't hold us up.'

'Oh, I won't,' I said. 'Goodbye!'

Vic looked at me. She clicked her fingers back at me. There was something final and bleak about the deadened expression in her eyes. Miss Parker tooted the horn.

Vic smiled at Miss Parker. 'I'm ready now!' she said and called up, 'Bye, Mother! Bye, Uncle Clive! Yes, I'll write! Bye, then, Sarah. See you soon!'

I wondered what Vic, honest to her core, would manage to find to tell Miss Parker as to the neglected state of the house. I watched them drive away, out towards the gates, the fresh gold haze of the spring afternoon casting sharp shadows on the newly green parkland. 'Goodbye, Vic,' I said to myself. I walked back up the steps of the silent house, and turned back. A black mark crested the undulating grounds, moving swiftly – I looked up, but it was only a crow.

Chapter Sixteen

'The best thing about a birthday in April,' Mrs Marshall-Wessendorf had told me after I revealed I'd had no cards on my birthday – I was ten – 'is that perhaps once or twice in your lifetime you will have a birthday on Easter Sunday, the day of renewal! And that only happens to the *very best people*, Sarah.'

I woke early, the promise of sun slipping into my small, cold room, easing itself over the fluted wooden casement, searching me out like a spotlight. I sat up in bed, and looked at my wristwatch: seven o'clock. I knew that I wouldn't get back to sleep – I had that fizzing, watchful feeling and my heart was racing.

In what one might cite as the ultimate example of the triumph of hope over experience I really always did look forward to my birthday. I enjoyed wondering what might happen, if it might be grand. If there might be a surprise – perhaps a party! The very same year I received no cards or presents, Melissa Hartley, one of our classmates at Minas House, had a clown at her tenth birthday party who gave us all a balloon and there had been a miniature Shetland pony we were allowed to ride around the garden square in front of her house, supervised by a taciturn, stiff-backed woman in a velvet riding helmet. There were two different cakes: *two*, at a time when there was still rationing and one rarely had one cake, let alone two, and meat paste sandwiches, tasting of meat for once, not sawdust. It was the most utterly wonderful afternoon of my life.

I hadn't given anyone at school my address and because of it being the holidays as well I told myself not to expect any cards. But the day after we arrived back from school a card arrived for me in the post, and I took it up to my room and hid it under the pillow in case my mother reappeared and tore it up, or threw it away, which she had been known to do. So I had something to open today. I sat up in bed, wiggling my numb toes, flattened under the weight of the heavy blankets gathered from empty rooms and piled on the bed. I opened the card, savouring the experience, stretching it out. It was of a girl acrobat standing on top of a prancing horse, about to dive into a glittering blue pool. In rainbow letters above it was the message:

Make a Splash on Your Birthday!

I opened the card.

Dear Sarah
Many happy returns!
Monica

PS I guessed your address!

PPS I'm sure hols at Fane are terrific but if by any chance you would like a change of scene Mummy says do come to Frencham Court – it's in Ripley just off the main road by the old manor house. We have no one else staying. It's wonderful to be back, but I'm already jolly bored. We'd love to have you.

Monica's looping, carelessly joyful writing took up all the space on the card, and went over the edge so some letters were missing. Vic had gone, my mother had gone, I had no idea where Clive was, how I would get back to school in ten days' time, what I would do with my time – but my childhood had taught me acceptance, and to just keep plodding on. I was tough. This card, so honestly sent and expressed, meant more to me than anything. I closed it, and held it for a moment, a sunny feeling of pleasure glowing through me.

'Happy birthday, Sarah,' I said to myself, and leapt out of bed.

I dressed in my ungainly holiday wardrobe of thick lumpy kilt and polo neck and opened the window, letting sweet spring air flood the room. I could smell wetness, chilled earth, new growth, overriding the stench that still, always, filled the house and never quite left.

I climbed up on the bed and looked inside Stella's box. Why? Perhaps I just wanted to know I wasn't alone. It was empty, as I knew it would be. My eye caught something moving in the breeze on the windowsill. A single soft white feather, long and edged with flickers of caramel-gold. I scrambled down, heart racing, and picked it up, staring at it as if it were a sign, a message of some kind.

Downstairs, all was very quiet, but in the daytime I didn't mind being alone. I went into the tiny blue kitchen where I never usually ventured, at the back of my mother's side of the house, and made some weak tea with yesterday's leaves. Mrs Boyes was not here this weekend; she had gone to visit her sister in Broadstairs. I found some bread and toasted it on the gas ring, biting down firmly on the stale crusts. I stared out of the window, at the bleak back courtyard of the house, until the stable clock stirred me out of my relative comfort in the warmth. It was eight thirty. I put on my shoes, pulled on my knitted beret and wondered whether to go to find Uncle Clive and make sure he was all right.

But I realised I couldn't face it. Not today. He wouldn't care that it was my birthday. He would say something nasty about me, or Vic, or my mother. I was so tired of it all. I was thirteen, and I was very tired. I crept out quietly through the front door, and ran all the way to church.

It was still very cold, but spring was here. I saw it now: the tiny yellow daffodils and narcissi shook in the sharp breeze as I ran, stumbling and skipping, towards the church. I could hear the bells ringing. I loved Easter, because it reminded me of my birthday and new beginnings, and didn't make me sad, like Christmas always did.

Last summer the grasses in the park had shimmered silver and gold. Now, in spring, they were bright green, and forget-me-nots poked through the iron railings that formed the narrow walkway. I pushed apart the old iron fenders that curved together, and walked down the path. The sun was warm on my face. I kept thinking of the increasingly deranged Miss Dunoon, who on our last day before the holidays had slapped her hands down on her desk so hard it wobbled, bellowing: 'O grave, where

IS THY VICTORY!' at us which had sent me and Monica, in the front row, into hysterics we only just managed to suppress. I thought about Monica, wondered what she was doing.

Inside I slid into a pew at the back of the church, still shivering. Someone had lit an oil heater which was more successful at dispersing a strong oil smell rather than any actual heat. I opened a Book of Common Prayer, and scrambled to my feet again as the choir processed past me. Tom, the vicar's eldest child, carried the cross.

'Jesus Christ is risen today! Alleluia . . .'

Tom had a beautiful voice, but today as he walked slowly past I could only hear it cracking and faltering, suddenly low then high; I couldn't understand why. Behind in the procession, his sisters were nudging and giggling.

First in the choir stalls was the aged Derek Adam, a man so old he had sung in the special service held when my great-great-grandfather, Lord Arthur Ashley, brought his fabulously wealthy bride, Lady Maria Capstone, back from Barbados. When slavery was abolished in 1834, her family had received £50,000 in compensation for the loss of their slaves, making them one of the richest families in the West Indies and financing the restoration and expansion of Fane Hall. There was a window celebrating this fact in the church.

I watched Mr Adam, his large ears flapping with the exertion of his singing. He stared back at me, and shook his head. I shrank into my seat; I didn't want to be noticed. As they went past, several other people gave me a quick look. Reverend Thomas looked over at me, then away. More and more people did the same. Glancing at me, eyes darting back and forth.

After a while, the congregation began to turn too, to openly stare at me. I could only stand there and pinch myself, wondering if this were a dream I'd had once where I was in the church with people wearing masks who all turned to look at me and then surrounded me. I looked down at feet, at my white, knobbly knees with the dusting of darker hair that had sprung up on them, which Susan Cowper had told me was a sign of lustful thoughts and an absence of good breeding.

'Aren't lustful thoughts needed for good breeding,' Monica

had said thoughtfully when I told her this, which was why I adored Monica.

I wriggled, trying to keep myself warm, and to shake off the stares. It was my birthday. How funny. I allowed myself to imagine what my ideal birthday might look like. A birthday breakfast on a long table on the terrace, decorated with primroses and royal blue muscari in little jars, and a cake with sugared eggs on top.

The hymn ended and there was silence. The chill in the church, the waves of incense lapping over the congregation, made the hairs on my arms stand up. I sat still.

'Lift up your hearts.'

'*We lift them up unto the Lord.*'

Reverend Thomas's voice was lilting and soporific, and I leaned back against the ancient wooden pew. It was very slightly warm. '*The first day of the week cometh Mary Magdalene, when it was yet dark, to the tomb . . .*'

'We pray for the souls of those recently departed,' the Reverend Thomas said, when he had finished the collect. He drew out a single sheet of paper, and closed the Bible. 'Of those who have died in the faith of Christ. On the day of his resurrection and glorious ascension we remember those who died in his love.'

Silence filled the tiny church, waiting to be broken.

'On this day we remember, O Lord, the soul of Clive, Lord Ashley, who departed this life last night and lies in the arms of God our Maker once more.' A silence again. 'Lord, in your mercy.'

'*Hear our prayer*,' the congregation said, and there was some rustling as one or two bold souls dared to turn round. Someone nudged someone else. '*She got* –' I heard them begin, but didn't hear the rest. My legs were stuck to my seat. I could not move. I tried to lift an arm, looking down at it, at my kilt. Nothing happened.

'Grant to Lord Ashley, O most gracious Lord, eternal rest and peace. And,' he said, clearing his throat again. 'Our most *sincere condolences* to the family. And so I call upon those persons here present . . .'

I realised he was talking to me. After a few moments, I was able to grasp my own arm, to lift it, rest it on the pew in front of me. I gaped at the vicar, but he did not look back at me.

When I could, I stood up, shaking so much that my legs gave way and I sank down. The second time I managed to make it to the back of the church, pushing the heavy padded leather door open with such force that it banged against the old stones as the congregation stood to sing again.

The door of the family mausoleum was open, the peeling black paint glinting in the spring sunshine. I saw stacks of stone coffins, piled up disappearing into darkness, like the glass bird cases in the house. Someone had unlocked it, had gone in. The coffins were cracked, the door broken, the mausoleum was collapsing.

I left the church, and as I ran back across the field, I could hear the voices floating across the headstones, across the boundary wall where Stella had flown overhead last summer, following me:

'The strife is o'er, the battle done.
Now is the victor's triumph won.'

As I rounded the parkland and came in view of the house, I saw a car, pulling away. I ran towards it, trying to see more clearly, but it hopped down the driveway, going unevenly from side to side. I ran as fast as I could, and hid behind the Burnt Oak as the car passed by.

It was my mother, her face grey, hands gripping that steering wheel tightly again. Her hair, always neatly twisted, hung about her face, tangled. Her eyes were blank and she was actually crying, her mouth twisted open; she looked terrified. I wanted to shout out, to ask her what she was doing. But I was frozen. I couldn't. Still, to this day, I can't explain why I couldn't call out to her.

I ran under the great portico and inside, feeling the chill spring air settle in on me, fighting as ever with the stench from the house. No banging from my mother's wing. No swearing from Uncle Clive. There was silence. The house was still. Not peaceful. I could feel its energy, something waiting to happen. A dangling banner of dusty cobweb, hanging from the giant carved lintel over the great front door moved very slightly in the breeze.

'Uncle Clive!' I called. 'Uncle *Clive*!'

I could hear someone in the East Wing, the sound of steps. Whispers, furniture moving.

I started walking down the corridor, my shoes echoing. I passed the old library, which always had its doors shut. Past Lady Ashley's drawing room, where Queen Charlotte had once taken tea. Past the state bedroom, and the dressing room, and the closet, and the private study, and the dining room, and the servants' hall, into the kitchen – all rooms, all shut away, once filled with unimaginable wealth, now closed up, full of dead things.

Still calling Clive's name, I arrived in the kitchen. The terracotta floor was still cold, the rooms dark, and smelling worse than usual.

I could hear the faintest sound of someone moving in the next room.

I was immensely relieved. I knew he was still alive; Reverend Thomas had got it wrong. 'Is that you? Uncle Clive? Happy Easter!'

Very, very quietly, I moved towards the door, and flung it open. I screamed. A girl in a jumper and a floral bunched skirt turned with a start, her hands in her pockets. She had short, curling hair, a slightly grubby face and a defiant smile.

'Who are you?' I said sharply. 'What are you doing here?'

She started to back away. 'They're pulling it down soon anyway – everyone knows that,' she said in a flat voice. 'Why can't I take a few souvenirs?'

She had a small suitcase with her, which she was struggling to keep shut. It flapped open, and two saucers and several cups tumbled out onto the floor. One of the saucers broke into pieces.

'Get out!' I shouted. 'You dirty thief! Get *out*, or I'll call the police!'

Her face slid into a sneer, her nostrils flared. 'That's a good one. Who'd come here? No one.'

The wolves are at the door, Uncle Clive had said. They'll crowd round the house, picking off what they want. And we'll tear ourselves apart first, rather than trying to get rid of them.

I yelled again and she laughed, and so I bent down and picked up the nearest thing to hand, which was a book, and threw it at her. 'Clear off,' I shouted, as loudly as I could, and she turned and ran, pulling the lid of the case up, clamping it under her arm. I glimpsed one shining blue-and-gold Spode plate in there, rattling around.

'Get *out*!' I yelled, realising I had to yell. 'And don't come back! No one's pulling this house down! Go away!'

In his bedroom, a dusty, dark dressing room at the back of the house, there was no sign of him, beyond the rumpled bedsheets and a few disturbed books, flung on the ground, spines down, but Uncle Clive was messy and that didn't prove anything. I went back to the kitchens.

'Uncle *CLIVE*!'

I flung the back door open, and called out one last time.

His name rolled around the hard surfaces, bouncing off the tiles and the enamel sink and in the stable and on the rusting corrugated-iron fencing. In the distance, by the ornamental garden, a group of crows in the tall elms took fright and flew away. The sound echoed back at me.

I went inside, and closed the door, but not before I noticed the stable was locked up. Normally, the top half of the big doors were left unlocked, as if the ghosts of old horses might still stick their heads out, watching the comings and goings of a great house.

Back in the kitchen, I found some Bath Olivers and munched them till the roof of my mouth was mealy and dry and I could hardly swallow. I ate a very soft, puckered old yellow apple, which was woolly but which had some sweetness to it, and drank some water, and then I wandered back to the Great Hall.

On the hall table there was an object, wrapped up in brown paper and twine, a piece of green card attached to it. I hadn't spotted it this morning, as I'd left through the side of the house. How long had it been there? I went up to it. There on the tag, was a scrawling message in my mother's handwriting.

For Sarah

I have business in town for a couple of days and will be staying at the flat.

It is your birthday on Sunday. Don't say I didn't remember. My main present to you is my mother's cello. This note is proof, should you need it, that ownership transfers to you. Don't let them forget that. Don't let them take it from you. What I did not tell you was that it is a Goffriller cello, and very valuable. My mother was given it by her teacher when she retired. She played it for many years. She made a beautiful sound. I can still hear her, when I close my eyes. My father loved the sound. I hear lots of sounds; I don't mind that one.

You are thirteen and old enough to do without me now I think. Here is another present I found last night by the Burnt Oak. I thought you would want her back. It was peaceful at the end.

Everything I have done has been for a reason. One day you will understand why.

I tore off the paper wrapping, then unfolded the thick heavy silk, left over from curtains upstairs. I thought I heard footsteps, running above me, and I jumped, but it was nothing.

It was very quiet in the hall, in the house. I kept unrolling. My fingers closed over the unwrapped package, its lightness, the soft smoothness. I looked down.

The dark eyes, now and forever fixed open in the heart-shaped face. The softness of her white down, the golden edging of her markings that was like gilding. The slight, very slight twist of the wing which was how I knew it was Stella.

Her eggs, delicately framed around her, resting on moss and straw. Unwrapped, she rested on my upturned hands. She was only a small bird.

You are old enough to do without me now, my mother had written.

I stood in the hallway for a long time. I don't know how long. Then I went and got some more water. I climbed the stairs to the top floor, and looked out of the window, thinking.

Eventually, I went to the spare bedroom and took the cello

out of its canvas case. I settled myself on the rickety old chair and balanced the Brahms sonata against another chair and started playing. I didn't cry. I played until the tips of my fingers were burning red and sore, my left forefinger was pale and starting to blister, and my back and shoulders ached terribly. I played, and played, alone in the house. There were times when I thought I heard movement coming from other floors. Running footsteps, whispers, floorboards creaking. But I knew it was ghosts. I simply carried on playing.

Chapter Seventeen

The men came early. I'd slept deeply that night, to my surprise. I heard a rumbling noise and turned to one side in the creaking bed, rubbing my eyes. A van was wobbling up the uneven surface of the drive. It drew to a halt, the doors flinging open, and four men jumped out and walked up the steps.

It was so shocking seeing them casually walk in. They didn't knock, or call out, just walked through the hall and towards my mother's end of the house, boots heavy on the rotten floorboards. I could hear sounds of chatter, the smell of cigarettes, someone laughing. And I realised: *they think there's no one here.*

I didn't stop to think. I dressed and grabbed my trunk, from under my bed, and threw my possessions into it. My uniform, home clothes, a jumper and skirt that were now too small, but I took them anyway. Vic's wristwatch, her pony books. My cello music, the stand, my birthday card. On top of them I laid Stella, carefully wrapped in her shroud. I dragged the chest downstairs and down the steps as quietly as I could, then ran back up for the cello, and just as I finished and was standing underneath the portico, I heard them behind me, come into the hallway. There were four of them: three younger men were in overalls. Two had thick, slicked-back hair, one with a cigarette behind his ear. The youngest stood chewing his lip, looking around him, wide-eyed. The older man was in a tweed jacket and baggy trousers, bunched up round the waist. He had a shining pate, carefully combed hair over it, and when he talked there was a huge gap between his teeth. He inhaled his cigarette heavily, then dropped it onto the floor, where it kept burning as he talked.

My things were at the bottom of the steps. I hid behind a pillar, watching the older one stroke the black marble statue of

Cassandra, almost as if she were real. The front door was open and I could hear them perfectly clearly.

'Nice place,' said one of the men.

'What about the lead?' said another. 'Be a good lot of lead up there.'

'It's gone already. Soldiers would've taken it. Shut your mouth, all right, Frank?' said the older man. 'Never know who might be around.'

'Where's the old man?'

'No idea, have I? He said he'd clear out. Now listen.' The older man moved his hand over his head, smoothing down the thin stripe of hair in a lightning, lizard-like motion. 'Out the back there's where the booty is. Just load those there crates up. Load it up and take it away.'

They nodded. The younger boy lit a cigarette. His hands were shaking, his eyes rolling around his head, like a nervous mare about to bolt.

'What for?'

'What for?' said the older man, mocking. 'We sell it, that's what we're here for,' he added. 'Then we give him half – or we tell him it's half, and we take the rest. Let's get on with it then we hop it. And when they ask, we weren't anywhere near this place, you got that?'

'What about the kids, and the mum?' said the boy. 'I don't like it, George. You said there'd be no one here.'

'He don't know what's he's talking about,' the older man said. 'He's lost the plot. I tell you, this is an easy job. Get in, get out, don't worry about the old man.'

'What about the kid?'

He laughed, scornfully. 'She's not here! There's no one here, Billy! Get that in your head. No one here at all.'

So I was the last Fane, here at the end. I thought about all the Fanes who'd gone before, all those who had lived on this very spot, for hundreds of years, the millions of hours spent polishing silver, dressing hair, waxing floors, giving birth to children, discovering new stars, carving wooden panels, planting vegetables, the thousands of people who'd cared for the house, and it came down to me, standing alone on the steps.

There was something I knew I had to do before I left. I walked round the outside of the house once, widdershins. I walked past my mother's wing, and through the stable yard, then the West Wing, Clive's kitchen door, the kitchen gardens, around the front of the house to the steps again. They did not see me – I knew how to move quietly. Then I picked up the cello and my trunk, and inhaled. Somewhere, someone had lit a fire. The spicy, heady smell of woodsmoke was like home. I breathed in, smelling the smoke, and the fresh air, and the wet earth, and walked away.

I turned back once, and looked at the house, then kept on going, as fast as I could. Halfway along the drive I put down the cello and removed something from the trunk and ran to the Burnt Oak. Using a small, flat slab of stone I'd taken from the terrace as a makeshift shovel, I scrabbled away at the loose earth until there was a grave. I placed Stella into it, silk shroud and all. I filled it over, then stood on it, tamping it down with my feet, and as I did I stared at the house.

I didn't know what to do next. I couldn't go back to the house or back to school, which was closed for Easter. It was a bank holiday, so there were no buses. I started dragging my trunk away from the tree, down the drive. *Forget about it all*, I told myself. *It's over. It's really over.*

'Good morning,' came a voice behind me, and I jumped.

I turned. There was the Bird Boy, a cricket ball in his hand.

He threw it in the air, and caught it.

He seemed to have stretched: he was tall and gangly, his thick hair flopping over his eyes. He wore a shirt under a navy jumper, khaki slacks, and slip-on leather loafers. He was the very embodiment of youth, and modernity, a figure from another world. For a few moments, all I could do was stare at him.

'What are you doing here?'

'I'm back to visit Mrs Boundy. I was out all day, but last night she said they announced your uncle was dead in church yesterday. I thought I'd better come down this morning and see if you're all right.'

I put the cello down. 'Actually,' I said, trying to stop my voice from shaking. 'I'm not all right. The thing is I'm not sure what to do. Or where to go. And um . . .' I swallowed. I would not cry like a little girl. I cleared my throat.

He just said: 'I see.'

I took a deep breath, and then realised I could tell the Bird Boy. That I could tell him any of it, all the insanity of it. On the breeze was still the scent of woodsmoke and I wrinkled my nose, noticing it yet paying no attention to it. 'I'm not even sure if Great-uncle Clive is even dead. Reverend Thomas said it in church, but I don't believe it.'

'Your mother telephoned the vicar to tell him, I heard.'

'But where? He's not in the house. I looked in every room.'

He shrugged. He didn't know – why would he?

'She left – she left me a present. Of sorts. Stella's dead. She wrapped her body up.'

'Oh, Sarah.' His thin face, grown to almost-maturity, was sad.

'I think it was the cold,' I said. 'She had eggs too . . .' I trailed off. Stella was under the ground and I was on my own now. 'But my mother was definitely here. And now she's gone, and I don't know where.' It was such a relief, knowing I could tell him and he'd understand.

'I saw her the day I came back, Saturday I think. Driving so fast she nearly jolly well knocked me down. I shouted at her.' He shrugged. 'She told me to watch out. Even for her she sounded – ah – jolly mad.'

I nodded. 'I have to get away from here, I think.'

He threw the cricket ball in the air, gently. 'Yes. I think so too, if you don't mind me saying so. Where will you go?'

'I don't know,' I said, and stopped, but suddenly I realised I did know. 'I'll go to my friend Monica's.'

'Who's she?'

'She's my best friend. She invited me.' I could see the writing on the card now. I'd filed it away, in my head, for when I needed it. 'She's in Surrey,' I said. 'It's a house called Frencham Court. Near a manor.'

The Bird Boy threw the cricket ball in the air again. 'Gosh, does everyone you know live in a stately home?'

'I don't think it's very grand. Her father sells cars. Very smart cars, but she's not a – a duke or anything like that.' We smiled at each other. 'It's in Ripley,' I said suddenly. 'That's the village.'

'I know Ripley,' he said.

'Really?'

'Yes. Mrs Boundy took me to visit her sister there once. It's a lovely place. Near Guildford.'

I shrugged, and he smiled at me. 'I haven't the faintest idea. Do you think there's a train there?'

He looked at his watch, and said: 'No trains today. But I'll drive you, if you want.'

'You don't have a car.'

'Dr Brooke has one. He lets me use it.'

I could have prevaricated; I could have fluttered and protested. I simply said, 'Would you mind? That's very kind.'

'It's not kind,' he said seriously. 'Everyone wants to get you away from here. But I'm awfully glad to see you again, Sarah.' He glanced up at the Burnt Oak, then over at the house. 'Shall we go?'

'Yes,' I said. I faced him. He was standing with his back to the house. 'Look, before we go – can you tell me something?' I froze, and caught his arm. 'No. Oh no.'

The Bird Boy was holding the cello. He turned round, following my gaze. 'Oh God. Yes,' he said. 'You have to leave now,' he said calmly.

The scent of smoke I kept smelling was not from a cottage fireplace, or a bonfire. It came from Fane. Flames were licking the house, curling from the inside out of the windows, at either end of the long façade. As we turned, on the ground floor of Clive's wing the glass blew outwards, glittering shards of glass flying into the sky leaving a row of rectangular spaces, through which one could see fire – purple, orange, red fire, white at the centre – and in the rooms it had already torn through, burning embers left behind, bright. Gilt-framed portraits now burning white-hot squares, dropping to the floor, rotten, moth-eaten brocade curtains blazing with fire, the sound of glass shattering as the stacks of bird cases started to explode, one by one. Smoke, thick and so black, not like a cloud but more like a cloak, rose above the house, whirling into a cone, twisting itself over the bare black branches of the trees behind the stables.

'What if there's someone still there?' I said. 'Look . . . There's two fires, one at either end,' I said. 'They –' My legs felt strange, woolly, and I staggered, trying to run towards the house, to be closer, to bear witness, to – I don't know what I wanted, but in that one moment the blood of my ancestors rose up in me and I was my mother, and I wanted to rush back inside, finally be subsumed by Fane. I steadied myself, then tried to run again, but I felt someone pulling on my arm.

'No,' the Bird Boy said. 'You're crazy. You can't go back there, Sarah. You know no one's there. You said so yourself.'

'Let me go. I'm not crazy. Of course I have to go back.'

I felt the pressure of his fingers on my arm. 'Listen to me. I went back to my house, and found it in ruins. And there was nothing to be done. Nothing at all. We're the same, Sarah, we know we are, except I'm older than you. I like you – you're a terrific girl. Please, get yourself away from here. If you didn't start the fire –' I opened my mouth to protest, but he shook his head impatiently – 'then the best thing you can do is drive to Monica's, and pretend absolutely nothing's happened. Nothing at all. Honestly. Trust me. Someone else – someone else will see this. Any minute now.'

He was hurrying me along the driveway. Outside the gates, I recognised Dr Brooke's maroon Morris Minor, parked on a verge.

'Let's open the gates,' the Bird Boy said. 'In case a fire engine comes in time. We can do that.' I nodded mutely, and together we dragged the rusting, ancient iron prongs across the scratchy earth, panting, my shoulders aching. 'There,' he said. 'Now – get in. Sit down.' I let myself be ushered into the car.

The cello and the trunk didn't fit in the boot. He lifted the trunk onto the back seat. In the rear-view mirror, I watched as he fastened the cello, carefully, onto the luggage rack on the back of the car, his long fingers persistent and patient with the leather straps and stiff buckles.

I saw in the rear-view mirror that someone had appeared and started talking to him, but all I could hear was the sound of the fire rushing in my ears, crackling, gaining hold. I got out of the car, and walked towards the phone box, outside the church. 'I'm so sorry,' I called back, not looking at him. 'I can't just leave the house like that. Let me call the fire brigade, at the very least.'

'Morning, Miss Sarah,' said a voice behind me. It was Mrs Boyes. 'I was just explaining.' I turned round. She was standing next to the Bird Boy, coat on, hat on, neat as a pin. Her face was pale, her mouth set. 'I've seen the fire. Saw it on my way in. I've called the fire brigade.'

'You have? Thank you.'

'Oh yes,' she said. 'They'll put it out – don't you worry. And I'll tell them you were away, staying with friends.' She came towards me as the Bird Boy gently shut the boot. She took my arm. 'You get away now. Go and stay with your friends. We all want you to go, my dear. Now's your chance.'

'It's not right –' I began. My throat hurt.

She leaned towards me, her slightly bulging eyes protruding even more than usual. 'It's not been right for ever so long, my dear. Long before you were born. This isn't your fault. It isn't your affair. You go off and stay with your friends and don't you worry. We'll never –' her fingers tightened on my arm. 'We'll never speak of it again. You weren't here. It'll astonish you, how little it's got to do with you, when you're older. It was always going to end like this. You don't need to worry, Miss Sarah.' And the pinch of her fingers became a soft stroke. 'Now off you go.'

I turned, and the Bird Boy was standing by the car door. He nodded at her. Behind them both, on the village street, I saw Mrs Boundy outside the post office. She bustled forward to the Bird Boy, and they had a quick exchange.

'You be off, you hear?' she called. 'And if it's no good at the friend's, you come back and stay here Miss Sarah. You don't go back to that house any more, understand, my dear? Come back, to me.' And she held out her hand. 'I'll be here.'

Unable to speak, I nodded gratefully, and I saw Dr Brooke had appeared and was standing in silence beside her. He nodded too. He raised a hand, his kind eyes watching me.

'Look after that cello, my boy. See you soon. Sarah – you ought to be on your way now.'

I got into the car. The Bird Boy closed my door for me. Smoke was appearing now above the trees, over the village. We drove away, the car starting first time, and, as we left, the three of them walked behind us, forming a row, and they stood in the middle of the road and waved.

Five minutes into our journey, on the London road, we passed the fire engine, clanging loudly, swerving from side to side.

Chapter Eighteen

I often wonder what would have happened to me if the Bird Boy hadn't, that bright bank holiday morning, decided to walk up to the house to make sure I was all right.

We talked in a general way, that journey. He didn't ask me to explain anything, myself least of all. I told him about school, the ghastliness of it, why Monica was my friend, the awful smells, the cold. I told him about the different teachers – the Loon, Miss Trubshawe, and I told him about Mr Williams, how wonderful he was, and the cello.

But mainly he talked, because I wanted him to, and he sensed that. He told me about his time in America: the neon lights in Times Square, the glittering bottles of Pepsi-Cola twenty-feet high, the long streets that ended at the river, buildings higher than five, six Fanes on top of each other, black metal fire escapes zig-zagging down the front. How he'd stayed in a boarding house in Brooklyn where everyone had a meal together at Thanksgiving. How cold it was, even compared to this last winter, how parts of the Hudson River froze for months on end. The smell of burnt sugar in the air, the rattling crowded subway, how friendly everyone was, bustling and kind. If you were lost and looked at a map, people stopped and told you where to go. How he didn't feel left out, or alone.

'What will you do next?' I said, when the landscape changed from chalk downland to hilly green, woodland and copse, and covered lanes where golden light flickered between the new green arching above.

'Me? I'm going back to America. As soon as I've finished the exams. I'll have two terms next year to fill before I go to Cambridge, if I get in, that is. I have an uncle there, my father's brother. I've never met him. He was older than my father. Left

Austria before my grandparents and father, went to Chicago. He's got a printing business there. He says I can come and stay with him.'

'That's nice of him.'

'He's family,' he said, as if that explained it. 'And what's almost as important is to get away from here. It's killing me, this country. Dead ideas, dead people, dead houses. America's where I want to be.' He accelerated. 'People see the future there, not the past.'

'But –' I began, and then I thought of Fane, I couldn't help it, and I blocked it out of my mind, blinking hard. 'What else?' I said. 'Tell me what else you like about it?'

'Well. I love milkshakes,' he said. 'Uncle Samuel, that's really his name, he says there's a milk bar just across the street from his apartment. And someone in a shoe shop needs a boy for the summer. Maybe I'll stay there, try and get a job as a writer. Maybe I won't come back and go to university.'

'If I was as clever as you,' I said, after a while, 'I'd *want* to use my brain. I'd *want* to show them all.'

'Well, you're not me,' he said mildly, after a pause. 'It's something I jolly well have to do – that's all.'

I understood, and didn't say any more.

As we rolled into Ripley, he said:

'Now, where would your friend's house be, I wonder?'

A woman with a toddler was standing by the little village pond, feeding some ducks.

I wound down the window and said, 'Excuse me. Do you know where Frencham Court is? The Powletts live there.'

Her face broke into a smile. 'Yes, of course. It's the last house in the village. Keep going, and then turn left into the little drive with the clumps of tulips outside. That's Frencham.'

'Thank you.'

'You're a schoolfriend of Monica's!' she said, delighted. 'She's been very bad with her asthma this holiday. How wonderful. She *will* be pleased.'

I was perplexed at the idea that other people cared about your business, and nodded politely, winding the window up rather too fast. My stomach gurgled embarrassingly, and yet I also felt very sick, with the culmination of it all, and weak, as my body slowly started to understand that I had left some part of my life behind, and could not go back.

We had reached the last house, and a wrought-iron sign said 'Frencham Court' in curling letters.

'Well, I think we're here,' I said, trying to sound formal, terror striking me suddenly at the enormity of what I had done, what I had seen. 'I'm so very grateful to you.'

'How polite. You're most welcome, Princess Margaret,' he said with a smile.

We turned into the driveway. My legs, in Dr Brooke's small, battered Morris Minor, felt like jelly. At the end of the drive was a square redbrick house with cream window frames and a black front door. The door knocker was in the shape of a lion. It gleamed golden in the midday sun. The windows sparkled. There was a lawn on the left and a woman laughing, patting her legs, gesturing at a dog to come to her. Her skirt spread out in the spring breeze. I got out and walked towards the door.

'Here, Sarah?' said the Bird Boy. 'Are you sure this is all right? I mean, are *they* all right, these Powletts of yours?'

'No idea,' I said, wanting to laugh suddenly, hysterical with it all. 'We'll have to see. And I'll come back to Mrs Boundy if not.'

People cared. People had made sure I would get out.

I knocked on the door, and the woman in the garden looked towards us, curiously. Sitting next to her, I spotted then, was a girl in shorts and plaits. She pointed at me, and stared.

'No, it can't be,' she said, her voice faint. 'As I live and breathe – just about. Goodness, Sarah, is that really *you*?'

'It is,' I called. 'Hello, Mon. How have you been?'

Her mother turned towards me. 'Hello, dear!' she said politely. 'I'm afraid I don't—'

'Mother, it's Sarah, Sarah Fox, my especial pal,' said Monica. She got up, and I saw the shadows under her eyes, and that she spoke haltingly, fighting for every breath. I walked towards her. 'You remember. I sent her the birthday card.'

'Oh! Of course.' She put her arm round her daughter's shoulder. 'Hello, my dear. Are you staying nearby? Have you come to say hello?'

I was suddenly overwhelmed. I wanted to crawl into the bush and lie down, or get back into the car and drive off. I turned round, needing to retreat, and saw the Bird Boy at the wheel of the car. He nodded at me. *Come on, Sarah*, his expression said. *Just one more step, one more white lie.*

'I'm so sorry,' I said, flustered. 'I opened the birthday card you gave me early and I wrote to you, last week, to take up your kind invitation.' I allowed myself to blush at this lie. It wasn't hard. 'Perhaps I misunderstood. Didn't you get it?'

'A letter – no! We didn't! It doesn't matter in the least. You are very welcome. Monica's told us all about you. We'd be *thrilled* if you can come and stay.'

'If Monica's been ill, perhaps it's not—'

'Nonsense,' she said. She smiled and pushed her chestnut fringe out of her eyes, which were just like Monica's, full of laughter, kind. In the bushes nearby, a bird was singing loudly with a repetitive, almost comic cheep. 'We'd love to have you. Monica's had a rotten time this hols, and she's been ever so lonely. Please do stay. It'd be such fun. Can we drive you to school? Shall I telephone your parents?'

'I'll tell them,' said a voice behind me. 'I'm a family friend. I live in the village. I gave her a lift. They don't have a telephone. Don't worry, Mrs Powlett.'

'Oh,' she said, and she gave him a sweet smile. 'Thank you so much. This is such a treat for us. Sarah dear, do come in. Let me take your things. Do you have much?'

The Bird Boy lifted the trunk from the back seat of the car, and then my cello. I swallowed.

'I don't have very much at all, really,' I said. 'But I don't want to bore you with it all.'

'It's not a bore,' said Mrs Powlett. She gave me a curious, direct look, and then dropped her eyes, and I knew she understood, not the whole of it, obviously, but something, enough. Some adults understand. Most don't. 'It's not boring, dear. We're very glad to have you. Come inside.'

Monica didn't like a fuss, so I was surprised when I felt her arm round mine, the squeeze of her fingers against my shoulder and arm. 'Golly, Sarah, you don't know how super it is to see you,' she whispered. 'Mummy and Dad are darlings, but they fuss about my asthma and I can feel it when they're sad about me, and it's too much!' I could see the shadows under her kind eyes, feel the bony shoulders against my frame; she hated eating when her asthma was bad. I wanted to hug her tight, to tell her I was here and I would make things better. 'Come inside. In we go.' She guided me into the hall and called out, 'Mary, could we have some hot cross buns? Are there any left?'

Mary, their housekeeper, greeted me with a smile. She folded her arms and said fondly, 'Just one, and I think your friend would like one, wouldn't she, and a little cup of tea? She must be famished after her drive.'

The thought of hot cross buns! Of food in general that wasn't the sawdusty porridge made of oat husks at Haresfield or the uncertain, cobbled-together, terrifying meals at Fane. My head swam.

'And your friend,' said Mrs Powlett. 'Do ask him in for a cup of coffee, or lunch. Would he like to stay?'

I turned, and went back into the driveway to see the car was already moving slowly away, towards the main road. I ran after him, suddenly panicking I wouldn't see him again.

'Hey!' I called, shielding my eyes against the spring sunshine that dappled the roof of the car. 'I say, do stop!'

He was at the turning, and cars were whizzing by. He wound down the window, stuck his dark, curly head out and smiled at me.

'You were driving off without letting me thank you,' I said. 'Mrs Powlett wanted to ask you to stay for lunch.'

'Thanks, kiddo,' he said. 'That's a lovely idea, but I have to go.' He gripped the steering wheel, and grinned at me. 'You take care, Sarah.'

'I will.' He was winding up the window as I slammed the top of the car again. 'Listen – thanks awfully again. For everything.'

'It was my pleasure. Let me know how you're getting on, won't you?'

'Yes,' I said, staring at him. We nodded at one another, me, thirteen and serious, determined and tired, him, eighteen and serious, hopeful and in a hurry. Always in a hurry.

'I forgot your map,' I said suddenly. 'It was under my mattress. I left the map you gave me behind.' Tears pricked my eyes.

'It doesn't matter!' he said softly. 'Here, Sarah, please don't cry, old thing. It'll come back to you if it's meant. Cheer up. What are you crying about?'

'I hope I did the right thing,' I said. 'Leaving when I did. What I've done . . . I don't know . . .'

'I didn't give you much choice. We all wanted you to get out of there. You know we did. I say, I do hope I'll see you again one day. We're the same, aren't we?'

'Yes,' I said. 'Yes, we are.'

I touched his cheek, holding my hand against his face, suddenly overwhelmed with the desire to hug him. We stared at each other, very calmly, and he smiled into my eyes.

'Don't stop looking up, will you, Sarah? Promise,' he said.

'I won't. And you too.'

Another car hooted at him. He waved them on, and caught my hand in his. 'Listen. Forget about that place. Don't go back. Put it behind you. Tell yourself this is the first day of your new life.'

'Yes.' I looked back at the house, and I squeezed his arm. 'That's an awfully good idea.' I breathed in, a long, shuddering breath. 'Thank you – Oh, tell me something, would you?' I said. 'Just before you go. I don't even know your name.'

He laughed. 'Really? Of course. It's Daniel,' he said. 'My name's Daniel Forster.'

'Daniel Forster.' I said his name for the very first time.

'That's me.'

I remember him exactly as he was that day, tall, thin, sort of stretched-out. But some of him was the same: his long slender hands, the intensity of his stare, his mind, his kind, kind heart that picks anyone and everyone up, dusts them off, sets them right. He still does it. Oh, Daniel. The miracle of the story is that I looked up, and I found you.

'Well thank you, Daniel Forster.'

'It's been my pleasure. Goodbye, Sarah. I hope I bump into you again, one day.'

'Goodbye,' I said.

'Go in now,' he said.

'I –' I was scared, suddenly. 'I don't want to.'

He laughed, and gave me a huge smile.

'Oh, go on. After everything else? It's all right. I promise you it's all right.'

It *was* all right. I turned, and left him.

Later that night, in a nightdress of Monica's, soft with repeated washing, in soft, starched sheets, lying staring up at the ceiling listening to Monica's wheezing breath as she slept, I worried I wouldn't sleep, that I would have nightmares. But when I slept, I dreamed not of the fire but of Stella, buried under the Burnt Oak. I dreamed she came to life and flew over the trees, over the abandoned house, under the stars, hunting, always hunting.

Chapter Nineteen

Vic had, in fact, left me an address to write to. Miss Parker's house was in Stanmore, in North London – and a few days after I'd arrived at Monica's and written to let her know my whereabouts I received this.

Dear Sarah

Thank you for letting me know where you are.

We are having a good time. We didn't go to Devon in the end, some difficulty about the accommodation, Miss Parker's friend was quite awkward about it so we have come here instead. It is a small house, attached to another house, which is called semi-detached. There is a small garden. We help Miss Parker catalogue her possessions and weed her garden. Kate Abbey is here, she's a ripping girl. She says next holidays I can stop with her.

I hope you're not being a burden on Monica's family. See you at school. I'm glad you got away.

Victoria
x

I was reading this at breakfast, the morning of my fifth day at Frencham Court, over a boiled egg and toast. There were eggs because Mrs Powlett's hens had started laying, she said. There was toast because Mary made fresh bread, every other day. There was white hawthorn blossom in a large copper jug on a tall table in the corner of the room, next to the French windows that gave out onto the lawn. Whilst I had been there, the little white flowers with the faintest hint of pink had started to drop petals onto the soft grey carpet and periodically Mary would sweep them gently up.

It was always quiet, and warm. It was wonderful to wake up after a good night's sleep, to stretch out in soft sheets, to hear someone call, 'Breakfast, darlings!'

Mrs Powlett had given me a heap of Monica's old clothes. 'She's much taller than you, and these won't fit her any more,' she had said on the second day. 'So you don't spoil your uniform, and your mother isn't cross with me – No, Monica, don't interrupt me, darling. That's what I'd like to do.'

I'd had a bath twice, and used Monica's bath salts, and washed my hair, and after that it was slightly different, lighter and softer than the dark grey-brown it usually was, especially after more than a week at Fane with the accumulated dirt and dust that hung everywhere.

Mr Powlett left early in the mornings and was back late, but he was jovial when we saw him, and Mrs Powlett was one of those people who woke up determined to enjoy herself. I don't think she had ever felt self-pity, and Monica was the same – she never thought how unlucky it was that she couldn't breathe sometimes, or had to spend days in bed, or couldn't do games and enjoy life the way others could. They simply got on with it, both of them. They were lucky in many ways: they had money and their lives were easy. But one couldn't help but like Mrs Powlett, adore her really. She'd had her own troubles – her mother had died when she was a child, and she was parked in boarding schools around the country by her grief-stricken father. I think she understood me better than I realised then.

Perhaps she is the heroine of my story, the woman who rescued me. I am certain she knew more – but she never, by action or word, gave me reason to suspect it might have been otherwise.

'What does Victoria say?' said Monica slowly. Her breathing was easing, she slept better, she smiled more. When she had an asthma attack, she liked me to sit with her, as I did at school, and sometimes I'd play for her, or she'd lean against me and I'd rub her back.

'She's fine. She's enjoying her holiday with Miss Parker.' I rolled my eyes. 'They've gone to her house to be unpaid skivvies, basically. She's got them cleaning her house and weeding the garden. Really, can you imagine?'

'Gosh no. Nosy Parker's house. How awful.'

'Exactly. I bet she doesn't even have another chair. I bet no one ever goes to visit her. Probably they have to sit on the floor.' We both giggled, speculation about teachers and their real lives being the most daring of conversations.

'Sarah, you are dreadful.' Monica smiled.

'Actually, I think she's dreadful,' I said, lowering my voice. 'She's awful. She's a liar. She lied about Mr Williams.'

'Really, Sarah? Do you think so?' Monica looked aghast; she did not like Miss Parker, either, but it was still the worst of all sins, to call someone a liar. And your headmistress, of all people.

'What's that, dear?' her mother called from the hallway, where she was talking to the postman. 'Who's a liar?'

'No one, Mummy.' The front door shut gently. 'I wonder where he'll go. Gosh, Mr Williams, I always thought he was . . . dreadfully handsome,' Monica volunteered, and we both dissolved into whoops of hysterical laughter at this, so much so that we didn't notice Mrs Powlett standing in the doorway, the newspaper in her hand.

'My dear,' she said, advancing towards me, and there was a kind expression on her face that I'd only ever seen before when things were bad, when people glimpsed the truth.

'Hello, Mrs Powlett,' I said. My stomach tightened. I thought she'd heard me talking about Mr Williams, and had something to relate. 'Is this about the cello lessons?'

'What? No, my dear Sarah.' She sat down next to me at the table, brushing imaginary crumbs out of the way. 'I'm afraid I have some terrible news. My dear, I am so sorry.' She put the paper down on the soft white linen tablecloth, folded onto page five.

TRAGEDY AT FANE HALL

***FIRE DESTROYS GREATER PART OF STORIED HOUSE**

***CORPSE OF PEER FOUND IN RUBBLE**

***ARREST OF EARL'S NIECE, LADY IRIS FOX**

Fane, Sussex. – Most extraordinary scenes at the seat of the former Earls of Ashley, one of the most noble families in Southern England, which it is the sad duty of this correspondent to inform readers is now an extinct line, the last earl having been discovered dead yesterday morning.

The body of Lord Clive George Rodderick Ashley was found in the stable block behind the house; he had died of natural causes. His doctor, Dr Francis Brooke said his heart had grown progressively weaker over the past year. Death was not unexpected.

Further compounding the tragedy is the news of the fire that engulfed the two-hundred-year-old stately home, often called the finest in Sussex. Fane Hall was built in the 18th century by 'Great' George Fane, first Earl Ashley. Today most of it lies in smoking ruins: the West Wing was entirely destroyed, along with much of the East Wing, including the panelled library and ballroom, both by Robert Adam. The hall's legendary collection of birds and paintings was destroyed in the fire, including several Canalettos, two Poussins, several Claude landscapes and innumerable valuable pieces of furniture.

However the great central hall, staircase and rooms above are still standing, as is the stable block.

John O'Reilly, the demolition expert responsible for the supervised destruction of many country houses, has been called in to flatten the remaining area and remove various sundry items of furniture.

Lady Iris Fox, daughter of the late earl's brother, had informed the local rector, Reverend Colin Thomas, of the death of her uncle early on Easter Sunday, but later disappeared. She was found in a gamekeeper's cottage on the edge of the estate, and charged last night with arson and attempted murder. A witness,

Mrs Deirdre Boyes, claims she saw the earl's niece walking towards the house an hour before the fire is thought to have taken hold. Relations between the earl and Lady Iris had broken down in recent years.

There were two pictures – one, very dark and grainy, of the house, which was strangely unchanged when you first looked at it, the central bulk of the frontage unaffected, and then you looked again and saw that the rest of the place was ruins, dark, waterstained and in places collapsing into the ground, windows blasted out. The second photograph was of my mother, sitting on the front steps of the house, a blanket round her shoulders, arms folded, talking to a policeman. Her feet were turned inwards; she looked like a child.

'Your mother looks all right,' said Mrs Powlett, reading over my shoulder. 'At least she wasn't hurt. Oh my goodness, Sarah.' She put her hand on my shoulder, and squeezed it.

I pictured Uncle Clive in the darkness of the stables. Stumbling, losing his way, sinking to the ground, shut away in there knowing he was going to die alone. All that time, as I searched for him, he'd been a few feet away.

I knew I mustn't cry. I knew I must not show any emotion. I could see Monica, opposite, watching me curiously. 'What's up?' she said.

'Fane has burnt down,' I said. 'My great-uncle is dead.'

Monica's mouth dropped open. 'My God. Sarah! I'm so sorry. He died in the fire?'

'He wasn't in the fire. They found him in the stables. He had a bad heart. I suppose that's what did it. She must have found him when she came back and just left him there . . .' I stood up, my hand pressed to my mouth. 'I – I – Oh God.'

'How did it start?'

'They don't say.' I was shaking. I remembered the phone call, all of a sudden; I'd forgotten it until then. *'It's the West Wing we start in?'* My mouth was dry. 'But each wing burnt down, and not the middle. So there were two fires. Look at the photograph.

They've – they've arrested my mother . . .' I stood up, pacing the room, trying to breathe. There was too much breath inside me. I couldn't sit down. I had to keep pacing. 'Nearly all of it . . . is gone.'

'How utterly awful,' said Mrs Powlett, turning back to me. The morning light caught her face; the laughter and frown lines made her seem so lovely: so real, somehow. She fiddled with her engagement ring. 'Dear Sarah, this is dreadful. I'm sure it's a terrible misunderstanding . . .' She trailed off.

I thought about how kind she was, and how Mr Powlett had proposed to her the third time he met her, and she had simply said: 'I thought you'd never ask.' There was a picture of them on their wedding day on the mantelpiece in the dining room, the frame polished and worn. It had stood there for fifteen years, and would likely be there in fifteen years' time, when Monica married and brought her children to visit.

'Perhaps you should go back,' she said. 'I could drive you? Wouldn't you like to collect the rest of your things? You're welcome to keep them here, darling—'

'Please don't go,' Monica begged, her voice thin. 'Sarah, it doesn't sound safe, apart from anything else. Mummy, you can't make her go. It's dreadful for her. And there's no one there for her.'

'But, Monica . . . !' Mrs Powlett folded the paper up. 'Sarah dear, we simply love having you – Monica's asthma's better than it's been for ever so long and you make her laugh and keep her busy – you've changed the house, you know.' She stroked my hair, her voice soft. 'You're welcome to stay here any time, to think of this as your home. But, Monica, this was Sarah's *home*. She has things there and – perhaps, Sarah, dear, you'd like to do that?' Her busy mind was planning, sorting, organising, smoothing the way for me. 'And if you want to stay the night there I could telephone that woman you mentioned your friend Daniel was staying with at the post office? Or the vicar?'

'Dear Mrs Powlett, you don't understand,' I said evenly. 'I don't have any things. I didn't have anything there. And now that I don't have to, I won't ever go back there again.'

She stared at me, a frown puckering her smooth forehead.

'Oh, my dear girl,' she said softly, almost without expecting an answer. 'What on earth happened there.'

I wanted to tell her the truth. And then I knew that I couldn't. If I told her everything . . . if I told her what I'd seen on that last day . . . how I'd driven away . . . I didn't deserve help, but I didn't want her to see the reality of the house even in ruins, its degradation and filth, the people who'd let it get like that.

I was silent because I didn't know what to say, and suddenly Monica coughed, and clutched at her throat, and Mrs Powlett turned to her, in consternation. 'What's wrong, darling?'

Monica was pointing to the newspaper, to an item below the one about Fane. Her hand was on her throat, and her face pale as milk.

'I'm fine. But – oh no,' she said. 'Oh, Sarah, no.'

Death of a Young Cellist

Sister attempts to save his life on train platform; family 'heartbroken' by tragedy

Additional information on the tragic death of Mr Sam Williams has been received today, *writes Hugh Johnston.* Mr Williams, most recently a teacher at Haresfield School, was jostled on a busy train platform on Tottenham Court Road when others were rushing for the doors. He plunged into the path of an incoming train and was killed instantly. It is not clear whether he fell or if it was a suicide. An inquest into his death opened yesterday at St Pancras Coroner's Court.

Mr Williams was a gifted young cellist, late a teacher at Haresfield School. He had recently returned to the family home from the school and on the day of the tragedy had travelled into town with his younger sister. Mr Williams was reported to be of a nervous disposition and apparently upset at the nature of his departure from the school, the circumstances of which he had repeatedly discussed with his family. He leaves behind his grandfather, his parents, and a younger brother and sister. Miss L. E. Williams, only ten years old, was praised by the judge for attempting to save her brother at the station. Giving evidence at the inquest, she said his mood was low but 'nothing that you would notice. He was simply the most wonderful big brother one could hope for. We will never get over it. Never.'

There's a service, you know, at the British Library, where you can look up any article in any newspaper. I did this many years after that spring morning. I wanted to see what I had missed. In any case, at the time, I did not pay enough attention. For a long time afterwards, I believed the event that destroyed our family had already happened: Fane had burnt down, my great-uncle was dead, our mother was imprisoned. How foolish. I was wrong – that wasn't it at all. It would take many years before I finally saw what the real threat to my family was.

Part Four

1974

Chapter Twenty

Twenty children lined up in the little square playground outside Miss Dora's Kindergarten, waiting for the bell to sound. Some stamped their feet, some swung their arms around to keep warm in the icy January cold, their cheeks pink. Parents waved, and retreated. Only one hung back – Friday Forster, clinging to her mother's leg.

'NO DORA!' she called loudly. 'WON'T!'

Ignoring Miss Dora, with her bell in hand, and the other children, Sarah bent down, rocking the pushchair behind her.

'It's only a few hours,' she said. 'And then we'll pick you up. Come on, Friday! You love it once you're in!' She looked up and said wildly, to anyone who'd listen: 'She loves it when she's in!'

'I HATE it! Won't go in!' Friday's eyes burnt black fire.

'We can go on the Heath afterwards. You can slide. It's frosty!'

'No, no, no, no, no, NO, no,' said Friday, her eyebrows rising so high they vanished underneath her fringe. She folded her arms.

'*Please, Friday*,' Sarah heard herself imploring. 'Darling, just go in . . . please . . .'

'Uhm . . .' Friday paused, and Sarah allowed herself to hope. 'NO, NO, NO, NO!' Friday finished, and a mother next to her sucked in her breath, teeth bared; as if Friday were unbearable, as if Sarah was too.

Rebecca, the baby, was crying; other parents were walking away, casting covert looks at one another or the ground, anywhere rather than at Sarah. It was the same every morning since Friday had started there the previous October. Every. Single. Morning. But you left them – that was what you did. 'Do her good to spend some time away from you,' Miss Dora had said firmly when she'd informed Sarah a place had been found for Friday at the kindergarten. 'She's very clingy. Don't want them clingy when they're starting at school.'

It *seemed* like a nice place, a dear little single-storey building behind Well Walk. It was rather like a gingerbread house: two rooms, a scalloped roof with small black dormer windows and a long chimney, and a jolly red front door. Inside were blue, red and yellow plastic boxes filled with board books, building blocks, large jigsaw puzzles for small fingers, and dolls, teddies and so forth. If Miss Dora was secretly torturing her charges, hiding the wooden blocks and puzzles and withholding food, she was doing a jolly good job concealing it. Sarah and Daniel had looked round it together, and Daniel had clapped his hands in joy. 'This is glorious. You're so clever for finding it.'

As if only a true superbrain could have located the kindergarten two roads away that every mother she spoke to said was the one to go for.

Last week, during an All Day Sunday, he'd complimented her on the potatoes. 'How did you cook them?'

'I boiled them in some water.'

Daniel had taken his time, wiping his mouth, swallowing again. 'Well, they're delicious. I don't know how you made them so delicious but you did.'

Sarah had murmured thanks as the other guests nodded in agreement. 'Delicious. Mm, yes, delicious.' One of them, a professor at Imperial College with whom Daniel was working on his new book, a sprawling project that was a people's history of Great Britain called *United We Stand*, had turned to him. 'Yes, yes, terrific boiled potatoes. Daniel, have you thought some more about beefing up the Chartists in Chapter Five? I'm concerned we're underplaying their influence.'

This had, in her grimmer moments, made Sarah laugh. *Yes, yes, terrific boiled potatoes, and now back to the relevance of Victorian parliamentary reform in today's febrile political atmosphere.*

Eventually, feeling like a brutal prison warder, having prised a screaming Friday's fingers off her wrist and handed her over to Miss Dora, who patted the child's shoulders kindly as Friday wailed, heartbroken, Sarah made her escape, pushing the pram back towards The Row. Her eldest daughter's bloodcurdling cries followed her down the road.

It was a gloomy day. The miners' strikes and the oil crisis meant there was not enough coal or oil, which meant there were planned power blackouts and a three-day working week, which meant the libraries were closed, the cafés had shut down, most shops on the high street weren't open, the buses didn't run and Daniel worked by torch and candlelight at night, wrapping himself in every spare blanket he could find. In addition, the street lamps were usually off, which in the dark meant it was sometimes hard to see people coming at you until they veered up out of the mist and made Sarah jump. Once, she'd screamed at Miss Barbara Forbes, who had been so upset she'd had tears in her eyes. 'My dear Mrs Forster! Please, forgive me!'

She kept meaning to make a fluorescent band to go on the arm of her coat, and one for the buggy. It was another thing she hadn't done.

Sarah didn't particularly want to go home to her freezing house. (Every child at Miss Dora's seemed to have beautiful hand-knitted jumpers, tank-tops, socks – not Friday, who had no kindly grandmothers to knit her jumpers.) Breakfast never seemed to get cleared in time before they had to leave: the dropped tea towels on the floor, the cereal detritus she hadn't had time to clean away, the good intentions of the day already scattered to the four winds. Friday needed a new overall for art, and new gum boots, and Sarah couldn't find the next tranche of baby clothes for Rebecca, which she had folded carefully and stored in the loft. She needed to go to the butcher to make sure they could still fulfil her order for the weekend, what with the food shortages, and then perhaps the chemist, to discuss Rebecca's cradle cap, which was really quite hideous, a raised brown and pink welter of shiny scabs that reminded her of the relief map of the UK Daniel had on his study wall.

She told herself Rebecca usually slept better when she'd seen some interesting things outside. Rebecca was alert – she had been from the moment the nurse had plonked her, screaming, onto Sarah's chest, and Sarah, screaming herself, pain that seemed to split her in two and sluice through her whole body, had paused to look at her, thinking it was like the offal you saw after a killing in the slaughterhouse, the peremptory, unceremonious nature of it. And now she couldn't stop thinking about how that had been her first reaction.

She had been afraid of Friday, of what she could do, of her power to disrupt. Rebecca simply wearied her. Sarah knew her eldest daughter, knew the bones of her, and she knew she was trouble, because she had done it all wrong. With her youngest daughter, she wasn't sure what she was doing wrong, not yet anyway. And, as ever, there was no precedent. All she knew was Rebecca had long black eyelashes, as long as the top joint of Sarah's little finger, and a tiny heart-shaped birthmark on her soft, dimpled shoulder, and she loved two things: her wooden hammer, which she used to bash anyone and anything she could; and her big sister Friday, her huge eyes following her round the room.

'I just know what she's thinking, I'm so much more relaxed this time round, aren't you?' a mother had confided to her at a Hampstead library sing-song, where they each sat on gingham mats and held their baby's hands and intoned 'Wind the Bobbin Up' even though, to Sarah's knowledge, no one had wound a bobbin since about 1786.

'Oh yes,' Sarah had said, tired mind racing, trying to remember into what expression she should arrange her face. Wry, nodding approval, that was it. 'So much more.'

She went to the butcher's, following Daniel's instructions, and to the cobbler's, to collect some of his shoes, and then to the wine merchant's, talking to Rebecca as she did so. At one point, Rebecca's small heart-shaped face broke into a half-smile and Sarah told herself today would be a good day: she had cracked it, she was able to do this – whatever 'this' was. She found with motherhood every small triumph or disaster felt like confirmation of the whole situation. The time she had stepped on a pin, barefoot, after a long day whilst Daniel was out carousing in Soho, and seriously thought about walking herself down to the Tube and jumping in front of a train. Quick. Clean. Done. But an hour later at bath-time, she was laughing helplessly as Friday made a cone of foam for her hair and put some on Rebecca's bald head and the two of them moved their heads together, giggling so much they both got hiccups. Or when Friday, just after she learned to walk, stumped over to her in the kitchen as she sat weeping one morning, clamping her hand round her forefinger, very firmly, and had stared up at her with her furious dark eyes.

'Laab ooo. LAAB OOO.' And Sarah saw she was trying to talk to her, to say: *I love you. Don't cry. I love you*, and that she'd already broken this little girl by being so broken herself.

As she heaved Rebecca's pram up the path, banging the door open just the right amount so it didn't rebound and whack the hood of the buggy too hard, as she had done a thousand times now, the telephone rang. Sarah assumed Daniel would answer, as he usually did – there was an extension in his study – but when it continued ringing she pushed Rebecca further down the hallway, and picked up the receiver.

'Hello?'

'Ah! Sarah. How are you? It's Oscar.'

'Oscar!' said Sarah, raising her voice in what she hoped was a sound of pleasure. She racked her brains. *Oscar.* Was he the man who'd been at All Day Sunday last week? The drunk TV exec who'd put his arm round her too tightly, so she could smell funky sweat, telling Daniel repeatedly how gorgeous his wife was?

'It's been an age, hun. How's motherhood?'

'Oh! It's – fine.' She paused, knowing whoever this man was, he wasn't asking because he was interested. 'How are you? What can I do for you?'

'Well, Sarah.' He cleared his throat with a high, guttural cough, and her mind raced, as it was so familiar to her. 'You might be able to help us out. Miranda's pulled out of the tour. Some boyfriend trouble I expect. You know – Well, you don't. You didn't work with her. She's a bit of a liability, I'm afraid to say. Jolyon and Peter say this is the final straw – they can't play with her—'

Oscar – Oscar Gould! Manager of the Pembroke Quartet. Lived in Kentish Town, but called it Primrose Hill. Wife called Polly who was into Eastern mysticism. Sarah smiled, twisting the phone cord round her fingers. Who was she, that she'd forgotten his name?

'I see. Listen, Oscar—'

He ploughed on. 'The first night's tomorrow. We desperately need a cellist. I can't find anyone. And there's no doubting the dolly-bird factor helps with sales. Sorry, Sarah, not very Women's Lib but you know what I mean. I don't care what Jolyon says – you were damned good, and we're in a hole. Would you consider coming back?'

'For one night?'

'No. For the tour. It's just a month, Sarah darling. UK only. All expenses paid.'

'A nanny?' she said, half laughing. 'You'd pay for a nanny?'

'Oh. Well. Yes, Sarah. I told you, we're desperate. It's sold out. And you *are* good.'

Briefly, Sarah thought of what would happen if she calmly told Daniel she was off for a month. What would need to happen for that to work. She leaned against the dark-green wall of the hallway, always cold, even at the height of summer, and looked down. She saw her skirt, pulled hastily on, the elastic frayed, the button popped off, her rayon brown shirt, covered with the remains of breakfast and baby and other, indeterminate stains. It had been clean that morning. In the oval hall mirror, her face stared back at her, white, hollowed-out eyes, hair vague, straw-like. She didn't know why it was always like this, but no matter how hard she tried it *was* always like this. The strangest thing of all was that no one had told her, warned her, it would be . . . like this.

Her mind wandered for a second as Oscar began listing venues, as if telling her she might get to play at Leeds Town Hall again would be what swayed her.

Last summer she'd locked herself out of the house. Daniel was away: the satirical revue he wrote for was at the Edinburgh Festival. Eventually Diana, who had their spare key, arrived back from supper. Friday was running round the front garden in Sarah's sheepskin jerkin, quite happy. Rebecca was quietly asleep, having been fed to distraction. Diana, taking one look at Sarah's pinched, glazed, tear-stained face, came in and shut the gate.

'You poor child. How long have you been out here?'

'An hour.' Sarah was too tired to respond, really. 'Friday found a woodlouse – it was easier after that. But they're both hungry, and Friday should be in the bath – I should have given them tea – I should have hung the washing out – I – I –' She cleared her throat, buying time, but a sob overwhelmed her, and she pushed one hand into her eyes, the other arm cradling a sleeping Rebecca. 'I'm so bad at this,' she whispered after a minute. 'I'm so bad. Monica does it so easily.'

'Your schoolfriend with the rich husband? She has a nanny, doesn't she?'

'It's not really the money.' Although they had no money, still, and she ought to just sell that damn cello and admit her career was over, bail the family out with it. 'Mon has the right *attitude*. She's grateful for everything. I'm not. It's getting things wrong. I get it wrong, all the damned time, Diana – I don't bring a spare nappy pin, or the right shoes, or an apple, or water, or a sunhat – I see all the other mothers, on the Heath, in the library, and they're getting it right, but I'm not. I'm . . . *not* . . .'

'You are,' said Diana. She sat at the edge of the step, and gingerly patted Sarah's arm. 'Oh, darling. You really are.'

'I'm not.' Sarah wiped her nose on her sleeve. 'Friday had her first party last week. A little girl on Well Walk, we know her from story-time at the library. It was on the Heath. We turned up with a present and Friday was in her new little Osh Kosh dungarees, she loves them, she won't wear anything else. But every other little girl was in a flouncy tiered dress, Diana. You know, homemade florals like they're in the Railway Children. I don't know the rules. I missed the part where they tell you the rules. I'm always getting it wrong.'

'Putting a little girl in a smart frock for a party on the Heath is madness. Far better to be in dungarees.'

Sarah gave a sniff. 'That's what I thought, and then it didn't matter if she fell over – she falls over all the time. Her shoes don't fit; I keep buying the wrong size,' Sarah said bitterly. 'The man at the shoe shop is no good. He's lying to me – I know he is. He sells single shoes. Who sells single shoes unless they're picking them up off the street where children have dropped them? He should be in prison – I'll complain to the council. I keep meaning to only I'm so tired . . .'

'Shhh a minute,' Diana said, holding up her hand. 'Forget about the man in the shoe shop. Oh, Sarah love. When I was your age, I had a lady called Mrs Tolliver who came to the house every single day. She cleared up after breakfast, she put the baby down for a nap, she did the washing, she played with my son, she cleaned, she prepared lunch, she cleared lunch. She did that every day. And there was just one of her.' Diana looked at her. 'I'd have gone under otherwise. Lots of us do, Sarah . . . But they don't tell you that.' She fumbled in her bag for her keys, then stopped, and wiped a tear from Sarah's cheek. 'Monica and I are the lucky ones. Most women don't have that help, have never had that help, for centuries and that's why,' said Diana, standing up now, and brushing the dust of the pavement from her black trousers, 'you don't hear anything from most women, especially women with children. They've arranged it like that. The whole damn world. And you don't see it till you're too far in it to get out.' She squeezed Sarah's shoulder. 'I'll pop home and get your key. Wait here.'

She was back before Sarah knew it, dropping a light kiss onto her forehead, opening the door. 'In you go, darling.' She took Friday's hand. 'I'll take Friday for tea. You get that baby in the bath and to bed, and I'll bring Friday back later. Listen to me. Have a gin. A large one. And don't worry. Everyone's getting it wrong. Hating yourself won't make it better. You're in a holding pattern for now. Liking yourself makes it easier, I promise.'

'. . . It's only for a few days in total, when you think about it,' Oscar was saying as Sarah dragged her attention back to the present. 'Only asking as otherwise the whole tour will have to be cancelled.'

He let that hang in the air.

'Oh,' said Sarah slowly.

A plane went by overhead, very faint. Even in her coat it was cold in the hall. She stamped her feet, wishing she could just hang up. 'It's just I haven't played for months now – years, really—'

'Sure, sure,' said Oscar, sensing he was close. 'But you're Sarah Forster. Come off it, my dear. I remember when you played the Elgar at college in one day after the examiner couldn't see you. No notice, just jumped right in.'

The pure, insistent sound of the cello solo in the first movement began in her head, between her ears. The feeling of the fingers, vibrating against the fingerboard. The intensity of the long, shuddering notes as the orchestra gently matched her, the sudden shift to jagged, sharp clawing at the strings, the longing of it.

Suddenly Rebecca, further down the corridor, began to cry. There was never just one cry – it signified the thin end of the wedge. Friday had been fractious, crying often, easily soothed. Rebecca was different. She'd start quietly, a snuffling sound, building in frequency and volume until she was bawling her head off, and the noise was something else. The window cleaner had actually covered his ears one morning, up on his ladder, and nearly fallen off.

'Jolyon has a *family*, Sarah. This is his future. And just think how much fun we'll have,' said Oscar as Rebecca's red fist shot out of the pram, followed by a bootee-clad foot.

And Sarah, suddenly, opened her eyes, as if she'd been asleep. Go on tour? It was almost funny.

'Listen, I have to ring off, Jolyon,' she said. 'I'm awfully sorry.'

'Oscar,' he said, half laughing, half disdainful.

'Oscar, yes, of course. Sorry. I have to go – the baby's crying. I can't come with you. The children are too small. There's no electricity. Daniel doesn't know how those tricky safety pins work – it's impossible.'

'Nothing's impossible—' he began.

'Yes,' said Sarah, pulling the receiver away from her ear. 'Yes, it is. You have absolutely no idea. Goodbye.'

Gently, she replaced the telephone on the stand, and lifted Rebecca out of her pram. She was making a huge racket, mouth open, little fists waving, but she stopped crying when Sarah looked at her, almost in surprise. Her eyes widened. She stared at her mother, and her face eased into a huge, ridiculous smile. Sarah smiled back, eyes, teeth.

'Come on,' she said. 'Let's get you a rusk.'

Later that afternoon as she was in the living room lighting the fire, she caught sight of her cello in the corner, gently gathering dust in the hard wooden case she had been given by the Royal College of Music, the dull gold music stand next to it. She stared at it, her tired mind trying to join the dots together, but already the morning seemed another lifetime away – Rebecca had cut a tooth, the milkman had dropped a bottle that had shattered over the front path, Daniel had come home in a towering rage because his editor had gone on holiday and wouldn't get to his manuscript for two more weeks – so many small, inconsequential, enormously aggravating tiny victories and defeats. A cello in the corner of the room was not a symbol of a former life – it was something that reminded her of an earlier conversation, but nothing more.

Daniel came in now, carrying Friday, pink from the bath, and deposited her on the rug in front of the fire. 'There, my precious,' he said. 'Get warm. Now, I've got this.' He pulled a Miffy book out of his back pocket. 'Can you read yet?'

'No, Daddy! Silly.'

'You didn't learn to read at nursery today?'

'No! My can't read! My three.'

'Well, when I was three I could read "antidisestablishmentarianism".'

Friday laughed uproariously. 'Silly Daddy!'

'Oh. All right. Shall I read you this, then?'

'Yes, please may you read this.'

She sat in his lap, pulling his dark hair up into stiff peaks, like a mountain range. 'My like diss beard, Daddy.'

He kissed her. 'I like you. Come on, then. Here we go. Oh, honey. I invited Lara and her husband for All Day Sunday this weekend.'

Sarah, absorbed in the twist of paper that wouldn't light, took a second to register this. 'Right,' she said, sounding vague. 'Are you sure that's a good idea? The joint of beef isn't that large – the butcher doesn't have anything better. He's a bigwig, is Tony Cull. He'll be dreadfully bored, unless you've got some other similar-level bigwigs coming.'

'Well, I've asked Terence.'

Sarah rolled her eyes. 'Oh cripes. Why? Terence is a grade-one idiot.'

Daniel turned to her, his face alight with mirth. 'He's interesting.'

'He literally was a member of the Flat Earth Society, Daniel. He's an idiot.'

'But he's famous. I know people like Cull. They're star fuckers.'

'Shhhh,' said Sarah mildly, nodding at Friday.

'Well, it's true. And Lara's given you the cold shoulder since the Missing Digit lunch, which is ridiculous. Hell, even *Georgina* came back at Christmas to say hello. It's all fine.'

'Georgina should be in prison!' said Sarah, and she was only half-joking. 'If Robert had decided to press charges . . .' She shuddered, involuntarily. 'Oh Lord, don't remind me.'

All Day Sunday had continued since the terrible events of the Missing Digit lunch, but it was mostly Daniel's friends from the Ox and Ass revue, a motley crew of writers and performers who vied with each other to see who could be the most piercingly, scabrously brilliant over moussaka and red wine, which left Sarah free to concentrate on cooking and clearing up and the children. It was easier that way. It just was. This would be the first All Day Sunday of the year because of the Three-day Week, and the butcher not having any meat, and the queues at the grocer's stretching down the block. Sarah knew how much Daniel had missed it. He needed people around, just as he needed to look after her and the girls, just as he needed to try to make things better by attempting terrible DIY projects, which is why they had no water last summer and Rebecca had crawled into a hole he'd made in the floorboards with a pick-axe whilst her father was looking for what he said was a funny smell. Rebecca had nearly been stepped on by her father and emerged covered in splinters and dust, extremely unhappy, so unhappy she didn't want to use her special hammer for three days and wouldn't look at Daniel for longer and even though Sarah was not even in the house, having gone to take Friday to playgroup, she blamed herself.

She knew it helped Daniel professionally to have people over, to be seen to be the ringmaster, the centre of the action. She knew, too, that if she had said to Daniel, 'I don't want to do this any more – this isn't what I signed up for,' that he would say, 'I know. Let's sell the house. Let's downsize to a flat, employ a nanny – you can go back to playing.' But she couldn't. Of course she couldn't, not after what she had experienced and what she wanted her children to experience. She was lucky – she had everything – she should learn to love it and in time she would, she told herself, so she did nothing, and the cello stayed in the corner of the sitting room, and one year Friday had decorated it with tinsel at Christmas.

Rudi Marshall-Wessendorf, her teacher at Boxers, the boys' school near Haresfield, had been one of those sorts who knows people, things, audition days. Via his mother, he had got her in for an audition at the Royal College of Music. When she was eighteen and offered a place at the college, he'd rung Mr Powlett, Monica's father, who had gone to see Mr Murbles, the old Fane family solicitor, and the result was a small allowance was made available to Sarah, barely enough to buy food, but enough to pay for rent, new strings, travel and shoes.

'Pa's disappointed you stopped playing,' Monica said to her once, as if this was the only way she could find to express what she really thought, and it was the only thing Monica ever said to her that hurt her.

But Sarah told herself this was how it was meant to be. She would never let her children experience what she had. She couldn't see similarities between their childhood and hers. She only knew she had to be different, as different as possible, and that meant doing everything: wearing the frilly apron and clearing up, smiling at the men's jokes about feminists at Miss World, ignoring the posters for the Proms plastered over boarded-up buildings, ignoring a part of herself.

The fire was lit now, white sparks catching on the edge of the dried, smoked wood and crackling loudly. She edged closer to the warmth and squatted on her heels, listening to Daniel's voice. Leaning back, she reached for the notepad on the table, and began writing a list, as she did every Thursday, for All Day

Sunday lunch. Lara was coming. For some reason, she was smiling as she thought about it.

Terence Wood was the main star of the Ox and Ass revue, according to Terence Wood himself, his agent and his new girlfriend, Judy, who'd worked as a secretary for a West End producer but made looking after Terence her job now. He'd been a big noise in the Cambridge Footlights, one of its undisputed stars. He was tall, good-looking in a patrician way, charismatic and articulate. He smelt heavily of spicy aftershave, wore a blazer and black polo neck, and kissed Sarah for a little too long as Judy hovered behind him, shivering in her mini skirt, thigh-high boots and oversized sheepskin jacket.

'Here's some wine, my sexy Sarah,' he said, placing a raffia-coated round bottle on the hall table, and squeezing her arm in an intimate gesture that enclosed them. 'We've heard so much about these lunches. What a thrill to be asked. Everything is so very grim at the moment. Do you know,' he said, turning to Judy, 'the first time I met Sarah, I gave her a standing ovation!' Judy looked blank.

'I was playing the Elgar Cello Concerto at Cadogan Hall,' Sarah told her, retrieving his coat and Judy's from her, squeezing them with difficulty onto a hook together amongst their own coats and scarves and mufflers, which seemed to have multiplied. She turned, smoothing down the skirt of the dress she had actually had time to iron, and said, 'Terence, you absolute liar, you fell asleep. My sister complained. She'd come up specially and she said you snored the whole way through.'

'Oh, Sarah, you divine little witch,' said Terence, pretending to look devastated. 'I wasn't asleep. I was bewitched by you into a comatose slumber of desire.'

'I believe you, thousands wouldn't,' said Sarah, nodding. 'Come through, why don't you. We've got some pâté and crackers and some lovely sherry.'

She could feel Judy's suspicious eyes on her – so who is she? I always thought/had been told she was a drab, downtrodden, mute housewife. This doesn't make sense – oh, Judy, Sarah wanted to tell her. Competition between women will never solve anything. Believe me – I've lived it. So, though she'd had no sleep and been in the kitchen either cooking children's meals or clearing them away and then clearing Daniel's mess away and hadn't sat down, she breathed in – *Channel Elaine Tynan*, she told herself. *Just be Elaine Tynan* – put her hand on Judy's arm and said kindly, 'Daniel's so pleased you could come. Here we are.'

Diana was there, of course, and kind Professor Gupta, who started talking to Judy whilst Terence and Daniel were deep in conversation and soon drew from her that she'd grown up in Broadstairs and never been to London till she ran away at sixteen, a detail that troubled Sarah but was one of many conversational loops she would fail to circle back into. Dorothea Minchin was next to arrive – a retired publisher's reader, another of Daniel's coterie of older ladies. She chain-smoked, had a short Oxford crop and wore a shirt with collars so long they drooped into the tomato soup and was a good person at a lunch like this as not only did she know every author and publisher in London, she could be relied upon to drink too much and regale the table with raffish literary anecdotes. She and Diana instantly settled into an involved conversation about publishing people who lived in Hampstead whom they both knew – a Venn diagram that was almost all central circle, no outer circles.

Last to arrive were Tony and Lara Cull. Sarah was listening out for their knock when it came. She wiped her hands on her apron and ran to the door.

'Oh, Lara,' she said involuntarily when she saw them standing there. Lara was dwarfed by the huge bulk of the man behind her, encased in a striped black suit with a watch chain. He reminded her of a badger, with a streak of white amongst his thick black hair and large jowls blackened with stubble. In front of him Lara seemed smaller than ever. She wore a simple pale blue woollen dress and a cream coat, and her hair hung around her shoulders. Her cheeks were flushed, as though the cold outside fed her, like a snow princess.

She hugged Sarah warmly. 'It's lovely to see you.'

'You too,' said Sarah, hugging her awkwardly back. Tony was

already looking past them towards the kitchen. 'Nice to meet you finally, Sandra. Are we in here?' he said in a great, booming voice. 'Grand. It'll be warm, at least.'

He strode past them like a beast drawn to the arena of the gladiatorial fight. Sarah watched him.

'Sorry,' said Lara. 'He's terrible with names.' She shrugged.

'People usually forget my name,' said Sarah, pathetically pleased that Lara was being friendly, that they were speaking again. 'I'm so glad you could come. It's been so awfully long.'

'Well,' said Lara. 'I – Never mind.'

'The tree and the finger and everything. I know, I still think about it all the time. I'm so sorry—'

But Lara waved her hand, quite frantically. 'Oh, shhh. Please let's not mention it. Anyway, it's not that. I find it hard to come back here, but I'm trying to get over it. Honestly, please let's not talk about it.' She threaded her arm through Sarah's as they went through to the kitchen. 'You look lovely,' she said, looking her up and down. 'Sort of fresh, and nice.'

'Oh, thank you,' Sarah said, taken aback.

'I'm very happy to be here.' And Lara looked around the kitchen. 'Very happy.'

The men were on to their fifth bottle of wine when the argument turned, as it always did. Sarah was clearing the bowls. 'Wonderful crumble,' Lara murmured as Diana stood up to help her stack.

'Yes, darling. Delicious,' she'd said. 'Now sit down. Daniel can make the coffee.'

'Yes, Diana's right,' Daniel said, half standing up. 'Listen, Terence. Just one more point on that – the miners don't ask for a monopoly. They simply want to earn a living.'

'That's poppycock, Daniel,' Terence said, laughing, with something like contempt. 'The NUM is in this up to its neck. They're a bloody disgrace. They have an easy time of it these days, and yet all they do is bloody well complain, and Britain suffers. Listen, I'm no particular fan of the Grocer, he's a contemptible little squib, but the Conservatives do at least understand that the free market—'

'Absolute rubbish!' Daniel banged his fist on the table with a fury that made the table shake, and caused even Sarah, who was used to his propensity for thumping items of furniture to make his point, to jump. 'The miners have an easy time of it! Good God, Terence, cool it on the Marie Antoinette talk, will you?'

Terence eased back into his chair, and folded one long leg over the other, his eyes glittering. 'I know you hate privilege, old boy, but there are millions out of work, and the way these fellows demand special treatment whilst others don't have a wage packet – well, it disgusts me.'

'Easy for you to be disgusted,' said Daniel, lightly jamming the cork back into the bottle with the palm of his hand. 'The Conservatives are trying to decimate their industry. No one wants to be a miner, old boy. Come off it. Do you know what it's like?'

'Do *you*, my little Soho roué?' said Terence, with a cool smile. 'When did you ever get your pretty Jewish hands dirty?'

Sarah heard Lara inhale, but she ignored it. Terence said things like that all the time: Daniel usually shrugged, laughed it off.

'I've been down a mine, you lanky shit, and it's horrific,' Daniel said. He was pale. 'I went down to show solidarity with the miners, to know what it's like. How can you write larky comedy sketches about the workers and not understand what it is they do? They're in total darkness most of the day. They never see the sun set, see the stars come out . . . You go down every morning and it's a miracle when you come out in the evening. OK, the unions are strong, but do you know how many miners die every year?'

'You sound like you want Gormley to call a strike. For this chaos to become endemic.'

'What an asinine thing to say, old boy.' Daniel spoke calmly. 'Terence, you have no idea at all what ordinary people have been through. You had a nanny, and a man to brush your father's jacket and bowler every morning. You write songs about it, and people cheer. Isn't he funny, he jokes about it, so it's satire. Our street was chock full of people, kind decent people, just trying to make a crust. Our neighbours had six children sleeping in one room. They got them up at five every day to help make wreaths and posies to sell at Covent Garden. And they still had nothing, no food, no shoes. Our other neighbour was a street fighter. He'd fight for money. Because there wasn't any other work for him. He lost an eye. Most of them were killed in the Blitz. Along with my mum. And most of them lost family in the Holocaust, because most of them were Jewish. And what did the council do after the war? Keep those who weren't killed in prefab houses for another twenty years, then scatter them to the four winds.'

'What were the Conservatives supposed to do? They had to build tens of thousands of homes. Millions of people, homeless. It's hardly their fault Hitler bombed everything to smithereens,' said Terence. The very tip of his nose was slightly pink. 'The way these days one simply blames the Establishment for everything – it's awfully *boring*, old boy—'

'I don't, you ass,' said Daniel, and there was an edge to his voice. 'But the Establishment is the root of most of the problems in this country. Class. Gender. Race – you must see that.'

Terence gave a short laugh. 'That's awfully rich, coming from you, Forster. I'm not the one married to a woman whose mother went to prison for burning down the family seat so she could make millions selling the land off.'

'Really?' said Judy, opening her eyes wide. Tony and Lara sat up. They all stared at Sarah with the exception of Terence, who inhaled his cigarette, deeply.

'I say, that's a bit harsh,' muttered Dorothea Minchin.

'You've no right to bring that up,' said Daniel, still very calm, but his tone was icy. 'That's got nothing to do with it.'

'It's fine, darling,' Sarah said. She turned to Terence, a tea towel in her hand. 'We don't know it was her.'

'You think it wasn't her?' Terence asked with a smile. 'She was convicted and went to prison for it, wasn't she? Forgive me, Sarah darling, raking over old ground. I'd always understood you weren't fond of your mother.'

'I'm not –' said Sarah, feeling her face turn red. 'I'm not – It's not like that. It's only –' She clenched her jaw. 'I don't see what it's got to do with this argument, that's all.'

'Who deserves what, Sarah. Who makes the world after it's been razed to the ground. Who builds it up again. And from what I see in the papers she's absolutely raking it in. Very nice work.'

'Terence,' Sarah began, and for a second she felt rage crawl over her, like a creature clinging to her skin, sucking the breath out of her, making her want to thrash, to writhe, to tear off the nice baby-blue dress so like one her mother had, to tell them all to piss off, leave her alone. 'You're an ass,' she said eventually, giving him a wide smile, and he looked back at her, eyes coolly raking over her. *She was a decent dolly bird once. Not now.*

'I say again, Terence, leave Sarah out of it. It's such a neat little trick to turn it back to her. It completely misses the point,' Daniel said, and he put one hand on the table, and held one hand back to her, grabbing her wrist, and his fingers were so warm, so strong, round her flesh she almost gasped. Sometimes, she had to remind herself amongst the daily chaos that he was there, her Bird Boy, that she had found him again.

Terence turned to Tony Cull, waving his hand with an apologetic air. 'I do apologise. Daniel likes to bait me. Always has done. We've been having this argument since Cambridge.'

Daniel said: 'Not like this. You're missing the point, as I say. You and your lot. My mother threw marbles out of the window when the fascists came marching for us in Cable Street. They were coming to kill us. We knew that and we fought them and the police stood there and did nothing. Because we were Jewish, and it's all right to joke about us. You always think it's all right to joke about the Jews – they can take it.' He stood up slowly, blinking, and, tall as he was, he still looked like a small boy. 'Thousands of Mosley's Blackshirts, they turned up, with sticks, with knives, and do you know what the police did? They told us they were there to protect the East End, to protect the Jews, and they didn't. The police let the Blackshirts march. Knowing what those fascists were like. Knowing Mosley, that he was an anti-Semite through and through, they still let them march. They were kicking children, Terence.'

Terence shifted in his seat, his face wearing the imperturbable mask upper-class Englishmen wore when discomfited. The others sat, transfixed, but Daniel went on.

'My cousin, she was five, one of them stamped on her hand. He – he called her a dirty Jew. They were beating people – my schoolmate's brother, Ray, they knocked him to the ground. This is in *London.* Where we'd been born and always lived, Terence, and we were being hounded out! I'm British, as British as you. But we didn't stand for it. The people of the East End didn't. Jews, Italians, Chinese, Blacks, we banded together and we damn well fought them. My uncle was hit with a stick. He broke a rib, Terence. He was attacked outside his own home, defending his own family.' Daniel's voice rose, and rose. 'But we shouldn't have had to. We shouldn't have been put in that position. Because posh men like you let Mosley charm them into not recognising him for what he was and they let the police get away with blue murder. The posh men didn't say to Mosley, "I say, go away, you little shit. You're a shabby, bad man trading on fear." They didn't tell him to clear out. They left it to the honest poor, the workers, to chuck that rabble out. It's always the workers, clearing everything up.'

He was leaning on the table, breathing hard, but now he shook his head. Sarah watched him, her lips parted, a stack of plates in her hand, frozen to the spot.

'Shame on you, old man. You preach the overthrow of the world order, you go after Sarah's family because they're dead and gone now, but you'd be crawling to them if there was still an earl and a flourishing estate and all of that. You're a damned coward like all of them.' He wiped his mouth, rather self-consciously. 'Sorry,' he said, looking around. 'We'll be friends again tomorrow.' He turned to Lara. 'My apologies, Lara. I promised Sarah there'd be no more incidents if we persuaded you to come here again.'

Lara smiled, and shook her head, and was about to speak, but her husband leaned forward.

'Young man,' said Tony Cull. He stubbed his cigarette out. 'That was magnificent.'

Terence Wood clapped, slowly. 'Very moving.'

Tony Cull waved him aside, like an annoying fly, and Sarah

saw the power of the man who makes things happen, the producer, not the performer. 'Listen to me, Mr Forster. Have you been on TV?'

'Me?' said Daniel, laughing. 'God, no.'

'You should,' said Tony Cull. He nodded. 'You should. This book you're working on, what's it called?'

Daniel said lightly: '*United We Stand.* It's a history of the United Kingdom through the eyes of the workers and inventors and outsiders who transformed the country. The Bodley Head is publishing it next year. Rick Blake is my editor.' He glanced at Sarah, complicit. She said nothing, but carried the plates over to the kitchen. It was growing dark outside, the last rays of the tangerine sun casting gilded light over the small back garden, its blackened branches and dirty London-stock bricks.

Sarah pressed her cool hands to her flushed face. As she bent over the sink, she heard Tony say: 'Let's talk. I know Rick; I'll call him. This should be on ITV. I'm going to make you the new Kenneth Clark, sir. The world needs to hear more from you, Daniel Forster – that's your real name, yes?'

'Yes,' Sarah heard Daniel say. 'My mother's family was from Ukraine. My father's was from Germany. They met in Spitalfields.'

'I always said he should be famous,' Diana interjected, and there was laughter, and the conversation became more general again, and Sarah started to do some washing up, just to get some of it out of the way. She glanced at the clock. Four forty. Friday was happily playing with her doll's house next to the range, and Rebecca was on Miss Minchin's knee, having a bottle. She needed tea soon, and to move towards bed. She needed these people to be out. She wanted five minutes to have a cup of tea, to restore some order. She didn't care any more about workers' rights and globalisation and the EEC and something called a thriller in Manila and – anything. She was too tired. Too boring and too damn tired.

A hand touched her shoulder, and she jumped.

'I'm going for a cigarette,' said Lara's voice in her ear, 'while the boys hammer out their new world together. Come with me.'

They stood in the front garden. Frost still glittered in little patches in the corners of the lawn. The setting sun was apocalyptic, streaks of blue and peach, the whole of The Row already in blackened gloom. The street lights had been dark for almost a fortnight.

'I love January,' said Lara after a few minutes' silence. She wrapped her cream coat more tightly around her. 'Can't explain why.'

Sarah shivered. 'I know what you mean. There's something about the depth of it. It's pure.'

'I knew you'd understand. I don't like it being so very dark on the streets, no lighting and all that, but I love the bare trees. More than when they have leaves. The tracery against the sky – look.'

She took Sarah's hand, and pointed it up to the tree in the communal garden, a beech tree, a tangle of black, knotted branches in silhouette against the streaked multicoloured flaming sky. She could see, right at the top, a little bird, hopping from branch to branch.

'We used to leave crumbs out for the birds, Sarah. They freeze on the branches otherwise. I wish you'd start it again. Sorry about Tony in there,' she said, inhaling sharply on the cigarette. 'He rarely bothers with my life, then he bowls right on in and takes over. But I think he's on to something with Daniel. I knew they'd get on. I hope you don't mind.'

'I'm so glad you brought him. I wanted you to come back.'

They were silent, the thudding emotion and atmosphere of the scene in the kitchen almost tangible still between them. Sarah could feel it.

'I didn't realise your mother was in jail.'

'She's not. She was released twelve years ago.'

'It must have been hard for you.'

'No,' said Sarah. 'I liked knowing she was locked away. She wasn't a good mother.' She saw Lara's expression. 'I don't want to go into it, if that's OK.' She stamped her feet on the cold tiles. 'Listen,' she said. 'I never really said sorry for that awful day. I know it's ages ago.'

'Don't. There's no need. I find the kitchen the most painful place, you see. There were so many good evenings there.'

As always, Sarah saw, in her mind's eye, Lara's mother, charming and lithe, with a fringe and a bun, dancing and singing, a baby on each hip, whilst her father played, and a brother strummed along on the guitar. And, as ever, it troubled her, and she couldn't remember why. It was always the same feeling – she was underwater, rising to the surface.

'You must both come back. Come back soon.'

'I don't think so.' Lara stubbed her cigarette out. 'I loved you living here at first. I enjoyed becoming friends, getting to know you.' She turned to Sarah, her small face pale, just the two spots burning, one on each cheek. 'I can't stand seeing you like this. Going down, further and further away from yourself. You weren't like this when you moved in.'

'Oh—'

Lara blinked. 'When I first met you, you reminded me of a wild spirit. You were shy, and bold, and unusual, and your cheeks flushed when you were excited, and you had all these plans, and there was something about you – I used to want to be next to you, just to feel whatever it was.' She looked at Sarah, eyes flicking over her.

Sarah nodded, and made to speak. She found she couldn't.

Lara said: 'You need to ask yourself something. What will you do when they're all gone?'

'What will I – I don't know,' said Sarah frankly. 'I don't think about it.'

'They'll go, you know. They'll leave you, one day. And what will you do? Don't you miss it? Don't you wonder if you're in the wrong life?'

'What?'

'You shouldn't be doing the dishes, Sarah,' and suddenly she had moved towards Sarah, and in the porch, quite unseen by the street, or the guests inside the house, they were kissing, her bony hips pressed against Sarah, her cool, smooth lips on Sarah, her slim hands on her neck, her shoulders, her waist, and Sarah felt as if she were melting, not sure if she were fire or ice. It was totally unexpected and yet as Lara's lips probed hers, as her tongue gently moved into her mouth, Sarah indistinctly felt that perhaps this was the mystery of Lara, and it made some sense. For a few seconds, she did not stop her, nor did she want her to. It was so surprising, and gentle, and nothing in her life was. Then, as the ice-cold air bit at the back of her neck, her ears, she suddenly broke away, pushing Lara back with her hands.

'No,' she said.

'I'm so sorry,' Lara said immediately. But she didn't look sorry. She took out another cigarette. 'I thought it might be fun.'

'Fun – Oh,' said Sarah. 'Yes.' She was so used to berating herself it took her a minute to realise this wasn't her obligation, much less her fault. 'Well,' she said, hoping she sounded like Diana, laconic and cool, 'sorry to disappoint you.'

Lara gave a short, dry laugh. 'You're easy to tease, Sarah. I won't, but I could if I wanted. I'm going home now. Tell Tony I left, would you?'

And she turned and walked away, shrugging her cream coat over her shoulders. Sarah stood shivering on the doorstep, then turned to open the door. She touched her fingers to her lips. The sound of men talking, braying really, came from the kitchen – the trouble with the BBC, the Ulster problem, whether Heath would call an election – neither one listening to the other, just talking, talking, talking.

Chapter Twenty-One

A year later

March 1975

'Jesus died on the cross.'

'He did.'

'For our sins, Mama.'

'Well – I suppose so. But some people—'

'So manandkind might be saved.'

'Mankind – well—'

'THAT'S WHAT I SAID, MANKIND!' Friday stopped pushing her little blue-and-white striped buggy and turned to Sarah, heavy tears immediately dropping from her blue eyes. 'Mum, I DID!'

Daniel was on an important telephone call, and Sarah had marched them hurriedly out of the house, but Friday did not like being hurried.

'I know you did,' Sarah hastened to reassure her, because once Friday had got herself revved up, like her father, it took a long time to calm her down.

'It a dog,' nearly-three-year-old Rebecca added from her own matching blue-and-white striped buggy, pointing at her toy dog. 'It a dog. DU-DOG.'

'Yes,' said Sarah. Sometimes she wanted to stop, press her hands to her eyes, scream *Shut up, just shut up and be quiet. Just for one second. Please.* But she didn't. She said brightly, 'Oh look, here's Diana doing the garden. Shall we go in?' She swerved the buggy away from the house towards the communal garden. As they stepped through the iron archway, Friday flung herself forward, running towards the flowerbeds where Diana and her companions, the Misses Forbes, the spinster sisters who lived at No. 3, were carefully picking grape hyacinth and daffodils.

'Good afternoon, girls,' Diana said, putting down her secateurs, for she and the girls were great friends. 'Did you have a good day at work, Friday?'

Friday giggled. 'I don't go to work! I was at nursery!'

Diana touched Friday's nose. 'It's Friday tomorrow, isn't it.'

'Dis Friday,' shouted Rebecca. 'HIYA FRIDAY!'

'Ah, but tomorrow is a *very special* Friday,' Miss Barbara Forbes said, leaning towards the girls. 'It is the day Lord Jesus gave his life for us.'

'For *manandkind* that we might be saved,' Friday said firmly.

'I see the nursery's got her,' Diana murmured, rolling her eyes.

'Hiya Friday,' said Rebecca sadly to herself. 'Mama, look. Dis Friday.'

'There's a marvellous *Good Friday* service tomorrow at St Aloysius, for the children,' said Miss Barbara, beaming at Friday and at Rebecca, who had picked up a daffodil and was staring at it, bemused. 'We stand a *bare cross* of *oasis and chicken wire* at the centre of the *church* symbolising Christ's agonising *death,* and all are welcome to come and decorate it with their *own flowers.*' Rebecca was still staring at her flower. 'Like that, dear,' said Miss Barbara. 'Oh! Oh – dear, should she –'

Sarah, who had been watching the front door of Lara's block of flats at the top of The Row, turned just as Rebecca bit the head of the flower off, and started chewing it.

'Oh Jesus,' said Sarah, and the Misses Forbes looked aghast. 'I'm *so sorry.*' She grabbed her daughter by the neck, prising open her mouth. 'Rebecca! Open! Now!' Rebecca's jaw was clamped tightly shut. Sarah could see the muscles working. Daffodils were poisonous – she knew it. Uncle Clive's gamekeeper's son had died after eating them – or was that bulbs? Her mother had laughed, and said he was so stupid it was a wonder he'd lived that long. Sarah slid her nail between her daughter's teeth but she would not open them. 'Rebecca!' she barked in her most martial, low voice. 'Stop chewing! *Now!*'

'Rebecca,' said Friday, staring in total horror at the situation, 'if you don't stop being naughty, no chocolates on Easter, the day of Jesus Christ.'

Rebecca opened her mouth and was slightly sick into the flowerbed.

Diana gave a great guffaw. 'Well *done*, Friday. Very politic.'

'Today is rather a big day,' Sarah felt she had to say. Suddenly, she saw Lara, approaching them now, rounding the hedgerows of the oval communal garden. 'Lara!'

Lara stopped at the sound of her name, just as at that moment Daniel burst out of the house. 'Darling! Sarah!' He rushed towards them, arms outstretched. 'The series is commissioned! We start filming in May!'

'Daniel! That's – oh my God! That's absolutely bloody marvellous!' Sarah flung her arms around him. He hugged her tight, pressing her to him, lifting her so her feet tickled the ground. He lowered her gently and she held his face in her hands, and they looked at each other. This was them. This had happened to them!

'My – our – series, for Thames Television!' Daniel's smile practically split his face in two, as he turned towards Diana, still clutching his wife's hands. 'It's based on my book, and it's a history of our country, the workers and the landowners and how we see ourselves, how others see us, down through the ages. We're filming at Stonehenge, and Arthur's Seat, the Lakes – all over! Tony says the chap at Thames is rather excited about it! Tony's been marvellous, introducing me to all the right people, you see. It's tremendously exciting, and – oh, Sarah!'

He clapped his hands to his face, kept them there, just smiling at her. His joy was infectious. She felt a grin break across her face, and their eyes met again. No one else would understand. No one had been up on the stargazing plaform that August night, when they had made a promise to each other. No one else knew how much this meant, how far both of them had come.

Friday clapped, and Rebecca, who had wandered to the furthest reaches of the garden the moment she could, tried to jump up and down, only couldn't. She yelled, loudly, from the flowerbed. 'Hayo! Hayo!'

'I know!' Daniel shouted at her. 'I know, darling! Hello, Lara!' He caught her by the elbows, and swivelled her round, so her hair rippled out behind her. Lara started, and pulled away from him, then laughed.

'Hey! Congratulations. That was Tony, calling to tell me,' she said. 'Wonderful news, Daniel.'

'It's all thanks to you, Lara dear,' he said, clasping her shoulder. 'You said to Sarah, you said Tony and I should meet – You made it happen. He's the chap who's pushed this whole operation through, from start to finish. Lara, I feel sometimes like –' He hugged himself. Sarah watched. 'Like there's a guardian angel, watching over us.'

'Oh God,' said Sarah. 'Get him away from here. He'll start crying and talking about ley lines soon. Daniel, would you start the lunch? I'll stay out with them for a while.'

Daniel flung his arms out. 'My darling, anything for you. I have to make some phone calls first, but then – then you shall have an *omelette*.'

He ran back to the house and jumped in the air, clicking his heels together before he got to the front gate. Sarah watched him, her heart full, a frown puckering her forehead.

'I've got some tea in my Thermos,' Diana said. 'Would anyone like a cup?'

'Oh,' said Miss Barbara brightly. 'No, thank you. My dear, you must be *delighted*.'

Sarah nodded. 'Oh yes.'

She turned, to see Lara smiling at her. *I know*, the smile said. *Goodbye to the next two years.*

She upended Sarah all the time – the way she knew what Sarah was thinking, how inscrutable she was, how frank and accessible the rest of the time. There were times when Sarah was driven quite mad by her, though she could never get up the nerve to ask her: *why did you kiss me? What did it mean?* She was so square, she felt, needing to know. Certainly she knew Lara wasn't in love with her. She was so helpful to Sarah, understanding sometimes exactly what Sarah would be going through ('I know Daniel's away on tour,' she had said a year ago, appearing at the door with a Chinese takeaway. 'And I know you've got flu, and

I know Friday loves noodles. I'll just leave these here, and go, all right?')

And sometimes she was haughty and childish, laughing at Sarah, enjoying the jabs she made about her marriage, her appearance, her career, her *life* in the house. ('You'll get there with this place,' she'd said a month or so ago. 'It'll never be how it was, of course. But you don't mind that, do you?')

Sarah watched as Lara took off her coat, carefully spreading it and sitting on the ground. Miss Barbara put her hand on Sarah's arm. 'How lovely to see you, dear. Now, I wanted to ask you a huge favour, one from which I trust you will not shrink—'

Lara bent down to stroke Friday's hair. 'Hello, Friday Forster! How are you?'

'Good,' said Friday blankly, and strode off.

'Lawah here!' said Rebecca, pointing at Lara, immensely pleased with herself.

'I am always here.' Lara smiled at the others.

'Oh. It is wonderful.' Miss Barbara clapped her hands together. 'I remember, when you were little, Lara, you and Henry used to play out here all day, no matter how cold it was.' She gave a little sigh. 'Summer, winter . . . in the pouring rain! You and your brothers.' She stopped, looking embarrassed, but Lara said gracefully:

'You're very lucky if you grow up here. We all are, aren't we.' She poured some tea into a camping mug, and handed it to Barbara.

'Thank you, dear. I will have one now, I think.'

'Girls, do you want a biscuit?' Lara said now to Sarah's daughters.

Miss Barbara turned to Sarah. 'My dear, I did have a favour to ask of you.'

'Yes, of course,' said Sarah, watching Friday out of the corner of her eye, accepting a biscuit from Lara. Friday didn't like Lara, and Lara didn't realise this, which was strange as Sarah thought Lara saw most things.

'Here,' Friday said, taking the biscuit and instantly slamming it into Rebecca's small palm. 'It's stinky – you have it.'

With a mighty will, Sarah ignored her children and turned to Barbara Forbes. 'How can I help you?'

'It's a charity reception. At our house. For Christian Aid,' Miss Barbara said. 'My dear, the pianist we booked has just pulled out. He has trench foot – most unfortunate, and especially given his profession—'

'I don't see what his profession has to do with having trench foot,' Miss Pam, the brisker of the sisters, put in sharply. 'Sarah dear, we're stuck. It's this Saturday, and we did wonder if you'd consider helping us out. Just a few pieces – anything you'd choose—'

'Me?' Sarah said, aghast. 'Oh, my goodness no. I haven't played in public for years.'

'Not at all?' Diana was watching her.

'Not once.' She turned to her. 'In fact, I've hardly practised. I tried, and it was – too painful. So I stopped. I always thought I'd find the right time, but . . .'

'But now *is* the right time, perhaps!' Barbara clapped her hands.

'No,' said Lara suddenly, and they all turned to look at her. 'I mean, if she doesn't want to play, she shouldn't have to.'

'Oh, I *am* foolish.' Miss Barbara gave a small moan. 'Father always said I had a distressing loose tongue. He said one day I'd have it cut off, and it'd serve me right. Oh, do forgive me.'

'Oh, Barbara, do calm down,' said Miss Pam, eyeing Sarah caustically, and Sarah felt, in a rush, the absence of her own sister, like lemon juice in a wound. 'If she can't do it, well, she can't do it.'

'It's perfectly all right,' said Sarah. 'Look – I would love to, but –' She turned to the children, who were in front of her, both patting her skirt. 'I'm talking. Eat these, and then roll down the hill for me, please. Can you do that, Rebecca? Can you roll, or are you too little?'

Rebecca waddled away, and Sarah watched her girls walk up to the top of the garden together, hand in hand, Friday officiously buttoning her little sister's cardigan up – 'So it doesn't come off, dess? DESS? Are you listening, Rebecca?' and the two of them rolling down the sloping garden, first slowly, then hysterical with laughter. She tried to work out why it felt strange, then she realised: they were looking after themselves. This state, this constant state of high alert, it would pass. They would grow up. They would leave.

Diana watched them. 'They're such ducks, both of them.'

'I'd love to do it,' said Sarah suddenly.

'Oh, Sarah dear! Thank you!'

'I'm sure we can arrange someone to look after the children, if Daniel's busy. Everything at the moment with the programme – it's all rather up in the air. His mind is full of only that and getting him to concentrate on anything else is very hard.'

'Well, of *course*,' said Miss Barbara immediately. 'It must be very, *very demanding* for him. When you know, just let *us* know, dear—'

'I'll look after them,' said Lara immediately. 'I can come and put them to bed. They know me, don't they?'

'Oh yes!' The sisters nodded. 'Wonderful!' said Miss Pam. 'Well, that's that.'

'Thank you, Lara,' Sarah said, turning towards her. 'It's so kind of you.'

'It's no problem,' said Lara, as she started to leave for home.

The afternoon sun was weak, and as the shadows lengthened it was cold. After the Misses Forbes had departed, carrying with them a trug filled with white, cream and yellow narcissi and yellow star-like aconites, Diana wrapped her scarf more tightly round her neck.

'Silly old biddies. That's very good of you.'

'Oh, I'm hopeless. I should do more –' Sarah waved her arms vaguely – 'of something. I need to start playing again, and I just thought why not.' Daniel's good news had made her feel breathless, light, full of energy. 'Daniel keeps saying I should perform something at All Day Sundays, but I somehow can't bear the idea. So self-indulgent, to subject people to your playing.'

'You are funny. I miss you practising. It was beautiful. No one's played in that house for years. It needs music . . .' A door slammed at the bottom of the road. 'Georgina's moving, did you know that?'

'I didn't.'

'Monty has finally persuaded her to go. They're buying a place in Suffolk.'

'Daniel will miss her.'

'Perhaps.' Diana was watching her. 'Look, Sarah. Do you mind if I say something?'

Sarah tensed. 'Of course not.'

'Catesby, my old man, he was a money man. He was a so-so husband. Very rich but very hardworking too. The money took over his life. Buying this house did too. Paying for it, as well.'

Sarah thought of the unpaid red gas bill, sitting on the kitchen table, casually, as if it were another piece of paper. She thought of the coal in the scuttle they hadn't paid for, and the one pair of thick woollen tights she had worn so often her toes stuck out through a variety of holes. 'Tell me about it.'

'I love it here, but would I have wanted a husband I saw for more than five minutes rather than this beautiful house? I think so. Houses can send people mad. Buying them, filling them full of . . . *things*. Just remember that.'

'I know that – believe me.' Sarah picked at a flower on the ground.

'You can't see a marriage,' Diana said. 'But it's more real than a house; it's more important. You have to look out for it. I wish I'd done that.' She nodded at the two Misses Forbes, who had worked their way slowly around the oval-shaped gardens back towards their own house, next to Georgina and Monty. 'I wish I'd had the chance to play it differently. Done things the right way.'

'How?'

'Oh, I don't know. Been braver.'

'You? You're the bravest person I know, Diana.'

'Oho, I'm not. I wanted a different life to this, Sarah. Do you know, I read Law? I wanted to be a judge. I had a mother who fought for that sort of thing.' She curled her hand into a fist, and uncurled it, then gripped Sarah's wrist. 'Dear girl. You have to get on with it. Do it for yourself. No one else will.'

Sarah nodded brightly. 'Oh. Yes.'

Diana looked at her shrewdly. 'I know you're trying to shut

me up. Listen, Daniel's series will be finished soon, won't it? Would you let me look after the girls for a night or two?' She stood up, and Sarah saw, for the first time, how slowly she moved, how she grimaced to straighten herself out. 'You could go away somewhere. The Chilterns. The sea.'

'Away!' said Sarah. 'You're very kind, Diana. That'd be wonderful. And the girls would love that. You know how much they love you.'

'I'm not being kind. I love you all.' Diana's voice was rough. 'You've brought life back to that dreary old house. It was a tomb for years, and I want so much to help you when I can.'

'Oh goodness,' said Sarah, laughing. She put her arm round Diana, who rested her white head briefly on her shoulder. 'You'll come round for a glass of bubbly to celebrate later, won't you? We've got a good bottle Daniel's publisher gave him.' She thought of the hours he'd spent on the TV series, drafting and redrafting ideas long into the night, of him retiling the bathroom after one long night, the cuts where he'd dropped a whole stack of tiles on the floor that had shattered and cut his bare feet to ribbons, how this morning, waiting for the call, he'd listened to the St Matthew Passion on the radio and conducted with two pencils at breakfast, with Friday copying him, both serious as anything. She thought about how hard he worked, never complaining, always cheerful, how miraculous a person he was. How very much she still loved him, maddening though he was. 'He deserves some champagne.'

'Oh. Well, that's an excellent idea.' Diana gave the quickest of smiles. 'How kind of you to think of me.'

'Think of you! The amount you've put up with, listening to Daniel jaw on about it night after night . . .' Diana's face broke into a smile. 'Most of the ideas in it are yours as much as his, the two of you together – you have to be there, Diana.'

'Oh, go on. He's a genius. I'm proud to be his friend. Listen, about that recital, I'd be happy to put the girls to bed, you know.'

'What?' Sarah took a moment to recall what she meant.

'Lara, looking after them. Sarah, I'm not sure if it's a good idea—'

But at that moment Daniel came hurrying out across the road, waving his arms. She saw him through the bare trees, then flinging open the gate to the communal garden.

'Sarah,' he said, and at the sound of his voice she froze.

'Yes?' She went towards him.

He held out a hand. 'My bird, come quickly. Vic's on the phone.'

She thought he said Rick, the name of his editor, and smiled. Then she replayed the phrase again. 'Vic? What on earth—'

'It's your mother,' he said, and his face was like a child's again, the boy she had known all those years ago. 'She's dying. She wants you both to go to Fane. She wants to see you. As soon as possible.'

Chapter Twenty-Two

Two sisters in their thirties stood in a churchyard, their hands sunk into their pockets in the chill spring morning.

'I don't want to go back,' said Sarah suddenly. Her legs were like water.

'She's dying,' Vic said. 'She can't hurt you now.' Her eyes gleamed, Sarah couldn't tell whether with tears or anticipation. 'Come on, for goodness' sakes, and let's get it over with.'

She turned, and stumped off, her chestnut hair gleaming in the watery sun. Sarah looked around at the unkempt graveyard, the wayward cracked gravestones, the decrepit Fane mausoleum, where Stella had tried to build her nest. *Oh, Stella. I owe this place nothing*, she thought to herself, and, jaw clenched, she followed her sister through the winding path out into the estate.

David Bailey had taken a photograph of her mother on her release from prison in 1962, but it had only come to light in the last year. It had been too controversial then, a comment on the state of the nation, a woman out of control. Even when Bailey published it himself in 1972 something about it chimed with the new wave of seventies unease – challenge the institutions, do away with the old ways – and so, despite being ten years old, it was instantly iconic.

Timing was on her side: the release of the photo coincided with the hugely popular Destruction of the Country House exhibition at the Victoria and Albert Museum the previous year where every day hundreds queued to hear, at the entrance, a mournful voice tolling the names of great stately homes lost since the war. There was something about the picture, and how Lady Iris Fane had served time for demolishing her own house to save it, so the story went. Because Fane had survived and, against the odds, was a remarkable example of what the old estates could become.

The photo showed Lady Iris in a bright peony-pink Schiaparelli ballgown with huge, puffed skirts like petals. She was facing the camera head on, perfect white teeth bared in a manic gaze, blue eyes ablaze, apple cheeks flushed. She stood in the vast hall at Fane, the few remaining cases of stuffed birds ranged behind her, mutely looking on – ducks shot on the lake, swifts and swallows and housemartins that nested in the eaves, a peacock that had once strutted across the lawn. In her skeletal hands she wielded a huge hatchet, knuckles white with the exertion of holding it above her head. She was laughing gleefully and her smile said: *So what? I don't care what you think about me.*

The new estate that had risen up in place of Fane Hall had won prizes for its planning, its architecture, the communal spaces thoughtfully placed around the grounds, the community hall and annual events such as the fireworks provided by Lady Iris every year, carol singing, the mobile library, and the summer fair, which took place on the front lawn outside the Old House, as the remaining section of Fane Hall was now called. Twenty years after many new housing estates were now falling into disrepair, and the planning decisions made for working-class families by young childless male architects who appreciated good design but didn't understand domestic architecture or family life, or community, were being called into question. Journalists were despatched to Fane to interview Lady Iris Fane to find out what she had done, and how, with no luck. Lady Iris never gave interviews.

The photo was published on the front cover of the *Sunday Times* magazine in a long piece on the rebirth of Fane Hall and Lady Iris Fane, and what other landowners were doing to preserve these houses and their heritage. Lady Iris was featured alongside the Marquess of Bath and his lions, the Duke of Bedford showing guests round Woburn Abbey, Lord Montagu of Beaulieu sitting in one of his vintage cars.

Perhaps most unusual of all stately-home owners faced with the small issue of several million in death duties and a crumbling estate is Lady Iris Fane, sole heir of Fane Hall who, after the death of her reclusive uncle Clive, Lord Ashley, and the catastrophic fire, faced financial ruin and the loss of an estate that had been in the family for generations.

Lady Iris did what no one has yet done. Before she was sent to jail, she had contacted developers and, in a unique partnership with the Regional Housing Board under then Housing Minister Harold Macmillan she gave over the land in a deed of trust so affordable housing might be built on the estate. It was here, of course, that the famous photograph was taken of Macmillan and Lady Iris breaking ground on the three hundred thousandth house to be built as part of the Conservative government's post-war pledge on housing. Twenty years after, Lady Iris is something of a recluse herself, not granting interviews, not discussing the cause of the fire for which she was jailed and about which she has always maintained her innocence – 'I would never, ever destroy my family's house,' is the only comment she has made on the subject, but the estate itself, home to eight thousand people, thrives.

SMASHING, the headline on the magazine ran, in bright pink, across the photograph. *The subheading: How Lady Iris Fane survived jail and saved the English Stately Home* was, at the very least, entertaining.

Sarah and Daniel read it together in the sitting room as the children ran amok, their mouths agape.

'That article could win the Booker Prize for fiction,' said Daniel when he finished it.

Her mother had, Sarah noted, entirely ditched her married name and reverted to Fane. She had always been a Fane – Sarah's father, Henry Fox, now utterly consigned to history. Sometimes, she would say his name out loud, just so someone remembered him.

As for the rest – she read it almost blankly, staring at the pictures of the neat black-and-white houses smothering the landscape of the park. She felt completely detached from it. Having to do without any input from Lady Iris, the *Sunday Times* had interviewed instead the residents of the housing estate, built over the old estate.

'I wouldn't want to have her round for tea, put it that way,' one man had said, washing his car when the reporter for the *Sunday Times* found him, in one of the three-bedroomed houses with drive on the main drive that once led up to the hall. 'She's rather an *odd* lady, shall we say? But doesn't one rather love an English eccentric?'

'She's ever so private.'

'Somewhat strange, if I'm honest, but a proper lady and we're ever so grateful to her.'

'We don't really ever see her, to be honest, sir, but we've been here for eighteen years and we love the place.'

'It's our home. We never had a home before.'

'Well, I'm not dashing down there tonight,' Vic had said when Sarah had spoken to her the previous day, stumbling into the dark of the house from the spring sunshine. 'It's three now. We won't be there till well after eight o'clock, and that's too late to visit a deathbed, surely. We can go tomorrow, and if she doesn't last through the night, so be it.'

Vic sounded older. Sarah, not having seen her since their disastrous visit three and a half years ago, wondered if she had changed in other ways. Did she worry about turning into their mother? Did she lie awake at night, still, listening for owls, just as Sarah did? Sometimes she thought about what Vic had done, colluding with Susan Cowper to get rid of Mr Williams, and anger filled her so full of adrenalin she couldn't sleep. Eventually, hours later, she would tell herself: she was a child. We were both children. It was so long ago. You ignored Susan that time in Peter Jones, because she doesn't matter. It was easy to ignore her. And it struck her that on the day she'd seen Susan and backed away so hurriedly she'd crashed into a mannequin she had been choosing curtains for her new house, 7 The Row, and that this was now four and a half years ago, and yet it seemed like yesterday. She thought of Susan, how she'd last seen her, her bucked teeth and raised top lip, her hooded, rather bulging eyes, her silk headscarf, her adherence to the old ways.

God, I'm so bloody glad I'm not Susan Cowper, she thought.

'You're right, there's no point in going tonight,' Sarah had said, realising going the following day meant she could have champagne with Daniel and Diana and one more night at home. 'I'll see you tomorrow.'

'Good. I'll meet you at the station at eight.' And Vic had put the phone down.

So now, on Good Friday, they walked through the estate in the bright spring sunshine. Sarah wanted to reach out, to take her sister's hand, but she knew she couldn't.

It was very quiet, hardly anyone out. The estate had wide pavements with slightly sloping banks leading down to the road. Budding blossom trees stood at equal distances along the road. She marvelled at the tidy lawns, the small, neat houses, where once she had run as a girl, watching Stella fly overhead, where she had sat out looking at the stars, night after inky-blue night. In one front garden a man was mowing an exact square of pristine grass and she stopped and stared, overwhelmed for a moment. Behind his house the Burnt Oak still stood, where centuries before Sir Rodderick Fane had taken a telescope and gazed up at the stars, where his son had built a manor house, and two hundred years later his ancestor a vast mansion, his son fifty years later giving it landscaped lawns, sweeping stone staircases and stable blocks and a portico so huge it could not be blown up. And their mother, the last of the line, had presided over its final decline, so the central heart of it still stood, but none of the vistas, the trees, the gentle English landscape, the sweep of the great drive and the breathtaking view of the greatest house in Sussex.

The man looked up and smiled at them politely, but with a slight wariness. Sarah understood that only she and Victoria knew what had been there before that day. A landscape destroyed, to be replaced by a man mowing his square patch of lawn for the first time that year, whistling on a spring afternoon.

'Look,' she said to Vic, who had marched ahead, and seemed to have missed it. 'Vic. Stop.'

Fane Hall Drive, the central road of the estate, curved slightly and between two houses one glimpsed the vast, grainy stone portico, looming over everything. It stood apart from the rest of the estate, encircled by a low stone wall. Once it had been the most spectacular house in the county, but now it was the oddest house she had ever seen, the wings simply cut off, the centre still holding, like a transit lorry cab without its cargo, a bird without wings. It did not seem real, but more like a façade from a film set, licked with dark rusting red marks on the white stone where the fire had spread on each side before being put out in time to save the centre. It was a ghostly contrast to the houses around it with their warm golden stone, the cars outside, the bird tables and hanging baskets and trappings of real homes.

'Pretty strange, isn't it?' Vic asked her with a grim smile. 'Let's go in.'

They craned their necks and looked up at the top of the building, flecked with lichen, pockmarked with age. They climbed the steps and went in. Sarah was conscious of her shallow breathing, of her heart beating in a slippery, fast kind of way. She felt she might just vanish into thin air, become a ghost, one of the ghosts of Fane.

She peered inside at the same vast black-and-white tiled hall, the stairs leading up to the same bedroom where she and Vic had slept that first freezing, bewildering night, where Stella had nested. This house where she had watched Uncle Clive catch mice, where she had organised the Star Study into some kind of order, looking out of the window at the vast, empty parkland and where one day she had run away down the steps, clutching all her worldly possessions, never to return.

She sniffed cautiously. But there was no smell other than damp and, faintly, sweet spring flowers. The smell had gone.

'Let's go up. Come on,' said Vic. 'The doctor said we shouldn't waste time so . . .' And she opened the great front door.

Sarah stepped inside the hall and stopped, confused, rather like when you put a foot down expecting a step but find only flat floor. The Rose-Red Drawing Room was half a room now, four yards long, blocked up at the end with no trouble taken to smooth it off, the bare bricks showing. It was lined with cases of birds, old chairs, the remaining debris of the house. But there was so little of it, compared to what there had been.

On the other side should have been the dining room, its rich oak panelling, the green paint, which, though peeling and cracked, still gave a taste of the house's former glory. But that, too, was gone – all gone. It was a bright bare room, with another door at the end, which formerly had been the corridor leading to Uncle Clive's quarters, the cold, tiled kitchen, the old copper pans and the range. Above the entrance was a sign: FANE ESTATE COMMUNITY HALL. A board below it was hung with notices:

Easter Bonnet Competition, 12pm Holy Saturday

Pet Rabbit for Sale, contact Doris Gooding, no. 12 Fane Hall Drive

Ham Radio Club – meets every Tuesday, Burnt Oak Pub, John's your man!

A pool table and a child's playpen were at the centre, plastic rounded chairs on the side.

'What *is* going on here,' Sarah whispered. She felt like Alice in Wonderland. Everything was topsy-turvy.

'I know,' said Vic. Their hands, at their sides, touched, knuckle to knuckle.

They climbed the stairs, and Sarah thought of the times she had looked down at events she didn't understand: her mother raging at Uncle Clive; Mr Murbles, foolish and gullible; the house-clearance men with their matches, their sly appraising glances. She had stood here scared, so often, alone and confused, knowing she was lost in this place and now she was back and nothing was the same. Her head didn't seem to be able to wrap itself round the new house. It was rather like jet-lag, or having a very small baby. She could see it all, but none of it really made sense.

Her feet sounded different on the black-and-white marble staircase. Deadened, muffled, whereas before they had echoed, and learning the art of creeping quietly had been essential.

Outside their old room they found a nurse, sitting in the

corridor in a cane chair, like a Victorian hospital. 'Oh,' she said, looking up, her face red with fresh weeping. 'You must be Lady Iris's daughters. Are you Mrs Howard?'

'Who?' said Sarah, but Vic stepped forward.

'That's me. Hello. You must be Carole.'

'Yes, Mrs Howard.' Sarah was still coming to terms with the fact she'd forgotten her sister's married name as Carole shook their hands, weeping profusely, then blew her nose into a large handkerchief. 'I'm sorry. What must you think – I'm Carole. I'm a nurse. I live over there, 14 Fane Hall Drive, that's me. Some of us have been taking it in turns to sit with her, you know . . .'

'Thank you,' said Vic, blinking slightly, disentangling herself from her handshake. 'What's happened to – her? We haven't seen her for some time,' she added.

'Oh, I understand that – she was most correct – you know what she was like! She always said you'd never come back, that she didn't want you to think you should. But she'll be thrilled you're here!' Her face shone. 'Now,' Carole continued. 'Don't think I'm trying to take your place—'

'Be our guest,' Vic muttered. Carole stopped, taken aback.

'My sister means we're very grateful to you,' Sarah said hastily. She wanted to laugh, all of a sudden. 'Thank you. You've obviously looked after her very well.'

'We don't want to tire her out,' said Vic, unwinding her scarf. 'What – what's happened, exactly?'

'A stroke, Mrs Howard. Yesterday morning. She was putting up notices in the village hall and she fell to the ground. I've seen enough like it. I think it's all those years of worry in prison. It's not good for you, is it? She's – poor dear, she's on her way out, but it's a peaceful end, even if she's relatively young.'

Their mother loomed over their lives with such a strange, spectral force that Sarah realised she never thought about how old she might be, whether she was ageing or not. So much was unexamined, so much unprocessed; Sarah had concentrated on getting away, on being different, on opening up a clear divide between her now and her childhood; she had never stopped to consider what it would feel like to be without her.

Vic's hand rested lightly on Sarah's, and she said, 'If you don't mind, we'll go in and see her. Carole, why don't you take a break, and go home? We'll make sure she's not alone.'

'Oh,' said Carole. She gave a thin smile. 'We're trying to – always make sure someone she can trust is here for her. So I'll stay, if you don't mind.'

Sarah was fascinated. A world where her mother was venerated, treated like a film star. She knew why. To some people, as with the article in the newspaper, her mother was a hero, because they wanted heroes in an age where everything was new and frightening. She was certain the Susan Cowper she'd glimpsed in Peter Jones would probably queue up to sit with her mother, telling people she was protecting Britain's heritage and ought to be treated with respect. She felt pretty sure the likes of Susan Cowper wouldn't have defended Daniel's neighbours back in Cable Street. She'd have made the policemen cups of tea. 'Do leave us, if you don't mind,' said Vic, and she briskly ushered Carole away, shooing her off like a pigeon inside a building. 'In we go,' she said, and Sarah opened the door.

She lay on the narrow iron bedstead in the Thin Room. One bed had been removed, so there was at least space for both of them to stand. Stella's shelf was still there. The curtains and wallpaper were new, though, and someone had, at some point, replaced the window frame. The room was still cold.

How pale her eyelashes were. Her huge eyes and round cheeks seemed to be sinking into the ghostly face. In her hair was the star hair slide she had always worn; Sarah hadn't thought of it for years. They stood, watching her, in the bed, her small hands peeking over the top of the dirty quilt.

Sarah often wondered what she'd say if she went back, if she saw her again. And now she was here and she couldn't speak. She was still very beautiful, the same fine features as when Sarah had taken Friday to meet her, three and a half years ago. Her eyes were open, and she blinked, and stared at them, as her daughters stood over her.

'Can you hear us, Iris?' Vic said, quite briskly. She drew the curtains back a little more, to let what light she could into the room.

There was a faint sound from the bed. One finger flapped, vaguely.

'We've come back to see you,' said Vic. 'We . . .' She trailed off.

Their mother made a small sound, and blinked. *Yes.*

Sarah found she couldn't say anything. Her throat had closed up. The thought that it might be a hoax flashed across her mind. She knew it was a dreadful thing to think, but she knew how many dreadful things there had been.

'Carole seems nice,' Vic ventured.

Another small groan.

Sarah said suddenly: 'Why are you in this room? Why haven't you taken a better room?'

There was silence.

'Why are you in our old room? To tease us?' Sarah nudged Vic. She felt sick, like when you run too fast for a train on an empty stomach. Adrenalin pumped through her, and the small room seemed to be closing in on them, getting smaller and smaller. 'This is ridiculous, Vic. We shouldn't have come. She's – she's playing with us.'

Their mother blinked, and made a tiny whispering sound. Sarah peered at her.

'I don't believe you,' she found herself saying, her voice thick. 'I don't believe you're dying.'

And, suddenly, Iris opened her mouth. Very slowly, her voice barely audible, she said:

'What a drip.'

Both sisters jumped, and Iris laughed, blinking, very slowly.

'You. Sarah. You –' She stopped, her mouth forming the words, and Sarah saw then that this was a further game, but she didn't understand it. 'I thought . . . you were the one who understood.'

'You're wrong,' Sarah muttered. She could feel sweat on her forehead.

Their mother laughed silently, opening her mouth, flashing her brown, patchworked teeth. She frowned, slowly, her eyes bulging with faux surprise. Sarah understood then this was the end, but she was playing with them still, like she always had done.

'What did you want?' Vic said, stepping forward and getting a little closer. 'You wanted to see us. Tell us.'

'They . . . think I'm their friend,' said Iris. She nodded very slightly and moved her eyes to the side, as if indicating the estate out there. 'Idiots. They like it here. My house. They like my house.'

'Oh God, this again,' Vic muttered, and Sarah saw her catch hold of the bedstead with one hand. Sarah took her coat off, and laid it on the chair, glancing as she did so out of the window. She thought of what she had done to escape, how hard she had worked, and she drummed her fingers on her thighs, feeling for the callouses that had once been there, the hours and hours of practice, what it had given her, what she had lost by leaving it behind.

'None of it . . . is for you,' their mother said, very faintly. 'You understand? There's no money.'

'Listen, we don't care about the money,' said Sarah, too loudly. 'We don't need your money. We wouldn't touch it.'

Her mother gazed at her, barely aware of where she was. She looked round the room, almost in surprise. And then she said:

'I didn't do it, you know.'

Vic was rubbing her forehead. She turned. 'What?'

'The fire. It wasn't me.'

They stared at her. 'Iris,' Vic said. 'It doesn't matter. It's in the past.'

'No. No. No. The Easter Monday. I came back. To get you. I saw them, laying the fire. Not. Me. I didn't do it.'

Sarah could feel her hands freezing, water trickling down her back, all of her icy cold. She said: 'What do you mean?'

Her mother fixed her with her pale-blue eyes, the long white lashes trembling. She drew in a breath, shallow, the base of her throat fluttering, the death rattle already at work.

'The fire was not me. I would never have got them in. I saw them . . . you understand me? I . . . *saw them.* It was him. Clive. It was him.' She raised herself up a little on the pillows, swallowing, and took a few breaths. She was very calm. 'Last thing he did. He died, in front of me. He told me they were coming and then he fell. Dead. They all fall down. I had to watch it burn. I sat and watched it, in the woods. I knew they'd get me. They all fall down.' She paused, her mouth open, not moving, her eyes fixed on the ceiling. White matter had formed in the corners of her mouth. She was so still they both leaned forward. Then, in a hiss:

'He planned it. He was so cunning; he always was. But it's my house now.'

'Uncle Clive started the fire?' Vic said.

Sarah knew, though. She said slowly: 'Of course he did. He hired the men who did. I saw them arriving, Vic. He hired the men and he framed her. Oh my goodness. I see.'

'Yes . . .' Iris said. 'You must understand. It's written down. It's written –'

'What's written?'

'It's written. My house. It's my house. My—'

She broke off, stared at Sarah again, not moving, not blinking, and she never said another word.

Afterwards, they sat in the little room, just the two of them, and their mother, Lady Iris Fane, last of the Fanes. She was very small. Death had pulled her further beneath the quilt, the hands that had slapped them, grabbed them, pinched them, disappearing into the bedclothes. Her lashes were white against her taut yellowed skin.

Vic sat with her hands in her lap, Sarah next to her. Once, Sarah leaned forward to adjust the bedclothes, and Vic reached out and patted her arm.

'It's over,' she said. 'It's over.' Neither of them knew what else to say, and they were old enough and wise enough to understand that, for the moment, that was all. It was over.

Chapter Twenty-Three

Walking down the street through the village, Sarah looked into the post office again, but it was Saturday afternoon and it was shut. Mrs Boundy had died five years ago, in Ripley with her sister; Daniel had given the eulogy at her funeral.

The high street was silent. Sarah wanted to ring a bell, to proclaim that Iris was dead. Vic was still at the house, dealing with the doctor, filling out forms. She knew she ought to go back and help her, but she sat on the War Memorial for a while, staring into nothing.

The sun was warm now, the daffodils bobbing around the sanded grit of the path leading to the old gates of the house. She could feel music now, flooding her, giving her life. She was alive. Her mother was dead, and she – she was alive –

'Miss Sarah?' someone touched her arm and Sarah jumped. A woman in a black coat and horn-rimmed glasses peered at her. 'Yes, it is you. Well I never. I'm so sorry.'

Sarah blinked at her. 'Mrs – Boyes? My goodness, it's been a long time.'

The old Fane housekeeper had not changed in twenty years, apart from the fact that now her hair was almost completely white. Her pale, unreadable face had settled into deep lines; she leaned on an elegant stick. She fastened her top coat button securely around her.

'I'm very sorry, Miss Sarah. I heard from the doctor about your mother. Just this lunchtime, I understand.'

'Yes,' said Sarah. 'It was very quick.'

She knew she'd have to have a stock of clichés to hand for this next stage, words that rolled off the tongue and didn't cost too much to say.

'That's a blessing.' The housekeeper nodded. 'Well, I'm ever so glad to have seen you. I suppose it's odd, coming back. I've not seen you here since the day of the fire.'

'I came back a few years ago. But other than that, no.'

'You'll be here more now, I suppose,' Mrs Boyes said. Her voice was flat, and respectful, as ever, but she stared at Sarah now and then, as if trying to read her.

'Us? I don't think so. Why?'

'To deal with the house, and suchlike.'

'Fane? Oh, not us. It's part of a trust. She set it all up when she built the housing estate. The building passes to the National Trust and they have to keep the community hall, but they'll open the rest of the building up, I suppose. It's such an oddity, and so remarkable, what she did – but it's nothing to do with me, or Victoria, thank goodness.'

'You've two little girls, I heard.' There was a pause. '*She* told me.'

Sarah didn't know what to say. 'So she knew that, then.'

'Oh, she knew. And when I see her around – saw her, I should say – she'd sometimes mention you. Or Mr Forster. I think she wanted to talk to people. About you, about Miss Victoria. She was happiest on her own, you know, more than anyone I've known, miss. But I do think she got lonely.'

'Well –' Sarah shrugged – 'it's too late now.' She wanted to leave, suddenly. Now wasn't the time for conversation. 'Listen, Mrs Boyes – I ought to –'

But Mrs Boyes leaned forward, and clutched Sarah's bag. 'You should know she wasn't always like this, you know.'

Her breath on Sarah's face was warm, and meaty. Sarah recoiled. 'What do you mean?'

'Well, she was a sweet little thing. Fluffy white hair. Always a bit odd. I wondered if she was – well, you know, some children are a little bit different.' She cleared her throat. 'But, if you ask me, I don't think she was ever right after your uncle came back to live here. She found it very hard.' She coughed again. 'I'm not saying anything. Forgive me speaking out of turn. I've lived here for seventeen years now, since they built the houses. It's a marvellous place. So I've some time for her. What she did, how she turned it all around.'

Sarah spread her hands. 'I should have made more effort, perhaps.' She smiled at her and there was an awkward pause. 'Well, thank you for everything you did for us all,' Sarah stood to move off, but the older woman blocked her way. Her grey eyes burnt. 'I said nothing. I saw it all. I couldn't say anything. I'd have lost my job and I had nothing.'

'Mrs Boyes . . .' Sarah put her hand on her arm. She looked into her eyes. Mrs Boyes had pulled her onto her knee once and hugged her when she'd come back limping after a fall, tears rolling down her muddy cheeks then, as her mother appeared, wailing and screeching about something, had thrown her off with such force, pushing her away that Sarah had stumbled over again. 'You mustn't apologise. I know you did your best.'

'Not really,' said Mrs Boyes. 'I kept telling myself I'd say something next time you girls were back from school. But then it was all over . . .' She leaned forward, her bird-like face pecking itself at Sarah. 'He was my employer. You understand? When he brought me here, in 1925, I had nothing. I'd lost my husband at Passchendaele. Lord Ashley . . . he knew Alf, my brother in the war. He knew him. Boys together. He understood, see? He knew – I knew what happened out in Canada, how he'd had to survive. I took the job because of it. All he wanted was loyalty. And silence. I gave him that. And Lady Ashley, though she was a fool. No interest in the estate, in what made the house work, in the villagers, in the old ways. All they both wanted was fine food, chocolates, fine clothes, the best of everything. Now I don't hold with all the old ways, but some of them helped people. They weren't interested in any of that – they were only out for themselves, for a good life. And there was nothing I could say, you understand?'

'Yes,' said Sarah. 'I understand.'

Mrs Boyes looked relieved. She nodded, and bowed her head. 'I kept his secrets. I'll never speak of it. But I knew. God bless you, Miss Sarah, you and your little ones and you give that Daniel Forster my best, won't you? He's a good one – I'll be off now.'

And before Sarah could say another word, she had turned and bustled away, down the narrow pavement abutting the church, still in the shade.

Outside the church there was a telephone box. Sarah dived into it, fumbling for change.

'Hello, hello, it's me.'

'My love.' Daniel's voice was close to the phone. 'How are you. How's your mother?'

'Well, she's dead.' It sounded so strange to say it. Very odd. She wasn't the sort of person you imagined being dead. 'It was a stroke. She just sort of . . . faded before our eyes.'

'Darling, I'm so sorry.'

'Oh, Daniel. My bird boy. You have nothing to be sorry for.' Her throat was closing up. Her eyes ached with unshed tears, and her head was pounding. 'I wish I hadn't come. And maybe . . .'

'It's good you were there. It's good, I promise.' Daniel's voice cracked and she knew he felt the pain she was in. 'Are you coming back today?'

'Absolutely. Look, kiss the girls, will you? And – my love oh, Daniel – thank you. Thank you for everything.' She was almost frantic with fear that she wouldn't make it back to him, wouldn't see him again. In the distance, she saw Vic, stomping across the churchyard towards her. 'Vic's coming. I should go.'

'Say hello to her, would you?' Daniel said.

Vic put her head inside the phone box. 'All right?'

'Daniel sends his love.'

'And to him,' Vic said, nodding.

'I'll see you this evening,' said Sarah. 'I love you.'

'Goodbye, darling. Just one more journey back. Then it's over. You don't have to go there ever again.'

Sarah emerged from the phone box, blinking in the afternoon light. 'Everything all right, up at the house?'

'Oh yes,' said Vic. 'Doctor was a sensible man. He said she'd been starving herself for the last few months. She was ready to go, even though she wasn't that old. I was cornered on the way out by some of her gang on the estate. There's some nonsense being talked about a memorial stone. But I say let them do it. We don't have to bother with any of it any more.' Her eyes were shining.

'We don't,' said Sarah. 'It doesn't feel like the same house, anyway. It's become something else.'

Vic didn't answer. 'The bus is at the end of the road,' she said. 'Come on, let's walk.'

So they walked along the new road with the painted yellow lines and road signs and Vic was silent, marching briskly, arms swinging by her side. But Sarah knew her sister. After a while, she said: 'I'd love it if you could come and stay with us soon. Friday would love to see you and you've never met Rebecca.'

'Hm,' said Vic. She scratched her ear. 'Do walk faster, Sarah. There's one bus an hour, and if we miss that we miss the train.'

'Yes, of course. Anyway, I'd love it too.'

'Look, Sarah,' said Vic. She blinked, very deliberately. 'I think it's best if we're not close. Let's stay in touch, of course. But this – it's all too much. We're very different. We always were. You've got your life in London, with the girls and Daniel and his books and show business.' She said it as if Daniel were running a casino in Vegas. 'I'm a simple soul, and I'm quite happy with my quiet life in the country. Let's just agree to – how does one say it?'

'Harmoniously live at a distance, you mean.'

'That's it! Exactly.' Vic picked up the pace, and smiled.

'But I don't want to,' said Sarah. 'I – I want you in my life. I want the girls to have an aunt, you see, and we don't have to live in each other's pockets, but –'

She wanted to say *I forgive you*. But it sounded so pious, and she was worried that she'd make things worse in this delicate balancing act.

There were wood anemones at the edge of the trees that still bordered the estate boundary – pale pink, and violet, and white, gently dancing in the wind. The sun had reached the dark tower of the church. Outside, a woman approached, carrying some green oasis foam, some flowers, a coil of green wire. She stared at the two sisters, blankly.

'Can I help you?' she said, with suspicion.

Sarah realised she had no idea who they were. She wasn't anyone here. She was free. Iris was gone, and she was free. She wished she felt clear of it all, but she didn't. Something was niggling at her. It didn't feel right, and it wouldn't ever feel right.

What was it Lara had said? '*What will you do when they're all gone?*' She gaped at the woman, holding her flowers and wire.

'Come on! The bus is here, Sarah,' Vic was calling, and together they ran to the end of the road, away from the house. They made the train, and it was never really discussed again, and after the funeral the following week it was easy, easy to tell herself she had left it all behind, and Vic was a part of that.

Chapter Twenty-Four

A year later

July 1976

'Sarah dear? I'm so sorry to bother you. It's another bill for you. I don't know why they keep coming to us.'

'Oh.' Sarah, who had fallen asleep at the kitchen table and been woken by the doorbell ringing, moved her jaw, trying to make her hot, flushed, stiff face work properly. 'I'm so sorry, Miss Barbara. It's the name. I think it confuses the postman – I'm certain of it. I'll talk to him again.'

A trickle of sweat ran, like an arrow, straight down her back as she straightened herself to read the neat, curved handwriting, rather like Friday's best efforts at school. She rubbed her face. 'Sorry. It's unbearable today, isn't it?'

'Worse than ever,' said Miss Barbara Forbes, grimly. 'Worse than Kandahar in August.'

Heat hung in the air. It gathered in pockets, in the kitchen, on the stairs, in the gabled room the girls shared on the top floor, which was like a furnace. They slept in the drawing room now.

It had not rained for ninety days. The Heath was brittle, dry like the end of August. They had found two bodies there in the last week alone, the first an old tramp called Lily whom Sarah used to chat to. She never wanted money; she simply didn't want to live in a house. The other was a young man no one knew, no ID on him, in a neat, worn suit, and a child's tiny toy bear in his pocket. Sarah kept thinking about the toy, whose it was.

The heat was killing people. It was driving them mad. Sarah felt *she* was slowly going mad. She had taken the girls on the Tube the previous week, and vowed not to step on it again until summer was over: the air had been like soup. Two people had fainted. A man in a white shirt had apologised for his soaked, scented appearance. At night, there was no wind, or refreshing summer showers. There was no relief. Even the shade was stuffy, the ground belching warm air.

She never missed Fane, nor wanted to be there, but in the last couple of weeks Sarah kept dreaming about it. About the parkland leading to the house, about simply lying in the cool of the trees, a breeze ruffling her, then running into the woods, letting the shade envelop her.

And it was still only July.

Miss Barbara lingered on the doorstep. 'Are you looking forward to tonight?'

'I am, though I'm rather nervous of course. Daniel isn't. He can't wait.'

'Well, we're all *very* proud of him. I can't wait to watch it. Professor Gupta's coming over specially, with his children. Eight p.m., is that correct?'

'Yes, Barbara. How kind of you.'

Tonight was the transmission of the first episode of Daniel's television programme. *United We Stand* had garnered huge amounts of coverage, in *The Times* and the *Observer*, on the radio, and even in *Private Eye* where Daniel had been given a nickname – the Guv'nor, on account of his gruff, overenthusiastic style of expressing himself – after he started appearing on talk shows and news programmes, a sure sign the Establishment had taken him in as one of their own: though Sarah thought this was unfair. Daniel was the sweetest-natured person she knew. He was a miracle, every day, to her.

'And my lesson? Is it as usual, tomorrow?'

'Of course, Miss Barbara!' Sarah smiled, realising this was the real reason for the older woman's visit. 'Nothing changes because of the series, you know. I'm still teaching.'

Miss Barbara Forbes clasped her hands under her chin. 'Oh! Oh, marvellous. I did wonder, because you must be so busy . . . and it is *so kind* of you to teach me . . .'

'It's not kind,' Sarah said gently. 'See you tomorrow. Goodbye.'

Shutting the door, she leaned against the wall in the hall. She took the date to be an auspicious one. It was on 30th July had been that they'd signed the mortgage agreement on The Row, though they hadn't moved until the following September.

Was it really nearly seven years they'd lived here? How could Friday be five, and finishing her first year at school, and Rebecca four? How was this possible? At times it seemed like a week had passed, that if she closed her eyes she could see it all on a carousel of slides, click, click: driving over the cobbles, Daniel painting the hallway, the first Christmas, walking back to the house arm-in-arm after she'd played a Christmas concert nearby and realising with a rush of joy this lovely, redbrick house was theirs, Friday as a tiny baby, screaming non-stop, those endless circuits around the Heath with the rickety pram, the day she'd run back to Fane, Friday strapped to her chest.

And yet, at times it seemed an endless amount of time, as if she'd lived through the entire age of the dinosaurs, a hundred and sixty-five million years in length, had experienced all feelings, emotions and ideas possible, multiple times.

The people they had met here – they were in archaeological layers in her life now, old friends. Diana was a quasi-grandmother, Professor Gupta's children were growing up and had offered to babysit a couple of times . . . And they got Christmas cards from Georgina and Monty, now established in the country, but they had almost passed out of their lives altogether – that was how long they'd been here.

Daniel had kept their last Christmas card as he said it was a perfect example of Britishness. It was propped up on his desk. Sarah did not like it being there.

We are very cosy here, Georgina had written. *A real change from The Row but probably for the best. There is a genuine community spirit here, and Communion here is from the Book of Common Prayer, which we are both pleased about. Monty is enjoying huntin' shootin' & fishin'! and I have become very keen on flower arranging! We have a trip planned to Chatsworth in February.*

I have never said so but I am extremely sorry for what happened during that unfortunate incident at lunch. I hope

you are very happy in number 7. Be careful, and watch out, as I am sorry to say others do not wish you well.
Georgina and Monty

Wails floated in like hot air from a garden nearby, a child come a cropper. Was it her child? Standing in the cluttered, still kitchen, a fly buzzing around the greengages she'd bought from the grocer's, Sarah put the electric bill into the beautiful creamy lemon glazed bowl they kept for keys and other household odds and ends – radiator keys, a Farley's rusk, a pressed flower, a stone, some old coins: farthings, threepenny bits, a shilling.

She'd bought the bowl on holiday in Italy the previous summer where all four of them had gorged on pasta and paddled in the stream near their tumbledown barn. She loved the bowl. It sat on the sideboard Daniel had picked up in Camden last week, which he had immediately scrubbed down and painted a loud thirties green.

'Like all the furniture at our school, Daniel,' Monica had pointed out to him, last time she'd come to London. 'You'll give me and Sarah terrible flashbacks.'

Sarah knew this frenzied DIY was a displacement for the nerves he felt about the TV series. He had decreed they had to move the old dresser left by Lara's family along the wall by about a yard, from the place it had stood for twenty-five years, so as to fit the sideboard in. They were going to do it this evening, before the first episode of *United We Stand.* Tony had offered to help.

Sarah had two pupils that afternoon, a boy of eighteen who was preparing for his Trinity College exam and a six-year-old who was too small for the cello his ambitious parents had bought him and who, she knew, would be happier building a den in the shade of the Heath than sitting with her in the stifling heat, learning first position.

She had started playing and teaching almost immediately after her mother died. The need she'd had to play as a child suddenly came back, with a force that surprised her. She took the Goffriller cello out of its case again and set it up in the corner of the drawing room, rearranging the chair and the piano so that she finally had a little space of her own. She left the girls grubbing about in the back garden for hours whilst she played. She let them forage in the bread bin for lunch whilst she played. They didn't have baths whilst she played. They taught each other rude words and wrote them inaccurately (ARCE) on slips of paper and left them in drawers around the house for her to find whilst she played. And they were happy. So was she.

The recital she gave for the Misses Forbes the week after her mother's death had confirmed it. Something had lifted and she could see clearly that she did not want to perform any more, but she had to play, to make music, to be herself again. After she had finished playing her favourite piece – the Brahms Cello Sonata in E Minor, accompanied on the piano by Miss Pam Forbes, who, it turned out, had studied at the Royal College too, in the 1920s – there had been a hushed silence, a moment of complete stillness, before the applause. She knew then it had been good.

As she was standing in the corner afterwards, rather shyly talking to Miss Minchin, a tall, stooped man had approached and stood patiently, blinking, waiting for them to finish.

'Here you go, then,' Miss Minchin had said briskly. 'Professor MacKay, how are you?'

At the name, Sarah started, and looked at the man again. 'Dear me,' she had exclaimed.

He was her old cello teacher from the Royal College of Music, a cousin of the Misses Forbes. And it was he who said, rather shyly:

'Dear Barbara is very nervous – I know she would be rather cross with me if I suggested it, but I know she wants to learn again. She was a wonderful cellist, in her day. I wonder if you'd consider – teaching her?'

It had never occurred to her, that teaching was the solution, what she wanted to do, what she and Daniel had talked about all those years ago, up on the Burnt Oak. Gazing up, looking around, passing what you saw on. But part of the beauty of the cello was the sense of continuity, the idea that a cellist hands down their teaching, from Brahms to Rostropovich and Casals, Beatrice Harrison, and her last teacher, Rudi Marshall-Wessendorf. And, of course, her dear Mr Williams.

She had started teaching Miss Barbara, who turned out to be the perfect first pupil. She wanted to relearn what she had forgotten, and was innately musical, and Sarah could try various techniques out on her without her crying or losing concentration. The corner of the drawing room worked well for lessons too: it was by the French windows, and seemed to be suspended in the trees, removed from the sound of the girls clattering about downstairs or in the back garden.

In the new year she had begun teaching on Saturdays at the Royal College of Music, sometimes on other weekdays too, if Daniel wasn't working that day or Diana was around and didn't mind collecting the girls. As they grew older, she could do more, and more. She could see it. As Monica had said to her, all those years ago, she could see her life stretching out in front of her, and it looked good, for once. She was the only woman she knew whose husband could help out with picking up and dropping off children, who had meetings but pushed them back so he could take Friday to a friend's house to play. She wondered how any of the other mothers stayed sane. Sometimes she wondered how she had.

'I don't want to go with Lara. I want to watch Daddy's TV,' Friday grumbled.

'Lara's going to have you for tea, just while I'm getting everything ready for the party. Then she'll bring you back over and we'll all watch Daddy's TV together. It's very kind of her.'

'I hate Lara.'

'I lub Lawa,' Rebecca rumbled, behind her. 'I lub her.'

'Well, I *don't*.' Friday folded her arms. 'She's mean, and she looks at me all the time, and I don't *like* her.'

Friday was always taking against people – Jacob at playgroup ('he doesn't like ORANGE'), Mrs Siezmasko after she grabbed her arm to stop her running out into the road ('she told me to *not be a silly girl and to look before I crossed the road in a MEAN WAY*'), the librarian who told her to shush ('SHE TOLD ME TO SHUSH, MUM'), but within minutes she would have changed her mind. Jacob at playgroup was her husband, as of last week. But she didn't change her mind about Lara. Sarah's fingers fumbled with the earrings she was trying to clip on; her hands were sweaty. The doorbell rang.

'There she is,' she said.

'I'm not going.'

'Are you there? The door's open.' Lara came in and shut the door. 'Can I come into the kitchen? Hello, Rebecca, are you ready? Friday! Do you want to come and play?'

'Not with you,' Friday said mutinously.

'Don't be rude, Friday,' Sarah hissed crossly.

'I don't care.'

The heavy heat and her nerves for Daniel made Sarah see red. She bent down and said sharply: 'Friday. Just for once, honestly, do as I ask and stop making a fuss about every little thing. Go and put your shoes on. Go *on*. And don't make that face. You're a big girl, darling. Stop acting like a baby.'

Friday stuck her jaw out, and gave her a curious look: a mix of anger and something else, which Sarah could not identify.

'You don't *LIKE* me,' she said, pushing past Lara as she ran into the hall. 'Good *BYE*.'

'Sorry,' said Sarah after she'd gone. 'I'm horrible today. Thank you so much for doing this.' She ran a hand over her face. Lara shrugged.

'I don't mind. Keeps me busy.' Her eye fell on the sideboard. 'Is that new?'

'Yup. Daniel's latest restoration project. We're moving your old dresser to fit it in.'

Lara's expression didn't change. She said: 'But you can't move it. It's been there for ever.'

'Oh!' Sarah felt that peculiarly awkward mixture of guilt and defensiveness she used to feel with Lara. Once, she had been aware of it all the time. But these days, with everything else, she forgot. She forgot because it had been almost seven years, and No. 7 was where she lived, she and Daniel and her furious first child and her thuggish second child, and it was their home. 'I'm not moving it out of the way. Just . . . along a little bit.'

'I bet it won't be moved. It liked being there.'

Sarah stared at her, and Lara shook her head.

'Sorry,' she said. 'I – it's none of my business.'

Sarah said, 'Are you all right, Lara?'

Lara rubbed her eyes. 'Just tired. The heat . . . I'm not sleeping.'

'Are you OK to have the girls?'

'Of course.'

But when they looked for Rebecca she had fallen asleep on a beanbag upstairs and, rather than wake her, Sarah thought it might do her good to have a nap before staying up late. No one was sleeping that well at the moment, they agreed. So she left her there, thumb plugged in mouth, face flushed, toffee-coloured curls plastered over her forehead and ear, and so only Friday, silent and furious, was borne away by Lara.

'We'll have some tea and take a walk on the Heath,' said Lara to her. 'OK?'

'No,' said Friday. She walked away without saying bye to Sarah. It was four o'clock.

'Next, after the break on Thames Television, we begin a new landmark series, a stunning evocation of our history and peoples, an examination of where we have been as a nation, and where we are going . . . Opening with a special two-hour episode tonight, "United We Stand", presented by Daniel Forster.'

'Doesn't say I wrote it,' said Daniel, chewing on the cigar Tony had bought for the occasion. 'Bloody rude.'

'Will do in the credits.' Tony sprawled further on the sofa, patting Daniel's knee. 'Don't be jealous, dear.'

'Where are they?' said Sarah, staring out of the window onto The Row. 'Tony, can you try your house again? Pop over there?'

'Sarah, it's starting in a minute,' said Tony, stretching out. 'I don't want to miss it.'

'Daniel!'

'Yes, Sarah.' Daniel stood up, coming over to the window. 'I'm sure they've got delayed somewhere.'

'They weren't at the flat. Where have they gone?'

'Lara's taken her for an ice cream – I bet that's it.'

'It's seven fifty, Daniel. Not five o'clock.'

Since six thirty, Sarah had called Lara five times, been over to the flat twice, and sent Daniel and now Diana out onto the Heath to look for her and Friday. But there was no sign of them. And now she was bargaining –

Don't be silly.

You're nervous because of the TV show.

Lara's a bit vague. She'll be back any minute then we'll all laugh about it!

Oh God. Please. Just send them back.

'Dad! Daddy! When are you on the TV?'

'Now, sweetie!' Daniel swung Rebecca up onto his knee. 'Watch!' He sat there, Rebecca on his lap, jiggling her hard so that she swayed and giggled. In her smocked cotton nightie, her shining hair bouncing around her, she looked like a little angel, as Miss Dora was always telling her. 'Your girls, Mrs Forster. You should get them modelling for Mothercare.'

Sarah, still staring out of the window, wanted to scream, to knock something over, pull down the curtains. No one else paid any attention.

Sweat trickled between her shoulder blades, between her breasts. She felt she was back in a nightmare, like Easter Sunday, the day she had sat in the church and heard that Uncle Clive was dead, as if it were a dream, and she was the only one in charge, responsible.

Don't be so silly, she told herself. *They're on the Heath and they've lost track of time . . . It's only just after seven thirty. Lara is always late . . .*

Rebecca settled back on the capacious corduroy sofa, determined not to waste the gift of being allowed to stay up to watch Daddy on the television, though her eyes were drooping.

'I'm going downstairs,' Sarah said. 'Get some more drinks.'

'OK,' said Daniel. He turned back towards her. 'Honey, don't worry. I'm sure they'll turn up any minute. Just watch the opening bit.'

She stood behind him, holding his outstretched hand as he clutched Rebecca with the other hand.

'*Welcome to my house,*' Daniel began, his face half in darkness. '*I grew up in a terraced house in the East End, and I saw my street destroyed in the Blitz. My wife grew up in one of the most magnificent houses in the country, and saw it demolished to make new homes for people to live in. This is the century everything changed.*' He stood up, and walked towards the camera. '*I want to tell you a story, the story of the United Kingdom, and thus of the world over these past two thousand years. It's a story of courage, of Empire, of derring-do, of man's artistic endeavour and it's the story of what it means to be British then, and now. We are all the products of this country's past. Welcome to "United We Stand".*'

The drumbeat of fear would not go away. The restless, surging wash of panic, of terror. Where was Lara? Where was Friday? Why were the others sitting there?

'Glad they kept that in,' Tony whispered to Daniel, and patted him on the back.

It was good. And Daniel – yes, he was good, that bearded, intense face so handsome on camera. He was young, but distinguished; he had a sparkle in his eyes, but a serious tone to his voice. He seemed friendly. Someone anyone might know, might meet at the pub or at a cricket match or down one's street.

Sarah couldn't watch any more. Clearing her throat, she went downstairs towards the kitchen, leaning on the cool wall in the corridor before stepping into the kitchen and looking around, blindly.

'Where are you, my sweet girl?' she whispered. 'Oh, why have you vanished?'

She knew then she had to go out and look for them, that she couldn't stay here. Her eyes ranged round the kitchen, looking for her sandals.

Then she turned, and stopped. The new sideboard Daniel had bought had been moved into place, as he promised, and the old dresser shifted along, into the corner.

It had stood in the same spot for twenty-five years or more. They had painted the kitchen a few years ago, but Daniel hadn't painted behind it. Possibly he thought they'd never move it. Possibly he couldn't be bothered. There, now revealed, was the oatmeal-coloured rectangle of unpainted wall, with writing on it; it had been that colour when they'd moved in, when it was still the Thorpe house.

Sarah walked towards the newly exposed wall. Every sense was alert, and she breathed entirely from her chest and throat.

And suddenly she remembered a rainy afternoon in spring, a few years ago, sitting in the unexpected quiet of the kitchen, both girls napping, hands wrapped round a mug of tea, Lara opposite her, and Lara had said, out of the blue:

'We each wrote a message on the wall before the dresser was put into place. It was New Year's Day, you know.'

How had she not seen it before? How had she not remembered? Sarah stared, as though stuck to the spot. She felt as if she might melt onto the floor, turn to water, dripping through the floorboards, the house finally swallowing her up.

Some of the letters were worn away, some were illegible, some had vanished when they'd painted round the dresser four years ago, but some remained, and what remained was enough:

HOPE AND WISHES FOR
NEW YEAR'S DAY 1950!
THE THORPE – WILLIAMS FAMILY

Adrian Thorpe
God Save the King (& the printing presses)

Tom Williams
God Save the King

Jane Williams
Happy New Year Darlings
To All Who Sit Round This Table For Years to Come:
Peace, Prosperity and Auld Lang Syne!

Sam Williams
Keep on playing. You have to play loudly to be heard!

Lara Williams
I love Sam + Henry + Pa + Mummy + Daddy

Henry Williams
Happy New Year!
1 January 1950

Daniel appeared in the doorway. 'Sarah, do we have some olives –' She turned to him, and her expression stopped him in his tracks. 'What?' he said. 'Sarah? What's happened?'

'Lara –' She pointed at the wall. Her hand was shaking. 'Her brother . . . Her brother was Sam – Mr Williams –' She started retching. 'I – I can't breathe, Daniel. She's taken Friday – she's taken little – our girl – She's always known – I understand now – All these years, Daniel – she was watching us – I've always felt we were being watched, didn't I say so? She's been waiting –'

She clutched at him, staggering towards him, and for a moment she thought she might fall over. Daniel was reading the words on the wall.

'She was his sister,' he said. 'Oh my God. Oh, Sarah. Of course. How did we not see?'

'When we moved in,' she said. 'I know it sounds ridiculous, but I thought, when you carried me over the threshold, I thought, I bet this was Mr Williams's house. You know, the way you think ridiculous things? I bet this is where he grew up, or somewhere like it. You know, you can't explain some feelings, some certainties, like that you've met someone before . . . But then I forgot all about it. Life took over. Of course it did. When I met her, I *knew* I knew her. I . . .' She pressed her face to her hands.

'Listen,' Daniel said. 'Sarah, oh Jesus. Listen. Tony's always said Lara's crackers, that she had some grudge against you. He wouldn't say what.'

She stared at him. 'You *knew* that? And you never said anything? And now she's – she's taken Friday? God, Daniel – how could you—'

'What could I do?' he said, coming towards her. His voice cracked. 'She was your friend, your only friend for some of the time. It was so bleak, us trying to find our way, playing at knowing what we were doing . . .' He caught her hands. He said in a hoarse voice: 'She won't have done anything to Friday, my bird. I promise you. I promise you. Let's go – let's go now –'

They ran out of the house, stopping to pick up Rebecca, who had climbed down the stairs by herself and was standing in the hall, watching them in surprise. Daniel clutched her under his arm, like a winger running for a try, and the two of them ran down The Row and out at the bottom, over the main road – all the cars, whizzing past, so many of them, so fast and so dangerous, and Sarah had to stop herself from being sick, just keep on breathing – and out onto the Heath.

It was like another country – the grass bone-dry, yellow-white, the trees in the distance the darkest green. Evening heat shimmered above the rolling heathland. There was hardly anyone around.

'Friday!' Daniel yelled. 'Friday, honey!'

'Friday!' Sarah screamed, going in the other direction. 'Lara! Friday! Where are you?'

'Friyay!' Rebecca boomed, under Daniel's arm. 'FRI YAY –'

'Keep on shouting,' she bellowed at Rebecca. Daniel set her down, and she screamed, at the top of her lungs.

'FRI – YAY!'

'Friday!'

'FRIDAY!'

'FRIDAY!'

Through the wooded areas, past the makeshift canopies where tramps slept, up through to Kenwood, down towards Highgate Ponds they ran up and down, screaming, shouting, crying. A crowd of people followed them – someone called the police – there was talk of the ponds being dredged, though they were so low anyway, because of the drought.

There was no sign of her. The police came back with them. Sarah found herself leaning on the arm of one policeman who seemed terribly young – she thought this, and then thought it was a cliché, and then realised this was insane, thinking about things like this, when Friday was somewhere, not with her, missing her – she started jumping up and down, drumming her feet into the dry, parched earth, sobs wracking her, bargaining with them to please, get more police, bang down Lara's flat, find her – anywhere, anywhere she had to go . . .

Tony, whom Daniel had called from a payphone at the other end of the Heath, had gone to search their flat at the top of The Row.

'I'm going to see if she's there,' Sarah said, turning away from Daniel on Lime Avenue. 'Let me go and check it out. You take Rebecca. You –'

Daniel nodded. He was green. It was worse, now that he was worried. It meant it was real. 'You go back to The Row. Find Tony. Ask him where she is.'

Sarah ran back to the top of The Row. The front door of the flats was open. Panting in the relentless heat, Sarah stumped up the airless dark brick stairs to the first floor where Tony was waiting at the door. She stopped, her hand on the railing, thinking she might faint. Tony shook his head.

'No sign of her,' he said. 'They *were* here – there's dishes in the sink. Two of them.' He folded his arms, his plump, nylon-clad frame slumped against the wooden door. 'I reckon she's taken her somewhere,' he said, pointing at the policeman, who had followed Sarah, and was making notes.

He seemed almost non-plussed – *What more can* I *do now? The whole thing is most inconvenient* – 'I'm not best pleased at being asked to open up my flat like this, without a warrant –' He jabbed at the policeman's notepad, with his finger, then reached into his pocket and took out a packet of Embassy Gold, lighting one casually, and blew smoke out of Sarah's way, down the corridor. As he did, she stared over his shoulder into their flat. Sarah watched him. Almost detached, she found herself thinking if she had a knife, or a gun, she would kill him. Stab him in the eye, shoot him in the head.

Lara had joked that Sarah hadn't been inside her flat after all these years. It reminded her of the local auction house she and Vic had used when they'd cleared out the rest of her mother's possessions. Chests of drawers, mahogany chairs, boxes, piled up one on top of the other.

'This is all her parents' furniture from the house,' Tony said, following Sarah's gaze. 'Wasn't anywhere else for it. I remember the day you moved in . . . dragging the rest of the stuff out across the road . . . Absolute bloody nightmare it was. She kept saying she was going to kill herself. Or kill you. She calmed down a bit, obviously. Thought it was OK for a while, you know?' He took another deep drag on the cigarette. 'Wouldn't have let her actually *do* anything, you know. But – you know what she's like!'

'No,' said Sarah, shaking her head, unable to believe him – this – any of it. 'I didn't know what she was like.'

'You didn't know any of – that business?'

Sarah gaped at him. She wanted to laugh. '*What* business? That she's Sam Williams's sister? Of course not. Her surname was Thorpe. I knew her as Lara Thorpe.'

But as she spoke she felt she was lying. As if she had always known some reckoning was coming, had chosen to ignore it, and now she was being punished for something – for what? For seeking happiness.

'Her surname was originally Williams too – she changed it when her grandfather adopted them, after her parents died.' Tony did actually pause for a moment, his face twitching, a wince of sympathy. 'Poor sodding kid. She did really go through it.'

'We all did,' said Sarah. She would not bend to this, not now. 'Where is she, Tony?'

'He killed himself, you know. Jumped in front of a train. She saw it happen. She was only ten.'

Sarah pressed her fingers to her mouth. She closed her eyes.

'I knew he fell in front of a train . . .' she said eventually. 'I remember there was a sister – I didn't know it was certain it was suicide.'

'He left them a note.' Tony ruffled his thick hair. 'From what she says he was very sensitive. Took things on, rather. He felt he'd let them all down. That he'd let you down, y'see. That you'd had this chance and he'd ruined it.' He was staring at her, with those drooping dark eyes, so arrogant, so casual – why was he so offhand? How could he be? 'And the whole family – it was never the same again. I suppose she couldn't—'

But Sarah pushed past him without another word. She strode into the sitting room, piled high with boxes and armchairs, then into a spare room, the one she could see from the front door, crammed full of furniture, a room of memories. Searching, calling out Friday's name in case she was there, in case – 'Friday! Friday darling! Are you there? *Lara! What have you done with her?* FRIDAY!'

'She's not here,' Tony said. 'I know Lara. She's gone – she's gone.'

Sarah turned, and nearly bumped into the policeman. 'Where is she,' she said quietly, her voice breaking.

'Now, Mrs Forster,' the policeman said, in what she presumed was his calming voice, hands spread wide, pushing them down towards the ground. 'We must try to keep things in perspective. If you come back to the house, we can all sit down and have a cup of tea, and I'll call into the office again. She's probably turned up by now.' He backed out again, onto the landing. Sarah could have screamed at him in frustration. She clutched her hands together, waving them at Tony.

'Why didn't she say something? Did she know, when we moved in?'

'Georgina – what's the name of that woman, the one who lived in the cottage at the end, who went nuts one Sunday?' Tony waved his cigarette towards the window, with the view of The Row stretching before them. 'Her. The estate agent told her. Sarah Fox, she's an earl's daughter, or something like that. Lara was full of it. What's the house called? Steyn?'

'Fane,' said Sarah. 'Fane Hall.'

'There. You're in some book – didn't you know that? We were standing out in The Row and I remember Georgina telling Lara. "She's an earl's daughter, or something like that. Grew up at a stately home. Fane."' His face twisted in disgust. 'Ghastly old biddy. And Lara's face changed. It was like she'd had an electric shock. She knew. She remembered Sam talking about you. He wrote letters to her parents about you, how good you were. Didn't know that, eh? You were the same age as her.'

Sarah pressed her hands to her ears. It was a nightmare, like being caught in a trap. 'Listen,' she said, 'I was a child. How could I have known? He told me to go off and play for my life and I did. He started me off, and I owe him – everything – but it was six months, less.'

Tony shrugged, his eyes turning towards the television, which was on in the background with the sound turned down. Daniel was walking up the drive of Fane, towards the house.

Tony, she saw, was one of those people interested only in what pertained directly to him. He had no empathy; she could almost feel sorry for Lara, the picture he painted, dragging the furniture from her beloved family home across the road, watching her, Sarah, and Daniel, move in later that day . . . Watching them, hating them from the start. She'd had Sarah in her sights, all those years here. And now . . .

'This is ridiculous. We're wasting time,' said Sarah, turning to the policeman. 'There must be something more we can do.' Her voice broke. 'She's five, for God's sake. She's only five.' She wondered if perhaps she hadn't explained how much Friday needed her, how little she was. If they understood how urgent this was, they'd do more.

'Ma'am – it's under control,' the policeman answered. 'Where is your husband? Is he back at the house?'

She gritted her teeth. He was no good. Neither of them were. She had to keep going. She had to find her. She looked at her watch. Two hours now. It was two hours. Despair flooded her. Her heart seemed to drown in it, her eyes hardly able to stay open. This was real – it wasn't a nightmare, it was real. Friday was gone. It was real. What could she do now? Where would she go next? She realised she would tear through every house on that street and the next, climb into every rubbish bin, open every drawer, shed, cupboard, car, treehouse. She had to keep going, she had no choice –

Friday's round, laughing face, her V-shaped frown, her still-dimpled little arms folded around her chest . . . 'Oh God,' she screamed. 'Oh God. Why? Why can't you give her back? Why? Tell me where she is . . .'

She heard her voice, an agonised, wailing howl, echoing around The Row, bouncing off the houses.

'Mrs Forster,' said the policeman uncertainly. 'If we just calm down now – the little one's not officially classified as missing as yet, you know. We have to follow the process—'

'Oh, be quiet,' Sarah said, pushing him aside. She could feel hope draining away from her, and she pressed her hands to her eyes, but, as she did, some movement drew her attention back to the window, the oval communal garden, the redbrick houses silent in the late evening heat. On the left, Daniel, jumping up and down, waving his hands, calling to her.

'Sarah!' he was screaming too, from down on the street, Diana by his side frantically waving her arms, and next to her Professor Gupta and the Misses Forbes in the garden, shouting her name, the whole street, as far as she could see, outside. 'Sarah, come quickly!'

And Sarah turned, and ran, and ran.

Outside the house, standing in the porch, was Friday, her hair covered in dry grass, barefoot, filthy, her face flushed red and covered in scratches. Her eyes were huge, absolutely terrified, wired, cartoon-like – that look, when everything was all over, was what Sarah remembered. That Friday had seen the dark in the world and could not put it back in a box again. She had her hands on her hips and when Daniel tried to go near her, she pushed him away.

'Sweetheart,' Diana was saying, stroking her small, dark head. 'Where on *earth*—'

'Not saying,' said Friday, but as Sarah batted open the garden gate with such force it broke off its hinges, Friday jumped and at the sight of her mother was still for a moment and then her little face crumpled into sobs, her mouth puckering, her eyes turning downwards, more red suffusing her cheeks, then her whole face. She buried her face in Sarah's skirt, clinging to her. But Sarah had to hold her, hold *all* of her, and she tore her clenched fingers from her skirt, falling to the floor so she could then wrap her arms round her small, slender body.

'Little one,' she said, rocking back and forth as Friday sobbed, and Daniel sobbed, and Rebecca, who was being held by Diana, wailed loudly. 'Where have you been?'

'I said I didn't like her,' Friday said. She kept saying it, over and over, her voice juddering. 'You didn't listen to m-me. I said I didn't like her.'

Sarah squeezed her eyes shut, then opened them. 'I know. I know and you were right. I didn't listen to you. What happened?'

'She – took me to the wooded bit. And she made me play hide-and-seek and shut my eyes, and then she ran away, and I could hear her, laughing and calling, so I kept followin' and followin', but I couldn't ever find her and my foots hurted, look –'cause I took my shoes off, Mummy, sorry, and I lost them. I'm sorry –' She started crying again, properly, her voice juddering. 'S-sorry, Mummy . . . I know they were n-new shoes.'

'It doesn't matter about the shoes, little one,' said Sarah. 'It doesn't matter.'

'But l-last week you said if I lost them again you would be so c-cross with m-me—'

'That's a different thing. It's all different. We'll get new shoes, sweetheart . . .'

'She kept saying all these things . . . She said you were bad. She said you were a bad mummy. She said you hated me. I said she was horrible. I said you weren't – you were my mummy. I said I wanted to go back and she wouldn't listen.' She took a huge, ragged breath. 'I don't want to go with Lara again.'

'You won't, I promise. Ever again. It's OK. It's OK.'

She pulled Friday into her again, so tightly as to swallow her up entirely in her embrace, make her invisible, safe from the outside world.

'Thank God for that,' Diana said, leaning against the porch. 'Friday, you gave us a fright, darling.'

'I didn't m-mean to!' Friday said, her breath coming in snatches.

'Of course you didn't. Now,' said Diana, fishing around in her pockets. 'I've got a Caramac bar in here. Do you want it?'

Friday's eyes grew round. 'Yes, please.'

'Is that all right, Sarah?'

Sarah stood up, lifting Friday with her. Diana handed her the Caramac bar and Friday stared at it, reverentially. 'Thank you, Diana,' she said.

Daniel, holding Rebecca, embraced them both. The four of them stood together, very still, and Daniel pulled Diana into the circle. 'Come here,' he said. 'Where would we be without you, Diana? Where would we be?'

'Oh honestly, Daniel,' Diana said, and she started crying, and Sarah and Friday both stared, astonished, at the sight of Diana in tears, as behind them someone gently cleared their throat.

'Mrs Forster . . .' The young policeman, looking considerably relieved now, rubbed his hands gently together. 'We've got her.'

'Who?'

'Mrs Cull. She's in the police car. She was on the Heath. Looking for the young girl, she said.'

Friday stiffened in Sarah's arms. Sarah said: 'Don't worry, darling. She won't hurt you. She's very sad. She's going away, for ever. Don't worry at all.'

'I'll go,' said Daniel, moving forward with Rebecca, but Sarah stopped him.

'No,' she said. 'Stay here. I'll deal with this.'

She handed Friday to Daniel, and he carried both girls over the threshold and into the house, as he had done with Sarah, nearly seven years ago.

Sarah stepped over the broken gate, onto the cobbles. There, in the panda car, sitting quite quietly, was Lara. She wore the same outfit she'd had on earlier – Sarah had noticed the long sundress, white with yellow flowers, the hoop earrings, the thong sandals. She looked, in fact, exactly the same. Her thin shoulders were hunched, her hair falling over into her face. Sarah could not see her eyes. She looked straight ahead.

Sarah realised that Lara had always frightened her – she'd just never known why. She was the embodiment of her fears. She had pushed the doubts about her to the back of her mind, and doubted herself instead at every turn, afraid of everything being taken away, convinced she didn't deserve this happiness, didn't deserve to have the life she'd longed for all those years ago when she sat on the Burnt Oak with Daniel and promised she would always look up.

The windows were rolled down. Sarah stood in silence for a moment, not saying anything. Lara's thin fingers, resting on her lap, plucked at her long skirt. Some more hair slipped over her shoulders in front of her face.

'What happened to your family was terrible,' Sarah said suddenly. 'I am sorry about Mr Williams. I didn't know he was your brother.'

Lara raised her head, and looked out of the windscreen.

'But you got it all wrong, Lara,' Sarah said. 'I was trying to survive. You have no idea what it was like. He made me believe I was good. That was immensely generous of him. He saved me. But I didn't deserve this. I don't deserve your hatred.' Lara didn't move. It was as though the windows were shut and she couldn't hear Sarah at all. So Sarah leaned forward. 'Don't you have anything to say?'

'You took my house.' Lara spoke so quietly Sarah had to move closer, towards her. 'You stole my life. You stole everything. You didn't even realise you were living in his house. That's what made me hate you. You forgot about him. You simply got on with your life and he was dead. What about the people left behind? You didn't care – care about our life in this house –' she jabbed her finger up towards the house, spitting slightly as she spoke – 'or the family we were, how happy we'd been. My grandfather after they all died – his heart was broken. You killed him, and you just walked away.'

'I didn't ever walk away from him. Oh, Lara,' said Sarah. The pain was receding. To feel it ebb away, slowly, was almost euphoric. She leaned in, hands on the car door. 'I was a child, Lara. Some girls at the school wrote a letter about him. It was all lies, and he was fired. It wasn't me.'

'We found the letter. He had a copy on him. Your surname was on it. Fox.'

'But that wasn't me, Lara. It was my sister. It was nothing to do with me. Oh, my goodness. All these years you've had that letter and been thinking—'

'It's not just about the letter—'

'Oh, Lara. I didn't ever stop thinking about him. But he told me I had to get on, and I'd promised I'd make him proud, and I did that. I'm here because of him. Listen, Lara. I didn't kill him. I'm so sorry he died. It's dreadful what happened to him.

But I didn't kill him, or your mum and dad. The girls who wrote the letter didn't kill him. I'm sorry. I'm *so sorry.* That's all I can say.'

'I wanted to break you into pieces,' said Lara. 'I wanted you to move out, to fail at everything. I'd watch you, cracking up, with your idiot husband getting you pregnant, your gifts, the talent you have that Sam saw – he talked about you! And you let it all slide away . . .'

'It's nothing like that,' said Sarah. 'How simplistic, to say it's one or the other. Life's not like that, Lara. It's so much more complicated than that. Can't you see?'

Lara looked up at her then, her dark-blue eyes like liquid metal, burning hatred. 'You're nothing,' said Lara. 'You took everything I had.' Her thin, white face was alight with hatred. It was astonishing. 'You don't care about what he did for you. You don't deserve it.'

'I thought I didn't deserve it,' Sarah said, and she was back on the road outside the church with Vic again, spring sunshine racing to catch them, running away from Fane, running for the bus, back to her life. She found she was dreadfully sorry for this dead-eyed, thin-faced girl whose hatred for Sarah seeped from every pore. 'I thought I'd never have it, this life. I thought I didn't deserve it, but I do. I deserve to be happy. So does Daniel. So did your brother. He was unlucky, and I'm so sorry. I thought it would never happen to me, but it did. And for you to try and take it away from me –' Sarah clutched at the window, her fingers white, and suddenly she saw her mother's knuckles on the photograph, bone-white. 'Oh, Lara, it won't ever bring your brother back. It's taken you away from what matters. Can't you see that? Me and Daniel – it's a miracle, our life together. The number of times we shouldn't have met but we did. How little we had and how lucky we've been. You have no idea at all.'

Chapter Twenty-Five

She didn't see Daniel for another four years after he dropped her at Monica's that Easter morning and told her his name. And even then she almost missed him again.

It was 1959. Monica's boyfriend Henry had a twenty-first birthday party at the Dorchester. It was a lavish affair: champagne, salmon mousse, black tie, ballgowns, kid gloves, fur stoles and matrons in heavy perfume. Each place setting at dinner had cigarette cases for the ladies and lighters for the gentlemen; the band had played two numbers from *An American in Paris*, Monica's favourite film. Rumour had it a second cousin of Prince Charles was in attendance.

Sarah was dancing to 'Hey, There!' from *The Pajama Game*, with a friend of Henry's called Guy, who moved her round the floor very dashingly. Guy was smooth, and fun, but he'd had, whilst with Sarah alone, three champagne cocktails. 'I say, Sarah,' he'd said, his eyes huge. 'Do a chap a favour and come outside with me while I have a smoke and talk about important things. Hurp.' And he'd hiccupped.

'Guy – I have an exam tomorrow. I really can't be too late.'

'Oh, please, Sarah – please.'

'Sure,' said Sarah, feeling rather queasy. She didn't want to have to fight Guy off, and she didn't really think he was like that, but she'd had a couple of encounters lately where knowing how to really slap someone hard – on the jawline, on the side of the head with the palm – had really stunned them, and given her a vital few seconds to climb out of cars or off bus seats.

Outside, it was still light. Sarah paused on the steps of the hotel for a second to rub her heel, where a blister was developing. She found herself looking up and down Park Lane at the sea of well-dressed people in black tie or elegant evening clothes, climbing in and out of cabs and smart cars. Her feet ached; she had a stitch, having eaten too fast, filling up on food at supper to last her till lunchtime tomorrow. One had to take these opportunities where one could. She wondered which was the quickest bus back to Earl's Court, and then remembered she had nothing to eat at home, and thought perhaps she'd better walk whilst she was full of food, blister or no blister.

The exam was for the end of her first year and even though she had two more years at the Royal College of Music it was important; if she did well, she would attract the right attention, be invited to audition for the right orchestras, be offered recitals, perhaps even find an agent. If she did well, she would put one more step between her and her mother. Soon, they said, Iris Fane would be released from prison. Sarah knew she had to be organised, be well on her way by then. She could not be dragged back into all of it. It was strange enough, to be back in that part of town. Sometimes a missed bus-stop would take her close to Pelham Mansions. Whenever it did, she would walk as quickly as possible, away from the memory, blanking it out.

Now she stood with Guy in the beautiful pale blue of a spring evening on the steps of the Dorchester. He failed to light his cigarette three times and when he did he told her with shaking hands he was hopelessly, helplessly in love with Monica and if he didn't declare himself soon he'd have to move to South Africa, or blow his brains out.

'Well, I'd tell her,' Sarah said, almost laughing with relief. 'Not tonight,' she added, as an afterthought. 'But, Guy – do tell her.' She knew Monica was going off Henry, who had large pink ears, a dolorous manner and liked to tell Monica what she was doing wrong. Guy, however, drove a sports car, liked weekends in Paris, made Monica laugh like a drain, plus he looked awfully dashing in black tie and looked a little like Gene Kelly. Sarah had long wondered why Monica was wasting her time with Henry when Guy was so obviously crazy about her. But Monica was decent. Sarah thought perhaps sometimes you needed to be indecent to get what you wanted.

'She's terrific. Darling Monica –' Guy said, shaking his head so violently that tears flew out, like a sprinkler.

They were at the top of the steps, Guy leaning against one of the pillars, flecked with shrapnel damage. A gaggle of young people gathered, waiting to get past them. Some of them stared at Sarah and Guy, but she ignored them. Guy swayed, and put his arms round Sarah. 'I'm sorry. Damn well drunk, that's what I am, on top of everything else – absolute blister of a man I'm being tonight . . . forgive. Forgive,' he muttered. 'Do you think there's any hope? Be honest, Sarah. Oh God. At another chap's birthday too. I'm the end. I'm a heel.'

Sarah, deeply touched, hugged him, and someone elbowed Guy in a sudden crush on the steps.

'Excuse me,' they said crossly. 'Could you move out of the way?'

'Sir!' Guy staggered to the side. 'Awf'lly sorry. This fair lady—'

'I'm late,' the stranger, who was also in black tie, said shortly. 'Would you excuse me?'

He pushed past them, so that Sarah and Guy fell against each other. They sort of bounced apart, and Guy caught hold of Sarah. 'You're absolutely ripping, Sarah,' he said. 'Monica's right about you.'

'What does Monica say about me?' she said, amused. She stared after the cross stranger, retreating towards the ballroom. He stopped, with his back to them, tapping his foot and looking at his watch.

'She says . . .' he said. 'Oh! That you're always the star, wherever you are, that you shine, and you're so comfortable with yourself you make everyone else feel they can be themselves too. Always 'member that about you.' He muttered to himself. 'I say, that's awfully good. She's awfully wise. Isn't she wise? Darling Mon.'

'I say,' said Sarah. 'That's lovely.' She stared at Guy. 'How kind of you. Thank you, Guy. Thank you for saying that.'

The man in the lobby turned as Guy kissed her on the cheek. 'Hey!' Sarah called, without meaning to, and the man came forward, as if he'd been waiting for her to beckon him.

Their eyes met. Sarah felt a jolt passing through her skin, into her body, into her bones. She couldn't ever have explained it to anyone.

'Hello, Daniel,' she said.

'Sarah. Hello.'

Sarah stared at his broad shoulders, encased in the smooth black cloth of the dinner jacket, at his large, sensitive hands, one of which gripped her elbow, at the curve of his lip. She felt her heart beating in her throat. She wondered what would happen if she took his hand, pressed his bare palm against hers, there on the steps of the hotel, felt his skin against hers.

I understand, she thought now, *why Monica doesn't want to be with Henry any more.*

'I don't want to interrupt,' he said, rather coolly.

He was quite different in some ways – he had filled out a little, grown into his face, and she had been only thirteen when she'd last seen him, and not even considered the possibility of – this. But his eyes were the same. She would have known him anywhere. She *knew* him.

Guy may have been drunk, but he gleaned Daniel's interpretation of events faster than Sarah, who was still staring at Daniel.

'I say, do you know our lovely Sarah? She's giving me advice. I'm hopelessly in love with her best friend, you see. Absolute disaster. She's been a darling.'

'It's really none of my business,' Daniel said coolly.

'I say,' said Guy suddenly. 'Would you do me a favour? Would you see Sarah home? She's awfully tired and she's got an exam tomorrow. I'm going back in, Sarah my dear. I'm going to ask Monica to dance—'

'Monica?' said Daniel. 'Isn't she Henry's girlfriend?'

Sarah and Guy looked awkwardly at each other. 'Good luck,' Sarah said.

'Oh, my dear girl,' said Guy, 'thank you. Thank you, sir,' he said, leaving the two of them on the steps. 'Do make sure she gets home all right.'

Daniel looked at her. 'Can I take you home, Sarah?'

She wanted to smile, but it wasn't funny – it was serious. He held out his arm to her, and they walked down the steps together. 'I can't afford the bus,' she said.

'Me neither. I say, what's wrong with your heel?'

'Ridiculous shoes. So how do you know Henry?' she said, trying not to look at him, unable to stop looking at him, and whenever she did he was looking at her too, both of them astonished.

It was a joke between them for evermore that she couldn't remember how he knew Henry, because she was staring at him, and not listening. But Daniel knew him from Cambridge, and he was arriving late because he worked in a restaurant. He was at Cambridge studying history, and was in a comedy group called Footlights. He was about to graduate and move to London.

'You never wrote,' she said as they stood side by side, looking out at the evening crowds.

'I didn't know where to write to,' he said.

'You dropped me there!'

'I thought you wouldn't want to hear from me. I thought we both needed to get on with our lives. *You* never wrote,' he said mildly. 'You could have written and you didn't.'

'I did,' she said triumphantly. 'I wrote to you care of Mrs Boundy.'

'I stayed with Dr Brooke. I don't know . . . I thought I should leave you alone,' he said. 'I saw what they were doing to Fane.' He leaned against the concrete wall of the hotel, staring out at the traffic on Park Lane. 'I thought about you often, Sarah.'

'Yes,' she said. 'Me too.'

'I knew – Oh, I can't explain it.'

She watched the way he folded his arms. Even that, he did enthusiastically, clamping his fingers round his ribcage, gripping himself tightly. He was the same sweet boy, but he was utterly different. She'd loved him before, but this – this was different.

'I knew I'd see you again one day,' she said. 'Is that what you were going to say?'

He turned to her, in the warm July evening, and she saw a lone star emerging above them, piercing the gentle blue of the dusky sky.

'Yes,' he said. 'Exactly.'

'How long are you in town?' she said, after they were both silent for a moment, simply gazing at each other. She could hear his breathing, see his chest rising and falling.

'I go back the day after tomorrow. Sarah—'

'What are you doing tomorrow afternoon,' she said quietly, and she took his hand, and she held it tightly, 'after one p.m.? What are you doing? Can you meet me, outside the Royal College? On the steps of the Albert Hall?'

'Yes,' he said. 'I can. I can.'

'I have to go,' she said. 'The bus – I can't walk. My shoes are worn through.'

He was shaking his head as she gripped his hand again, pressing it against her stomach, where the warmth of his skin penetrated her thin dress. She wanted to lean against him, to simply stay like that for ever. But she had to go.

'I'll see you tomorrow.'

'And the day after,' he said. 'And the day after that.'

She was smiling as she ran down the steps towards the approaching bus.

'And the day after that!' he called after her, his voice carrying in the evening air.

The next day, she ran up the steps of the Albert Hall, lightheaded with lack of sleep, and food, and nerves. She had her cello strapped across her back, and more comfortable plimsolls on.

He was waiting for her on the top set of steps, legs apart, leaning on his knees, reading a Penguin, and he looked, she thought, like a film star, his dark, serious face, his sweet lips, the strong hands that turned the flimsy pages. And when he looked up and saw her his expression changed, and he smiled.

'Daniel,' she said, holding out her hand, and he took it, and held it.

'Hello, Sarah,' he said. 'How are you?'

'Wonderful,' she said. 'I'm wonderful. Listen, would you do something for me?'

He nodded. 'Of course.'

She pushed her hair out of her eyes. She was slightly out of breath, and shifted the cello on her back. 'I have to play for

Professor MacKay in twenty minutes. He was late this morning for my exam – his wife's ill – and so he's coming in to watch me perform the Elgar Cello Concerto – only the first movement. It's our end of term concert. I wasn't even supposed to be playing, the soloist's ill. They asked me this morning. So I was nervous before but now – well, now I'm terribly nervous. I have to show them – prove to them. Would you—'

'Yes, of course,' he said, standing up, sliding the book into his back pocket. His eyes met hers, with a look only for her. 'Sarah, I've wanted to hear you play for years.'

So he came into the old building, and walked with her down the wood-panelled corridors lined with portraits of men and women who'd composed and played there, and as they approached the concert hall he could see her shoulders rising and falling, and he took her hand, and it was quite natural that he did. At the entrance to the green room backstage, she stopped, and turned to him, pointing through the doors.

'Would you go and sit there – front row, middle of the balcony? Then I'll know where you are. Would you?'

'Yes, yes. Of course.'

He pulled her slowly towards him, so the cello on her back dug into his shoulder, and she was between both of them. Neither of them spoke. She stood up on tiptoe, brushing something away from his face. She had to stretch to reach him, but she kissed him, her soft cheek feeling his gritty, scratchy chin. He kissed her back, slowly, deliberately, holding her shoulders, then sliding his hands down over her arms, so they were holding hands. It was as though he were creating her, making her come alive, waking her up from a dream.

She vanished through the doors, with a wave.

As she came onto the stage and sat down, arranging herself, the cello stand and her skirt, the lights dimmed, and a hush swept across the audience, and it sounded to Sarah like rustling branches in late summer oaks. She closed her eyes, very briefly, and raised her right hand, with the bow. She glanced out to the balcony and saw him there, perfectly still, perfectly calm. She started to play, the first, broken-up, melancholic chords of the Elgar, and it was like music torn from the wind, the sky, music that echoed over an empty country churchyard, taking flight. Her bow worked across the strings, drawing out the notes, dancing, and Sarah was half there, half air and light, in another place altogether. It was her, only her, filling the silent hall as the orchestra waited, then joined in, a wall of sound that ebbed away, leaving her alone again. She was lost, as ever, the moment her bow touched the strings, but she played, as ever, as if it were the only thing in the world that mattered.

At the end of the first movement, into the awed hush, Sarah looked up, brushing a lock of hair from her face. She could just make him out, sitting back, keeping himself separate, letting her have her space, giving her freedom, so she could fly, soar, like Stella. But she could see his face, and she knew. She played for him. Perhaps she always had done, since the night on the Burnt Oak.

Recalling herself to the present, Sarah stared at Lara as the policeman nudged her. 'Mrs Forster? I need to drive the lady to the station. Ask a few questions. We'll charge her there if you want to –'

But Sarah shook her head. 'One minute.' She cleared her throat and crouched down, peering into the police car, so her face was inches away from Lara's.

'You need to leave,' she said. 'You need to not be here any more, looking over at the house every day. Get out of here. Go away, Lara. I won't press charges if you do. Go away and start a new life,' she said again.

Lara said nothing, just gazed ahead.

Sarah said softly: 'If you don't, I swear to you: I will hurt you. I'm my mother's daughter, and I know how to hurt.' She took a deep breath. ''Cause this is my house. It's *my* house.' The policeman, who had turned to answer to one of the neighbours, looked back.

'Right,' he said. 'We'll pop back to check on you and the little one later, Mrs Forster,' and Sarah dropped her hand, turned and walked away, towards No. 7. She didn't even look to see what Lara did, just stood on the doorstep for a moment. Then she crossed the threshold, slamming the door behind her, and as she did she felt a puff of air, as though the last of the bad spirits was leaving the house.

Daniel had put Friday into her nightie, and washed her face and feet, and she was curled up in between him and Rebecca very slowly eating her Mars Bar, drinking some cold milk.

The television programme was still on – it was unbelievable that this should have all happened, and it was still on. There were still fifteen minutes to run. Daniel was standing in front of a small, half-timbered cottage, where flowers swayed in the breeze.

'This is where Anne Hathaway lived,' Daniel was saying. *'And nearby, the forest of Arden, a place of myth, of stories, of chaos, which Shakespeare loved. All of it is gone now, cut down to build the English navy that sailed around the world. It's all gone.'*

Sarah heard the police car drive away. It was quiet on The Row. Friday slid her hand out towards her, and Sarah took it, wrapping her arm round her, squeezing tight against her, against Daniel, feeling his hand warm in hers. His hands were always warm. She sat between her husband and her daughters. At some point Friday moved, putting her head on her mother's lap. Diana, in the wingback chair in the corner, had fallen asleep, snoring very lightly. Sarah knew she would have to get up in a minute, take the half-full wine glass out of her hand. But not just yet. The Forsters sat huddled tightly together, in silence, and when it was over Sarah clapped, like you did at the end of a show.

Iris

1925

Later that evening as they survey the damp, cramped flat with bare black floorboards and thin curtains reeking of fried fish, her mother grips her daughter's hand. 'All is not lost, my love,' she says, reaching down. 'Here.'

They have two trunks between them, from which to form some kind of life. There are eighty rooms at Fane Hall. She knows, because she has counted them all. She likes counting things, sorting things, collecting things. She knows, because she has spent every night of her life at Fane, apart from the night she was in hospital with influenza, and the five nights she and her mother were in Bognor Regis for a change of scene after Daddy died. She knows Fane so well – it is part of her – and so the shock of *not* being there has not yet hit her.

She knows the hole in the floorboard outside her bedroom through which one could gingerly insert a big toe. The round window above the Star Study, which showed you the stars on the clearest nights. She knows the orange and red poppies that spring up in the vegetable garden in June, and the drifting golden light that shimmers across everything in September. She knows where barn owls nest, in the family tomb next to the church.

But now there is so much she does not understand. Or, at least, she understands it, but no one else does. She sees everything clearly, and no one else does. *For now we see through a glass, darkly; but then face to face: now I know in part; but then shall I know even as also I am known.*

She sees it all, so clearly, but no one else does.

For it comes down to one afternoon. The afternoon when she

had said to Uncle Clive, two days after his arrival, 'Do you want to come and see the Burnt Oak again?'

She didn't know how to ask: 'Daddy wrote to me about it. Daddy wrote that it was your favourite place. Daddy said you used to dream about going back there. About sitting up in the branches again with Bramble.'

But she has come to see something is not right with this man who says he is Lord Ashley. And she has been thinking. She is clever, little Lady Iris. She is too clever.

They walk out across the empty parkland, the house behind them. Her uncle is impatient, obviously regarding the trip as a waste of his time. He walks fast. Iris's legs are much shorter and she stumbles frequently, trying to keep up with him.

'The burnt oak . . . Rodderick's oak, yes . . .' Clive is muttering as they get closer to the tree. 'What is it?' he is saying to himself. 'What did he say about it?'

He looks so tired, craggier than ever, and he smells a little, and she really does not like him, and feels sad she cannot bring herself to love her father's brother, and she looks at him again, at his dark lashes, seeing something that had never occurred to her before. She doesn't answer him, doesn't keep up her usual nervous chatter.

When they arrive at the centre of the field, he looks around.

'The oak tree. Where's it gone? Hm?'

She points. 'You know where it is.'

'That's not an oak tree,' he says with a thin, over-eager laugh. 'Good grief, young woman. That's a wreck. But whatever it was, it weren't ever an oak tree.'

They gaze up at the frame of the Burnt Oak, wizened, jagged and rusting.

'I – know that,' she says. 'It's not a tree. There hasn't been a tree there for seventy years. I know that. My father knew that. His brother knew that.'

He gazes up at the iron tree. For as anyone who has seen it knows it is not a tree at all but an iron tower, a contraption bolted together with a viewing platform halfway up. It is one of the oldest steel structures in the country, built in 1880 using the newest technology developed by someone called Bessemer. She knows this; everyone knows this. They are proud. Her family has always been first with new things. It is built in place of Rodderick's beloved oak tree, where he tracked Betelgeuse and spotted new stars. There is even a plaque to this effect, in thick metal letters, on the side.

She knows this. Her father knew this. They are proud of this oddity, of its role in the history of the country. Now Iris clears her throat and says in a small voice:

'If you were who you said you were, you'd know what the Burnt Oak was too.'

He wheels round, small eyes fixing on her.

She is afraid, but she takes a short breath. 'I don't think you're my Uncle Clive,' she says after a pause, but she keeps her voice steady. 'I – I don't know how you've tricked Mama.'

His face looms down over her. She flickers her eyes, trying to keep them open.

'I s'pose you've given Mrs Boyes money to work here, that's why she's nice to you and ignores us now. My father and Uncle Clive spent hours up here. Yet you thought there was still a real oak here. I don't think you're the real Uncle Clive. I think you've taken his place somehow and now you're taking our house.'

He doesn't answer. Above them, swifts wheel and swoop, screeching loudly.

'So what if I'm not?' he says after a while. 'If I met your uncle again in Canada? If we joked about our faces, how unsettling it was? What if we fooled the others in camp, playing practical jokes, and he thought it was rather a jolly jape, the idiot, but I started to see . . . see what might be?' He stands with his legs a little further apart on the ground, clapping his hands loudly, so the echo disturbs the birds in the nearby trees. 'What if I had listened to his stories, over and over again in the camp whilst we waited to strike gold?' He gives a little dance and leans close. 'Say . . . say my name isn't Clive at all, it's Donald, and say I'm sick of poverty and scrabbling to live, and he didn't deserve it, any of it, that he was an intemperate fool? Say I watched him die of malaria, little Iris? Say he gave me his watch, and he trusted me, and I promised I'd return it to his brother's widow and her child?' She can hear the steel in his voice now. It is a different voice altogether. Lower, harder. 'Does it matter? Someone needs to live here. We all need a roof over our heads. Even you.'

Iris doesn't understand. But she knows she must save the conversation to sift over later, and in the long years to come.

'Then if my poor Uncle Clive is dead . . . it's my house.' She says for the first time, 'It's not yours. And you shouldn't be here.'

He says in his Uncle Clive voice again: 'I am here, though, my dear.'

'I'll go back and tell my mother,' she says, as calmly as she can.

He laughs, throwing his head back, displaying the reddened rash across his neck.

'You can tell anyone you want,' he says, and he grips her arm, and it is painful. He is pulling her up by the arms, his fingers sliding up to her armpits. Her small feet dangle just above the ground, and tears sting her eyes. 'Do you think anyone will believe you?'

He drops her, and she stumbles, falling onto the ground, bruising herself and scrambling to stand up immediately again.

'Yes—'

He interrupts her. 'No. No one will believe you. I took great care to make it all stand together. You like people to tell you you're a bright little thing, don't you? So let me explain it to you. I came over a year ago, and my Dolly and I took a tour of the house on an open day. I watched you and your mother, in your ridiculous white lace and parasols, little girl. Nodding and smiling as though you were Queen bloody Mary. I saw how stupid your mother was. How most of the servants had left because you had no help, the place was falling down, and those that were there wouldn't remember your father. So many people are dead now after the war. Most of your father's friends, Clive's friends, they never came back either. And I saw it would be rather nice to live his life. Damned funny.' He moves closer, his spit raining on her face. 'And do you know what else I saw?'

Tears pool in her eyes. She will not let him see it hurt.

'I saw that you weren't a nice little girl. You're unattractive, and strange, and they don't like you, none of 'em. So listen to me. If you were a boy, it'd be different. But it's not your house.' He laughs. 'It's my house now, to do with what I want, and what

I want is to live here and not have to earn a living breaking rocks and panning for specks, and flecks, of gold. I've got all the gold I need now. See? It doesn't matter what you think you know. They won't believe you. No one will believe you. They'll think you're mad, and gradually you'll get madder and madder. And long after I'm gone that's what you'll be remembered for.' He puts his hand on the iron tree, brushing off the orange rust.

Her throat hurts. She bites her lip so hard she tastes blood. She says in a quiet, choking voice: 'You can't do that. It's not your house.'

His fist closes round the front of her blouse, pulling the material into a twist, lifting her off the ground. Iris cannot breathe. 'Don't I deserve something? Don't I deserve to live and enjoy life after what I've seen? After the things I've had to do? What would happen to this place? It'd go to ruin. He was dying anyway – he was never coming back here. Why shouldn't I have something? Have a bit of something good for myself? Instead of grovelling in the muck for the rest of my life?'

He lets her go, and she drops to the ground. She swallows down a sob, struggling to breathe, refusing to give in.

'But . . . it's – not – your – house.'

He raises his hand, and hits her, across the face, so hard that she staggers, and falls to the ground partly with the force of it, but partly in shock, because it is so unexpected, and so brutal. She stares at him, her jaw aching, her ears ringing, head spinning. Her brain buzzes, filled with thoughts like bees humming inside her, wanting to break out, to swarm over him. She feels murderous rage.

'Listen,' he says as she stands up again. He is calm again, laughing at her. 'I don't like you, but I don't want to kill you. That needn't be a problem. I've had a fresh start, so can you. I strangled men in the war, and out in Canada, strangled them for their guns or in the forests for their furs. I'll do it again.' He closes his hand round her neck. Very gently, but his entire hand fits around it, with room to spare. She would snap; she can feel it. She elbows him, and backs away. 'Try to understand,' he says. 'I can't have you messing things up for me, so what I think is you'd better clear out, you and that silly mother of yours. The sooner you accept this situation, the better. Your old life is over, Lady Iris. Just like that.' He clicks his fingers.

Iris nods, mutely. As he walks round the Burnt Oak, muttering, she rubs her cheek, eyes stinging, and drinks in the sight of the house. She wonders again what would have happened if she had been born a boy. As she stumbles back alongside him, tripping and scrambling to her feet, racing across the land she knows so well she wonders how on earth she will take revenge. For she understands already that is what her life's work will be. It will take time. She understands that too.

'But it is my house,' she says quietly to the air. And months later she repeats this, in the dank, sad flat, on that first evening there. 'It is my house.'

Epilogue

August 2020

'Well, Mum,' said Friday, buttoning up her army-surplus jacket. 'We'll be off, then. I tell you something, leaving your childhood home after lockdown to just go off on holiday feels weird. Very weird.'

'I don't want to go,' said Esmé. 'I want to stay here with you, Gran.'

'No,' said Sarah firmly. 'You don't. Have a great time. Go surfing. Eat crab. Try new things. Wear masks. Give Rebecca a big kiss from me. And send me a postcard from Cornwall. Have a wonderful time, darlings. I'm very jealous.'

After a week of rain today was gloriously, lazily hot, the wood-pigeons cooing ecstatically in the gardens of The Row. 'Mum –' Friday clutched the sleeves of her jacket. 'Are you sure you don't want to come with us?'

Sarah was tidying the kitchen. She looked confused. 'Take me with you? Good God, no.'

'I don't mean on holiday. I mean we could come back early. Take you to the reopening . . .'

'Of what?'

'The reopening of Fane? I spoke to Rebecca. We thought it might be a good chance to say goodbye properly. Or something. I don't know. I just know that letter from Vic has made you very strange the last couple of days.'

'I know. I'm sorry.'

'What was in it?' Esmé said.

'Well . . . I haven't read it yet.'

Friday did a double-take. 'What?'

Sarah said gently: 'Darling. I'll tell you all about it one day.

When you're back from your holiday. It's a long story and parts of it are rather sad. But it ends happily. I promise.'

'What was that crazy woman called? Laura. She took me for a walk and ran away and shouted loads of crap at me.'

Sarah sighed. She took some juice out of the fridge. 'Lara. Oh dear, yes. She was a very unhappy person.'

'God, I'd forgotten all about her! Lara. Didn't her husband have a heart attack at Buckingham Palace or something?'

'At the Ritz. At the afterparty for the Baftas. He keeled over and hit a waitress. Very sad. He worked with Dad.'

'*What?*' Esmé looked up from her phone.

'What happened to her?' Friday said. She put her head on one side, her empathetic dark eyes watching her mother.

'Lara?' Sarah said: 'She moved to Wales. Became a wildlife photographer, last I heard of her from someone on The Row. Listen, don't worry about her. She's way back in the past.'

Spring at No. 7 had lasted for ever, and then it had suddenly been late summer, out of nowhere. You were allowed to go wherever you wanted now, provided you wore masks. Masks in shops. Masks to walk from your table at a pub to go up to the bar to order a drink. This was . . . normal. Everyone kept saying this was all . . . normal.

Sarah barely noticed Friday and Esmé leaving. Her mind was off again, humming with thoughts, and memories. In the still quiet of the hall after they'd gone, she stood at the bottom of the stairs, listening to the old sounds of the house – the ticking under the floorboards, the burr of the hot-water tank, a fly buzzing in rectangles.

She had been here for fifty years. Here she had stood when Lara was driven away, slamming the front door on her. Here she had sat, listening to a baby's cries, day after day. Here she had wept in the front garden when she and the girls were locked out and Diana had rescued her. She had also laughed till she was gasping, despaired at the mess, the clutter, the vanishing years.

Here the house had echoed with All Day Sundays, and the screams of children's birthdays, and now the pandemic: the socially distanced meetings when the residents of The Row would stand outside their front gates, chatting and waving at a distance, banging pots and pans every Thursday, listening as ambulances charged up and down the road abutting the Heath, racing to the hospital. Fifty years, and at times she had hated it all with so much passion she had wanted to melt into nothing, and yet the house had held her up, every time and she had turned, turned towards the love it held inside it.

Sarah walked slowly up the wide, shallow, curving stairs to the first floor, where the boxes Friday had brought down from the loft sat in the corner. Old music, letters, endless exercise books – why had she kept them, and how could she now ever throw them away? The birthday card from Monica. Her and Vic's tickets to *Peter Pan*, neatly labelled by Vic with the date and time. Old, yellowing pages from school stories. The scant clothes she'd had. And now the map of the stars Daniel had given her, all those years ago, that she had stuffed under the mattress in the Thin Room and forgotten to take with her. Packaged up, posted back to her. She wondered if her mother had looked at it. Had ever gazed up, wondered what was above her. She thought she probably hadn't.

Inside the map were the sheets of her mother's writing. She unfolded them. The sheaf was thick, and wedged at the edges with dirt. She glanced at her mother's handwriting, a jolt of jagged-edged italics that she had forgotten. There were pages of it. At first she thought she couldn't read it, that it would be too much, and then she realised it didn't matter. Nothing she could do now could hurt her. Vic had sent it to her, and she had wanted her to see it too.

As she is dying, she remembers it all once more, piercingly clearly. As if to die, she has to live through it again.

Her mother's hands stroking her pale hair, how soft it always felt, a caress every time.

'It's my house; I don't see why I should give it up.'

'It's not your house, darling. It belongs to your Uncle Clive and he will live here when he returns. If he returns.'

Across the top she has written, in large, shaky black letters

THIS IS THE TRUTH

Sarah read it all, the story of her mother's early years, the arrival of Uncle Clive, the dismissal from her home, the trip to the Burnt Oak . . . a small mind, broken by a liar and a bully, like Cassandra, doomed to shout the truth into the darkness for the rest of her life.

At the end she looked up, blinking. She remembered the number of times her mother had yelled: *It's my house. It's my house.* A sort of tic, she'd thought, a sign of the madness. Tears pricked her eyes. Her joints ached from their kneeling position. She felt old, and this was all so long ago, so why did it matter? Did it change anything? She had just told Friday to forget Lara, that she was in the past. Did knowing that her mother had been right about one thing change anything? She stared at the star map, and at the letter. Across the decades, and she is there again, back at Fane, a child, setting out into the starry night, a crumbling house behind her.

Sarah is old now. She has not been back to Fane since her mother died. She sometimes thinks of the good, true houses built over the estate for people to build a community in.

Yes, she thinks, standing up very slowly, her knees creaking. *Yes, I am proud I walked away that day.* She puts the map and the papers on the dresser, and picks up her keys. It is time to go.

He turns to greet her as she calls out to him, his face crinkling with joy when she appears. The wrinkles are ironed in, like pleats on a curtain, like a map. He is bowed with age; he forgets names, histories, where he is; she does not want to think about that too much, as she knows in her heart there is not much time left for them when everything is normal, when life carries on. Things will change, and soon, but for the moment –

But his eyes, his eyes are the same. He rescued her, and she him. As Sarah walks towards him, the years fall away, and it is only them again.

He's sitting on their favourite bench on the Heath, with the same binoculars he had sixty years ago, his birdwatching book by his side, and he's looking down towards the ponds, and the city in the distance. Someone is flying a kite.

'Did Friday and Esmé get off all right?' he asks, blinking at her.

'Fine. They sent you a hug. They'll come and collect their things when they're back.'

'Did you read your sister's letter?'

She nods, and sits down next to him.

'What was it?' he asks her.

'The past,' she says. 'The past arrived in an envelope. I'm going to invite Vic to stay. It's time to make it better. It will be better.'

'What on earth was in that envelope?' he says with a twinkling smile.

'I'll tell you about it later. Let's go for a walk. It's so lovely now.'

The sound of a funfair in the distance swells, a breeze carrying the carousel music towards them. They set off, hand in hand, across the uneven, dry ground. His hand clutches hers, so tightly. She doesn't let go: years ago, she used to want to. Now, she holds on to him. He is her home.

Acknowledgements

This book has been a pleasure to write from start to finish. I am so lucky to be able to make use of the London Library and to find inspiration, information and new ways of being a better writer in its hidden corners and on its shelves. I am also grateful to Bath Central Library for its quiet spaces and its collection, and the efficient central heating.

At Headline, I'd like to thank Imogen Taylor for the fantastic work she did on *The Stargazers* and for guiding me through her edits with commitment and diligence and wisdom. I'd also like to thank Zara Baig in editorial, Lucy Upton for her fantastic marketing, Caroline Young for the most stunning cover, Louise Rothwell for her legendary production skills, Rosie Margesson, publicity genius, sales supremo Rebecca Bader, Rebecca Folland, international rights community genius, and Marion Donaldson for reading it and for long ago getting me into stargazing. With especial thanks and love, as always, to Mari Evans.

At Curtis Brown, I would like to send huge thanks to Stephanie Thwaites, for her commitment and kindness and top, top agenting. I'd also like to thank Sheila Crowley, Gordon Wise, Jonathan Lloyd, Helen Manders, Annabel White and Grace Robinson.

I came to having lady novelist friends relatively late, as I was always suspicious of writers, having been an editor. It has been the greatest gift and I am hugely, properly, tearfully grateful to some wonderful women for their support, cheerleading, advice and inspiration over the last year. In particular Tasmina Perry, Kate Davies, Lissa Evans, Ronnie Henry, Sue Mongredien and all the Swans, and with a special shout-out to the post-Tom crowd, my dear Jane Casey, Anna Carey and Sarra Manning, and in loving memory of Sarah Hughes.

One of my oldest friends, Jen Arnall-Culliford, was able to help me finish the book with her hugely helpful, lyrical and practical information about the cello and what it means to be a cellist. And this will sound cheesy, but I wrote so much of *The Stargazers* listening to Jacqueline du Pré and Daniel Barenboim's recordings of the Brahms Sonatas for Cello and Piano and also the Elgar Cello Concerto, on repeat, and it would be strange not to acknowledge that.

I lost two people who meant so much to me writing this book: my darling old boss Jane Morpeth, who changed how I saw myself and the world, was a true champion of writers, and whose approach to life informs mine every day, and my wonderful dad Philip Evans, whom I miss more and more but whose voice is never far from me all the time, and I absolutely love it.

Finally I'd like to thank Hannah Gilbert and Julia Marshall-Wessendorf for their generous donations to appear in this book, Penny Clayton for the wisdom and walk chats, James Coleman for writing and life conversations, Shona Beats for so often picking me up, holding me up and dusting me off over coffee YAS SISTER, to Chris for making our house a home, to Cora for the chats about books and stars (we're still not getting a dog baby girl I'm sorry), and Martha for the beautiful pictures of owls saying Hoot.

Discover the enchanting world of . . .

Harriet Evans

'Spellbinding' ***Independent***

For the latest news about Harriet's books,
exclusive content and competitions,
visit www.harriet-evans.com.

And you can follow Harriet on:

/HarrietEvansBooks

@HarrietEvansAuthor